# The Longest Night

# The Longest Night

## GREGG KEIZER

G. P. PUTNAM'S SONS

NEW YORK

This is a work of fiction. Names, characters, places, and incidents either are the product of the author's imagination or are used fictitiously, and any resemblance to actual persons, living or dead, businesses, companies, events, or locales is entirely coincidental.

G. P. Putnam's Sons
*Publishers Since 1838*
a member of
Penguin Group (USA) Inc.
375 Hudson Street
New York, NY 10014

Library of Congress Cataloging-in-Publication Data

Keizer, Gregg.
The longest night / Gregg Keizer.
p.   cm.
ISBN 0-399-15170-2
1. Lansky, Meyer—Fiction.   2. World War, 1939–1945—
Netherlands—Fiction.   3. Holocaust, Jewish (1939–1945)—
Fiction.   4. Jews—Netherlands—Fiction.   5. Jewish criminals—
Fiction.   I. Title.
PS3611.E37L65     2004                    2003066667
813'.54—dc22

Printed in the United States of America
1   3   5   7   9   10   8   6   4   2

This book is printed on acid-free paper. ∞

BOOK DESIGN BY AMANDA DEWEY

*To the real rescuers, to those few saved,*
*and in remembrance of the many who were not.*

Whoever preserves a single life,
it is as if he had preserved an entire world.

—TALMUD: *SANHEDRIN* 37A

# Prologue

Weiss stood beside the empty train and listened to the huge black locomotive tick and click as its firebox cooled. He caught a whiff of coal smoke from its open furnace door.

Those he'd lifted and helped out and down from the cattle car, the mother with her little girl, the angry man with glasses, the old woman, all the others, had long disappeared into the dark behind Paul Kagen, the fuckin' mamzer who still thought he ran this crazy business. The rest, freed from their rolling prisons, had followed, all heading for the shores of the Waddenzee. When Weiss looked past the front of the locomotive, the light from the flickering parachute flare swinging above was just enough to show the last shadows vanishing down the roadbed. The smart thing was to walk after them. A month ago he would have done just that, no question.

He fingered the yellow star sewn to his coat. He was still Weiss, dropper for Meyer Lansky, still Weiss, son of Ruth Weiss out of Brownsville,

Brooklyn. He would always be those things, yellow star or not, but now he was also something more.

He looked up as the stick-shaped German airplane whirred over the train, heading south, the way they'd come on the tracks from Uithuizen. It dropped another flare, the light popping under the silk with a noise like a faraway shot. The engine faded until the only sound was the sizzling of the flare lighting them up for everyone to see.

Weiss took a deep breath, smelling the coal smoke still, but as the breeze shifted, it brought the tang of salt in the air, just like at Coney Island. Close now. Real close.

"Leonard, what should we do?" the woman behind him asked. He turned to face Reka, and the rest of those who made up the knot of dark shapes beside the locomotive. Her voice wasn't angry, like he'd expected. The rain had stopped, but her long dark hair was still wet and it hung in lines along her cheeks and across her forehead. Mouse wanted to see the expression in her eyes, but they were only black ponds. In his imagination, he filled in the love he needed to see there.

He counted the figures behind her. Eighteen, all silent. Waiting for him to say something.

He wished he could tell them to run after the others for the Dutch coast and the boats that should be there soon. Instead, he put his watch close to his eye; there was just enough light from the still-falling flare to tell him the time. Half-past nine. The boats would be offshore in an hour. But although they could walk the last kilometer to the water in those sixty minutes, it would take twice, three times that to load the boats. And the Germans were somewhere out in the dark, coming for them.

They had to buy time.

"Leonard, what do you want us to do?" Reka asked again. Few of the Dutch men and boys behind her could understand the English, but as he looked at their darkened faces, he knew what he would see if there was more light. Like in the cattle car when he'd shouted down the panic. They expected explanations. Wanted help. Waited for orders. They thought he had the answers.

Whatever he told them, they would do. And there was the problem.

From the start, he'd only worked the angles for himself. Now he had another chance to do for himself—run for the shore and maybe get away. Or, for once, work the angles for others. So he decided, and what was a surprise to him was that it wasn't a surprise, for he knew this had been a long time coming.

"We have to keep the SD from following the others," he said, and when the shapes behind Reka shoved closer, as if being nearer would make his English understandable, she translated. "We have to stay behind to give them a chance," he said. She translated again.

The flare floated over the train, and there was light enough now for him to see each face. It was sinking in. They would not reach the boats. Some faces got tight and almost angry, others looked away as if they could pretend they hadn't heard. Reka was the first to nod, though slowly—even she didn't want to do this.

"We can use the train as cover," Weiss said, feeling his way. "They'll come along the tracks, it's the only way. If we can keep them here for—" He stopped to think. "For two hours, or three, the others can get away." Reka spoke again in the Dutch. Another one, then two, nodded. Understanding, as he had made himself understand.

A drop gone bad had put him on this path. Meyer Lansky, or more on the mark, Lansky's money, had pushed him down it. And the Jews, the thousand walking now for the ocean through the night, they had made him take it to its end.

"You're right, this is what we must do," Reka said, her voice firm, and she stepped close enough so he could smell her wet hair. She put her hand to his cheek. *"Mijn lief,"* she said, but he knew what that meant, even in the Dutch.

How the hell did I get here? he asked himself as he touched her hand with his own.

# PART ONE

# Mouse

. . . and the abomination, and the mouse,
shall be consumed together . . .

ISAIAH 66:17

# One

Mouse Weiss slouched in the doorway, lit a Chesterfield, and kept an eye on the big bulky man in the barbershop across Canal. It wasn't hard. The man filled the chair to overflowing and the chair was the one at the front of the shop and the plate glass was clean as a whistle. Tootles always kept his shop neat as a pin—Mouse appreciated that. But after today he would have to find himself another barber.

He turned his back on the street and pulled up the collar of his overcoat against the wind. Even in April, a New York breeze could cut right through. He stared at the reflection in the glass window in front of him—the store was Bauman's, cheap jewelry—to keep an eye on the big man in Tootles's shop.

Mouse used the faint mirror to adjust his hat, tilt it a pinch more to the side. He pulled at the lapels of his overcoat and gave himself the up and down. Five eleven, a real giant in his crowd. Weight one sixty-five, not bad, though he'd eaten like a horse night before last at his muter's and now the coat was snug across his stomach. His nose was small, his shoulders wide, his eyes dark gray, his chin a good strong chin, not the nothing chin of a rabbi or a rackets man; and then there was his skin. Mouse paid attention to his skin. It was why Tootles was such a great barber; he shaved without damaging the skin. Mouse pushed at first one cheek, then the other, to tighten it up. He was coming up on thirty-one, and the wrinkles still didn't show.

The ladies liked his looks, he thought, because of his skin. No swarthy, pockmarked face, like most guys he knew. A good face, one the ladies liked to touch. Mouse smiled to himself, saw the smile in the reflection in the glass, and in that reflection, saw the big man pull himself out of the barber's chair, put both hands to his hair and brush back the sides, and use the towel Tootles held to wipe off the pomade he'd gotten on his fat fingers.

Mouse didn't know the big man's name because he'd not bothered to ask. That wasn't his way, that slippery Meyer Lansky way of talking until a guy spilled his whole life's story before he knew it. Anyway, Mouse didn't need a name to pop the fat man. All he needed was a reason, and Lansky telling him to do it was reason enough. Lansky said, Mouse did. That was how it worked.

The big man said something and Tootles laughed a phony laugh. Mouse knew he didn't laugh like that, head back with his mouth open like a circus seal waiting for fish. He helped the big man into his overcoat and handed him his hat. The big man adjusted his hat and Tootles held open the door. That was Mouse's first hint that the big man was someone, well, big. Tootles never held the door for him.

Mouse let his almost-smoked cigarette fall to the sidewalk at his feet, didn't bother crushing it under a shoe, and waited. The big man was deciding which way to go. East to Ludlow, or west to Orchard. What's it gonna be?

It didn't matter. Mouse had Dukey waiting at the corner of Ludlow, and Little Farvel was down on Orchard. If he missed his chance, one of them would do the pop.

West it is, Mouse thought, and the man turned and walked toward Orchard. Mouse spun on his heel and took a step that way, figuring the reflection in the glass would flip the direction of things. But the big man was really heading east, toward Ludlow. Sometimes he surprised himself how stupid he was. He had to turn on a dime and kind of hop a step to change direction.

And that was why the big man saw him, or so Mouse thought later. The big man must have caught Mouse's strange step and he stopped, just for a second, and stared across the street. Mouse didn't know how the big man knew who he was, but he could see the big man's eyes go, well, big. The big man turned and tried to run.

It was a howler, later, when Mouse told Little Farvel and Dukey, but at the time he didn't think it so much funny as just feeble. The big man couldn't run, and when he tried, his overcoat couldn't hide the way the fat at the back of his neck flopped as he lumbered toward the corner at Ludlow.

Mouse was sure as shit not letting Dukey do this pop, so he took off running too. He had trouble pulling the revolver out of his overcoat pocket because he had to reach—the ends of the coat were flapping behind him like in the breeze on the Staten Island ferry—but he got it okay, and as he ran he held the revolver alongside his leg and managed to pull back the hammer. He was gaining on the big man fast, real fast.

"Wait!" Mouse yelled, hoping to make him turn around, make him think he'd seen things wrong and this wasn't some guy after him with a gun. Mouse wanted to shoot him front, Lansky had told him to do the big man in the face. Whatever he'd done, it must be serious—maybe cheated Lansky outright or welshed on a deal—but like the big man's name, the reason why he was to get it in the face was none of Mouse's business, far as he figured.

Mouse shouted "Wait!" once more, but the big man wasn't fooled this time, either. He kept jiggling down the walk.

So Mouse stopped, raised the revolver—a heavy Smith & Wesson .38 Military and Police with a four-inch barrel—and shot the big man in the back. One, two, three, working the action just like that, and the three slugs caught the big man to the left of the spine halfway on the shoulder—a lung shot, Mouse knew—then to the right, an inch higher, and the last one, as the big man was already falling with his hands flung out, at the elbow. The big man crashed to the walk, skidding like, and flopped just a foot from the curb and gutter.

Mouse stopped, his breath ragged, and he stood over the big man's big bulky body. All the plugs around had gone frozen or crouched down at the first shot. The nearest was a young girl, no more than eighteen, cute in a Lower East Side way with too much lipstick, and their eyes, hers and Mouse's, locked for a moment. Mouse smiled at her, and taken by surprise, he supposed, she smiled back. Think of that, him having a Smith & Wesson in his hand.

Dukey hoofed it this way, not running, but walking real fast to cover Mouse in case something went wrong. Mouse wanted to finish it himself, but he had a hell of a time heaving the big man over. He figured two-eighty, easy.

Finally, though, the big man came faceup, a tree-limb arm hanging over the curb now, and Mouse saw that he was still alive. There was blood on his white starched shirt where it showed under his overcoat, a splash of it at the elbow. The .38 slugs had gone through him, big as he was. Blood leaked over his gums and down both sides of his chin. But the big man's eyes were still alive, and they looked at Mouse.

Mouse bent down, ignoring the noise he heard from the plugs around him, forgetting the sound of Dukey's shoes on the sidewalk as they came closer too. He leaned in to make sure the big man saw his face.

"Meyer Lansky sends regards, you fat fuck," Mouse said quietly so that the girl, huddled in a doorway a few feet away, couldn't hear. And Mouse stood, pointed the Smith & Wesson at the big man's nose, and pulled the trigger. One, two, the second going in higher, right in the forehead.

The big man's body twitched each time a slug hit home, but Mouse knew that the first had zotzed him sweet. What a fuckin' mess, Mouse thought, taking one more look. Guess that cut and a shave went to waste.

Mouse put his hand in his overcoat and pulled out a deuce, folded the two-dollar bill, and stuck it in the dead man's mouth. Just a sign how unlucky it was to cross Mr. Meyer Lansky.

"Leonard?" a voice behind him asked, a small voice, tired or scared. Mouse knew who it was before he turned around, but he was disappointed all the same. Tootles. The old man had come out of his barber-shop, rousted by the pop-pop-pop of the first three shots.

Ah, Tootles, Mouse thought, looking at the guy's rheumy eyes, you should've kept cleaning your scissors in that blue water or stropping your razors to make sure they were extra sharp.

Mouse had the Smith & Wesson up and pointed at Tootles in a heartbeat, and since the barber was just a few feet away, the shot would have been a cinch. Mouse knew he had one more left—Mouse was a careful man when it came to business—and he should have shot Tootles right then and there. For Tootles knew him not just as Mouse, but also as Leonard Weiss, the name almost nobody but his muter and Meyer Lansky called him.

But Mouse couldn't do it. Tootles was a mensch, really a mensch, and although Mouse knew when he'd gotten this job that he'd have to stop coming to Tootles for a while, he hadn't expected this. He hadn't expected the big man to run, and make him chase and catch him so close to Tootles's place, and Tootles to get curious and come out and see it all.

Mouse didn't pop Tootles. He just couldn't. Although Lansky telling him to was the reason why the fat man lay there on the walk, Tootles wasn't part of the deal, making it Mouse who had to come up with a reason for the barber. He couldn't. This was all an accident. Anyway, he couldn't shoot a man who shaved as sweet as Tootles.

Instead, Mouse just smiled at Tootles, knowing this would probably come back at him, but he still couldn't help it. He'd save this one, he thought, thinking first of the last cartridge in the revolver, but realizing he meant Tootles really.

He put the Smith & Wesson back in his overcoat, and as the sound of Dukey's shoes slap-slap-slapped up alongside him, Mouse took off running down the north side of Canal toward Orchard and the car that Little Farvel should have turned the key on by now.

You're a putz, Leonard," Meyer Lansky said from the deep cushions of a chair so large that it made the small man, all five feet and no inches of him, look like a kid. "Do you know that?"

Little Man was right, and when he was right, he was right. Mouse nodded.

"I know, I know, but that Tootles, he gives a great shave, you know what I mean? We go way back. I just couldn't do it. If I'd had more time to think it out," he lied, knowing he'd had plenty of time to decide, but he'd rather Lansky think he was stupid than soft.

Mouse tried not to look in Lansky's direction. He would have to look in his eyes then, and Lansky had eyes like little ice ponds.

"Leonard, Leonard," Lansky said quietly. "You put me in a situation. This Tootles talks to the police, there's a chance they haul you in, and if you spill . . ." And here Lansky held his hands out in front of him. "I know, Leonard, I know, you'd never do that. But I have to think of every eventuality. What if you spill and it comes back to me?"

Mouse looked up and dared to glance at Lansky. "You're not gonna pop him, are you?"

Lansky folded his small hands over his small stomach and smiled what Mouse thought was an awfully small smile. He didn't think Meyer Lansky meant that smile.

"You have to go away for a while, you know that. At least until I have someone talk to this Tootles."

Fuck. Go away, that meant Lansky sending him somewhere to keep an eye on him. Just in case Tootles talked, to make sure Mouse didn't spill. And Tootles was probably a dead man anyway, the way Lansky liked neat tidy ends.

Lansky didn't say anything, only tugged at his bright blue and white bow tie, and Mouse couldn't think of anything, so there was a silence in the wide room with the low ceiling. It was in the back of Ratner's on Delancey, a special room they'd given Lansky where he could do business. Lansky had decorated the place himself and it was filled with dark furniture and musty books and red drapes that covered nothing. There were no windows in this room. Lansky had proudly showed him that when he'd come here the first time, years ago. Safer without windows, Lansky had told him.

"I'll think of something," Lansky said finally. "I never leave you Brownsville boys in the lurch, you know that."

Mouse nodded. He was one of the few left of the old bunch. He'd been with the Brooklyn gang since he was eighteen, when he had no idea there was more to life than sticking up corner stores in Queens. But he'd been tough, even then, and mean as a snake, like Lepke Buchalter had said to him just before he'd brought him to meet Lansky for the first time. So he'd become a dropper for Lansky and Lucky Luciano's syndicate—a kind of cop really—and drew a steady twelve grand a year.

Murder Incorporated, the newspapers called them, like it was a business, which was how it was. Crime was business to Lansky, and those who didn't play by the business rules had to pay. Then Lansky would call the Brownsville Troop, the proper name for the gang—Mouse hated Murder Incorporated, that name too showy—to pop some bum. Mouse was proud to be a dropper for Little Man.

But now the old bunch was nearly gone. Lepke was out at Leavenworth trying to stay away from New York and Sing Sing, where the state D.A. would strap him into Ol' Sparky if he could get the feds to give him up. Then there was Kid Twist Reles, who had turned rat and for his troubles gotten tossed out the sixth-floor window of the Half Moon Hotel out in Coney Island, half a dozen New York dicks watching him be damned. And the others, like Bugsy Goldstein, burned in the chair thanks to Kid Twist, and Mendy, stuck so far into a cell he'd never see daylight, and . . . Mouse could run his brain over names of the dead-and-gone or just plain gone until it was dark and still not be done. Even Mouse saw the way things were going. Twelve years, that was forever being a dropper. He was an old guy to the trade, and he couldn't think of many old guys who'd made it. He'd been lucky, but sooner or later luck ran out. That was why he'd been thinking about a change.

Not that he would ever say anything to Lansky. Little Man wouldn't understand, and then he would get suspicious. You didn't want Lansky suspicious.

# Two

Friday: April 2, 1943

So this is the man?" asked Lansky from the cheap chair in this cheap office they'd climbed four flights to find.

Mouse leaned against the wall and looked over Lansky's shoulder. The sound of traffic below on Broadway came through the half-open window beside him.

"Yes, Mr. Lansky," said the man with the dark eyes. That had to be Peter Bergson, the guy Lansky had told him they were coming here to meet today. "And this is Paul Kagen, Mr. Lansky," said Bergson. "Paul, I'd like you to meet Mr. Meyer Lansky."

This Kagen stood up, leaned across the scratched-up table, and shook Lansky's hand. Kagen had a black patch over his left eye. He was young, twenty-five maybe. Mouse wondered if Kagen was as tough as he looked. His square face was nut brown, like he'd lived in the sun all his life, and he was whip-wiry, small, though he had a good four inches on Lansky. Kagen wore a suit—something borrowed, from the way it hung on him.

He caught Kagen giving him the up and down with that one eye. Something about the guy rubbed Mouse, and not the right way. Mouse smiled, hoping that it was a small, nasty smile like Lansky's.

Bergson pushed a newspaper across the table. "Read the piece I've marked, Mr. Lansky." Mouse could see that it was the *Daily News*, but that was all. Bergson had an American name, but his accent sounded from the old country. Polack, perhaps, Mouse thought, a word he would never dare say in front of Lansky, who had been Polack once, too.

Lansky read from the paper in his high voice. "'U.S., Britain Map Plan to Save Jews,'" he said. He looked up, expecting someone to explain it to him—Lansky always expected that. "I'm not following you, Peter." He put down the newspaper, and because Mouse could see his face, he could see Lansky give Bergson those cold eyes.

"The Nazis have always hated the Jews," said Bergson, getting right to the point, which Little Man liked. "But until last November, we had no idea how deep their hatred ran. The Jews are not being resettled in the East as we thought, Mr. Lansky."

Lansky listened, not saying a word.

Bergson looked away for a second, then back. "Now we have proofs. Last year, Hitler and his kind made a decision; they would evacuate the Jews."

"But—" Lansky started, and Bergson held up a hand and Little Man went quiet. Mouse had never seen someone shut him up that way.

"For the Nazis, Mr. Lansky, 'evacuate' means a different thing. For them it means exterminate. When they say they evacuate Jews to the East, it means they exterminate them there. They've sworn to evacuate every Jew in Europe, Mr. Lansky, annihilate the Jews. Annihilate. The. Jews," Bergson said, each word in Mouse's head like the sound of one of the three slugs from his Smith & Wesson hitting the fat man on Canal.

"They round up every Jew, Mr. Lansky, and put them on trains and take them to special camps in Poland. We have the names of these camps. Sobibor. Treblinka. Belzec. Auschwitz. And in those camps, the Germans put Jews in airtight rooms and poison them with gas, like you would rats or roaches. Then they burn the bodies to hide what they've done." Bergson reached for a Lucky Strike from a package on the table and struck a match, the smell of it sweet and sick together. Bergson struck the match that moment on purpose; he knew what he was doing. "They even have a polite word for this. *Sonderbehandlung*. Special methods, it means."

The yids over there had been pushed around for years, Mouse knew that. But *trains camps gas fires*, those were words that could change everything. *Trains camps gas fires*. And the German word. *Sonderbehandlung*. It was long, like a snake stretched out in the sun.

Lansky seemed surprised by the words, too, for Mouse saw Little Man's face go cold-cold-cold. He'd seen that look only once, when Lansky had told Mouse to find Kid Twist after he'd ratted out Lepke.

"You're sure about this?" Lansky asked. Mouse's head was still spinning, and he tried to remember Bergson's words, the exact words.

Bergson nodded. "Yes, Mr. Lansky." He put two photographs on the table and slid them toward Lansky. Mouse could see them over Little Man's shoulder. The first showed a line of railroad boxcars and a bunch of people in ragged clothes, women with scarves over their heads, men with the flat caps he saw on old guys down on the Lower East Side. Two women were climbing into an open boxcar while a German in uniform, a rifle over his shoulder, stood beside them and grinned at the camera. The second photograph was another train, but a different place with trees in the distance. People crowded around this train, hundreds already lined up in a long column and walking away from the camera. In the background was a tall pillar of black above those trees.

"Look carefully at the second," said Bergson. "That's Treblinka, one of the special camps. The black cloud, see, in the distance? That smoke comes from the pyres where the Germans burn the bodies. They stack corpses on steel rails, drench them with petrol, and burn them. That cloud, Mr. Lansky, is Jews going up in smoke."

Little Man picked up the second photograph again, looked at it again, and put it on the table again. "You're sure?" he asked.

Bergson nodded. "These were smuggled to the Polish government in exile, in London. Friends among the Poles sent them to us. We only received them Monday."

Lansky touched the second photograph again. "How many?" He didn't look up from the picture.

"Two million. Perhaps more. Many, many more."

"Two million . . . ," Lansky said. Mouse wondered at the number. That would be everyone in Brooklyn. His muter, Little Farvel, old Mrs. Biernbaum, everyone in his neighborhood, everyone in the borough.

"We had no idea at first," said Bergson. "Then, in November, we began hearing of talk about the evacuations. The exterminations. We raised nearly half a million dollars to tell the world and we spent it on newspaper advertisements and on rallies. The one at Madison Square Garden last month drew forty thousand, Mr. Lansky. Mrs. Roosevelt was there, justices of the Supreme Court, over three hundred from Congress. They all pledged to save the Jews. But now . . ." And he nodded to the photographs on the table. ". . . rallies aren't enough." Bergson picked up the *Daily News*. "And this is to be our salvation."

"I don't understand," said Lansky. Neither did Mouse.

Bergson tossed the *News* aside. "The U.S. State Department and the British Foreign Service are meeting in Bermuda for twelve days, starting on the nineteenth," he said. "At this conference they will discuss ways to protect Europe's Jews from Hitler, or so they have promised. But it will fail. It has been designed to fail. They will delay and postpone and submit to their committees. They are afraid to turn this into a war to save the Jews, Mr. Lansky. They will say they will help, but in the end they'll do nothing. And every hour, more smoke."

Mouse was confused. He wished Little Man had told him what this was going to be about. But maybe Lansky hadn't known either.

"And they will not let Jews take part," Bergson said. "The State Department says no organization, not even Rabbi Wise and the Jewish Congress, may send a delegation. All they will accept from us is a list of proposals. And those they will ignore." Bergson paused, looked away, then back to the ice-pond eyes. "Anti-Semitism runs deep, Mr. Lansky, in the State Department."

"I don't know how I can help," Lansky said. "I'm not a politician, you know." Lansky pulled a cigarette from the fancy silver case he always carried, the cigarettes, Mouse knew, rolled by hand for him special. "You asked me to help, Peter, and I will do that. But I'm not the man for this." Lansky lit his cigarette with a polished Zippo, clicked it shut, and set it on the table beside the silver case.

As Bergson nodded, his head bobbed up and down. "Yes, Mr. Lansky, yes, you are the right man." Mouse tried to remember where Bermuda was, down by Cuba maybe, but Bergson's words and the photographs wouldn't let him concentrate.

"How can I help from here—" Lansky got out.

"Some think we could buy Jewish lives," Bergson said, interrupting again. "The Nazis won't bargain, but other governments might. Romania has said it would let go its Jews if we paid."

"A ransom?" Lansky asked. "That's never a good—" But Bergson ran over Little Man's words.

"Others want to convince the Americans and British to bomb the camps and destroy the railroads that take our people to the gas. And there are more ways. Perhaps countries like Hungary could be pressured to free their Jews. If the war turns against the Nazis, especially in Russia, some might reconsider how they treat Jews. It's possible, but . . ." And Bergson shrugged.

"But neither Roosevelt nor Churchill will listen," he went on. "So we must make them listen. We must show them that Jews can be saved. Not by pleading or signing petitions or even paying ransom. Something more. Something that would make them help."

"What do you have in mind?" Lansky asked.

"We must rescue Jews, it's that simple. And we must do it ourselves. Jews saving Jews," Bergson said. Mouse was getting to like Bergson. The way he talked he made you believe it came from God's own mouth, like a rabbi. "It must be something big, very big. Very dramatic. So the world will sit up and take notice. Not just one here or there. Not just a few."

"You have some ideas," said Lansky. Bergson nodded. "And these ideas will take resources." Bergson nodded again. That was when Little Man reached for the tired leather briefcase with the brass fasteners he'd carried up from the car, the one that he wouldn't let Mouse touch.

Lansky set the briefcase on the table and began pulling out bundles of greenbacks, stacks of new hundreds, crisp and clean. Each stack was held together by a wide paper band. A hundred bills, Mouse knew, in each stack. A hundred times a hundred, and here Mouse had to think for a bit, was ten large. Lansky laid the last stack on the table, and Mouse did a count. Ten. Ten times ten, that makes a hundred grand. A hundred fuckin' thousand dollars. That was more than enough to change a life, Mouse thought.

It seemed that was how Bergson and Kagen saw it. Both of them stared at the money like it was a plate of steak and potatoes and they were starving.

"When we talked on the telephone, you asked for a contribution," said Little Man. Lansky slid one stack toward Bergson, another to Kagen. The man with the patch reached for it, touched it, flipped the edges of the bills.

"I don't know what to say," said Bergson.

"You have some ideas," Lansky said again. Mouse could tell that Little Man was giving them the up and down, seeing how they took to his money.

Bergson nodded, his eyes off the money. "Yes, Mr. Lansky, Paul and I have ideas. It must be something big, as I said. And it must be soon, before the Bermuda conference concludes. That will be on the thirtieth." Mouse did the arithmetic. That was four weeks from today. "We must show that Jews can be saved, while the diplomats are in the public eye. Then they will have to do something. The people will demand it."

Lansky looked at Kagen. "Peter tells me you're German." Mouse wondered where Little Man was heading now.

Kagen tugged again at the patch over his eye. "Not since 'thirty-four. My family emigrated to Palestine." Mouse heard the accent in Kagen's voice and it made him think of his muter, who had an accent just like that.

"And you've been where in the meantime?" Lansky asked.

"Here. There," Kagen said. He acted like he didn't need to be straight. He must not know who Lansky is, Mouse thought, or he wouldn't do that.

But Bergson butted in. "Paul was last with the British Army, in the Long Range Desert Group. They raided behind Rommel's lines in North

Africa," he said. "When he was injured, they said his wounds would keep him from the front. Which meant he couldn't kill Germans, so he left." Bergson smiled. "Isn't that right, Paul?" Kagen didn't say anything.

"Peter also tells me that you were in the Irgun," Lansky said. "You made bombs for the Irgun in Palestine, is that right?" Mouse now knew why Little Man had let Kagen get away with his crap. Lansky had a soft spot for Palestine. He was always talking about how the Jews should have Palestine, about how the British were fucks for not giving it to them, and how, someday, Jews would own the place.

Bergson answered for Kagen. "Yes, Mr. Lansky. Paul and I were with the Irgun. Paul was . . ." And he stopped for a moment, as if deciding what to say. "How should I put it? Paul was very good at what he did."

Lansky nodded. "Peter's told me you like to kill Germans. Do you? Like it, I mean?" he asked quietly, the question a shocker to Mouse. Lansky never, as far as he knew, put it like that. Little Man never was so direct about the work. He even hated the way Happy Maione talked about popping bums like he did, plain and straight, like it was nothing.

Kagen helped himself to one of Lansky's hand-rolled cigarettes from the silver case in front of Lansky, lit it with Little Man's Zippo, looked up, but didn't answer. He's really pushing it.

"Paul, Mr. Lansky asked—" began Bergson. But Lansky waved him off. He leaned forward in his chair.

"You don't know who I am, do you? I wouldn't expect you to." Lansky smiled one of his very smallest smiles. "I'm a businessman. But sometimes my business, well, sometimes it skirts the law. Do you understand what I mean by skirt? Go around, that's what."

Kagen looked like he was thinking. "A thief?" he asked, smoking Lansky's special cigarette. Mouse almost laughed. Lansky had been called a lot of things, but a simple thief, a ganef? That was rich. It was like saying the Rockefellers were regular Joes who punched a clock.

Lansky did the laughing, a high laugh. "Not quite. Now I own houses of chance. I used to run bootleg, illegal liquor from Canada. But mostly gambling now."

"A gangster," Kagen said, still smoking. Mouse got the idea that Kagen knew exactly what he was doing. He was pushing Lansky on purpose.

"I've seen gangster movies. Edward G. Robinson," said Kagen, like that told him everything he needed to know. "You're a gangster."

Lansky's face changed back to that cold-cold-cold look. Mouse told himself to remember this day, when he had seen Little Man's face twice like that. "No one calls me that anymore," Lansky said.

"Mr. Lansky is a very important man in New York, Paul, and he deserves our respect," Bergson said, his voice getting loud. Even Bergson was getting pissed at Kagen.

"Peter asked me to meet with him and you, too, and possibly make a contribution," Lansky said, lighting another cigarette, but this time he put his silver case and Zippo in his pocket. "From what Peter's said, I'd like to. But I'm not a generous man by nature. As I said, I'm a businessman. And I am very careful about who I do business with. I know Peter and trust him, but I don't know you. Do you follow me?"

Kagen nodded, though Mouse thought the German didn't really get it.

Little Man looked at Bergson. "You have some ideas," he said for the third time. It wasn't a question now. The dark-eyed man better have something grand, Mouse knew.

And Bergson nodded again. "Yes, Mr. Lansky. Something big, very big." Mouse waited to hear this big, very big idea.

"We will seize a train from the Nazis, one of the transports that take Jews to the camps," said Bergson, the words tumbling out. "We will seize this train and turn it from its usual route. And we will rescue the people on that train and bring them to safety. To England."

Mouse wondered if he'd heard right.

"You can do this?" Little Man asked after a bit. Bergson nodded one more time, his head up and down like before.

"Yes, Mr. Lansky. We have friends in London who have a plan, a good plan. There's a track, these friends say, right to the coast, near a small town called . . . ," and Bergson paused, as if remembering. "Uithuizen is the place. In the north of Holland. The boats will pick them up there." Another pause. "Yes, we can do this, but we need your help, Mr. Lansky," he said, nodding to the hundred large on the scratched table. It sounded crazy to Mouse, this idea.

Mouse could almost hear the little wheels turning in Little Man's little head and he thought Lansky would say the thing he was thinking, that this was nuts, meshuge. But instead, Lansky twisted in his chair and gave Mouse a strange look before turning back to Bergson.

"Mr. Weiss goes along. To watch over my contribution."

Had he heard right?

"I don't want this money wasted," said Lansky, touching the closest stack of dollars. "So Mr. Weiss will make all decisions involving my money." Little Man must have seen how Kagen and Bergson looked at the stacked hundreds.

Kagen didn't waste any time and butted right in. "No. We're not criminals." He pointed to himself, then to Bergson. "We're Zionists, Mr. Lansky. We're not criminals." Now Mouse knew why Kagen baited Lansky. He thinks he's better. Mouse wanted to reach across the table and show the guy who was better. "And he's no soldier. He'll be in the way," Kagen said.

But Little Man didn't get upset, even though Kagen was way out of line. Maybe because of the Irgun and Palestine. "This isn't negotiable. No Mr. Weiss, no money," Lansky said to Kagen. "Don't worry, Mr. Weiss can take care of himself. And he speaks German besides. That may prove useful."

The room was quiet, the only sound the car horns down on Broadway coming through the open window. Mouse waited, like Lansky.

Kagen tugged at his eye patch again. "No," he said, now aiming his good eye at Bergson, talking as if Meyer Lansky wasn't there. "This is wrong. Bad enough we take their money, but this . . . this poisons everything. Do we want the world thinking all Jews are criminals? They say that about us now, Peter, the British do. Do you think they will help us create Eretz Yisrael if they find out we trusted gangsters? Not even the politicians will trust us then. No."

"I'm sure Mr. Weiss will do just fine," Bergson said, looking first at Lansky, next locking looks with Kagen. Mouse got the feeling that Bergson and Kagen had had this argument before. A lot.

"No, this is our plan, Peter. Not theirs. Take their money, yes, but bring one along?" asked Kagen. "No. It will ruin everything."

Mouse couldn't help himself. No one talked to Lansky like this. He

leaned over the shoulder of Little Man and stared into that eye of Kagen's. "Who the fuck you think you are, chochem, talking to Mr. Lansky like—"

Lansky held up a hand to stop Mouse. He didn't bother to turn around,
but kept his eyes on Kagen. "We're all Jews here, aren't we? We all want
the same thing."

"Paul, please," said Bergson. "This is how it must be."

To Mouse, the silence in the cheap office lasted forever. Finally, Kagen nodded. "Yes," he said, breaking his stare with Bergson and looking
at Lansky. "We do want the same thing, Mr. Lansky. Yes, I'll do as Peter
asks. Of course. Because he has convinced me that this is the best way
to work a miracle." But Mouse could tell this wasn't the end of it. Kagen
was a chochem, a wiseheimer, a wise guy.

Kagen thinks he's too good for us, but not too good for our money.
Mouse had seen the way Kagen's eye took in the dollars spread across the
table. He would have to watch him. If anyone was going to get that fortune, it sure wasn't going to be this yid who insulted Mr. Meyer Lansky.

L ansky sat in the too-big chair in the room back of Ratner's and stared
at the book he'd pulled from a shelf almost as soon as they'd returned
from Bergson's cheap office. Mouse saw the big letters WORLD ATLAS on
his side of the book.

Lansky caught him looking. "It took me five minutes to find that town
Peter mentioned. Uithuizen."

"Yes, Mr. Lansky," Mouse said, paying attention.

"Leonard, I want to make this very clear," Lansky said as he set the book
on the small table beside his chair. Lansky never called him "Mouse," although Mouse didn't understand why, since Little Man called everyone
else by their nicknames, Dukey, Little Farvel, Longy, and the rest. "I want
an account of what you spend." Maybe Mouse didn't nod quickly enough,
since Lansky went on. "I want an explanation for every dollar, Leonard."

"I'll write it all down, don't worry."

Lansky shook his head. "No, not just that. You're my representative,
Leonard, on this . . . this expedition. In other words, you speak for me,

do you understand? And I want me—that means you—to make every decision that involves the money. Do you understand?"

The "me and you" part was a bit confusing, but Mouse figured he had the drift. He tested the waters. "If this Kagen wants to spend money on guns, and I don't think we need that many, or those kinds, I say no. Yeah, I got it."

Lansky nodded. "Exactly. I don't think either Peter or his friend realize how generous I've been."

Mouse thought about that. Lansky was afraid they would piss away the money, maybe even think they had a right to it, since it was gangster money. Mouse looked away. Here it might get tricky.

"I don't think I'm the right guy, Mr. Lansky. Maybe Kagen's right."

Lansky shook his head. "You're perfect, Leonard."

It was the way Lansky said "perfect" that made Mouse understand how things were. Ever since Tootles, Mouse guessed, Lansky had been thinking this. He had known Bergson wanted money, even if he didn't know exactly why; he knew Mouse had to go away, he knew he needed someone to watch that money. Like always, Lansky thought too far ahead for Mouse to follow or second-guess.

"You meant all along for me to go with Kagen," he said.

"And people say you're slow on the take," Lansky said, smiling his small smile. "Not until you did this stupid thing with Tootles, no. But you're perfect. You speak German. And I can trust you, Leonard." Lansky unfolded his hands, folded them again.

Mouse tried another way. "It's just that . . . maybe I could go to Saratoga Springs, lay low there, do some work up north for you." Mouse had been to the tracks and gambling joints Lansky owned upstate, like the Piping Rock. He wouldn't mind playing the ponies, even working the tables for a few weeks, long enough for this thing with Tootles to straighten out. "I mean, Mr. Lansky, I'm making good money. I get myself killed snatching some yids . . ."

Mouse wasn't sure he wanted to keep going. But he'd come this far, and the money in the briefcase now at Lansky's feet weighed on him. That was a lot of money, and he didn't see why he shouldn't see some, not if he was gonna stick out his neck. And Mouse was smart enough to know that this would put his neck on the line, right on the line. He had his muter to take care of, after all. His twelve thousand a year—a lot of money, sure—would be gone just as soon as some Nazi put a slug in his skull. And then where would she be?

Lansky wasn't stupid. He figured out what Mouse was after. "Tell you what, Leonard. I'll give you a bonus, how's that, if everything works out."

"Bonus, Mr. Lansky?"

Lansky looked up from his folded hands. Mouse had to stare into those ice-pond eyes for a second.

"Three thousand when you bring our people home," Lansky said. Mouse heard the hint in "our people," and reminded himself to lay off the "yid" in front of Little Man. He didn't like that word, Mouse remembered, though Mouse didn't see the harm in it, long as you were one yourself, not like some goy giving you shit calling you names like yid or kike or sheenie. "That's three months' salary, Leonard. You can buy your mother that house she wants." Lansky seemed to know everything, but how did he know Ruth Weiss wanted a house with a yard?

Three grand. What crap. Put my head on the block for a lousy three grand. But what choice did he have? He was Lansky's dropper, wasn't he, and he did what he was told. Or he just might end up like Kid Twist, flying to the sidewalk six floors down.

Mouse played his last card, hoping it would call this off. "That Kagen, I don't trust him," Mouse said. "I think the first chance he gets he'll put a hole in my head and take your money." It wasn't much of a lie, as far as lies went. He'd only spent a few minutes with the German, and he'd already taken a dislike.

"That's why you'll need to be extra careful, Leonard." Lansky smiled. "There's no one else. You heard Peter. This needs to be finished by the end of the month. And Kagen's a soldier, he's had experience with this kind of thing." Mouse doubted that; no one had done this exact thing, had they?

"Kagen's in charge," said Lansky, who must think the case was closed, even though it wasn't, not as far as Mouse was concerned. "Listen to him. But watch him, Leonard. Carefully. You understand?" Mouse got tired sometimes the way Lansky talked to him like he was stupid, but like always, he played along.

"I got it, don't worry, Mr. Lansky. He's the one gives the orders, but I hold the money. I won't let it out of my sight." Not for one second, Mouse thought.

"You'll go to London first, you and Kagen, then you'll get into Holland from there. Stay in touch from London, Leonard," said Lansky. "Cable me when you arrive. And remember, they read cables, so pick your words carefully. You understand? Don't give anything away." As Mouse nodded, Lansky reached for the phone. The talk was over. Mouse stood and went to the door, but when he had his hand on the knob, Lansky said his name again. Mouse turned.

"You have a job when you come back." Mouse nodded. So? "What I mean, Mouse," said Lansky, using his good name for once, which made Mouse pay attention. "Don't you be tempted by the money. Don't disappear on me, Mouse." Lansky smiled his small smile.

Mouse nodded. Lansky must be a mind reader. He'd been thinking of just that very thing.


Horst Preuss stood in the center of Amsterdam's Plantage Middenlaan and listened to the Jews wail from the Joodsche Schouwburg. They had been packed into the theater an hour ago and still they made noise enough to hear from the street.

It was going to be a beautiful day, warm even this early in the morning—and not a cloud in the sky. He looked up, tried to ignore the noise of the Jews, and wondered what the weather was like in Vienna and what Marta was doing now. He looked at his watch. Getting dressed for work.

"We're finished here, aren't we?" the Dutch policeman beside him asked, bringing Preuss out of his Austrian daydream. Preuss turned to look at his shadow, Piet de Groot. The detective—seconded to the Sicherheitsdienst as Preuss's link to the Amsterdam police—wore a too-tight suit, dark blue, and held his fedora in his hand. The man was in his middle thirties, his blond hair beginning to recede, with a face and frame gone to fat. No rationing for him, Preuss thought.

De Groot even spoke passable German. "All accounted for. Three hundred forty-nine. Exactly. Just like your list says." The Dutchman waved the sheaf of papers in his hand, today's names.

Preuss looked at de Groot, who didn't blink but wore his usual bitter expression. Not that it mattered. Preuss was the one in charge, and if de Groot didn't like his place, well, that was simply too bad.

Preuss switched to Dutch, proud that it was better than this policeman's German, just as he had been proud of picking up Russian before that. "As always, your men have been very cooperative," he said to de Groot. "Give my thanks to the young corporal." He gestured to the Amsterdam policeman in the blue tunic and tall, stiff hat who stood with his men at the theater doors. He and de Groot had only supervised; the police had sweated the roundup.

"Of course," said de Groot, having turned to his native tongue, too. It was clear he was anxious to leave.

"Go on," Preuss said. "I'll stay for a bit. It's such a fine day, I think I'll walk. Take the car back to Euterpestraat and leave it there."

"As you wish," de Groot said, settled his fedora on his head, touched his finger to its brim in a mock salute—he's getting entirely too forward, thought Preuss—and walked to the black BMW, turned its key, and drove off, the car's rough engine a bother to Preuss's ears. Just like those Jews.

Today's *Aktion* had gone well. The Jews didn't come when they were summoned anymore—they knew better—but they still didn't put up much fuss. No one had gotten hurt, none of the police anyway. The police corporal—young and, unlike de Groot, eager—had dragged them from their homes at dawn and shoved them into the street before too many Amsterdammers were up and about. The corporal and his men had marched them here, as always, and packed them in. On Monday, they'd herd them two kilometers to the rail station, put them on a train, and ship them to Westerbork. Another three hundred forty-nine off his hands and onto his ledger.

Preuss walked west on the Plantage Middenlaan, the sound of Amsterdammers, walking and pedaling their bicycles and twitching their bicycles' bells, slowly replacing the noise from the theater. A tram rumbled by on the tracks that divided the broad avenue.

Most of the people he passed glanced away from his gray uniform, the lightning bolt runes on his collar, and the death's head on his cap that marked him as SS. But as Preuss took a seat at a café table in the morning sun and told the waiter he wanted a coffee, he didn't concern himself. The waiter saw the silver SD on the black diamond patch at his left elbow, smiled wanly, and hurried off. Even waiters respected and feared the Sicherheitsdienst, the SS security service. He was as safe here as if he was home in Vienna. Not like Russia. In Russia, partisans had guns and sometimes shot at those with the runes, especially those with the SD diamond.

He'd come far, Preuss thought as he sipped the ersatz coffee, the burnt barley tasting foul on his tongue. Far from Vienna, far from that dead-end job as a postal inspector. Marta was proud, as she should be. Wasn't he now a Hauptsturmführer? And once the war was over and his job done, they would marry and he would settle in Vienna. Work for the Party, perhaps. Or perhaps remain in the SD. He wasn't sure.

That reminded him. Preuss pulled out the signal that the Unterscharführer had handed him as he'd left the old school on Euterpestraat, the building that housed the Gestapo and the SD. He read it quickly, adding up the tally as he did.

Brigadef. E. Naumann; Obstuf. W. Gemmeker
Stubaf. W. Zoepf; Hstuf. H. Preuss

The following deportation transports for special action have been authorized this date by Gruppenführer Müller, RHSA Amt IV.

| DATE | SOURCE | DESTINATION | NUMBERS |
|------|--------|-------------|---------|
| 6.4.43 | Westerbork | Sobibor K.Z. | 2020 |
| 13.4.43 | Westerbork | Sobibor K.Z. | 1204 |
| 20.4.43 | Westerbork | Sobibor K.Z. | 1166 |

| 27.4.43 | Westerbork | Sobibor K.Z. | 1904 |
|---------|------------|--------------|------|
| 27.4.43 | Westerbork | Theresienstadt | 196 |

*(signed) Franz Novak,* Hstuf., Amt IV B-4-a, 1.4.43

More than six thousand Jews would leave the transit camp at Westerbork this month, evacuated to the East, and it would be his job to replace them. March had been a bad month; he had not met the quotas that Eichmann in Berlin and Zoepf in The Hague had set. He had heard about that, of course, a screaming telephone call from Zoepf and a slyly worded teletype from Eichmann. But three hundred and forty-nine was a good beginning for April.

A muffled explosion washed up the street and dully echoed off the buildings, but it was enough to scare up a huge flock of jackdaws in the Wertheimpark across the way.

Preuss ducked, toppling his chair as he fumbled for his pistol. But the gunshots that chased the fading sound of the blast were over almost as soon as they started, and he suddenly felt foolish as the Dutchmen in the café looked on. He brushed a hand across his tunic, dropped some coins to the table, and righted the chair before walking as steadily as he could for the Muiderstraat bridge where it crossed the Herengracht.

From a street away, he saw the burning car. He trotted toward it, his pistol still in his hand, ignoring the Dutch standing beside their bicycles. There were three bodies, two lying on the walk near the Renault, a small Juvaquatres, the third hanging out of the opened driver's door, his black tunic afire. The Renault's hood was peeled back like a tin of herring, and the nearest shop front was a shambles of broken glass and splintered wood.

One of the men lying on the walk was dressed in black. NSB, Dutch Nazi. Preuss glanced at the Renault's front fender, noticed the small pennant—a yellow wolf's hook on a black background. The two in black had been high-ranking NSB. The other figure on the walk was just a boy, his clothes old and washed-tan and patched. He was sprawled against the smashed shop, his head a bloody ruin, an ancient revolver in his hand. The boy was dead, but the NSB man was not.

"Did you see anything?" he shouted at the nearest Dutch, a middle-aged man who looked like he would faint from the question. The man dumbly shook his head. "Call for help," he said to the man. "Call the police." And the man finally turned and walked briskly up the street. Preuss doubted there was a phone box that way. Damn Dutch.

Preuss knelt and put his face close to the NSB man. His blood had run from the wounds on his chest and neck and across the concrete and into the gutter.

"Did you see anyone?" he asked softly, using Dutch. "Who did this?"

"Grenade," the man whispered and he was gone, one eye screwed tight, the other wide and staring at the cloudless sky. Preuss stood, and as he looked over the husk of the Renault and through the smoke from the flames that licked its shattered interior, he saw a young woman ten meters away, perhaps in her early twenties, with dark hair tied back and a plain face. There was something about her . . .

She stared at the car, next her gaze shifted to the dead boy against the shop, and then she looked at Preuss. He noticed a scratch on her face, a long, thin line of blood that started above the corner of her left eye and ran back toward the ear. She turned her head to hide it.

"Come here, girl," he said loudly in Dutch. But she turned and began to walk away. "Girl! Come here!" Preuss shouted, remembering he had a pistol in his hand.

She was fifteen meters away now, her legs striding quickly under her yellow print dress. "Stop!" Preuss yelled, and brought the pistol up. Her back was to him, so he couldn't see the blood on her face, but he was certain she'd been too close when she'd thrown the grenade. Without calling again, he fired.

Preuss knew he was a poor shot. Even in his Russian days, he would sometimes miss when he fired at the Jews ranked before the pits.

The first bullet from his pistol smacked at the wall beside the woman, and she was off running. Preuss fired again, and again, and a fourth time, too, each shot wider from the mark than the last. But as she turned the corner, he fired a fifth, and because she stumbled before she disappeared, he thought it had struck.

With police sirens warbling in the background, he sprinted toward the corner, where he was sure he would find her lying dead on the pavement. She wasn't there. Only a tiny splash of blood on the brick marked her passage. Preuss looked down the narrow street, the canal on the left, five-storied houses on the right. She was gone.

Partisans, he thought. And put his pistol back in its holster. The Gestapo would find her. It wasn't his job. But he still wished he was a better shot.

Preuss waited for the Amsterdam policemen and the Gestapo to arrive so he could tell them what he'd seen and what the NSB man had said. But he was anxious to get to his office on the Euterpestraat. He knew that the Gestapo would round up scores to shoot in reprisal, and he wanted to make sure they kept their hands off his Jews. He needed them for his own ledger.

As he waited, Preuss lit a Nil, savored the thick Turkish tobacco, and when he looked at his watch, wondered what Marta was doing this very minute.

# Three

Mouse looked down at the water and hoped the big airplane would stay in the air.

He'd never seen so much water, even when he'd looked out from the tallest hump of the Cyclone at Coney Island back when he was a kid. Just water and water and more water. The whole Atlantic Ocean, so much water. And him not able to swim.

Kagen slumped in the seat next to the window, but Mouse knew the German was only pretending to sleep. Mouse looked past him to the engines on the wing above, their propellers just a blur. Below, all that water.

The plane bounced, just a bit, and Mouse grabbed for the armrest.

"Nervous?" Kagen asked. The German's eye was still shut. The big plane trembled again, moved up, down, and to the side before straightening out.

The two of them had gotten on the four-engine Pan Am flying boat in New York the morning before, landed in a blue bay just after dawn today beside an island that rose up out of the ocean like a mountain. The Azores, Kagen said, and they were off again, the small waves slapping at the bottom of the plane as it bounced across the water and into the air. They were bound for Lisbon, said Kagen, and from there, on to London.

Half the passengers were in uniforms, the other half in suits, like them. Bergson had pulled strings, Lansky said when he'd seen him off at Ratner's and handed him the case with its hundred grand, the case that now sat between Mouse's feet. Bergson had friends in high places, Lansky said. Even I couldn't get you on this plane. Mouse didn't believe that. No one was connected like Lansky.

"How much longer?" Mouse asked. It had been twenty-five hours already.

Kagen grunted but kept his eye closed. "Another two hours to Lisbon. We'll change planes there. Should be in London by tomorrow noon."

The German straightened out of his slouch, opened that one eye of his, and pulled out a Lucky—he smoked Luckies, just like his pal Bergson—and lit it with a beat-up lighter, round like a lipstick tube. It had a palm tree and tiny swastika scratched on its side. Kagen caught him looking. "Souvenir," he said, showing Mouse the lighter. "My days in Africa." Mouse looked up. He'd taken a hate to this guy from the moment Kagen had put on airs and talked crap to Lansky, but he tried to keep an open mind. Lansky had told him to listen to Kagen.

"Get it off a dead guy?" he asked, trying to keep the conversation going. Kagen nodded.

"We drove trucks behind Rommel's lines, shot up airfields and supply columns. And killed Germans. This was a German's."

Mouse thought of newsreels where tanks spurted sand behind them like water from boats, and men in shorts wore flat steel helmets. That was where Kagen got his tan. "You pop him?" Mouse asked.

"What?"

"You shoot him? Or was he a prisoner?"

"No prisoners," Kagen said, smoking his Lucky and giving him the eye. "Never prisoners." He smoked some more. "The British Army . . . ,"

Kagen started, and sucked hard on his cigarette. "They wanted to put me behind a desk after this." And he touched the black patch. "It would have meant no more killing Germans. So I walked out."

"Just like that?"

"Just like that."

"So you walked out. Aren't they after you?"

"They're after Paul Kagen," he said, quieter now, though Mouse was sure no one in the airplane could hear. Mouse himself could barely make out the words over the noise of the engines. "But not David Tucker, citizen of the United States." Kagen patted his suit jacket. He had showed the customs guy an American passport, its cover blue like his. Bergson or his friends must have arranged that, too.

Mouse pulled out a Chesterfield and put it in his lips, but before he could reach for his lighter, Kagen was clicking the dead Nazi's to light him up. His one eye met Mouse's for a moment.

"What's your story?" Mouse asked, direct.

The German looked down for a moment, pulled at his patch. That was a habit with him. "My family are Zionists. I am a Zionist. Do you know what a Zionist is?" Mouse nodded. Sure. Those crazy yids who yammered on about how everyone should move to Palestine and be a farmer. Like Little Man, but more so—that was a Zionist.

"I fight the enemies of Eretz Yisrael," Kagen said. "First British and Arabs, now Nazis. Today I kill Nazis, tomorrow British and Arabs again. Besides, what else is there to do?" He shrugged.

"No, I mean, why you? This trip?" He waved his cigarette in the air.

Kagen pulled at his patch. "Peter says this is better than killing them one at a time. Peter says if we make them afraid of Jews, perhaps they won't kill us so quickly." He shrugged again. "And one must be practical. If the Nazis kill us all, there will be no Yisrael." Kagen drew on the cigarette again. "And you?"

"Lansky trusts me." Not you, Mouse thought.

"Yes" was all the German said at first. He half turned and stared out the window. He talked to the glass circle of the window, its shape reminding Mouse of portholes in boats. "That morning we met, the newspaper said a man had been murdered by a gangster. In Canal Street. There is no canal, is there?"

"Not that I know," Mouse said after a moment. He had seen the paper, too. The *Daily News* used big headlines—LABOR BOSS SLAIN, GANGLAND LINK—with a picture of the fat man, dead on the walk, his face the mess Mouse had left. The *News* liked that kind of thing. Sold papers.

Kagen turned from the window and looked back at Mouse with his one eye. "The newspaper didn't say who killed him."

Mouse kept his mouth shut. Kagen was trying to get to him, just like he'd tried to get to Lansky. But Mouse wasn't ashamed of being a dropper. He just didn't want to end up like Lepke, in prison, or Kid Twist, dead with his neck broke from a long fall.

"How many have you shot, gangster?" Kagen asked, and it took Mouse a moment to realize Kagen said it in German. *"Wieviele hast du erschossen, du Gangster?"* Kagen had asked. He kept using that word "gangster" as if it would hurt Mouse.

Mouse stayed with English. "None of your business." He smoked, felt it slide down into his lungs. He wasn't ashamed of the number, which was eight, but he didn't go around telling everyone, either.

In German again Kagen asked, "Any of them shoot back?"

Mouse knew Kagen meant it to get under his skin. Most people figured you just gunned down the guy; that was how the movies made it out. Sometimes that was the way, but not always. "Sure," Mouse said, still in English. "Once a schvartzer came at me with a shotgun. A few other times."

Seemed like Kagen thought some more. "How many do you think I've shot, gangster?" Mouse looked up from his cigarette. Kagen had a small grin, almost a smirk, on his face. "How many? Make a guess."

The only Brownsville boy he'd ever known who bragged like this was Happy Maione, another one ratted out by Kid Twist and burned last year in the chair for it. Happy had loved his work, not that that was how he got his name—the way he scowled all the time was reason enough to call him Happy—and he used to button guys for hours to tell and retell how he'd gone at this bum with an ax, done that bum with wire. And he had kept a count, Happy had, with a silver dollar minted to match the number he'd claimed he'd popped. He still had that '27 silver dollar in his pocket when they burned him, that's what Mouse had heard.

Happy Maione was the craziest fuck Mouse had ever met, and other than Kid Twist himself, the only dropper he'd known who loved the work only for its own sake.

"Take a guess, gangster," said Kagen.

"No, you tell me," he said, still looking at his smoking Chesterfield.

"I went back and counted after Peter first told me they murdered two million." When Mouse looked up, Kagen still had that smirk. "Fourteen. Fourteen, and never prisoners," Kagen said, crushing his Lucky into the ashtray on the armrest. "You're not so tough, are you, gangster?"

"Call me Mouse," Mouse said very very quietly. "Everyone calls me that."

Kagen shook his head. "No, I don't think so." He stared with his one eye. It was like the air between them got thick, like summer air, Mouse thought. It was hate both ways, that thick summer air.

Mouse stared back. He remembered something then that Lansky had said in that office over Broadway. "You made bombs in Palestine. Blow up women Arabs? How about kids? Don't bombs do that? Count them too, do you, *Wichser*?" Mouse asked, switching to German only at the end. Kagen's eye went angry when he called him a fucker.

"At least I don't do it for money," Kagen said, still in German, ignoring his questions. "I'm not a whore like you and your Pole," he said, *Hure*, the German for "whore" not sounding half as bad to Mouse as calling Lansky a Polack. Lansky would surely have somebody beat Kagen's brains in for calling him that to his face, Irgun or not.

"You're the worst kind of Jew," Kagen said, changing now to English. "You're the kind that makes the gentiles think they're right when they think of Jews. You care only about money."

"I'm not the one who kills women, am I," Mouse said, not looking away.

"That's enough," the German said, his voice low and hard, intending to scare him with the sound. "I'm in charge of this . . . this . . . and you'll give me the proper respect, even your fucking Pole said you were to do what I say—"

"*Leck mich am Arsch*," Mouse said, leaning in until his elbow was on the armrest and knocking the ashtray into Kagen's lap. "You're no more a real soldier than me, are you? *Gangster?*" Mouse put the weight on that last word. "So just kiss my ass." And it was Kagen who broke the stare first. He brushed off the butts and ash from his pants, turned to look out the porthole window again, and didn't say another word.

It was going to be a long, long trip, Mouse thought. The big flying boat slipped and slid through the air again, and he hung on to the armrest and pinched his feet together to keep the briefcase from sliding on the floor.

R eka breathed. The footsteps above faded to the far end of the shop. "Close," Johannes said quietly. "That was very close." They had been surprised when the bell over the shop door jingled, and with Henrik's help had only made it back to the cellar in time.

In the dim light of the one electric bulb, Reka looked at Johannes and the two others in the short-walled cellar: Annje, and her backward brother Martin. Annje had her head down, but Martin, now that the footsteps were gone, was again humming to himself. He stopped his mindless tune. "Jew?" he asked. He asked the question so many times she had given up being angry.

"Yes, Martin, Reka is a Jew," said Annje, so patient. Martin made a face, as he always did.

"Jew, Jew, I smell a Jew," he said, slowly saying the words. Reka wondered how he could smell anything, what with the stink in the cellar. The bucket in the corner behind the blanket smelled like what it was: a bucket of excrement. Annje shushed her brother.

Reka heard the scrape of the bureau above and the sound of the trapdoor opening. Henrik called down. "It's clear now. Only a late customer." Johannes led the way up the ladder, and in a moment they stood in the back room of Henrik's used clothing shop. Henrik closed the trapdoor and shoved the bureau on its hinged side back over the trap. The old man, who always seemed nervous, wiped his brow. "I can't take any more of this," he said. "You have to find a new place to hide."

"No one knows," Johannes said. "We've been here for weeks, no one suspects."

Henrik shook his head. "No, it doesn't matter. My nerves. I can't stand this. You must go," he said.

Reka wasn't surprised. Since yesterday, when she'd come back with blood on her from Gerrit's grenade, Henrik had been beside himself. That he'd come up with the courage to tell them he would no longer hide his comrades in the Resistance was astonishing.

But Johannes frowned at Henrik, who melted into the frightened old man he was. Johannes was good at bullying Henrik. "You have a message for me?" Johannes asked, pointing to the piece of paper Henrik held. He's so stupid, thought Reka, to write it down. The old man did it because he was afraid he would forget, but it was stupid. If the police or the Gestapo caught him with the message, he was dead.

Johannes took the paper from Henrik, read it, and tore it into tiny bits, dropped them into an ashtray on the small desk, and lit them with a match. They curled into black snowflakes. Drama, she thought, was Johannes's second love, right after bullying.

"They want us to meet an old man," Johannes said. "We're to bring him into the city and hide him until they send for him."

"Who is he?" Annje asked. Johannes shrugged. Reka, who had been with the Resistance since she'd fled Mrs. van Mieps's farmhouse five months before, knew that was how it should be. The less one knew, the less one could tell.

"We're to meet him at the Diemen-Nord," Johannes said. "Someone else is bringing him that far. I think it best if you and you meet him," he said, looking first at Annje, then Reka. "You two will be less conspicuous." Reka knew the real reason; Johannes's third love was himself. He was afraid of the police, who had a habit of snapping young Dutchmen from the streets for labor service.

"Martin?" Annje asked.

"He'll stay with me," Johannes answered.

"When?" Reka asked.

"Seven tonight. He's old, tall and thin, and he'll wear a brown cap, the message said. Look for a man in his fifties standing alone," said Johannes. "Ask him if he's from Groningen, and he's to tell you that, no, he's come from Leeuwarden to visit his sister." Reka nodded. The train station was six kilometers away, and they had only an hour. They had to leave immediately.

"I'll be back soon," Annje told her brother, her hand on his arm. "Mind Johannes," she said. Martin nodded, as if he understood.

She and Annje left Henrik's shop on Lindenstraat and walked to the tram stop at the corner. The tram would take them as far as the Sport-park, but from there they'd have to walk.

They rode the tram in silence. There was nothing they could say in public, and in any case, the only thing they shared besides the hiding place in the cellar was their age: twenty. Reka felt the tram bump over its tracks and felt, too, the ghost of Mama's hand trembling in hers. Trams did that to her now, took her back to the afternoon five months before, when she'd stood on the Appelplatz at the camp of Westerbork and waited while a policeman read names that would fill a train with dead people.

The wind had been cold that day, Reka remembered, although most of all she remembered Mama's hand in hers, squeezing first, then trembling as their names, Mama's and Papa's and hers, were read by the thin-shouldered policeman. "Dekker, Jacob," first, "Dekker, Meijer" second, and finally "Dekker, Reka." Everyone in the family but David.

"Our end has come" was all Papa said, and he took Mama back to Barracks 65, their Westerbork home. In the morning, they'd be marched the five kilometers to Hooghalen and board the train that would take them to the East. And they would never come back.

She and David had argued one last time about her plans, David telling her she could not abandon Mama, Reka saying if she got on that train she would die like Mama and Papa. For proof she had pointed to the spot just outside the camp gate, where the work gangs had been laying rails for the past week. "Soon they'll bring trains into the camp. Why would they do that unless they're worried about what other Dutch think? And why would they worry if the trains only take us to work camps? They'll murder us in the East, I know it. I won't die where they want. Or when they want. That's all we have left."

But David wouldn't go with her. He thought himself safe because he was the camp's assistant chief electrician, just as Mama and Papa thought themselves safe because they believed the German tales of re-settlement and hard work in the East.

And so that night she stole out of the barracks alone, felt her way to the spot at the wire fence where David had broken the light—his one concession to her escape—and cut the strands with the metal snips he had given her from his workshop. The silent watchtowers at either end of the long fence stayed silent, and the dark outside the wire stayed dark. And there in the trees fifty meters from the camp, she heard the long, low whistle of a train from the direction of Hooghalen and the railway that Mama and Papa would march to tomorrow. That was why she hated trains, and trams.

Reka looked up from her seat and caught a man standing in the aisle glancing at her hand, which was trembling now for real. The man looked away and she touched the cloth of her coat where the yellow star should be. Perhaps he knew. Perhaps he knew she was Jew pretending to be not.

Mrs. van Mieps had known, or seemed to. But still the old widow took her in, hid her in the barn where she'd found Reka cowering after that long night of running from Westerbork. It had been a miracle, but with the handful of guilders Mrs. van Mieps had given her, she made it to Amsterdam. She had been twice blessed, for once in the city, she had found a gentile who had worked for her father's company, who still worked for its new Aryan owner, and the boy had taken her to the Resistance. They made false papers for her and gave her to Johannes, who found a place for her to hide in Henrik's cellar.

The tram squealed to a stop, rocked one last time, and was still. They walked, she and Annje, the rest of the way to the station, and were only ten minutes late. A locomotive huffed alongside the platform, sinister in its polished blackness. Perhaps this very one had strained against long lines of wagons and dragged Mama and Papa to the East. Reka put her hand over her breast, thinking that might make her heart beat slower.

Annje spotted the man, gray hair poking from under a brown cap, and pointed him out. He stood alone near the ticket windows, tall, with a long, thin face and a narrow, pinched mouth. Reka started to walk toward him—he was farthest from the platform and the locomotive, a safe place she thought—but Annje put out her hand.

"I'll do it," she said. "You wait here." Reka nodded, and as Annje walked toward the man with the brown cap, Reka took one more look at the crowd. But she saw no police, no one in uniform, and no one paid attention to Annje as she pushed through the throng.

Reka leaned against a pillar and pretended to study the departures board with its chalked cities and times. Annje had reached the man. She spoke a few words to him and he answered. Reka glanced away to watch the platform again, and movement caught her eye's corner. In a swirl of arms and legs, men in plainclothes came out of nowhere and grabbed Annje by the wrists.

Reka ducked behind the pillar, her heart thumping in her chest. As she peeked around the column, she saw one man either side of Annje, their hands wrapped around her upper arms, a third at the front plowing a way through the crowd. When she looked for the tall man with the brown cap, he was gone. She put the pillar at her back and listened to her heart hammer. But no one came for her.

After five minutes, when her pulse had returned to nearly normal, she fled the Diemen-Nord and its locomotive. She must get back to the shop. The others must be warned. Sooner or later Annje would talk and tell where they hid. Everyone talked.

Hauptsturmführer," a voice said, and Preuss looked up from his desk and its ledger. A tall man, thin like most Dutchmen, dressed in a worn coat frayed at its cuffs, a brown cap clutched in one hand, stood just inside his office door.

"Yes," Preuss said, irritated that a sentry had let the man in. That someone could just stroll into the Euterpestraat was unacceptable. The guard's ears, or more, would sting for this. "What?" He closed the ledger on those he'd marched from the Joodsche Schouwburg to the Muiderpoort station this morning for the transport to Westerbork: one thousand, two hundred and nineteen, off his hands.

The man gave Preuss a Soldbuch, the identity booklet all soldiers carried. So this one was German, not Dutch, Preuss realized. He flipped open the cover and inside saw the thin man's photograph, on the opposite page his name and rank handwritten. Hermann J. Giskes, Oberstleutnant. So, a lieutenant colonel, and of the Abwehr, military intelligence no less.

"I'm not in uniform," said Giskes, the older man sounding apologetic. He must be pushing fifty, thought Preuss.

Preuss didn't bother to stand, but waved to the chair on the other side of the small desk. This Giskes outranked him, but he was only Abwehr, of the Wehrmacht, not of the Reich Security Main Office, SS or Gestapo or SD. Giskes didn't seem to take insult, but he did take a seat.

"I've brought a woman here," he said. "Someone I just snapped up. I thought perhaps you'd like a word with her." Unusual, an Abwehr officer bringing someone to the Euterpestraat. Preuss got suspicious and curious, all in the same moment.

"Why should I talk to her?"

"She says she was with a Jewess when we arrested her. Unfortunately, the Jewess escaped."

Preuss snorted. That would be just like the Abwehr. Those fools wouldn't know a Jew from a Romani. "What do you want?" he asked, lighting a Nil and snapping shut the blue tin so that it made a satisfying click. He hadn't bothered to offer one. The Nils were too good for the Abwehr. The SS and SD, they traveled in style, lived deluxe. The Abwehr . . . well, he didn't know how they traveled, but he guessed it wasn't first class.

Giskes smiled at him. "Since she mentioned Jews, I thought you might shed light on the Hebrews," he said. "You're the expert, aren't you?"

Preuss nodded. He was the head of Amsterdam's Reich Security Main Office Amt IV B-4, Department of Jewish Affairs. Everything that involved Amsterdam's Jews, that was his purview.

"Let's talk to this girl of yours." He stubbed his cigarette in the tray on the desk, slipped the cigarette tin into his tunic pocket, and followed Giskes from the office and down the narrow, whitewashed stairs of the old schoolhouse. The cellar was low-ceilinged and made Preuss uncomfortable.

Giskes opened a door, stood aside, and Preuss hesitated for a moment before walking into the claustrophobic room. A young woman was slumped in a chair in the corner. An hour or so ago she might have been pretty, in a country sort of way, with her wide face, bluest of blue eyes, and corn-silk hair. But bruises now marked her arms, marred her face under her eyes and along one cheek. Blood trickled from a split lip, more from a nostril. And she shook in the chair enough to make its old joints creak like a very small, very poorly strung violin.

"You've questioned her," he said, not asking.

"Nothing serious," the Abwehr man answered. "We talked in the car. She admitted she was with the Resistance soon enough." Preuss noticed that there was no blood on Giskes's hands. "When she started babbling about Jews, I had my man drive us here."

Preuss switched to Dutch to talk to the woman. "Do you know who I am?" She shook her head. Her eyes were wild. "But you know what this means," and he pointed to the SD diamond stitched on his sleeve. She nodded, and he went on, "My friend here says you know something about Jews. Do you?"

She seemed to seize on this, like a shipwrecked sailor reaching for the one bit of flotsam on the waves. "Let me go," she said, her words slurred from the blood in her mouth. "I can give you Jews."

Preuss looked at her carefully. She would, of course, have every reason to lie. "How many? Ten? A hundred? What are we talking here? Precisely?"

The woman hesitated. "More than one," she said finally. Her eyes were even more frantic. She was lying. He had better things to do than worry about one Jew or two. He had scores to find every day, hundreds every week, thousands every month. This was a waste of time.

The woman must have read his face. "I can find more," she said. And the words rushed out. "There are hundreds hiding, thousands. They're like mice, they're everywhere. We help them hide and protect them. I can find them, every one." She looked at Preuss, at Giskes, back at Preuss.

Preuss said nothing but instead looked at Giskes, nodded, and led the way out of the room. Giskes closed the thick door behind them and they stood in the narrow corridor, the bright electric bulbs at either end making for dim light here in the center.

"She gave up fast enough," Preuss said.

Giskes smiled. "Some aren't so brave," he said, and shrugged. He was disarming, in a way. Preuss heard the Berliner accent in the man's voice now.

"Where did you find her?" Preuss asked.

Giskes smiled still. "An operation of mine." And that was all.

"What do you want?" Preuss asked, the question the same as upstairs. He expected a different answer this time, something a bit more honest.

"My task is to roll up the Resistance. Yours is to find Jews. I propose a partnership. If I find Jews during my work, I call on you. And if you, in yours, discover evidence of the Resistance, you telephone me. A simple exchange of information, that's all. I'll give you the girl and the Jews she says she'll find. You can have her, as a token of our agreement."

"She's no good to you, is she?" Preuss asked.

Giskes's smile broadened. "You're wasting your time working for the SD. You should be doing detective work, like me." His smile disappeared. "She's nothing. I thought her group might lead to greater things, but it seems not. Hers is a dead end, a handful who do nothing more than paste leaflets to posts and harass collaborators, she says. I'm after bigger game." Giskes dipped a hand into a tunic pocket and came out with an identity card. "Hers. She lives on Van Breestraat, Number Ninety-seven. With a mother and a brother, she says." Preuss glanced at the name, "VISSER, ANNJE," and flipped the card to look at the address. Near the Vondelpark, south of the Singelgracht. A pleasant part of the city.

Preuss nodded. He liked Giskes's offer. As the Abwehr rooted out partisans, they would certainly uncover the Jews who dove deepest in Amsterdam. And as Preuss combed the city for Jews, he would surely find some who hid with help.

"I agree," said Preuss, and Giskes put out his hand to shake. The old man's grip was strong, but Preuss squeezed back all the harder.

Preuss pulled at the thick door and stepped back into the too-close cell and up to this Visser and her noisy chair. Her eyes were wild yet. He held her identity card so she could see it and only it.

"You must give me Jews each week," he said. "Each week, do you understand, some Jews. Or I will come to your house. Number Ninety-seven, Van Breestraat, yes? Do you understand what I mean by coming to your house?" She glanced away from the identity card and her photograph, which looked little like her now. "Yes, I think you do. Your mother, yes? And brother?"

"Yes, I understand," Visser said very quietly. "Jews each week."

"Your mother, she's in good health, is she?" Preuss asked and laughed, and tossed the identity card on her lap. Visser's only answer was to make the chair noisier than before.

R eka stood in the shadows across from Henrik's shop and wondered if it was safe. Even after two hours in this doorway, she still hadn't come up with the nerve to test the street. The police might be waiting in the dark to snap her up.

She'd run from the station to the Sportpark until her legs gave out, but the tram had made its last trip. Sometimes they did that, stopped the trams without warning. She had three hours, then, to walk back into Amsterdam before curfew, each step another second when Annje might have talked and brought the police to their hiding place.

But as she stood, uncertain whether to dare the Lindenstraat, Annje came out of the shadows across the way. Annje turned to look the way she'd come, fit her key in the lock, shoved open the door, and slipped inside the shop.

Reka waited more minutes. How had Annje escaped the police; where had she been these hours? Reka knew the only way she would have answers was to go inside and ask her questions. She looked up and down the empty Lindenstraat. It would be easier, she thought, if she could see a policeman lurking somewhere. Then she could simply turn and run. Instead, she stepped out of the doorway.

A nnje was in tears, her head buried in Johannes's shoulder, his hand stroking her hair. The way he pressed himself against her gave more than comfort.

In the smoky glow of the oil lamp here at the back of the shop, Annje looked terrified. Her face was wet with tears and her shoulders trembled. There were broad bruises on her face, under her eyes and over one cheek where she'd been beaten, and her lip was split and swollen.

"There, there," Johannes muttered, still stroking Annje's hair. Reka caught his eye.

"They questioned her," he said quietly, Reka barely hearing his words over Annje's sobs. "But her papers were in order and they let her go."

"I don't understand. The police . . . ," Reka said, remembering how quickly the plainclothes policemen—Gestapo or Amsterdam's own police, what did it matter—had swooped in and yanked Annje away.

"They . . . they said . . . said they were looking . . . looking for someone else," Annje sobbed, the words choked out. "They . . . they said . . . said they were looking for Jews," and she glanced at Reka, but looked quickly away. "And . . . and this man . . . this man . . . the old one we met . . . they . . . they thought he was a Jew, but he wasn't . . . wasn't a Jew . . . no . . . and they thought I was a Jew, too, for talking to him, but no . . . ," and her voice was gone.

Reka remembered the man in the brown cap, how he'd managed to disappear. How the policemen had not paid him the slightest mind as they reached out and grabbed for Annje. She didn't believe her story, not for a moment.

"You say the police thought the man was a Jew." She looked in Annje's puffy eyes. "But they didn't put a hand on him."

The cellar was quiet but for Martin's small singsong voice as he stood behind his sister. "Jews, Jews, Jews," he repeated. Reka could see she'd sown some confusion in Johannes's head.

"You think she's lying?" Johannes finally asked. "If anyone betrayed you, it was Henrik. Not her. He was the one who sent us to the Diemen-Nord. Not her."

He clasped Annje even tighter. With Joop gone, it was clear that Johannes now thought it was his turn to get up Annje's dress.

Reka looked at Annje, who stared back through watery eyes.

# Four

Mouse was too tired now even to hate this German beside him. But he'd kill for a shave from Tootles.

The flight from Lisbon had been bumpy but they'd made it, joined by a sleek British fighter as they neared the English coast. Landing at a place on the shore called Poole, they took a jerky, three-hour train into London. Mouse tried to sleep but couldn't; a kid in the compartment cried almost all the way. Then a ride on a creaky subway that looked like it had been built when Moses was a baby. And finally, finally, onto an underground platform with big signs that said KING'S CROSS on the tile wall, and up and out to the street.

He held the handle of Lansky's briefcase tight in his left hand and his small suitcase in his right. He didn't like that neither hand could get to the Smith & Wesson if he needed it, but there wasn't any use complaining. Kagen wasn't about to carry his suitcase.

Mouse looked around. "Where we staying?" he asked. He didn't see any hotels. All he wanted was a room, so he could lock the door and take his hand off this pile of money, slide into a hot bath, and crawl into a soft bed. Maybe some Scotch.

Kagen set down his bag, pulled out a small black notebook, flipped through pages, looked up, and pointed. "There, Argyle Street, Number Forty-seven." It was a narrow house, with a raised stoop and tall, thin windows. Two stories, pale red brick, and about as ordinary here as a slice of white bread. If someone wanted to disappear, this would be a good place. But not exactly the Ritz.

Kagen picked up his bag, and they walked the half block to the house and up its stairs. The German knocked on the door. Mouse set down his suitcase and put his right hand on the .38 tucked into his waistband.

"You let me do the talking," Kagen said to the door, and for a moment Mouse didn't get that the German was talking to him. "Keep your gangster mouth shut—"

But Mouse didn't let him finish. "You can kiss my—" he started.

And a woman opened the door. A real knockout she was. Blond hair to her shoulders, a thin nose, full lips, and he swore her eyes were first blue, then green, then blue again as he looked over Kagen's shoulder. She wore a blue-green dress belted at the waist, the fabric tight at her hips. But she wasn't looking at him. She was looking at Kagen and his damned black patch.

"Peter Bergson said I should stop by and say hello," Kagen said, stiff. "My name is David Tucker."

"We're expecting you," she said, her voice carrying an accent Mouse couldn't place. Not British like he'd heard on the train, and not quite German. She stepped aside, holding the door open.

The first room was a parlor and they set their bags in a corner, though Mouse kept his hand on the briefcase. The girl stood in the center of the room, and the light through the window turned her hair gold. She held out her hand to Kagen. "Rachael Schaap," she said, and shook Kagen's hand. "Paul Kagen," he said, and held on to her hand a moment too long.

Mouse stepped forward, stuck out his hand, and said, "Mouse is my name. All my friends call me Mouse." The woman let go of Kagen's hand and turned to him.

"That's a very unusual name, Mr. . . ."

"Weiss. Like White."

"Mouse Weiss," she said, smiling now. Was she laughing at him? "You must be the American Peter cabled us about." She glanced at his briefcase. "The others will be here soon," she said. "Can I get you something to eat?" She was looking again at Kagen. The German nodded.

"Where can I wash up?" Mouse asked. He hadn't had a bath since . . . and suddenly he couldn't remember what day this was. They'd left on Sunday, that's right, so it was Tuesday.

"The stairs at the back, the WC is at the top, on the left."

A few minutes later as he came down the stairs, feeling cleaner from washing his face, Mouse heard laughter from the parlor. She was sitting in one of the two chairs, Kagen in the other, their knees almost touching. Kagen said something, but Mouse couldn't catch the words, and she laughed again, this time putting her hand on Kagen's leg. A knock at the door, and she got up. Mouse took her chair, set the briefcase beside his feet.

Kagen pointed to the briefcase with the chunk of cheese in his hand. Rachael had put a plate of cheese and bread on a tiny table near the window. "We should do something with that," he said.

"Like you'll watch it for me?"

"If we lose the money, we lose everything," Kagen said, giving him a hard look.

Mouse understood what was itching the German. Kagen was smarter than he looked, or maybe he'd just seen how Mouse had given the money the up and down in Bergson's office, like Mouse had watched how Kagen and Bergson had looked at it. "You don't trust me with the money, do you?" Mouse asked.

"I never said—" Kagen started, but Mouse didn't give him a chance to finish.

"It's Lansky's money, not yours. Don't forget that," Mouse said.

"It's our money, gangster," Kagen said.

"Fuck you."

Kagen leaned forward in his chair as if he was going to stand up, but voices floated into the room from the front door then, and Rachael returned with two men. The tall one with blond hair was dressed in a brown British uniform and held a green beret in his hand. The other was shorter, more Kagen's height, with dark hair and round glasses. He wore rubbed-smooth corduroys and a bulky sweater. His hands looked like he worked for a living.

Rachael stood between the two men. "Paul," she said, already calling Kagen by his first name, "this is my brother, Kristiaan Schaap." The tall one nodded in Kagen's direction. "And Joop van der Werf, my brother's friend, not long from Holland," she said, touching the shorter of the two on the shoulder. She said to the two newcomers, "This is Peter Bergson's friend, Paul Kagen, and Mr. Mouse Weiss, from America." Kagen stood and shook hands with the two; Mouse pulled himself out of his chair and did the same.

"Mouse?" the tall one asked. Schaap, the woman's brother. His accent was like hers, the English easy to understand but sounding different. Mouse nodded. Schaap's uniform was a plain brown jacket and brown pants. The only colors were the patches sewn on both shoulders. The top one was a thin red bar stitched with 10 COMMANDO and below that was one larger, a circle that showed a red Thompson submachine gun under a pair of wings. So this one's a soldier, but the other, van der Werf, he was dressed like a plug.

They stood, all five of them awkward in the silence, until Rachael asked them to follow her, and they went past the stairs he'd climbed a few minutes before and into a kitchen at the back of the house. There was a narrow table and enough chairs for everyone, and they sat while Rachael pulled a pot off the stove and poured coffees, steaming and strong.

"We've told Peter of this idea," she started, "but we need help. Money and help." And she looked in Mouse's direction. He nudged the briefcase with his foot to remind himself it was there. That was when he noticed the plain gold crucifix on a chain around Rachael's neck. No Jew, this one. He had thought they'd all be Jews. So Schaap was gentile, too. What about van der Werf? It was suddenly important to Mouse to know who was, who wasn't.

She spread a map on the table. It was of Holland, the word "Amster-dam" printed large beside a stain of yellow. "The Jews are taken by train from Amsterdam every Monday," she said, getting right to it, putting a finger on the city, "and brought here, to Westerbork, in the north." She pointed to a spot on the map. "From Westerbork, other trains leave each week, always on Tuesday, for the East. Each train carries hundreds, some-times as many as a thousand." It was Tuesday today. That meant a train left today, maybe right this minute, with a thousand Jews. He remem-bered the photographs of people crowded around boxcars. "And that's all we know. We don't know the exact route the trains take or the schedule they keep."

"We must do this before the end of the month," Kagen said. Rachael nodded, as if she knew that.

"Then the Westerbork transport three weeks from today, the twenty-seventh, that's the best for us. It gives us time to make arrangements here, travel to Holland, and still meet the deadline." They talk like it's simple, Mouse thought, as if all they had to do was show up and it would happen.

"Joop is an engineer," she said. "He worked for Nederlandse Spoorweg, the Dutch railroad. He will operate the Westerbork train after we take it." Van der Werf nodded as she talked, but didn't say anything.

"Drive it where?" Mouse asked. This was crazy, talking about stealing a train with a one-eye deserter, a woman, and only one real soldier, Schaap.

Rachael's answer only made him madder. "That's a good question, Mr. Weiss. At the moment, we only have ideas—"

"You don't know—" was all Mouse got out.

"We won't know all the details until we're in Holland," said Kagen, butting in. "We can't make precise plans from here when we don't know how it is there. We must think on our feet. Do you see?"

Mouse let Lansky talk to him like he was stupid, but he didn't have to take it from this one. "No plans? You were full of plans in New York, you and Bergson. Big ideas, he said you had. From what I've heard, all you got is your putz in your hand." They glared at each other in the thick quiet that was like the time in the flying boat.

Schaap broke the moment. "Paul here is right. Until we scout out—"

"But we do have ideas, Mr. Weiss," said Rachael quickly. She nodded to Joop, the train engineer with the rough hands and glasses.

"To remove Jews from Westerbork, the Germans would use the closest rail line. Here, at Hooghalen," he said slowly, as if he thought hard before each word. His English was understandable, but his accent was thicker than the Schaaps'. "From Hooghalen, the way to Germany is north to Groningen," and his thick finger, dirt under the nail, stabbed at another yellow spot. "From Groningen, the train would take the Bremen line, through Hoogezand and Winschoten, and into Germany at Nieuweschans. This is the most efficient route. And Germans are always efficient." Mouse thought the little guy looked Kagen's way for a moment.

"But at Groningen, there is track that heads north toward the Waddenzee. I know this line." He pointed now to a spot in the blue of the ocean north of the city named Groningen. "If we seize the train before it reaches Groningen, I can guide it through the yard and onto this track. The line comes close to the Waddenzee, perhaps five or six kilometers, closest at this place. Uithuizen." He put a thumb on the green of the land again.

"And near Uithuizen," said Rachael, "Joop says there is unused track, a spur that ends at the coast. A place where fishing boats once docked to unload their catch at a cannery. There we meet boats that will take us all to England. With enough money, we'll find Dutch fishermen to take everyone from the train."

"You're going to drive a train of Jews halfway across Holland?" Mouse asked, wanting to laugh. "And when the track ends, everyone just waltzes onto the beach? Lady, you are crazy."

"It sounds fantastic, I know," said Rachael. "But we think it will work."

"Patrol boats offshore?" Kagen asked, tugging at his black patch, as if Mouse hadn't called the whole thing nuts.

Schaap shrugged. "The Waddenzee is very shallow. At low tide, almost impossible to navigate. Even at high tide we think their S-boats stay outside the Waddenzee." And Schaap put his finger on the map, on a string of islands close to the coast. "Joop thinks the nearest Kriegsmarine are in Den Helder, a hundred and twenty kilometers away. Hours, even for their S-boats."

"What of help?" Kagen asked. "Will we have any help in Holland?"

It was Joop who answered, talking slowly like before. "I come from Amsterdam, three weeks ago. I had to leave . . ." And he paused, as if thinking of the words again. "I was of . . . the underground. Resistance, you say? My friends will help us if Kristiaan can get word to them." And van der Werf looked at Schaap. "There are five in my group. One is a Jew who was deported from Amsterdam but escaped Westerbork. She was the one who told me of the trains from Westerbork each Tuesday. She will help, and the others, too."

"From Amsterdam, how do we get to the camp?" Kagen asked. There was a long second, then two, of silence. Rachael looked at her brother, next at Joop. This wasn't good, Mouse thought.

"To seize the train that leaves Westerbork, we must get into the camp," said Rachael. "We must be on that train from the time it departs Westerbork to be sure we can take it from the Germans. Joop says it's the only way to stop a train without risking it jumping the tracks." She looked at him and made a small smile. "Taking a real train is not like in your cowboys-and-Indians stories, Mr. Weiss."

Oh, shit. Mouse had a feeling where she was going with this.

Kagen wasn't as fast. "Yes?" was all he asked.

It was Schaap who took over. "The only way to get into the camp is to be Jews." He looked hard and long at Kagen's one eye, steady and not blinking. "We will all be Jews for a day, and steal aboard the train that leaves Amsterdam for Westerbork on Monday, the day before. Ride that train into the camp, and the next morning, onto the train for the East from Westerbork."

"You're kidding, right?" asked Mouse. He made up his mind, right then and there, that he wouldn't do what Lansky had told him to. This plan was a joke.

"We need guns," Rachael said, ignoring him. "And a way to Holland, the five of us. By boat, perhaps. We need time in Amsterdam, more than a week, we think, to prepare. The eighteenth or the nineteenth, that is when we should leave." She reached out and touched Mouse on the sleeve. "The money you brought will buy us guns here and a way to Holland. And once there, the boats we'll need. We just have to find them. But with enough money, anything's possible. Isn't that right, Mr. Weiss?"

She was right. Worse, Mouse knew where he might find such things. The piece of paper in his jacket pocket, the one he'd slowly copied out as Little Man talked in that back room of Ratner's, might take him to such things. The idea meant spending some of the money he already thought of as his, but there was nothing else to do, not yet. He had to play along until he could figure out a plan of his own.

"Yeah, you're right," he said. "You're absolutely right."

You're not a Jew," Mouse said to Rachael. The others, van der Werf and Kagen and her brother, were in the parlor, but he'd stayed in the kitchen to put some distance between himself and the German. She poured him another coffee.

"Does that surprise you?" she asked. "That I do this?"

Mouse shrugged. "Maybe. Yeah, it seems strange." He looked at her through the smoke from his Chesterfield.

It seemed forever before she said something. "My brother married a Jew," she said. "Vreesje, my best of best friends, from before the war. I introduced Vreesje and Kristiaan, and then they married. She's my sister."

"Sister-in-law," he said through the smoke, correcting her.

"No, like my sister. I know English, Mr. Weiss. I know the difference."

He didn't understand, but he shrugged it off to her being Dutch and not knowing English as good as she thought. "So where is she? Is she around somewhere?" That she would do this just because her brother married a Jew, that didn't make sense.

Rachael shook her head. "When the Germans came, Kristiaan was in the Dutch army." She sipped at her coffee. "He wanted to keep fighting the Germans, and after the surrender, he fled here with his comrades. Now he is a commando, with other Dutchmen. But he had to leave her behind. She . . ." and her voice tailed off.

Mouse got the drift. Maybe she was alive, maybe she wasn't. Maybe she'd been grabbed by the Nazis and shoved into a boxcar. Maybe she was smoke.

"But you, Mr. Weiss, you're Jewish," she said.

"Yeah, I'm a yid." She raised her eyebrows. "Yid. It means Jew. Yeah, I'm a Jew, like Kagen."

She motioned for a Chesterfield, he gave her one, and she lit it with a match she plucked from a box behind her near the stove. "He loves her so," she said, talking to the room, not to him.

"She's probably dead by now, you know that, right?" he asked. "And even if she's not, how can you find one person in a whole country?"

Rachael stared at him with eyes that went from green to blue and back to green, all in a blink. If she wasn't wearing that crucifix, he would have taken her home to meet his muter. "We know where she is, my Vreesje. Joop says she and her family disappeared from their house, taken away almost eight weeks past in a *razzia*. A roundup of the Jews, Mr. Weiss . . ." And she stopped, drew on the Chesterfield. That hand shook, Mouse noticed, and she used the other to wipe at her cheek. "She's in Westerbork. You heard what Joop said. That's where all the Jews go."

She looked at the end of her smoking Chesterfield. "Kristiaan left and I was alone, Mr. Weiss. My father and mother, they were killed in Rotterdam when the Germans bombed the city," and she wiped her cheek again, the cigarette almost brushing her blond hair. "Vreesje took me into her family's house on Wijttenbachstraat. They wouldn't flee or even hide. They could have, they had enough money to hide or buy false papers and dive underground, but her papa was too proud to hide in someone's attic and her mama didn't believe the rumors then." She wiped at her face again. "Nearly a year ago, Vreesje paid a man to take me to England on his boat. I begged her to come with me, but she couldn't leave her mama." Another tear.

"So you think you owe her . . . ," he started, thinking what a sap she was, how Rachael should count herself lucky, that's all. But what she'd been saying finally worked its way into his brain.

"You mean we're doing all this to save one girl?" he asked. "You cooked this up so you and your brother can get into that camp?"

"I have to try, Mr. Weiss."

"That's crazy." He wondered what Lansky would say if he heard this. Or Bergson.

Rachael shook her head slowly. "This is larger than Vreesje now," she said, drawing the last bit from the Chesterfield. "At first, when we found Peter Bergson, it was about Vreesje. But he would help only if it was more than just one. So now we're to save hundreds."

"But you?" he asked. She looked at him square, those eyes of hers going between colors in the sunlight coming into the kitchen.

"I only know one Jew, Mr. Weiss."

"No, now you know three," he said.

She nodded. "Yes, it seems so. But your money, Mr. Weiss, only buys one for me."

Mouse glanced at the briefcase there on the floor, half under the table. Her reason made no sense, but the mention of the money convinced him that his reason made all the sense in the world. That much money would change things. He could stop being a dropper, for one, before his luck ran out and prison or a slug got him. Head for California maybe. He'd heard California was wide open. Move his muter to California, start something on his own. Maybe make book.

But he couldn't just disappear with the money. That was too obvious, even Mouse knew that. Lansky would hunt him down, and he'd end up like Kid Twist, screaming six stories to the sidewalk. No, that wouldn't work.

Not for the first time, Mouse wished he'd never, ever set foot in Tootles's barbershop.

M ouse let the barber pick coins from his hand, confused as he was by the whole pence and pound thing. He rubbed his jaw, pushed first at one cheek, then the other as he looked in the mirror the barber held in front of his face. The guy was no Tootles. He'd cut him, just a bit, under the nose, and he hadn't even said sorry.

Mouse touched his shirt and felt the metal key cold against his skin. He'd found a bank three blocks from Argyle Street, Barclays, a name he remembered seeing in Manhattan. He'd told the queer behind the high wooden counter that he wanted a safe-deposit box, and although the guy had looked down his nose at him, he'd nodded. Mouse had to show his passport, which was fine—it wasn't like he was wanted for any-thing—and the queer took him to a room behind a cage with rows of metal boxes built into the walls. He slipped a key in a small door, slid a box from its metal tray, and put it on a wooden desk. For a moment, the queer looked like he wanted to stay, but Mouse gave him the eye—he wished he could show him the Smith & Wesson, but that would be stu-pid in a bank and all—and the man huffed and left.

Mouse stacked the bundles of greenbacks in the box, thanking Kagen for giving him the idea earlier when the German hinted that he didn't trust him. Here it was safe.

He kept out two grand, twenty hundreds, which he put in his front pants pocket. He wished he'd brought a money clip. He shoved the box back into its tray, closed the metal door, locked it, and took the key.

He changed a hundred American into English, twenty-five pounds for his trouble, the bills big and floppy and too plain to be real. Even the coins were off, too big, too small, and none jingled right in his pocket.

Mouse paid the queer for the safe-deposit box—five pounds for the year, like the money would be there that long—and left Barclays. He tossed the briefcase in the first bin he came to, found a shoe shop, bought a packet of laces, and used one to tie the key around his neck. He used the other lace to tie the nineteen hundreds into a tight roll that felt bet-ter in his pocket. Then he went looking for a shave.

And now he felt himself again. He pulled the piece of paper from his pocket, looked at his own writing, and waved down a hack, big and boxy and black. "Two Whitechurch Lane, Stepney," he told the old man driving from behind the wrong side of the car.

Mouse looked at the name he'd copied. "Jack Spark," he'd written. "Call on Jack if you need anything," Lansky had said there in Ratner's. "He owes me favors. Big favors."

Mouse smelled the East End long before the hack got him there. Fish, just a bit, like the East River, but other odors ran up his nose—shit and sour beer—before being trampled by the stink of burnt things. Wood and rubber and oil and, Mouse wondered, maybe something else, too.

The East End looked like Hitler had squatted there and taken a giant crap. Whole blocks of buildings were missing roofs and slices of walls and every piece of glass in every window. Bricks were piled into off-center mountains in the street, the piles thick with weeds taken root and covered with playing kids whose faces hadn't seen soap since soap was invented. What a place, he thought, for a big man who runs big action. But then, Ratner's was a dump, too.

The driver took coins from Mouse's hand and drove off. Two Whitechurch Lane was a butcher shop—the sign painted above the greasy glass-plate window said JOHN MARLEY & SON, MEATS—but Mouse doubted if anyone bought meat here. Two guys in cheap suits sat in straight-backed chairs on either side of the door. They had beefy red faces, the both of them.

He didn't bother going up to the door, but waited in front of the two ganefs. This was something he knew. This was comfortable, not like talk of stealing trains.

"I'm here to see Jack Spark," he said to the one on the left, who looked the smarter of the two. "Is he here?"

The man, a bit soft around the middle, growled, "Piss off, wanker."

Mouse knew he had to play along. It was the rules.

"Tell Jack Spark that Mouse wants to talk to him. Tell him Mouse is a good friend of Mr. Meyer Lansky of New York, who said he should come by if he was ever in this shithole." Mouse smiled.

"Meyer who?" the ganef asked. He still hadn't gotten up, which was starting to make Mouse mad.

"Meyer Lansky, you dumb fuck."

The other one, the one who looked even dumber, moved in his chair like he was going to get tough, but a new voice, bigger, boomed and Mouse looked up.

"Meyer? Did I 'ear you right?" A third man, a big round man, stood in the doorway of the shop. He was in his late forties, with a big round head that looked like a ball, his hair cut so short he was almost bald.

Mouse could see right off that this was a mean one, he could see that in the strange little smile and the little pig eyes.

"Meyer Lansky, yeah, that's what I said. Now who the fuck are you?"

The dumber one was out of his chair, starting to move for Mouse. Mouse thought he could take him, but the second would be on him before he could finish. That's why there were two here, just for that.

"Si' down, Richie," said the big man's big voice, and then he looked at Mouse. "I'm Jack Spark, 'at's who," said the man with the big bald head. "An' unless yer Meyer Lansky yerself, which yer not, you should learn 'ow to talk to yer betters."

"Meyer didn't tell me what you looked like," Mouse said, trying to smile to make it clear he meant no offense.

The big bald man laughed, a quick bark that came and went fast. "S'all right, just watch yer mouth an' manners 'round me, son." Mouse nodded, even though he didn't want to. This was still part of the game. "Come in, tell me all 'bout Little Man. Okay?" And Spark's arm motioned him into the shop.

Mouse had been right; no one had bought meat here in ages. There wasn't even a butcher's case or block. Instead, there was a tiny table and two chairs in front of the dirty window, the furniture looking like it had been glommed from a museum, it was so old.

"Yer late for tea, son, but 'ave a seat. I'll get Richie to get us somethin' to drink." Spark sat down, the thin chair creaking under his bulk, and yelled for Richie. "Get us somethin', Richie. Make i' strong. Right?"

"Sure, Jack." And the dumb one hustled through a doorway to the back.

"Lansky sen' you, did 'e?" Spark asked, but went on, no time for an answer. "What's 'at yid midget up to these days?"

Mouse might have taken offense in other circumstances, but there was no profit here. Anyway, Lansky *was* short.

"He said I should come by and see you if I needed a favor. He said you'd be happy to do me a favor, since it would be doing him a favor."

Richie returned with two glasses. Mouse smelled the Scotch as Richie put one glass in front of him, the other in front of Spark. "'Ere's to midgets," said Spark, and raised his glass.

Mouse let that go, too, even though he knew Spark was pushing, see-ing if he would push back, and instead he drank the Scotch in a single long swallow. He lit a Chesterfield, flicked ash off his sleeve. It was time to stop playing the game. "Mr. Lansky said you owed him a favor or two. I'm here taking care of business for Mr. Lansky, and I need a favor. Or two. So let's cut the crap, how about it, Jack, and get down to it?"

Spark looked at him, the pig eyes in his big round face not blinking. No one talked to him like this, Mouse figured. Fuck him. Mouse knew Lansky's name was plenty of protection.

"Yes, I owe Meyer a thin' or two. But I'll be sure to tell 'im 'bout you when I see 'im next."

You do that, Mouse thought, but he didn't say it. "I need guns," he said.

Spark nodded, like it wasn't out of the ordinary, this request. "What kind of guns?"

"A pistol or a revolver, I'd like the revolver if you can find one. With a silencer." Spark's small eyes got a little bit bigger. That was as much as his big face could show surprise, Mouse figured.

"More'n 'at one, then?"

Mouse nodded. "Yeah. Some Thompsons."

"'Ow many?" Spark leaned back in the creaky chair and Mouse won-dered if it would hold the weight.

"Ten."

"Really?" Spark lit a cigarette—Player's, the pack said—and called again for Richie. The dumb ganef went for more whiskey while Mouse breathed the cheap tobacco from Spark's cigarette. Richie returned with a bottle of Black Label and went back outside to sit in his chair. When he was out of earshot, Spark said, "Plannin' on invadin' Fortress Europe, Mr. . . ."

"Mouse. Call me Mouse."

"I asked you a question."

"Don't worry, I'm not dipping my bill here. Neither is Mr. Lansky. Let's just say I'm passing through."

"'At's a lot of guns, son. What you gon'a do with 'em?"

In the hack, Mouse had wondered what he would do if Spark put him on the spot. He'd decided to ask himself what Lansky would do, since that was the safest way Mouse knew to keep from saying something stupid. And Mouse was sure that Lansky wouldn't tell Jack Spark jack shit, as it were. Little Man's business, no matter what it was, was his business. No one else's. Certainly not this English goy's. So Mouse said nothing, just stared at Spark and tried not to think too much about the man's mean little smile. He was a bad one, this Jack Spark. Mouse could tell.

"Five I can get," said Spark finally. "Ten, don't know 'bout ten. An' not Thompsons. Stens. But they won't come cheap. Right?"

"Then I'll need revolvers, too. Say ten. Automatics are okay, but revolvers even better." Spark nodded. "How much?" he asked Spark.

Spark fiddled with his cigarette for a moment. "Two 'undred quid each fer the Stens, oner each fer the revolvers. The one with the silencer, don't know. I've never 'ad use fer one. But I'll see what I can find, right?"

"Oner?" Mouse asked.

"'Undred. 'Undred quid, son."

Mouse did the adding in his head, fast as he could, figuring ten of the Stens, hoping they were like Thompsons, submachine guns. "Three thousand. Dollars?"

"Quid, son, what means pounds," Spark said, sounding impatient. Mouse did more arithmetic. Twelve grand for twenty guns? That was four or five times what they cost back home. But he wasn't home, he was here.

"Throw in cartridges and extra clips for the Stens, and do it for nine thousand. My money."

"Eleven," said Spark, not hesitating. Spark knew what dollars were worth.

"Ten and a half," and Mouse stuck out his hand. Spark was smiling that nasty mean smile, but he took Mouse's hand and shook it.

"Let's 'ave a tiddlywink on 'at," Spark said, pouring another finger of Walker into each of their glasses.

Tiddlywink? "I need something else," Mouse said over his whiskey, giving up trying to puzzle out Spark's mumble-jumble.

"Don't tell me. Tanks an' a submarine, now?" And Spark laughed that short, doglike laugh again.

Mouse shook his head. "A boat or a plane. I need the name of a man with a boat or a plane. I'll pay you another five hundred for the name. Five hundred *quid*," and he rapped the glass on the table. That would be two grand real money. Spark should be happy, since it gave him back the twelve he'd asked for to start, and then some.

Spark leaned forward, his chair groaned unnaturally, and for a second Mouse thought the big man was making a move. Mouse put his hand under the table and touched the butt of the Smith & Wesson stuck in his waistband.

But Spark only talked. "You must 'ave somethin' very special in mind, you an' yer midget. A boat now? An airplane? Sounds like you need some 'elp, Mouse, from the locals. 'At's me. I'm the local."

"I just need a name, Jack, that's all. Either you give me a name or you don't."

Spark's answer was to blow a stream of smoke right into Mouse's face. He almost coughed at the stink.

Mouse knew that the big man's wheels had to be turning, wondering what he was up to, and wondering which was more important, what he might make by pinching Mouse's play, or how much he was afraid of Lansky.

Finally, Spark nodded and said, "I may be able to come up with names. I know a lad who flies, and I 'ave occasion to call on a boat. Fast boat you'll wan', right? I 'ave friends with one, even 'as Vickers guns, if 'at's what you need."

Mouse stood, slowly so as not to make Spark nervous, and reached into his pants pocket and pulled out the roll of hundreds. He untied the shoelace and counted out ten on the table, tied up the roll, and slipped it back in his pocket. "That's a thousand to show my intentions. A plane's better," he said. He didn't like the idea of taking a boat to Holland, the way he swam for shit. "I'll give you the two grand for the name when I come tomorrow. The rest on Friday, when I come for the guns."

Spark's big head jerked. "Friday? I can't get—"

"Then just the name. I'll find someone else for the guns," Mouse said. If Spark couldn't get them in three days, he couldn't get them, which meant that they'd need to find another way.

Spark shook his head, said nothing, but his face got red all over. "Friday, five in the afternoon, 'ere. Not a tick-tock earlier."

"And the name . . ."

"Come tomorrow, 'round tea. If I 'ave something, I'll 'ave it then." Spark put out his hand again and they shook on it. But this time his smile was meaner still, his pig eyes smaller yet.

"Pleasure doing business with you, Jack," Mouse said, and turned to walk for the door.

"Tell Lansky," Spark said from behind him, and Mouse turned back. "Tell Lansky he and me 're evens. You understan'?"

Mouse nodded. "I'll be sure to tell him the next time I see him, Jack." And he walked out of the shop into the fading sunlight, past the pair on watch, and took a right, heading for the busy street to find a hack to take him back to No. 47 Argyle, where he hoped there was a bath so he could wash off the stink of this place, Spark's cigarettes included.

# *Five*

The closer Johannes stepped toward Henrik, the more afraid the old man got.

"I swear," Henrik said, using a handkerchief to dab at the sweat pooled above his lip. "I simply brought the message. You saw it. I had nothing to do with what happened at the station. I swear." Henrik put weight on one foot, then the other, as if his bladder was full.

"I think it was you," Johannes said, his face now only centimeters from the old man's. Henrik quaked, but didn't change his story. That was when Reka knew Henrik said the truth. If he stood up to Johannes's bullying, it was because he told the truth. And for all his faults, Johannes wasn't stupid. He understood. He was letting it go now, satisfied.

Henrik wasn't. "Please," he said. "Leave tonight. I can't take this any longer. I have a wife." Johannes just shook his head.

"We have nowhere else to go."

"No, you must leave. Tonight. I'll help you find another hiding place, but—"

"Henrik," and Johannes's voice got firm. "There is nothing to worry about. We're perfectly safe. No one will find us." The old man didn't seem convinced, Reka thought, but he didn't argue. Johannes had won again.

Johannes looked finally at the paper Henrik had handed him before the argument began. "Interesting" was all he said.

"What?" Reka finally asked because no one else did. Martin was too dimwitted, and Annje . . . Annje seemed too shaken, even now. Or was she? The woman's bruises had turned yellow and purple, and her lip was swollen twice large. She'd been beaten, yes. But Reka still thought there was a lie behind those bruises.

"Another message to meet someone. But it doesn't say much."

"Another trap," she said.

"I don't think so. It has Joop's name on it," he said.

Joop. Reka didn't believe it. "What does it say?"

Johannes let the silence stretch out. "Joop's coming, on the eighteenth or the nineteenth. Others, too, it seems. But it doesn't say where. Or why."

Little Joop. Four weeks past he had helped them ruin the electric switch controls in the railyard outside Amersfoort, but he had not shown up at the designated time for their next meeting. Two days later they'd heard he'd been betrayed by someone at the Nederlandse Spoorweg, but that was all. Unsure if he'd been arrested, they'd all been forced to come live in Henrik's cellar, a place Joop had never been. Johannes left his job as an apprentice printer, Annje and Martin moved out of their mother's house. Reka, of course, had been here all along. Jews had no jobs, no homes, only hiding places.

"Where is he?" Reka asked, seeing in her mind the short man with the dark hair and the spectacles and the slow words. She had liked little Joop. He had been the only one who didn't fret that they had a Jew among them.

"It doesn't say," said Johannes, looking at the paper again. He handed it to Reka.

CHOSEN PARTY COMING 18 OR 19 DETAILS LATER JOOP VDW

*Chosen party.* What did that mean?

"Joop is back?" asked Martin from his place beside his sister. No one answered him.

"Perhaps he thinks it's safe," Johannes said, shrugging. "Did they say where this came from, or how?" he asked Henrik, but the old man just shook his head.

Reka looked at Annje. She was quiet, which was odd, Reka thought; they'd been lovers, she and Joop, hadn't they? Or so Martin had blurted— not in so many words, but he'd said that Joop had been spending nights at their mother's house. Annje should be happy at this news.

"Joop is back?" asked Martin again, and Annje touched her brother's massive hand and patted it.


Mouse was nearly late to the butcher shop. He'd overslept—twelve hours and more, making up what he'd missed traveling from New York—and he had to walk to the Barclays and wait while the same queer as the day before led him to the room with the safe-deposit boxes. He took ten grand this time, jotted down the numbers in the little brown book he'd bought at a news shop at the corner. He rolled twenty of the bills into a tight bundle and tied them with the shoelace, but the rest, still with the paper band around them, went in his jacket. He was getting to like the shoelace idea. It had a certain character, he thought.

Next he stopped at a Commercial Cable office Rachael had told him about. He'd printed Lansky's name and the address of Ratner's in block letters on the cablegram form, then spent ten minutes thinking up the words.

HERE SAFE STOP MET JACK YESTERDAY STOP HE WANTS IN OUR DEAL STOP LEAVE EIGHTEEN RETURN TWENTY SEVEN WITH THOUSAND PACKAGES FROM MISTER UITHUIZEN

Twenty-four words, and he'd handed the impatient clerk a pound note and some coins after he'd given the words a last up and down, looking for anything that would give him away.

The hack today was a different car, with a different old man driving, but it smelled the same. He told the driver to let him off on Whitechapel Road, and he walked the fifty yards down Whitechurch Lane to No. 2. On the way, he checked out doorways and the one alley—to see the lay of the land, so to speak. Spark might try something stupid.

But Spark just greeted him at the doorway where the same two sat in the same two chairs, dumb Richie on the right, the other on the left. Both looked like they'd love to beat his brains in, but they stayed in their chairs.

"Jus' in time fer tea, son," Jack Spark said, his big body making a big voice that went up and down Whitechurch Lane. Spark motioned him into the shop. There were cups, a pot, and a chipped plate piled with small cakes on the museum table. Spark sat down, the chair creaking like before.

"Si', 'ave some," Spark said. He stuffed one of the cakes in his mouth, crumbs flaking onto his suit. The mean smile was still there, even around the cake. Mouse sat, poured himself a cup of tea from the pot, and sipped. It was crap. He wished Spark had made coffee, or at least offered him some Johnnie Walker.

"Got a name for me, Jack?" he asked, shoving the cup to the side. He lit a Chesterfield to chase the taste.

"'At I do, son, 'at I do." Spark brushed cake crumbs from his belly. What a shmok, Mouse thought.

Spark reached inside his jacket and by habit Mouse watched the hand, felt his own edge to the Smith & Wesson stuck in his waistband under his suit jacket, wondering if he could get to it in time. But Spark's hand came out with only a piece of paper. He slid it across the tiny table.

HARRY
GOLDEN PHEASANT, BIGGLESWADE, BEDFORD

"Harry? That it?"

"'Arry O'Brien. You said you wan' to fly, 'e's yer man," said Spark, shoving another cake in his trap. He mumbled around it. "Irishman. Pilots fer One-six-one Special Duties Squadron, up at Tempsford. Takes agents in'er Belgium an' 'Olland, secret sort of thing, to bother the Boches. 'E's done some jobs fer me this last year. Knows 'is way around, knows 'is airplanes an' all. 'E wants to meet you tonight at the Golden Pheasant. Nine o'clock. You know where Biggleswade is? Straight up the A-One, on the way to Peterborough. Car'll take you there inside an 'our an' a 'alf. The train—"

"I'll find it," Mouse said, pulling out his roll and counting out twenty hundreds to the table, saying the count. He pushed the pile of curled bills toward the big man. "Two grand for Harry's name, like I said. The rest for the guns when I come on Friday." He looked at Spark. "You'll have the guns Friday, won't you, Jack?"

The big man nodded and filled Mouse's cup again so it overflowed with tea. "Got a line on 'em. Maybe not ten Stens, like you wan', but enuff, I think. Revolvers won't be trouble at all, right?"

"The one with a silencer?"

Spark reached inside his jacket again, and this time, he did pull a piece. It took Mouse by surprise, and Spark pointed the gun in a careless kind of way before he could do more than move a finger for the Smith & Wesson. Spark didn't pull the trigger, just smiled that mean smile.

The gun was an odd thing, a black tube mostly, twelve inches long with a short grip at one end. The barrel was thick all the way from muzzle to butt, the silencer probably. It was an automatic and looked like something a mechanic would use to squirt grease into places.

"They call this the Welrod," Spark said, still pointing the pistol carelessly Mouse's way. He twisted a flat knob on the butt of the barrel, pulled it back and pushed it in, twisting the knob again. Mouse heard the action's gentle click-clack. He hoped like hell the thing wasn't loaded. "Quiet as the proverbial mouse, i' is," and Spark grinned large at his own joke. "The SOE uses 'em. 'At's the outfi' O'Brien flies fer. 'E pinched a pair of these fer me ages ago."

Mouse remembered how Spark had said he had no use for silenced pistols. That he was a liar didn't surprise Mouse, but that he didn't hide it did.

Spark held the gun in two hands, one under the barrel, the other on the grip, the thing pointed at him now for sure. "Single action," and he squeezed the trigger, the clack of the hammer making Mouse jump. Spark smiled that nasty smile at the fun he was having. Spark pulled the bolt from the butt again, pushed it in again, twisted the knob before and after, and the striking of the hammer filled the old butcher shop again.

"I's thirty-two caliber, good fer forty, fifty feet. 'At far away 'e won't even 'ear i'." Spark laid the Welrod on the table.

"How much?" Mouse tried to keep his voice even, though he was hot at what Spark had just done. Fuckin' mamzer, fuckin' bastard, Mouse thought.

Spark put his hands on the table, one each side of the Welrod. "Gratis, son. Free."

"If . . ." Nothing was free.

"If you tell me what yer midget's up to, 'at's the if. 'E's got some jelly cooked 'ere, don't 'e? 'E's not satisfied with all 'is money, is 'e? 'E wants a piece of me and mine." Spark pulled out a Player's and lit it, sending the stink into the place like before.

Mouse shook his head, remembered his promise to himself that he would always ask what Lansky would do. Lansky would stare down this East End putz and tell him to fuck off. But not if the guy pulled a trigger on him, empty chamber or not. Then all bets were off. Then Lansky would play it plain for the moment, but not forget, not ever. So that was what Mouse did. "I'll have to pass, Jack." His voice, he was glad to hear, was flat level.

"All I wan', Mouse," said Spark, "is a sliver of the pie. Just a very small slice. I'm not greedy." Spark sent a breath of that shit-smelling Player's Mouse's way.

Mouse stuffed the piece of paper with the address of the pub into his pocket and stood up to get out of the stink. "Like I said, Jack, this doesn't have anything to do with you." He watched Spark's hands, still alongside but not touching the Welrod.

Spark didn't believe him, Mouse could see that. "You wan' this fer somethin' special," Spark said, twitching a finger at the Welrod. "Somethin' you don't wan' anyone, much less bottles an' stoppers, to know." Bottles and stoppers? Again Mouse had no idea what Spark was saying. "Whatever i' is, I wan' in. You make a play on my fiefdom, as i' were, an' I get a taste. 'At's the rules. Know what I mean?"

"I'll do without the gun," Mouse said. "See you day after tomorrow." And he turned and walked out of the shop. There, calm and calmer, he thought, proud.

He stepped past the two ganefs in their chairs, their asses glued there; neither had left to wait for him down the street. Mouse turned right, like yesterday, for Whitechapel, crossed the street, and started walking.

By the time Mouse got within spitting distance of Whitechapel Road, he knew one of Spark's ganefs was following. Mouse caught a glance of him in the reflection in a plate glass window he walked by, the guy across the street. Just like in front of Tootles's place.

It was Richie, the dumber one. Figures. If Mouse listened carefully he could hear Richie's footsteps, clumsy and loud.

Just before the corner, with Whitechapel Road in front of him and a hack rolling by, Mouse stopped and pretended to be thinking. Maybe which way to go, Richie would figure. He used the moment to unbutton his suit jacket to clear the butt of the Smith & Wesson. He turned left at the corner, and as he heard Richie's footsteps pick up, he moved quick into the second doorway he found. Not the first.

Richie was dumb. Although Mouse heard him stop at the first doorway to sniff it out, he was careless after that. Probably because Richie didn't see him at all, he must have thought he'd hoofed it all the way around the next corner. No one was that fast, except maybe that schvartzer Jesse Owens.

Richie didn't see him tucked into the blind spot of the store's doorway until it was too late. Mouse kicked him, hard, just below his left knee. Richie yelped and started to go down.

Mouse grabbed the shoulder of Richie's cheap suit and yanked hard so that the ganef made acquaintance with his knee, which was coming up at the same time. There. That felt bad. From the sound and the blood, Richie'd just busted his nose and maybe a cheekbone. Richie made a sound like a balloon losing air as he sagged to the concrete, both hands out now to catch himself.

But Mouse gave him no time. He turned, slipped a step around Richie, and shoved the man to the ground, the back of Richie's head slapping the brickwork beside the doorway. Richie, now sitting with his legs stretched in front of him, moaned. Mouse made a fist and, leaning over Richie, punched him once-twice, bang-bang, first hard on the nose then on the cheek, maybe busted. There was blood all over.

When he knelt, he saw from the corner of his eye a couple of plugs behind the glass in the door. Let them look, Mouse thought—he'd be gone in a moment. Mouse pulled aside Richie's suit, found the gun in the holster under his armpit, and tossed the revolver to the other corner of the doorway, out of reach.

"Don't ever follow me again," he said to Richie, who was still awake, though not so much that Mouse could be sure he was listening real good. Richie didn't say anything, not words anyway, just gurgled a bit and moaned. Mouse punched him again, hard, on his nose. "Understand? You follow me again, and I'll do more than this, Richie." Richie moaned again. "You make sure you tell Jack, Richie. My business is none of your fuckin' business."

An old guy tried to push open the door to come out of the store, but Mouse was in the way and the old guy froze. Mouse turned and walked down Whitechapel Road, leaving Richie in the doorway, waved down a black car, and got in.

Too bad Kagen hadn't come along, Mouse thought as the hack took him away from the East End. Too bad. He wouldn't fuckin' talk about who was the wrong kind of Jew now.

It was dark in the car, dark outside, even the road was dark. The headlights of the little car—Rachael called it a Morris—barely lit the way. Every once in a while, a sign or rock along the road glowed like a little ghost, special paint, Rachael said, that showed in the dark to keep people on the straight and narrow. Even so, she drove no faster than thirty.

The last sign in the weak headlights said STOTFOLD and Rachael said it was just another ten minutes. Mouse snapped open his lighter and looked at his watch: quarter to nine.

When he'd come back to the house at No. 47, Rachael was alone. Kagen had gone out for cigarettes, she said. Mouse told her they couldn't wait, he needed to get to Biggleswade by nine to meet with a pilot who might fly them to Holland. But the truth was, he was glad the German wasn't around; the last thing he wanted was to be cooped up in a car with Kagen.

Mouse could tell Rachael wanted to wait for Kagen by the way she looked at his right hand, where it was red from Richie's blood and where he'd bruised his knuckles. He'd wiped it off on the seat of the hack, and he'd missed some. But she scratched out a note and left it on the kitchen table, and grabbed her coat and bag.

The Morris was parked in a small garage out back, facing the alley. It was her brother's, she said, and the petrol—she used that word—was his by rights from his ration as an officer. He'd left the car when he returned to his duty station by train.

She drove badly, like most women, Mouse thought. She gripped the wheel too hard and let out the clutch too fast, but at least she never stalled it. What with her troubles driving and their trouble seeing the road, it was no surprise that they didn't talk. Mouse smoked and thought, and rubbed his right hand.

The whole thing with Spark was fucked. If he'd told the big man what he was here for, why he wanted the guns and the plane, maybe things would've gone smooth. Now it was too late, what with Spark pointing that silencer and pulling the trigger—what balls—and then the thing after with Richie. What a mess.

The Morris rolled on. He wanted to lean over—he could smell her in the car, a nice smell, something like perfume but under it he could smell her—and press his foot on hers to make the Morris go faster, but he didn't.

"What happened today?" she asked out of the dark. She meant his hand and the blood.

"Nothing really," and he flicked the butt through the crack at the top of the window.

She was quiet for a mile or more. "Did you shoot someone?"

He laughed. "No, not today." He meant it like a joke, but she didn't laugh along. "I had to settle for something else."

Again the quiet. Mouse saw a dim sign that said BIGGLESWADE 1 MILE.

"Paul says you are a gangster."

He wasn't going to argue. The papers back home called him that, the three times they'd used his name, but it wasn't a bad word, not by itself. He thought of himself as someone who made sure people followed rules, and if that was a gangster, fine. At least he wasn't like Kagen, who had packed bombs in Palestine that killed anyone unlucky.

"Paul says you'll get us in trouble before we leave."

What did it matter, before they left or after? It was trouble all the same.

"He says we can't trust you, Mr. Weiss."

Big surprise, Mouse thought. Kagen had said as much, though not as straight. But although he was tempted, Mouse kept his mouth shut, knowing nothing would change her mind if she was sleeping in Kagen's bed, which was what was happening. He'd heard them through the walls, hadn't he?

"There," he said, pointing, but in the car's darkness she might not have seen. "Turn here." And they drove down a darkened street, only a chink or two of light showing from behind tight curtains, and into the center of the village. Even in the dark, Mouse found the pub, what with the big wooden bird swinging from a pole over the door. Rachael saw it too.

Mouse was out of the car and at the door to the Golden Pheasant before he heard a car door slam. Rachael was beside him. He could smell her in the dark.

"Wait in the car," he said, trying not to make it sound like an order, but wanting to.

"I want to meet this pilot."

"It'll be better if you wait."

"What if he asks where he's to take us? What do you tell him, Mr. Weiss? Holland? Holland may be a very small country, but it's still a big place."

She was right. He pushed open the door—a sign on it said "No dogs during lunch"—and he stepped into the pub. It had a low ceiling, with a bar farthest from the door, bottles stacked behind the bar, glasses in racks overhead, a balding man, maybe fifty years old, standing between the bar and the bottles. Two guys stood at the bar. Mouse counted five tables. At one was a man and woman, old people. At another sat a man alone. That was all. Mouse sniffed, smelling Rachael behind him. Even in the pub's stink of spilled beer and cigarettes, he could smell her.

Mouse walked to the table with the one man, stood there until the guy looked up. A wide face, red hair cut short on the sides. He wasn't wearing a uniform, just a faded denim jacket. His nose had been broken once and he could use a better barber; there were two nicks on his cheek where he'd shaved.

"O'Brien," Mouse said, not putting it as a question. The man didn't nod, but with his foot pushed out a chair. Mouse sat down.

"Who's the bird, boyo?" O'Brien asked. Mouse heard Rachael scrape a chair over the floor from another table and then she was sitting beside him, facing O'Brien too.

Bird. Mouse liked that word.

"Is there a problem?" Rachael asked. Mouse wished she would shut up.

O'Brien shook his head. "No, though you're a fine bit of stuff, dear. I was expecting one, not two, that's all."

Mouse didn't bother to put out his hand to O'Brien. That would come later, if at all. He leaned forward and felt the pressure of the Smith & Wesson, like always in his waistband.

O'Brien beat him to the conversation. "Jack Spark, what do you think of him, la? One wit more and he'd be a half-wit. Always with that fuckin' Cockney Rabbit way wid words. Rhyming and all. 'Bottles and stoppers' for coppers, that kind of thing. Drive you off your nut jus' tryin' to get the meanin'." He was looking at Mouse now, though every few seconds his eyes would dart Rachael's way.

"He said you had a plane," Mouse said, ignoring the language lesson. "I'd like to hire it for a night."

O'Brien looked him over. "I freelance on the occasion, true." O'Brien had dropped his voice some. They were maybe ten feet from the old couple. In the background, Mouse could hear the guys at the bar talking, but he couldn't make out the words.

"For Spark," Mouse said.

"Sometimes. Sometimes for meself."

"What do you do, Mr. O'Brien?" Rachael asked. Mouse wanted to nudge her knee, but she'd sat just out of reach. "How do you come by an airplane? There's a war on, I hear."

O'Brien's smile was wide and showed that he was missing one of his front bottom teeth, on the left. "I heard some talk of that, too."

Mouse could see Rachael getting angry. The muscles in her neck tightened and she stared straight at the mick. "Don't talk to me that way, Mr. O'Brien."

"Don't talk to *me* that way, then," O'Brien said. He looked over at Mouse. "Who am I speaking to here, you or your bird?"

"Me. I'm the one with the money, so you talk to me."

"Good to know."

"Where does your plane come from?" Mouse asked, lighting a Chesterfield. He shut up for a moment as the bartender came to the table and asked what they wanted. Rachael said brandy, Mouse said whiskey, and O'Brien lifted his empty glass and said, "Another jar of your finest, good publican," laying on his Irish accent thick.

"It's a Lysander," O'Brien said when the bartender was gone. The name meant nothing to Mouse. "I fly Joes who need to go places without a lot of attention." Belgium and Holland, Spark had said. Agents, he had said.

"So you're a soldier . . . ," Rachael said, and this time Mouse didn't worry what she would think, and kicked her lightly under the table.

O'Brien caught the kick and smiled again, said, "The Royal Air Force frowns on civilians flying its aircraft, yes, it does."

The bartender brought their drinks, set them down on the table, and took Mouse's pound note. When the guy was back at the bar, Mouse took a sip of the whiskey, lit a new cigarette off the ember of the old, and laid out the deal. "I want you to fly me and my friends to Holland. I want you to put us down where we tell you, safe and sound."

O'Brien drank his beer, and for a moment Mouse thought this was going to be over quick. But the Irishman put down his glass and shook his head. "Never done that," he said. "I've done jobs for that Cockney wanker, some things for meself, but strictly within the U.K.," he said. The mick took another gulp of beer, shook his head again. "Flying over the waters, that's not business. That's the war. I do that for king and country, not for money."

What a sap, Mouse thought.

O'Brien shifted in his chair. "If Jack had told me this, I would've told him to sod off."

"Spark doesn't know nothing. Spark had better never know, either."

"Why do you want to go all the way to bloody 'Olland anyway, la?" O'Brien asked. "Germans there, I hear." And now he looked at Rachael who, Mouse noticed, was glaring at him. She was wasting her time.

"That's our business," said Mouse. O'Brien shook his head again. Mouse reached inside his jacket slowly. He brought out a stack of bills and put it on the table, his hands around it and over it to hide it from the plugs in the pub.

"Four thousand, in dollars," Mouse said. "A thousand pounds. Another thousand quid when you put us on the ground in Holland." He was offering the Irish a fortune.

O'Brien looked at the money under Mouse's hands. He was trying to decide. Mouse moved his hand so O'Brien got a better look. He wanted the money, Mouse saw that as he watched O'Brien chew a bit on his lower lip. Finally.

"Another thousan' quid up front," he said, very quiet. Shit, thought Mouse. The pile in the safe-deposit box was getting small fast.

"Four hundred," Mouse said. "And when you get us there."

O'Brien thought again, but not so long this time. He nodded. "Where to and when, if you please."

Mouse waited for Rachael to say something, but she didn't, so he looked to her and she understood.

"Outside Amsterdam," she said. "Somewhere close enough that we can walk to the outskirts by dawn. South of Amstelveen, perhaps. There's a tram we can take from Amstelveen into the city. And it must be the night of the eighteenth or early morning of the nineteenth," she said.

O'Brien seemed to be thinking again. "Almost full moon that night. Good. I need a big moon to find me way." He looked up, smiled. "It must be someplace easy to spot from the air. Near a river, that's best. Or some water. And not close by city or town, that's where the German are, la? 'Em and their guns."

"The Westeinderplassen," Rachael said. "It's a large lake south of Amsterdam, you won't miss it. Not more than ten kilometers from Amstelveen. And there's nothing along the east and south shores."

"You'll have someone meet you on the ground, I don't wonder," said O'Brien.

Rachael nodded.

"Tell 'em to bring torches," O'Brien said. "They need to mark the landing site. Tell 'em at least three, and make an L shape. That's how we'll find 'em." He went quiet again, thinking again. "We'll want to leave around twenty-one 'undred, once it's dark here. That should put us over Amsterdam 'bout midnight. Tell your people to meet us at midnight, on the dot. You'll tell me exactly where later?"

"Yes," Rachael said. "But perhaps not until we leave."

"You'll want a return ticket, I assume. Or is this a one-way?" O'Brien asked.

"One-way," Mouse said. And as he said the words, the idea came to him. How he could have the money and stay on Lansky's good side, both.

"And how many in the party? Just the two of you, then?"

"No, us and three others. Five. And some gear," said Mouse.

"Five . . ."

"Is that a problem, Mr. O'Brien?" Rachael asked.

O'Brien looked at her, at Mouse, back to her. "The Lysander's small, miss. I've never taken more than three. I don't know if me flying carrot can manage. We won't be taking off at a proper airfield here, you'll know."

"Just get us there," Mouse said, the idea firming up in his mind. He wondered why he hadn't thought of this before. It was the simplest way.

Mouse looked over his shoulder, saw that no one watched, and he slid the dollars across the table. O'Brien set his hands atop the money and pulled it off the tabletop.

Mouse stuck out his hand. O'Brien shook it, his face grinning like he'd swallowed the actual canary. "Pleased to be doing business with you, Mr. . . ." O'Brien said.

"Mouse, just call me Mouse."

One of O'Brien's eyebrows went up, but he didn't laugh or smile. "Mouse" was all he said. "Well, Mr. Mouse, we'll meet here, on the eighteenth, twenty 'undred. That's eight in the P.M., la? Don't be late."

Mouse nodded, but leaned forward so O'Brien could hear him when he said very softly, "No one hears of this. Especially Spark. Right?"

O'Brien's eyes got smaller, but he nodded. "From what I know, Jack Spark has no business interests in 'Olland. Why should he care what you do?"

Mouse stood and helped Rachael from her chair. He let her head toward the door, but turned and said quietly to O'Brien, "We both know what's what, Harry. I would hate to get in an argument." That was as much as he figured he should say, the most that Lansky would say if he had met O'Brien and seen him for the kind of guy he was. And Mouse followed Rachael out the door.

The Morris was just a few miles down the road, not even as far as Stotfold, when Rachael asked from the dark, "Do you trust him?"

He knew what she meant. She knew where he'd got O'Brien's name and she had seen the blood on his hand.

"It's a lot of money," he said. He lit a cigarette, and in the flare of the lighter he saw the side of her face. Her hair had fallen a bit across her cheek. "He'll play it straight for the money, you can bet that." But as Mouse chewed on the idea in his head, he was thinking more of Rachael than of Harry O'Brien.

She didn't say anything at first, and another mile or so slipped behind the Morris. "He flies for the Royal Air Force, but he works with gangsters. I don't trust him."

"You're working with a gangster now, aren't you?" he asked. "Isn't that what you called me before?" He wanted to tell her that she was sleeping with one worse, but he didn't.

Even with the window rolled down some, he could smell her in the car. Mouse wondered if he could pop her, a woman. He'd never popped a woman. Women weren't part of the deal, being a dropper. But there was no way around it, not with his idea storming in his head.

Funny thing, but it was the kind of idea that Lansky might like, Mouse thought, if he was in my shoes.

# Six

M ouse lay in bed, his hand off the edge of the mattress, in his hand a Chesterfield, and listened to Kagen and Rachael. The walls of the old house were too thin to muzzle the sounds from the next room. He heard her call out something, over and over. Maybe it was Dutch.

He dropped the butt into a half-empty cup alongside the bed and listened to it sizzle. He couldn't think with that going on next door.

He dressed, picked up his shoes, and padded in socks to the kitchen. He lit the gas ring, put the pot on the stove, and while the water warmed, sat at the table. This was more like it. The kitchen was quiet, only a little traffic noise from the street reaching the back of the house.

"You'll want a return ticket," O'Brien had said night before last. "Or is this a one-way?" The mick's words had given him the idea.

Fly to Holland sure, Mouse thought. I'll do that. But I won't let O'Brien leave without me. I'll climb out of the plane, make O'Brien wait. Pop Kagen, the two Schaaps, and the little one, Joop. Not here in London,

which had crossed his mind, which was, in fact, why he'd asked Spark
for a silencer, but pop them over there. Then get back in the plane, back
to London, lie low for a week, pull the money out of the box in Barclay's
and find a way home to New York. It was foolproof.

It was better than anything else he'd cooked up. He couldn't disappear here before the others left. Kagen would cable Bergson that Mouse
had vanished with the money and then Bergson would tell Lansky. And
this was better than popping them in London. He didn't know London
and so didn't know where to plant them. The cops might find them and
if the cops knew them dead, Lansky would too, sooner or later. In Holland, they would just disappear.

So he would have to pop them. If he didn't, and by some miracle they
made it back, well, that meant Lansky would learn the truth. Mouse
couldn't leave witnesses, not again. He didn't want to spend the rest of
his life looking over his shoulder.

With the four of them gone—he tried to put Rachael out of his head,
but she kept coming back, her face on the wrong end of his Smith &
Wesson—he could make up any story he wanted. How they were am-
bushed when they got off the plane, or how the Germans had grabbed
all but him. Maybe that was it. "We almost did it, Mr. Lansky, but the
Nazis got 'em, I got away, and here's how I escaped." He would have to
work out a story, a good story, a story without kinks or leaks so Lansky
couldn't trick him into revealing the truth or track his trail, but he'd
have plenty of time to dream up the story. For now, all he had to do was
play this out the way it was going, and step off the plane in Holland and
pop the four of them.

Just one thing about it bothered him. He'd never popped a girl, and
didn't know how it would go. But there was no other way as far as
Mouse could figure. Not if he wanted to keep the money.

The water boiling, Mouse made coffee, strong like Rachael had the
morning before, by pouring the grounds into the roil and then taking
the pot off the ring to let them settle. He poured a cup, sat back down,
lit another Chesterfield.

He would have to pay Spark for the guns, there was no way around
that. To do different would make Kagen all suspicious and maybe queer

the plan. With what he'd already given Spark, that made more than twelve grand. Another four to O'Brien night before last, almost another six when he got them to Holland. That came to—Mouse had to stop to do the addition—about twenty-two large. Say another five for incidentals now and expenses later when he lay low in London and then getting back to New York. That would leave seventy-three grand. Take him six years to make that kind of money working for Lansky.

It was a good plan. It would work.

He pulled Lansky's cablegram from the pocket of his pants, where he'd put it yesterday after the boy came to the door.

EAGER TO RECEIVE THOUSAND PACKAGES FROM MISTER UITHUIZEN STOP DEAL NOT JACKS BUSINESS

Thirteen words. Lansky never wasted a dime, did he? But the part about Spark he wasn't sure how to read. Was he to warn off Spark, tell him Lansky's words exactly? Or was it just a reminder of something Mouse already knew?

Rachael stepped into the kitchen. "I thought I smelled coffee," she said, reaching for the pot and a cup, and he slid the cablegram under a short stack of papers on the table, maps and sea charts and lists and such.

"Where's Kagen?" Mouse asked. Rachael didn't answer, just sat down at the table. Her hair was tied back.

"Still sleeping," she said to the cup in her hands as she blew on its surface. She didn't look up.

Mouse wanted a reason to hate her. That would make it easier when the time came. He got right to the point.

"Why you sleeping with him?" he asked.

She blew on her coffee again. She wasn't going to answer.

"It won't work out, you know," he said. "He's Jewish, isn't he, and you're not, that's one. And he's crazy, you know that, right? Has he told you how many Germans he's killed? If he hasn't, he will. You can bet that."

"Where I come from, Mr. Weiss, people don't ask such questions."

"You're fooling yourself if you think he's right in the head," Mouse said. He tried to work up some anger—tell himself that she was a stupid shikse that chased Jewish cock because it was different, or that she slept with bad news like Kagen because she was bad news herself—but it didn't exactly work. He'd never known someone like her to cry over a Jew, for one. "He's German, too, in case you forgot. And he's—" he said, intending to tell her Kagen had probably put holes in women and kids once upon a time, but he stopped, awkward. He was going to do the same, he was planning on popping her, wasn't he?

"You are such a strange man," Rachael said, now looking over the rim of her coffee. "Why say these things to me? Why do you care?"

Mouse didn't have an answer he could tell her.

"I like Paul because he's simple, Mr. Weiss," she said finally. "For him, things are black-and-white." She put down the coffee now and looked him hard in the eyes. Hers did that change from color to color. "When I'm with him, I can also see things are black-and-white."

Mouse lit a Chesterfield, then another, and handed her the second. She smoked, still looking at him.

"Black-and-white, I think like that, too," he said.

She shook her head. "You're a funny one, Mr. Weiss. I think things are more complicated for you." Could she see into his head and read the plan printed there?

Rachael used the back of her hand to wipe at her eye. "I'm here because my friend Vreesje isn't, Mr. Weiss. I would like to know the reason for that. If things were black-and-white, one or the other, it might be easier to know the reason."

She stood up, the chair making a scraping sound on the wooden floor and the half-smoked cigarette spitting when she dropped it in her coffee.

Mouse listened to her footsteps on the stairs, then heard a bedroom door open and shut.


Reka watched from the deep shadows of late afternoon, tucked in a doorway. Annje was in the crowd up ahead, walking east on the Herengracht, past flower stalls and vegetable sellers, threading her way through children and mothers, a policeman here, a shuffling old man there. She was impossible to lose as long as Reka kept an eye on the blue scarf Annje wore over her hair.

As Reka stepped out of the doorway, she collided with someone. A paper-wrapped package skittered into the gutter. Reka fell.

"I am so sorry," a voice above her said as Reka got to her hands and knees. "Please, let me help," and a hand came into view. As Reka stood, she first saw the woman, old, and then the six-pointed star, JOOD in black across the yellow fabric stitched to her coat. The old woman, gray-haired and parchment-faced, smiled and bobbed her head, saying she was sorry, so sorry as she scurried for the package, reclaimed it, and pressed it against her chest. That was how she had been hiding the star.

Reka looked over the old woman's shoulder and saw Annje's scarf half a street away, still marching east. There was time to be polite.

"No, it was my fault," she said to the old woman. She couldn't look her in the eyes. Her forged papers promised she was Aryan, a good Dutch girl of standing, not a Jewess, and she felt a moment of shame for the lie the old woman lacked.

Reka lowered her voice for the people walking around and past them. "Do you want to get caught, *oma?*" The old woman's eyes went wide. "No," Reka whispered. "I won't tell, Grandmother. But go. Go home where it's safer. *Barukh atah Ha-shem, Elokaynu, melekh ha-olam,*" Reka said, the Hebrew coming slowly because it had been months. And the old woman looked at her, surprise on her face, but her head bobbed again.

"*Barukh atah Ha-shem, Elokaynu, melekh ha-olam,*" she said quietly, like a bird's wing, and with the package tight to her, walked away. Reka shook her head. Stupid old woman was tempting disaster.

She put the *oma* out of mind, and caught up with Annje and her scarf as she turned where Herengracht met Reguliersgracht, then left at Utrechtsedwarsstraat. Reka followed, and Annje crossed the street and knocked on the door of a three-story house across the way. While Reka stepped into another dim doorway and wondered what Annje was doing, the answer came.

The door opened. It was Henrik. This was his house.

Henrik said something—Reka could see his mouth move but couldn't hear the words—and he opened the door wider for Annje. Henrik glanced this way and that, and then the door closed.

Annje, with the old man? Conspiring with him?

She waited. But after long minutes she knew Annje was not coming out. Curtains moved at a second-story window and there was Henrik. Even from here, even within the shadows of that room, Reka saw Annje standing beside Henrik. She was naked, and just before the curtains ruffled shut, she put her bare arms around Henrik's neck and pressed herself against him.

Joop was still alive, Reka thought, and coming back. He would not be happy to find his lover shoving herself against the old man. What was Annje thinking? What was going on?

N o," said Mouse. "This is my kind of job. You'll queer it." He was at the curb, where the hack and its wrinkled driver waited for him, its engine idling.

Kagen wasn't buying it. The German tugged at the patch over his left eye, shook his head. "Rachael said you fought the last time you met with this man."

"He won't give me trouble," Mouse said, but Kagen shook his head again.

"You say you've arranged for guns and spent our money," said Kagen, and Mouse couldn't miss the "our." "But other than the meeting with the pilot, it might just be talk. I'm coming with you."

Kagen didn't trust him. Fine. He didn't trust the German back. But Mouse decided, why rock the boat when it didn't matter whether Kagen came along or not?

"Okay. But keep your mouth shut. Spark's my kind and I know how to talk to him." Mouse got in the hack and slid over so Kagen had a place to sit. "Corner of Whitechapel Road and Whitechurch, Stepney."

The old driver nodded and said, "Right, Yank," and the cab slowly pulled into traffic.

He said nothing to Kagen while the taxi wound its way to the East End. The smell was the same—fish and beer and things burnt—and he said, "Here's fine," as the taxi closed on the corner. There on his right, across the street, that was the doorway he'd beat Richie's brains in, but there was nothing to mark the spot, not even red against the doorway.

No matter what he'd told Kagen, Mouse wasn't sure how Spark would behave. He looked to see if he could catch any of Jack's boys lounging in doorways or staring into shop windows or crouching in the one alley they passed as they walked the block from Whitechapel down the right side of Whitechurch. But as he and Kagen crossed Whitechurch and walked up to No. 2, it was the same as always.

"Richie," Mouse said, stepping up to the two ganefs. "How you doin'?" The man's face was thick and puffy, his left cheek a spread of bluish bruises. He'd not broken Richie's cheekbone after all. But the wide white strip of tape across his nose told the story there; Richie's nose was busted.

Richie looked up, a whole lot of hate in his eyes. "Piss off you fuckin' kike," he said, the words hollow from the busted nose.

"Don't close your mouth when you chew, Richie, you'll suffocate yourself," Mouse said, ready to step up and bust that nose again.

"Richie, is 'at a way to talk to guests?" And Mouse looked up from Richie's messed-up face to see Jack Spark, big as life, standing in the doorway. "You've brough' a friend, now 'ave you, son? Afraid you'll get los' finding your way back 'ome?"

"Hello, Jack," Mouse said.

"Come in, come in. You've missed tea, but I think we might find somethin' stout for a tiddly. Come in." Spark waved a big hand to motion them inside, the hand holding one of those smoldering, stinking Player's. The old table was set with a pair of glasses and a bottle of Black Label, two chairs pulled up.

" 'Ugh, go get us another fred astaire and a clean glass fer Mr. Mouse's friend," Spark called. "Who's your friend, son? Long John Silver?" Spark asked while they waited for Hugh to come back. The big man laughed at his own joke. "Cat got your tongue as well as that one eye? Right?"

"His name is . . . ," and then Mouse couldn't remember the name on Kagen's passport.

"David Tucker," said Kagen after a beat or two. He didn't bother to put out a hand to shake. Hugh came in carrying a caned chair in one hand, a glass in the other. He set both down, then left to take his place outside. They sat, Mouse and Kagen beside each other, Spark across the table. Mouse unbuttoned his jacket. He didn't want to be surprised by Spark or that Welrod again. While Spark paid attention to his cigarette, Mouse put a hand under the table, touched the butt of the Smith & Wesson, and gently eased it out and laid it on his right thigh.

"That name's not yers, innit?" Spark asked as he poured the Black into each of the three glasses and looked hard at Kagen. "You sound Boche to me. Been away from the Fatherland fer a long time, 'ave you?" Spark dropped the butt to the floor and crushed it with a shoe.

"A while," said Kagen. "Where are the weapons?" he asked.

Spark looked at Kagen, that mean smile on his face again, then turned toward Mouse. "Richie 'ad an unfortunate acciden' the other day, son. Know what I mean?"

The question didn't exactly take Mouse by surprise. "I don't like being followed, Jack."

Spark nodded, then said, "Most people 'round 'ere call me Mr. Spark, son." The mean smile was there. "I let i' go the other times, but now I insis'. I may not be as big as 'at midget of yers, but I'm no piker either, son. Remember 'at."

Kagen saved Mouse from saying something stupid. "The guns, Mr. Spark. Do you have them?"

"Down ter business? No time fer social pleasantries, I take i'."

"Something like that," Kagen said.

Spark called for Hugh again and said, "Bring Mr. Mouse's packages, please." Hugh disappeared again into the back; Mouse kept an eye on that doorway.

"Well, well, well," said Spark. "A four by two *and* a Boche. 'Ow cozy. 'Err 'Itler wouldn't approve, would 'e?"

"Four by two?" asked Kagen.

The big man laughed. "Four by two. Jew. Rhymes, see? Just a phraseology, that's all. Don't get bunched. Mean no offense. Right?"

Hugh dragged two army-issue duffels across the floor by their straps. He let them fall beside Spark's chair. "Go ahead, 'Ugh, show our friends their pret'y toys." Hugh stood up one of the bags, unsnapped its neck, and pulled out a cheap-looking submachine gun. It was short, with a simple metal stock. Hugh reached in again and came out with a long box magazine that he snapped into place on the gun's left. Mouse curled his fingers around the grip of his Smith & Wesson, but Hugh just set the gun on the table. Kagen picked it up, pulled the magazine out, looked in its open end, jammed it back into place, then pulled back the bolt. He pointed the gun at the floor, pressed the trigger, and seemed satisfied with the clack it made.

"Stens, like I said. Yer Thompsons can't be got," said Spark. "Not enuff of you Yanks yet. Maybe if you check back in a few months."

"These will do," said Kagen.

"How many?" asked Mouse, looking now at Spark, not at Kagen, who was still examining the gun.

"Seven. I couldn' find ten in such shor' time. An' ten pistols in 'at other bag. Along with surplus magazines fer the Stens, an' enuff cartridges to get you goin'."

Spark had told him two hundred pounds for each of the Stens, but that was before Mouse had driven down the price. He tried to figure how much he owed now, but there wasn't enough time to do the arithmetic.

" 'Ugh?" Spark said, and pointed to the second bag. Hugh opened that duffel too, and took out ten revolvers, one after another. They were a mixed lot: three Smith & Wesson .38s with five-inch barrels, military issue, the rest some sort of make Mouse had never seen. "Smith & Wessons an' Webleys. The Webleys take the same .38 as the Smith." Some of the Webleys were still coated in a thin layer of Cosmoline. Spark had glommed them from the army for sure.

Hugh moved away from the table and near the back door again, but Mouse didn't worry. Spark wouldn't make a move here, even if he was pissed about Richie. There was no percentage in it, not with the money involved, not with Lansky looking over Mouse's shoulder, so to speak.

Mouse reached inside his jacket and put the stack of dollars on the table, the paper band still around the notes, though he'd pinched five bills from the pile. "Nine thousand, five hundred, my money," he said to Spark. "Count it. That's what I was to owe you for the revolvers and ten of the Stens. You found just seven. Hand me the Welrod and we'll call it even." It was a lot of money—three Stens' worth, over two grand he figured, finally working the numbers—just for the Welrod, but Mouse wanted that silencer. Especially now.

Spark seemed to think for a few moments, but then he shook his head. "Same as before, son. This is my cat and mouse, my 'ouse, London is, and Lansky 'as 'is. You don't see me pissin' on his shoes, right? Let me 'ave my rightful slice of what you 'ave goin' and i's yours. No charge. Otherwise no jelly." Spark smiled. "No deal, 'at's what it means." He lit another Player's.

"No, like I already said," Mouse said, closing his eyes against the smoke. "Can't do that. No jelly, Jack, like you said." He put on a smile too.

The big man bristled. "You don't know what yer doin', son. I'm not some cheap East Ender on the make. I'm Jack Spark, an' I run things this side of London. I've tried ter be reasonable." He pointed the Player's right at Mouse like it was a bony gun barrel, pointed it right at Mouse's eyes. "But you try my patience, you an' yer Boche friend. 'Ugh!"

And Mouse saw the man near the back door move, and as Hugh moved, Mouse pulled the Smith & Wesson from its place on his thigh under the table and stuck it in Spark's face, the tip of the four-inch barrel as close to Spark's nose as it was to Mouse's hand. It wasn't that he was faster than Hugh, but the way Spark had pointed that cigarette at him, he knew what Spark was gonna do before he did it.

"Four by two, am I?" Mouse asked. "I should get one and beat your brains in with it, Jack, to show you how things are."

Spark just glared and said nothing.

"Looks like we're even, Jack, you and me," Mouse said quietly as he stood from the table, the Smith & Wesson still aimed at Spark's nose. "You point one at me, I point one at you. But should I pull the trigger, like you did?" Spark's eyes got as big as eggs and his mouth opened then closed.

"Put it down, 'Ugh, an' kick i' this way, right?" Spark said finally. Hugh set his gun on the floor and pushed it toward the table with his foot.

Mouse nodded to Kagen, who picked up one of the unloaded Webleys from the table, then stood and moved to the doorway. He rapped on the jamb with the barrel, and when Richie looked up from his chair, he motioned him inside.

As Richie moved past Mouse, he reached inside the ganef's jacket and took the revolver from the holster there. Just like before. "You are as dumb as you look, do you know that, Richie?"

"You don't 'ave any idea of 'ow much shit you just got in," said Spark.

"Hey, Jack, here's news," said Mouse. "I could give a fuck." He bent down and picked up Hugh's revolver, opened the cylinder, and let the cartridges clatter to the floor, then tossed the gun into a far corner. Richie's revolver he kept for a moment, but then handed it to Kagen.

"Nothing we do in England is your concern, Mr. Spark," said Kagen. "We are not all . . . gangsters . . . here."

"Don't matter now, right?" Spark asked and nodded to the gun that Kagen held.

Mouse saw his opportunity, what with him and Kagen with guns, Spark and his without. "How about that Welrod, Jack?" he asked. "That's a lot of dough for one gun," he said, pointing to the stack of hundreds. "Six hundred quid by my count. I call that a good deal. A good jelly, how's that, Jack?"

But Spark shook his head. "Sod off." And he crossed his arms over his chest like he was daring Mouse to call the bluff.

Mouse had an idea, so he walked the two steps and pointed the Smith & Wesson at Richie's head and pulled back the hammer. "Maybe you know where that Welrod is." And he touched the ganef's nose with the muzzle of the revolver, right on the white tape. "Jack may not care, but you do, don't you, Richie?"

"Mr. Spark?" Richie said. Mouse wondered how much Spark liked Richie.

"Pick, Jack," Mouse said. "Richie here or the Welrod. You can't have both, can you? So you say which."

Spark said nothing, but he nodded, and Richie moved to a shelf at the back of the shop, Mouse right with him. Richie moved aside a stack of old, yellowed newspapers and pulled the Welrod from its place. Mouse took it, motioned Richie to stand beside Hugh, and put the Welrod in the duffel, dumped in the rest of the revolvers, then the Sten still on the table. He slung one duffel over his shoulder, the other he dragged to Kagen.

"Thanks, Jack," Mouse said. Kagen was already on the walk outside.

"You'll wish you never met me, son," said Spark.

Mouse nodded. "I already do, Jack. But there's nothing for it, is there?" He reached toward Spark, plucked the Player's, or what was left of it, from Spark's hand. "My advice, Jack, is to use that money," and Mouse nodded to the table where the money lay untouched, "and buy yourself a better brand of cigarettes. These'll kill you for sure. Right?" He tried to put a Cockney accent on that last word, just for a jab, but it came out sounding wrong.

"Piss off," said Spark, quiet at first, but then his voice got louder and braver. "You got no idea of 'ow much trouble I'm gon'a make on you, Jew."

But Mouse just shook his head and flicked Spark's cigarette to the floor. He backed out the door, then followed Kagen down the walk, across the street, and for Whitechapel. Kagen took the lead, he the rear. He kept an eye on Spark's place.

But no one came out of the shop. At Whitechapel, Mouse hailed a hack, tossed in his duffel first, then Kagen's. The car was off and running, and Mouse told the driver to head for King's Cross.

They rode in silence for a bit, but as they passed the Tower—a familiar sight to Mouse, this being his third time to and from the East End—Kagen turned from his window and said, "I knew bringing you people into this was a mistake. I told Peter this would happen. And look what you've done."

Mouse tried to keep his temper, and managed to keep his mouth shut. There was no use in arguing with a dead man.

"What did Spark want?" asked Kagen.

This one he'd answer. "He thinks I'm here to work a deal for Lansky and he wants in."

"You've made him angry," Kagen said. "And angry men do stupid things."

"I can handle Spark."

"Thieves falling out, that's what you've got us into."

"Listen to me," said Mouse. "I'm not a ganef, I'm a dropper. I pop ass-holes like you, but I haven't stole since 'thirty-one. If you're gonna keep calling me names, at least get the names right."

Kagen gave him an up and down with that one good eye. "We don't like each other, Mr. Weiss. But we must get along well enough to work together."

Mouse said nothing. Neither of them said a word the rest of the way.

The car pulled up to the curb in front of No. 47, and Kagen climbed out, dragging his duffel with him. Mouse followed, but standing there on the step, waiting for someone to answer Kagen's knock, he felt a prickling on the back of his neck. He didn't have a sixth sense—he didn't buy that—but when he got this feeling, he knew something needed attention.

Mouse set the duffel on the step, turned slowly, and looked around. Checked up the street, down the street, even looked at the flower store opposite.

There. A car, black like every other car in London, idling half a block down, back toward the Underground, a small cloud of blue exhaust curl-ing up behind its roof. The giveaway was the two guys in the front seat. He couldn't see faces, too far away, but he could tell from their hats that they were guys.

Cops? Mouse didn't think so. Spark's men. Spark was smarter than Mouse gave him credit; he'd had a backup plan, and put guys in a car, probably on Whitechapel, to follow them.

Kagen went inside, but Mouse wasn't sure what to do. Now Spark knew where they lived. Nothing good could come of that. But what to do. What would Lansky do?

Nothing. That's what. Guys in cars watching, that was only business. Spark wouldn't dare anything more, not with Lansky's name over him like a shield. It wasn't like Mouse had done more than Spark had done to him.

"Coming in or staying out?" Kagen asked from the doorway.

"Comin' in," he said, and grabbed the duffel.

# Seven

## Monday: April 12, 1943

This was a bad idea, but Mouse was done arguing with Kagen.

"Someone will hear," Joop said. Which was what Mouse had been saying all along.

They stood in the middle of a grassy clearing, a hundred yards by fifty, fenced by trees coming into green. The four had driven out from London in the Morris, Rachael at the wheel, Kagen beside her on the left, he and Joop in the back seat. Kagen said they needed to learn how to fire the Stens, but Mouse told him it was a dumb idea, thinking they could shoot without someone wondering what was going on.

"No, this will do fine," said Kagen. "The last village was back a kilometer at least." Mouse looked at Joop, who just shrugged. The little guy was thinking like he was, that this was stupid at best, dangerous at worst.

Kagen pulled a white sheet from the duffel he'd dragged through the woods and wrapped it around the trunk of a tree at one end of the clearing. He grabbed the bag, paced down the meadow, and motioned them over.

From the way Kagen held the Sten, Mouse could tell he was comfortable with it, like he was with the Smith & Wesson. The Sten was stubby, shorter than the Thompson he'd used the once. Maybe thirty inches long, almost half of which was a plain metal stock that ended in a T.

"The Sten is very simple, very rugged," said Kagen, "about three kilos, with a thirty-two-round magazine." He pulled the box magazine from the side of the weapon and handed it to Joop. "You load and cock by pulling back here," and Mouse watched as Kagen pulled back the bolt along the right side of the gun. The Sten clacked as the bolt locked. "Press the trigger," Kagen said, and he did and the Sten clicked. "Keep on the trigger, and the Sten cycles until the magazine is empty. Release, and the bolt's caught here at the back." He pointed to the Sten. "To put it on safety, you simply push the bolt up, like this." And he pulled the bolt back again, but this time let it catch in a small slot above the bolt path.

"And careful for your fingers," he said, pointing to an opening on the right, opposite the magazine. "The casings fly out here. I've seen men lose fingertips."

Kagen dragged the duffel over and kneeled in the grass. "The best thing about the Sten is that you can break it down in just a few seconds and hide the parts." He pulled off the metal stock and turned a cap on the butt to let a spring and a couple pieces of metal drop onto the duffel. A few more twists and turns and he held the barrel, now in two parts. He tossed those onto the duffel.

Kagen made them watch as he put the gun back together; made them do it themselves once each, too. Finally, he braced the Sten's stock against his shoulder and pressed the trigger. The shots were loud—not as loud as a .38, but plenty loud, Mouse thought. The ba-ba-ba-ba-bang was slow enough to hear each shot individual, and all he could hope was that the trees around them muffled the noise. The burst struck the sheet-wrapped tree about shoulder high. A good shot, Mouse thought, for a one-eyed guy.

"The muzzle climbs, so keep it down," Kagen said, and handed the

Sten to Mouse. "Give it a try, gangster," he said, smirking. Mouse grabbed the Sten, pointed it at the tree trunk, and pressed the trigger.

The gun bucked against his hip—he'd not put it to his shoulder—and although he pressed the trigger for a couple of seconds he missed the tree completely.

"Don't worry, it won't shoot back," said Kagen. Mouse glared at the German, put the Sten to his shoulder and fired, a shorter burst, and this time hit the tree. You had to aim low and pray. Not that it mattered. Mouse didn't figure to stay in Holland long enough to use it.

Joop was next, and he wasn't any better, missing the tree completely the first burst, chewing up some low branches the second. Rachael, though, turned out to be a natural. With her blond hair moving in the slight breeze, she put the Sten to her shoulder and tore a tight circle through the sheet, laughing as she lowered the submachine gun and Kagen put his arm around her waist.

"No, I've never," she said when Kagen asked if she'd shot before. She raised the gun again and fired, shredding more of the sheet.

But as she handed the Sten to Kagen, a dog barked just beyond the trees.

Kagen caught the barking too, but he looked uncertain.

"We got to go. Now," Mouse said. They had enough problems without someone calling the cops about people shooting up his woods. "Come on." Mouse knew when to cut and run—he'd dodged cops all his life— but the German seemed lost. If he was a soldier like he said, he should know what to do. But Kagen just stood there, a strange look on his face. Mouse saw what he was looking at. An old man had come out of the woods on the far end of the clearing fifty yards away. He was in brown pants and coat, a wide-brimmed hat on his head, a shotgun in the crook of his arm, and a big dog at his side. Mouse didn't know dogs, but it was big.

"Rachael, grab the bag," Mouse said, taking charge. That was when the German pulled up the Sten and pointed it at the old man. He was going to shoot the farmer, no question in Mouse's mind, like it was the only way the German handled anything. Kagen drew back the bolt. Mouse was a good ten yards from Kagen and he knew he couldn't get to him in time.

"Paul, don't," Rachael said. And she did what Mouse would've done if he could, put a hand on the barrel of the Sten and push it down. "That's not necessary."

"You! Stand fast, you with the guns!" the farmer called.

Kagen's face was tight, and as he looked at Rachael it got tighter, like he was going to do it anyway, but then the moment must have passed, because that look faded. He stuffed the Sten in the duffel, shouldered the bag, and headed for the trees and the road beyond. Mouse picked up the other.

"I said, you there!" the farmer yelled again. Kagen and Rachael ducked into the trees, Joop right behind them. Mouse took a second to swing his duffel to his shoulder and stumble after.

He heard the old man yell again but he didn't slow down to pick out the words, afraid of losing Joop. The dog barked closer. Mouse stepped in a hole, the mud sucking the shoe right off his foot. Fuck. He dropped the duffel, reached down and pulled the shoe from the muck, and shoved his foot into the wet leather. But he heard the dog moving through the underbrush, close.

Mouse fumbled with the duffel, got it open, and pulled the Welrod from the top of the pile inside. He worked the Welrod's action fast, a bit frantic, twisting the knob at the butt counterclockwise, pulling at the bolt, pushing it back in, twisting the knob clockwise to force a round from the magazine into the chamber just as the dog thundered out of the thin brush and stopped a few feet away, teeth showing in a snarl.

It had taken him too long. The dog came at him with a mouth as wide as the croc he'd seen once in the Bronx Zoo, and clamped its teeth around his left hand. He didn't drop the gun. With the smell of the dog in his nose—dark, musky, wet fur—he tried to pull out his hand, but the dog had a grip like a sharp wrench and he felt the teeth rip the skin as he yanked. Panicked now, he hammered at the dog's head with the heavy muzzle of the Welrod, again and again, connecting finally with bone, and the dog let loose. It backed away, growling.

"Cromwell! Cromwell!" a voice called through the trees. Mouse brought up the Welrod, the big gun hard to hold in just one hand, and hesitated. It was just a dog. But the old man yelled "Cromwell" again, and the dog padded forward. Mouse pulled the trigger. The gun made a quiet noise, a *phfft* of a sound, as mum as Jack Spark had promised. The bullet knocked the dog down, Cromwell whining and thrashing his legs.

"Cromwell!" the old man called. Mouse grabbed the duffel and punched through some low branches to get away. A minute it took, and he stepped out of the woods, right along the road, just twenty yards ahead of the Morris. Joop was waiting at the back of the car.

"Here!" Joop called, and Mouse staggered to the Morris, tossed the duffel into the open trunk, and fell into the back seat. The trunk lid slammed and Joop was beside him on the seat.

"You're hurt!" Rachael said as she twisted behind the wheel and looked at his hand. Mouse looked down, too, and almost passed out. His hand was slick with blood that dripped steady onto the floorboard.

"Go, get going," he said in a quiet voice that sounded far away. He laid the Welrod on his lap to cradle his torn left hand in his right.

Rachael put the car in gear, and as the Morris moved off the shoulder and onto the road, the old man came out of the trees ahead. He raised the shotgun to his shoulder. She shifted and stomped on the accelerator, and the little car roared ahead, brushed past the old man, and was a good thirty yards past when the farmer finally fired. Pellets pinged off the back of the car, one punched through the rear window, and then they were out of range, roaring down the narrow road, Rachael having trouble keeping it straight.

"Here, let me help," Joop was saying as Mouse closed his eyes against the pain and the sight of his own blood. He opened them to see the little guy holding a handkerchief. Joop pressed and held it on his hand. "You're going to need a doctor," Joop said softly.

"What happened?" Kagen asked. Mouse opened his eyes. "What happened back there?" Kagen asked again.

"What happened? You said no one would hear us, that's what happened, you dumb—"

Kagen turned to look over the front seat. "Hold your tongue, gangster."

"I killed a dog back there. But you were ready to pop the old man. We'd have the cops on us for sure—what about your fuckin' plan then?" And Mouse held up his left hand wrapped in Joop's blood-soaked handkerchief.

"Is this how you're gonna handle things? You do something stupid like that over there and you'll get us all killed." The rage was thick in his throat and if he didn't think he might pass out, he would have climbed over the seat and beat Kagen's brains in with the Welrod, just like that dog.

"Wait—"

"No," interrupted Joop. "Mouse is right. It was stupid, what we did. Dangerous." The little guy didn't talk so slow now. Kagen was ready to say something, but Rachael took one hand from the Morris's wheel and touched him on the arm. He muttered, German it sounded like, but turned to face forward again.

"You need a doctor," Joop said again.

"No, no doctor," Mouse said. "I'm all right. No doctor." He pulled at the makeshift bandage to see the damage. Blood welled up from the two gashes, straight lines an inch apart across the top of the hand. They were deep. He flexed his fingers. They moved, but the pain put black around the edges of his vision. He rewrapped the handkerchief around his hand.

As Rachael drove them back into London, the too-green countryside giving way to the grays and reds of London's brick, Mouse leaned back, staring out the window, wishing it was time to climb on O'Brien's plane so he could pop Kagen.

That was how, when Rachael pointed the car down Argyle Street, Mouse happened to see the ganef standing at the corner.

P reuss stepped aside. No one had answered the door when he'd pounded it with the flat of his hand. "Break it down," he said, nodding to the two SS, an Unterscharführer and a Rottenführer, both wearing gray like himself. But they had machine pistols slung over their shoulders, while all Preuss had was his Walther in its holster.

The Rottenführer, a bulky boy with acne, stepped up to the door and slammed a heavy sledgehammer into it, splintering the frame. He struck it a second time, and the wood shattered and the door swung open. The Rottenführer dropped the hammer and disappeared inside, the Unterscharführer following.

Preuss didn't join them, but took the blue tin from his tunic pocket, fingered a Nil, tapped it gently against the metal lid, lit the cigarette, and looked at his watch. Almost noon. Marta would be taking coffee, perhaps a Sachertorte, at the café across the street from her office in the Economics Ministry.

De Groot stood a few meters away with his clutch of Amsterdam policemen. The Dutchman had the fingers of one hand stuck through a suspender under his jacket, his big belly pushing out. His face was set in a grimace. He was not doing enough to disguise his distaste.

As Preuss half-heard sounds from inside the house, some dull shouting, a piece of furniture overturning, he looked at the blond policeman and asked, "Something bothering you? Something you'd like to say?"

De Groot surprised Preuss by answering with a question of his own. "You are sure there are Jews here?"

"Yes, Detective-Sergeant." Preuss drew again from his cigarette. "And perhaps some of your fine countrymen, too, harboring those Jews." Preuss smiled at the Dutchman, watched his grimace get even tighter.

The traitor Annje Visser had given him the address this morning, delivered as Giskes had suggested by dropping a copy of today's *De Telegraaf* in a waste bin on the Stadhouderskade, with the address written in a margin. Preuss had paid a boy to fetch the newspaper from the bin and bring it to him where he waited a street away in his black BMW. He was not used to such ruses, but Giskes had convinced him this was how it must be done to make sure the woman's treachery went undiscovered.

As more sounds of struggle came from inside the house and while Preuss wondered if he should send in de Groot and his policemen, a Kübelwagen, the small car painted army gray, rolled up the street and stopped at the curb. Giskes climbed out, followed by two others, the last barely able to squeeze himself from behind the rear seat. All three were in plainclothes.

"What took you so long?" Preuss said as the tall, thin officer came near.

Giskes shrugged. He wore a well-fitted suit this time, not the farmer's clothes of their first meeting. "Found your Jews? What about mine? You said there were some here for me." The sound of more shouting from inside the house reached the street. "How many are there?" and Giskes nodded to the house and the noise.

"I don't know. Two of mine are inside now." More sounds from the house, and from an open window on the third story, loud in the quiet of the morning, a shot. Another. And as Preuss watched, a body, arms like windmills, fell backward the ten meters, like a diver who had stumbled on the board, and landed on the walk close enough to touch. Blood flicked across Preuss's boots and trousers.

"Shit," he yelled, covering himself in sparks as he knocked the cigarette against a leg in his panic to jump out of the way. An old woman lay faceup, the back of her skull flat against the concrete walk.

"It seems two was not enough," Giskes said calmly. He motioned to his men and the pair entered the house. Preuss heard their shoes on stairs.

Belatedly, Preuss gestured to de Groot. "Send in your men as well," he said, his voice unsteady at the sound of another shot echoing from the open window. He flinched, expecting another body to come sailing to the street.

But de Groot was fixed to his spot—neither he nor his policemen took as much as a step toward the house. Preuss stared at the old woman. Her gray hair was tinted red, but from a bullet, not a bottle. "She's no Jew," the Dutch detective said.

"I don't care if she's Queen Wilhelmina herself come back to Holland, go in there and drag them out!" Preuss shouted. The old woman's eyes stared at him. De Groot was right; she lacked the yellow star. A crowd was gathering behind the Dutchman.

Still, de Groot didn't move. "Sergeant!" Preuss yelled.

Finally, de Groot urged his men forward and followed them, his bulk skirting the dead woman. His grimace was gone now, replaced by a new look. Stronger than hatred, whatever it was. Loathing, that was it.

"Get in there!" Preuss yelled, pushing the fat man toward the door.

But Giskes's two men were already stepping from the shadow of the broken door, followed by three Dutch, a boy barely twenty and two girls even younger. The girls wore the *Jood* on their coats and looked enough alike to be sisters. One was in tears, the other silent and glaring. The boy only had eyes for the old woman. The two SS brought up the rear, their machine pistols pointed at the Dutch.

Giskes walked up to the boy and asked, *"Bent jij joods?"* The boy looked blankly at Giskes, at the dead woman, back to the Abwehr man. He'd been beaten during the raid. One eye was already half-hooded and there was a smear of blood on his forehead. *"Bent jij joods? Begrijp je me?"* Giskes asked.

*"Nee,"* the boy said.

"These two are mine," Preuss said, pointing to the two girls. Only now did he realize that he had pulled the Walther from its holster.

"Just two?" Giskes asked. "It hardly seems worth the trouble, does it?" Preuss glanced toward the Abwehr officer. The bastard was right. Preuss stepped up to the Jewess who glared still, and slammed the Walther against her cheek. She staggered and crumpled to the walk. He was getting set to bend over her and smash the pistol against her head again.

But de Groot squeezed between him and the Jewess. "Please, let me take care of this," de Groot said. Through the haze of his anger, Preuss heard the murmur of the crowd. This could go bad in a second, and he didn't have enough men to handle the small mob staring at the dead old woman. Preuss stepped away, his anger dissipating. De Groot pulled the girl to her feet, took her by the arm, led her to Preuss's BMW parked at the corner, its cloth top down, and put her in the back seat. All too gently, Preuss thought. The other girl followed, arm held in the grip of another of de Groot's men. The rest of the Dutchman's policemen pushed back the crowd and in their Dutch told everyone to go about their business.

Giskes turned to Preuss and said, "I'll have this one," meaning the boy. One of his plainclothes cuffed the boy's ear, grabbed him by the coat sleeve, and shoved him into the rear of the Kübelwagen.

"The next time you telephone," he said to Preuss, "have the courtesy to stay out of the way." He pointed to the old, dead woman. "She was the one who knew the next contact, says the boy, and the only one worth my trouble."

Preuss could only stare back. How dare he? "I have had more experience with Jews than you will ever—" he began, his voice thick, but Giskes had already turned toward his car.

At its door, Giskes turned again to face him, removed his hat, and brushed back his gray hair. "We'll never have to worry about work, will we?" he asked. "At this rate, we'll both be old men by the time we've cleaned out Amsterdam." And he laughed as he opened the Kübelwagen's door and climbed in. The small engine turned over and the little car drove off.

Giskes was right again, and Preuss hated him all the more for it. He had scores to deport each day, hundreds every week, like the one thousand, four hundred and twenty-two he'd seen to Muiderpoort and the train to Westerbork just after dawn. And here he had wasted over an hour on only two.

Just two. The image of his blank ledger was stronger even than the old woman who'd flown from her window. He stepped past her to the BMW, and the thin semicircle of Dutch parted to let him by.

K eep driving, don't stop," Mouse said, leaning forward, putting his bloody left hand on the front seat.

"What? Why?" Rachael asked, and the Morris slowed.

"There's guys watching the house."

The ganef at the corner wasn't the only one. Mouse saw another on the same side of the street as No. 47, but three doors down.

The two were easy to spot, not good at what they did. Their clothes were the same ganef clothes as Richie and Hugh, badly cut suits and hard shoes. They stood the same way, stiff and heavy. And they were stupid, like Richie. The one at the corner didn't even pretend to be doing something else, while the other made like he was reading a newspaper in the shadow of a doorway.

Rachael let the Morris coast. "Don't slow down," Mouse urged. "Step on it, drive past!"

"Do what he says," Kagen said, and Rachael finally put a foot to the accelerator. The Morris sped past No. 47. When it reached the corner where they would normally turn for the alley at the back of the house, Rachael asked, "Where to?"

"Anywhere," said Kagen. "It doesn't matter." Rachael kept the Morris straight and another three blocks down turned right.

"What's going on?" It was Joop. "How did that farmer know where we live?"

"It's not the farmer," said Kagen.

"No," Mouse agreed.

"Your Mr. Spark."

The German was right. But what was more important was that the ganefs weren't watching from a car like before, but on the street. That meant only one thing. Spark was planning to pop him. Him at least. Maybe the others, too.

"Yeah, it was Spark," Mouse said.

Rachael drove on. Mouse looked out the window and caught a street sign that said GRAY'S INN ROAD. "Where do we go?" she asked again. "All our things are in the house. Our clothes, all our things. We have to go back."

"We have the guns," Joop said. Mouse leaned back into the seat, pressed the handkerchief against his hand. It was throbbing.

"Our maps, the maps are in the house," Rachael said. "The charts of the Waddenzee, Paul, the tide tables. Plans, plans, too. Everything we've written down is in there." Mouse remembered the stack of papers on the kitchen table. "What if they're in the house already?" she asked.

"They're not in the house," Mouse said, squeezing his eyes tight against the pain. "If they were in the house, they wouldn't be out on the street waiting for us."

"What about the money?" It was Kagen. Mouse had his eyes closed now, feeling the Morris start and stop. "What did you do with the money?" Kagen sounded worried. Mouse smiled, but kept his eyes shut.

"Don't worry, the money's safe and sound."

He heard Kagen shift in the front seat, maybe turning back to face forward again. "Then we can replace anything we've lost," he said.

"But the maps, Paul. We've marked on the maps and the charts, made schedules on paper. They'll find out about our plan and—" Rachael's voice was climbing.

"We just need to lay low until Sunday," Mouse said. He was so tired. Spark wouldn't care about their plans once he saw they had nothing to do with London.

"A hotel," Rachael said after a few seconds. "We could live in a hotel for a few days."

"Great idea," said Mouse, feeling the Morris spin, but he knew Rachael was driving it straight and true. He thought he might pass out. "A place with some class. Spark won't think we'll go to a hotel that costs a bundle."

No one said anything for a moment. "I know the place," Rachael said. "The Chesterfield. In Mayfair. On the other side of Green Park from the Palace. I've had tea there. Very posh."

"Perfect," said Mouse. The hotel had the same name as his cigarettes. He liked that.

"The Chesterfield's expensive, very expensive," Rachael said. She shifted gears, braked.

"Money doesn't matter," Mouse said, hearing only a whisper. So tired. He had to sleep. The last thing he felt was the Morris turning again to the right.


I think this hurts me more than you," Mouse said. Rachael looked up and gave him one of her smiles. He smelled her clean soap smell. She held the needle over the flame of a match.

Mouse closed his eyes when she said, "Yes, this will hurt." He felt Rachael's fingers on the top of his left hand, felt them gently squeeze together one of the slashes. He felt the needle. It was still warm.

"Fuck," Mouse said, moaning. He couldn't help it. Shit, it *hurt*. He felt the tug on his skin as Rachael pulled the needle through, the thread dragging like sandpaper.

"Ah, fuck," Mouse said again. "I need another drink." He opened his eyes and tried not to look at Rachael's work, instead toward Joop, who sat on the other side of the bed. The little guy got up and poured a few fingers of Scotch into a glass.

"No ice," Joop said, and Mouse nodded, took the glass, and drained the whiskey. It burned, but that felt better than the stitching Rachael did.

She'd called the hotel's kitchen for a pot of hot water—for tea, she'd told them—and dumped in the white thread she'd bought along with the needles at the druggist down the street. That was as good as they'd get without going to a real doctor, which Mouse refused to do.

Ten minutes and two more Scotches later, Rachael said, "That's all I can do," and swabbed iodine over the stitches and dressed the hand with a clean cloth bandage. The iodine's sting reached Mouse, drink and all. Ah, fuck.

She stood, smoothed her dress over her hips as she did. "You're a fine bit of stuff, dear," Mouse said to her, liking the way O'Brien's words sounded, liking the drunk that was on him, the first since he'd left New York with Lansky's briefcase in his hand. Rachael smiled.

"Thank you, Mr. Weiss."

"Call me Mouse," he said, swallowing the last of the Scotch.

Kagen stirred from the chair near the corner. He'd been quiet since they'd come up to the room. He walked to the bed, stood over Mouse.

"Where's the money? Where did you put the money? If you left it in that house—"

"In the bank," he said, slurring the words a bit. "Safe and sound in the bank." He looked up at Kagen and stared at the black patch over the German's eye. Mouse was glad he wasn't going to see this through. Kagen was crazy careless. He didn't think, that was his problem. The gun, that was his only answer, Mouse thought through the haze of the Scotch. "Don't be worried 'bout the money. You should be worried 'bout how you got my hand bit off."

"Your scratch is the least of our problems," said Kagen.

"Paul, leave it be," Rachael said.

"No, I won't. He dragged us into this thing with his gangster. It *is* your fault," Kagen said, talking to Mouse. "I *knew* bringing you people into this was wrong."

Mouse was too tired, or too drunk, to argue. But if he had, he might have said it wasn't him who'd gone for his gun first, it was Spark and his ganef Hugh. What was he supposed to do, sit there and let them take his money? Mouse didn't say anything, but he was feeling good, really good, about the idea of popping Kagen. Rachael, now, that was another story. But not the German.

"If this falls apart because of what you've done—" but Kagen couldn't finish. Joop broke in.

"Rachael's right. What good does it do to argue?" the little guy asked. "How else were we to get the guns?"

"Rachael's brother might have found them," Kagen said. Yeah, thought Mouse, then why hadn't he? "Our business is at risk now, because of what he did," said Kagen.

It was the money, Kagen was worried about the money and what might happen to it if something happened to him. Like maybe Kagen killed him, Mouse thought in his drunk.

Rachael had her hand on Kagen's arm now, and was leaning her head toward the German, whispering something. Kagen nodded, stared at Mouse a moment or two with that eye before he walked for the door.

"Everyone needs rest, I think, and time to calm down," Rachael said. "We'll go to our room now, and let you sleep." And she smiled at him again. The two of them, her and Kagen, left.

The room was quiet. Mouse wanted another drink—there was still a good three inches of Scotch in the bottle—but he didn't think he could stand up and walk to it so he stayed on the bed, sitting with his feet on the floor.

Joop broke the silence. "He wants this to work," he said, shoving his round glasses farther up his nose.

Mouse nodded. "But he's still a prick."

"Prick?" Joop said, trying out the word. "Ah, yes. *Pik,* we say. *Groot pik.* Big prick. Yes." And Joop laughed. "More than that, I think. He is also a *Duitser.*"

Mouse tried to keep his eyes open. "Jew, you mean?"

Joop laughed again, louder this time. "No, no, no. Not a *jood.* German. *Duitser.* Kagen is German. I do not trust any German, Jew or not."

Joop brought the bottle to the bed, poured Scotch into the glass Mouse had forgotten he still had in his hand. Mouse sipped long, felt the liquor slide down his throat and warm it and his face as far as behind his eyes.

Joop leaned in, like he was afraid someone would hear. "I want to ask you something . . . Mouse," he said. He was almost whispering. "Ever since we met, I have wanted to ask this."

Mouse looked at the little guy. Joop's dark hair fell over one eye; he brushed it back. "Sure. Shoot," Mouse said. He was slurring for sure now, but he didn't care. He felt great.

"Shoot," said Joop slowly, as if not understanding.

"Yeah, ask me."

Joop paused a moment. "You are a gangster? A real gangster? Yes?"

Mouse smiled. When Joop used the word it sounded different than when Kagen said it. Mouse found it hard not to like the little guy. "Sure."

"I have seen the picture *Enemies of the Public* many times," Joop said. "With Mr. James Cagney. About gangsters."

*The Public Enemy*, that must be what Joop meant. "Yeah?" Mouse asked. Cagney had sure been fun to watch, maybe because he reminded Mouse of Little Farvel.

Joop hesitated again, swallowed, and looked at Mouse. "You know James Cagney, yes? Do you think you could get his . . . how do you say it," and Joop made a motion like signing a paper.

Mouse laughed, his head spinning from the Scotch and the pain in his hand, and he couldn't stop. "An autograph?"

Joop nodded, all serious, Mouse could see.

He loved this guy. Too bad he had to pop him, too. But business was business. Rachael, though, that was going to be different.

# *Eight*

M ouse tried to lift the coffee cup, but the makeshift stitches tugged under the bandage and made him wince. He set the cup back on the small table.

"It still hurts?" asked Joop, sitting at the chair near the window. Behind him, Mouse could see green through the window. Hyde Park, Rachael had told him.

Mouse nodded. "Like hell." He gently flexed the fingers.

"You can hold a gun?" the little guy asked, fiddling with his glasses, pulling them off, wiping them with a dirty handkerchief, putting them back on his nose.

Mouse knew what he meant. "I'm still going, don't worry." He'd thought about saying he couldn't get on O'Brien's airplane, that his hand was too bad, but there was no way he was handing over the money to Kagen, who would demand it to pay for the Dutch boats. No, he had to stick to his plan, even though the more he thought about it, the less he liked it.

"I hurt my hand once, in the switchyard," Joop said, drinking his coffee. His glasses steamed up as he brought the cup up to his face. He held up his left hand. For the first time Mouse noticed that the middle finger was missing its last joint. "I caught it between two goods wagons," Joop said slowly—he talked slowly again—"when I was hooking one to the other." Joop paused. "Sometimes I wish I had kept to trains, even though they did this," he said, and put down his hand. He looked at Mouse. "But then I would not have met an American gangster who knows James Cagney." He smiled. It was their joke; Mouse had had to tell the little guy that no, he couldn't get him Cagney's autograph. Joop drank more coffee, stared into space.

"Joop?" Mouse asked, wondering what the little guy was thinking, saying the name like Joop had told him, "yoop."

"I think of a woman. What else do we think about, yes?"

Mouse's answer was sitting in the safe-deposit box in Barclays, so he said nothing.

"Annje is her name," Joop said. "Annje Visser."

"She'll be waiting when we get there?"

Joop shrugged. "Perhaps. She may think that I . . . ran out on her is the way you would say it? After we wrecked the switch circuits and my friend Dirk . . . rat me out," he said.

"Ratted you out." Mouse was proud that some of what he'd taught Joop had stuck.

"Ratted me out, yes. I couldn't stay. But I couldn't get word to Annje before I ran to England."

"Not your fault."

"I want to see Annje again," Joop said quietly.

"That all?" Mouse fumbled a Chesterfield to his lips, lit it with his lighter.

Joop wasn't stupid; he got the drift. "Jews, you mean." He pushed his glasses back into place; they had a habit of slipping. "Vreesje, yes? Kristiaan I've known since we were boys, I tried to look in on Vreesje after he went away, but . . ." He paused, sipped again from his coffee. "One week they were there, the next not. I told Rachael when I came to England, but I did not think it would take us to this."

"You don't think it's a good idea." Mouse meant it less a question than it sounded.

Joop shrugged, pushed his glasses again. "I like Vreesje. But I do this because it will hurt the *Duitsers*. If we show my countrymen that the *Duitsers* can be beaten, perhaps they will fight back again." Joop made sense, more sense than Rachael, anyway. Someone tried to muscle you out, you had to stand up. If someone pushed Lansky, Little Man pushed back.

Mouse smoked, waiting for more, and wasn't disappointed.

"Most of all, I miss my Annje." The little man looked up and smiled. "If I return and do this, I can bring her back to England with us. Foolish, yes?"

Mouse didn't know what to say. Put your neck on the line for a girl? Yeah, he guessed he thought it was foolish, but he didn't say that to Joop, not wanting to hurt his feelings. "You know the people we'll meet in Holland, right?" Mouse asked.

"Kristiaan thinks he got a message to them, yes," Joop said, sounding glad at the turn in the conversation. The little guy didn't smoke, and he opened the window beside him. Traffic sounds from the street below came up to this fourth floor; it reminded Mouse of Bergson's office over Broadway.

Rachael had phoned her brother the day before at his barracks south of London, told him not to go near the house on Argyle Street, and he said that he'd used his commando's radio to send a message on a frequency that the Dutch underground was supposed to listen on, all arranged long before the Germans goose-stepped into Amsterdam back in '40. They had to take on faith that the word got through.

"There are five," Joop said. "Three men and two women. But one of the men is *achterlijk* . . . how you say it . . . stupid?" Mouse didn't know if Joop meant mental or just not smart, like Little Farvel. "My Annje's brother is stupid. But the other woman, she is even smarter than my Annje. Reka. Reka Dekker." Joop set his cup on the table beside Mouse's chair. "She is the *jood* among us. She has a lot of hate in her heart, Mouse. The *Duitsers* already send her *vader* and *moeder* to the East. But she is fearless. You will like her, I think."

Mouse knew he wouldn't even meet her. Off the plane, a few *phffts* with the Welrod, and back to England.

When he glanced Joop's way and nodded, Mouse couldn't look the little guy in the eyes.


W hat do I owe the pleasure, Brigadeführer?" asked Preuss. "You didn't come all the way to Amsterdam to visit. The Hague isn't so close as that."

Erich Naumann was commander of all Holland's security police—the Gestapo, the Kriminalpolizei, the SD—and even ran the camps, Wester-bork included. He smiled a thin smile at Preuss.

"No, Horst. I was in Berlin, endless meetings with Himmler and his toadies." Naumann, his face middle-aged but still taut, looked at him. His eyes were dull gray and peered from under thick brows. Preuss had always had trouble keeping his look locked on Naumann's. "At least Heydrich isn't there anymore. That's the one good thing those Czechs did for us, eh, when they murdered him last year in Prague. They got rid of that madman Heydrich for us at least."

It was dangerous, talking of the Reichsführer this way, speaking of Heydrich, Himmler's dead protégé, like that. It made Preuss uncomfortable.

"They're worried about an invasion by the Allies, can you imagine? This year." Naumann shook his head. "But I can afford a few minutes to have a drink with my favorite apprentice."

"Forgive me," said Preuss, taking the hint. He leaned back in his chair and pulled a bottle of Pierre Ferrand from the lowest drawer of the wooden file cabinet behind him, a pair of nearly clean glasses, too. "One of my last bottles, I'm afraid. The French aren't much as friends, are they, if they can't keep us in this." He poured the burnished gold cognac into the glasses, gave one to Naumann. They leaned across the desk, clinked glasses together, Naumann saying *"Prosit"* in salute, Preuss ready to say "the Führer" in reply, but changed his mind and mimicked his mentor.

"I wanted to talk, Horst, that's the real reason I stopped on my way back to The Hague. There are things I've heard, things you should know." Naumann settled back in the chair and put one of his dreadful Russian *papirosi* between his fingers. He pinched first one end of the cardboard tube, then the other before lighting the cigarette. The coarse tobacco popped and sparked, and the cardboard wrapper made snowflake-sized flecks of ash that fluttered down onto his gray uniform. Naumann brushed them off as soon as they touched. He leaned forward, as if sharing a secret. "Himmler wants Holland *Judenfrei* by the end of July. He wants it cleansed of Jews before the Allies get here. *Alles ausrotten,*" he whispered. All eliminated.

Preuss knew his mouth hung open. That was impossible. "Surely not."

"Surely," said Naumann. "Himmler himself told me he wants Westerbork torn down and plowed under no later than the end of July." Naumann shrugged. "I asked him where the Jews would go, and he said there would be no Jews left." The stink of Naumann's cigarette hovered in a cloud over Preuss's desk and drifted out the door, where the others, those of the Gestapo whose offices he shared, would have to smell it. Naumann smoked these things, Preuss knew, to remind everyone that he had been in Russia during the old days, the glory days.

"We have known each other a time, haven't we, Horst?"

Preuss nodded. Yes. Naumann had watched over him, had watched out for him, in '41 and '42 while he had led a Sonderkommando in Naumann's Einsatzgruppe B. Naumann was the one who taught him to scour Russia for Jews, round them up, and march them to pits dug in the forests, where his men shot and shot and shot until their guns cooked off rounds and their heads reeled with drink. It had been horrible work, horrible. But necessary. Naumann was the one who had made him see the necessity of it. More important, Naumann made possible his transfer to Holland, where he didn't have to shoot Jews but only arrange their deportation. He owed Naumann much.

Naumann pulled a piece of paper from inside his immaculate gray tunic and held it between thumb and forefinger. "Read this, then."

Ogruf. H. Rauter
Brigadef. Dr. E. Schöngarth

Brigadef. E. Naumann
Stubaf. W. Zoepf

The most important thing for me, now as before, is to see that
as many Jews as humanly possible are dispatched to the East.
In the brief monthly reports of the Security Police I want only
to be informed about what has been carted off during the
month, and what Jews are still left at this juncture.

*(signed) Heinrich Himmler*, 9.4.43

It was bland, like every signal from Berlin, even Eichmann's when he
was on a rampage, but reading between the lines was something Preuss
had practice doing. And as he read the spaces, he felt a small chill at the
back of his neck.

"The Reichsführer's unhappy," said Preuss.

Naumann's cigarette cracked and popped again, and he nodded.
"When did you last talk with Zoepf?" he asked.

Preuss had to think. "A week at least. He called to thank me for cognac I sent. Some of this." Preuss raised his glass. "Why?"

"He's not told you he was called to Berlin? He and I left for Berlin together, four days ago, but he returned to The Hague after just a day."

"No, nothing about Berlin."

"Zoepf was called to Berlin to meet with Eichmann."

Nothing unusual in that. Preuss reported to Zoepf, but Zoepf, who
oversaw all Holland's Jewish matters, reported directly to Eichmann's Department of Jewish Affairs, Amt IV B-4. Eichmann was Zoepf's master. All
deportation directives came straight from Berlin, right from Eichmann's
office. So if Eichmann had concerns, he would naturally summon Zoepf.

"It's getting more difficult each month," Preuss said, coming up with
a reason why Eichmann would send for Zoepf. "Perhaps that's why the
Sturmbannführer went to Berlin, to explain this to Eichmann. I called
up two thousand the first of the month and fewer than one hundred
came. I had to send men house to house, and even then I was eight hundred short for my first transport this month."

Naumann leaned back in the tired chair, brushed more ash from his tunic. He was a lawyer by training and he had a lawyer's fastidiousness still. The way he held his head cocked to one side—as if not believing for a moment the defendant's alibis—that was from his lawyer's days, too. "No, that wasn't the reason. This is what I heard, Horst. Eichmann demanded that Zoepf hasten the Jews' departure. And Zoepf agreed. He guaranteed he would deliver nine thousand in May. And seventeen thousand in June. That's a lot of Hebrews, my friend."

Nine thousand. Seventeen thousand. Ridiculous! He had managed, just barely, to ship three thousand in March, and if the new deportation schedule was any sign, he must gather more than six thousand this month. Nearly double that for May, doubled again in June?

"And they must all come from Amsterdam. This is the only place where there are still Jews," said Naumann.

Preuss nodded, able only to think of how they wailed when he packed them into the theater on the Plantage Middenlaan. Nine thousand? Seventeen thousand? Insane!

"I thought you should know this," Naumann said as Preuss imagined the old building expanding like a balloon while he squeezed Jews through every door and pushed them into every window.

"Zoepf will put the blame on me if the quotas are not met," Preuss said.

Now it was Naumann's turn to nod. "As surely as Jews go East." He brushed more ash from his tunic as the *papirosi* sparked and made snowflakes. "He's still upset you have this chair. He has friends of his own he'd like in your place, I think," Naumann said. "He hates me for setting you here, but because he can do nothing to me, he hates you instead. And then there is the other thing."

Naumann paused, took a swallow of cognac. "He was never in the East. He worries whether you'll take his place, perhaps, because he has not done what we have done. Stood where we have stood," Naumann said, now holding the snapping *papirosi* so it was in front of his face, as if to say "Russia." "To stand at the edge of the pit and . . ." Naumann's voice disappeared for a second. "He wants to rid himself of you, and so he will lay the blame on your shoulders as soon as things go badly. I'm afraid you're on the stove now, my friend."

Naumann was right. Preuss had never trusted Zoepf; the man never looked in your eyes. If the quotas weren't met, Zoepf would remind Eichmann it was Hauptsturmführer Preuss who had failed. And Eichmann would report to Kaltenbrunner or Himmler that it was not Zoepf, his handpicked expert in The Hague, but this Preuss in Amsterdam who had ignored the Reichsführer's directive. And he would end up somewhere unpleasant, someplace dangerous, like Yugoslavia, fighting partisans, instead of herding docile Jews onto trains. Partisans had guns. And they used them.

"Perhaps you can intercede again . . . ," said Preuss finally, looking at Naumann.

"I wish I could help," Naumann said, shaking his head. "But Eichmann wields all the power on the Jewish question here. This isn't the East. I have no authority over Jewish matters." True enough. Naumann might command Holland's security police, but he had little to say about deportations. That was run directly from Berlin, Himmler to Kaltenbrunner to Müller to Eichmann to Zoepf to Preuss. Except for holding them at Westerbork and shipping them to the East, Naumann had no say where Jews were concerned.

"At least lend me some men. I rely too much on Dutchmen. If you could spare a few, if only for a short time, I might make the quotas."

"I don't really have . . ."

"Please, Brigadeführer, just a few." Preuss heard pleading in his voice and hated it. But he didn't care.

It worked, and Naumann nodded again. "Perhaps a few men, for old times' sake. I'll send ten or twenty, some Kripo, some SS. But you can have them only for a few weeks."

"Thank you," Preuss said again. For a moment he had been afraid the migraines would return.

Naumann smoked more of his sparking *papirosi*. "You can return the favor," he said.

"Brigadeführer?"

"Kaltenbrunner mentioned something about the Abwehr running an operation here." In his mind's eye, Preuss saw Gruppenführer Ernst Kaltenbrunner, the huge alcoholic Austrian who since Heydrich's death had headed the Reich Security Main Office. "Something called Nightingale. The Abwehr has penetrated Churchill's Special Operations Executive."

Preuss had no idea what Naumann was talking about, and perhaps it showed.

"Churchill's SOE, that gang of criminals who work for the fat man with the cigar," said Naumann. "Spies and saboteurs, that's the SOE. They come from England by plane or parachute to make mischief here. Kaltenbrunner said the Abwehr has turned several of these SOE spies. But they're also crushing the Resistance with Nightingale. Counterfeit orders from England to draw the partisans into ambushes and arrests, that sort of thing."

Naumann waved a hand—like he might to a jury, Preuss thought.

"The one in charge is named Giskes. An Oberstleutnant of the Abwehr. Kaltenbrunner wants us to keep an eye on him. You'll let me know if you hear of him, won't you, Horst?" Naumann looked at him carefully, as if he knew. Preuss made his decision quickly.

"I've met him, Brigadeführer," he told his old chief. "We've talked, we've worked together, in fact." And Preuss explained how he and Giskes had agreed to share information, how Giskes had given him an informer, this woman Visser—whom he must have caught in this Nightingale snare, Preuss now realized—and how it had led so far to just one small raid. Preuss didn't bother the Brigadeführer with the story of the old woman who sprouted wings.

Naumann smoked his *papirosi* for a moment, its sizzling the only sound in the office. "Officially, we cooperate with the Abwehr. But I have heard things, Horst," and Naumann put his finger along his nose to show that this was a secret. "Dangerous things. Traitorous things. The Abwehr is full of traitors, I've heard it even harbors traitors who plot against the Führer. One day they'll regret what they've done and we will take over their business as well. Watch this Giskes. Stay close to him, in case we need to take this Nightingale from the Abwehr. Tell me what he does. Will you do that?"

"Of course," Preuss answered automatically. But his head began to throb with the effort. Himmler wanted Holland *Judenfrei;* Zoepf schemed at his expense. Now he must watch Giskes, too, because of bad blood between the SD and the Abwehr.

"Superb, Horst. Superb. Thank you. Now, if you have more of that Ferrand, we should drink up. No need for you to give it to Zoepf." He smiled. Preuss filled Naumann's glass to just below its rim.

Naumann leaned forward and held out his cigarette case, the one dented and scratched from months in Russia, *papirosi* inside, lying beside each other like fat little logs waiting at the mill. But as Preuss looked at the cigarettes, another image came, of Jews lying side by side, down in the pit.

Preuss picked one of the *papirosi*, spent a moment pinching the ends to filter the worst of the smoke, accepted the Brigadeführer's light, leaned back in his chair, and tried to force the harsh smoke into his lungs.

He had put Russia behind him, he thought, including these horrible things that reminded him of the glory days, the early days. But here he was, with one in his hand.

The *papirosi* popped and snapped like so many small shots.

W e have a problem," Mouse said. Kagen glared at him from across the table. They sat in a pub, THE DOLPHIN, the sign outside said, a block or two from the house at No. 47 Argyle Street. The place was dark—it was coming down in buckets outside, the rain hammering at the window they sat beside—but the bartender had left them alone once he'd brought their warm beer.

"And you're the one made it," Kagen said. Mouse flexed his hand, felt Rachael's stitches tighten up.

"Spark won't stop," Mouse said. "His boys are still there, which means Spark still wants us." They'd scouted Argyle Street a halfhour before, and he had pointed out the ganef standing inside the flower store across from the house, his face pressed against the glass pane in the door. Mouse wasn't sure, but from this distance it looked like Hugh.

"It's you he wants, gangster."

It was getting harder to keep quiet each time Kagen opened his mouth, but Mouse held his tongue. "If he wants me, then all of us are in trouble, aren't we? You are, Rachael is, her brother, Joop, too." He couldn't tell Kagen that the four of them were all in trouble anyway, even if Spark was out of the picture. Mouse touched the butt of the Smith & Wesson tucked into the front of his pants.

Kagen sipped his beer, looked out the water-streaked window at the people passing by, umbrellas up against the rain. He nodded after the longest time. "Yes" was all he said, quiet like. Now he looked at Mouse, but he didn't hold the gaze for long. "But what does it matter? He can't find us, not in that hotel."

Mouse drew on the Chesterfield. He'd been thinking about this all yesterday, some today too. "There's one place where he knows we'll be," Mouse said. "And when. O'Brien, the pilot. Spark will put the heat on O'Brien, and the mick will tell him when and where we're leaving. Spark will put a gun to his head. He'll tell Spark, you can bet on it." Mouse knew he was right. Spark had to know by now they were meeting O'Brien in Biggleswade on Sunday.

He had to get the others as far as Holland. Without that, his plan was for shit. Once he'd done the pops and come back to London, he could dodge Spark and his boys long enough to get home. But getting the other four to Holland, that was important.

"When we walk into that pub in Biggleswade, Jack Spark will be waiting for us," said Mouse. "He wants to set things right, for what we did to him. He'll pop me for sure, you too for being there. The others, just to keep things neat. That's how things work." Mouse remembered Lansky, and how he liked tidy ends. He wondered if Tootles was dead, tossed into the East River or hauled out to Long Island and buried in a hole along a dirt road.

Kagen shook his head. He looked up, his good eye half closed from his anger. "You people" was all Kagen said.

This was too much. "You ran with the Irgun," Mouse said. "Done time in jail. Don't tell me you never had someone after you. This is just like that."

"No, it's not," said Kagen. "Not at all. I fought for a home, not for money."

Mouse laughed and it caught the bartender's attention. "You're some great hero, are you? How many Arabs you kill with those bombs of yours? Women, right, kids? Rachael know all about that, does she? Brag to her how many you kill yet, *Wichser?*"

Kagen stood up, the table shifting and some of the beer sloshing out of the two tall glasses, his fingers curling into fists.

"Sit down," Mouse said. "Sit down." The German sat and the bartender, who had been watching them, went back to his rag. Mouse lowered his voice so that it wouldn't carry past the table.

"We need to work together, like you said, or we're not going to get out of here alive. Understand?" He'd settle things on his own time, but not here, not yet.

Kagen took another swig of beer, set down the glass. His voice was low and quiet too. "Yes, you're right. You're the one with the money, aren't you?" Always about the money.

"We have to pop Spark," Mouse said after a moment.

"Pop?" Kagen asked.

"We have to kill him."

"Is that all?" Kagen asked, snide-like.

Mouse shrugged. "Look, we have to do it before we leave London, otherwise he'll be waiting for us. Him or us, that's it. But I can't do this on my own. Not with . . ." And Mouse raised his hand, the white bandage wrapped around it making his hand easy to see in the dim light of the pub. "Spark has two ganefs, that Richie and the other one, Hugh. Maybe more, but at least those two."

"You need my help."

"Yeah," Mouse said. Kagen still sat silent. "You said we have to think on our feet. Well, this is one of those times. I don't see any other way."

Kagen was thinking it over. Probably weighing the ups and downs of the idea. But Mouse was sure this was right. Lansky would do this, Mouse thought.

"On one condition," Kagen said in a whisper so Mouse had to lean over the table to hear. "You bring the money from the bank, so we can both watch it." Mouse shook his head at first. Fuck no. But Kagen went on. "In case something happens to you, when we do this . . . pop . . . on Jack Spark. The money won't be lost and the rest of us can continue. Otherwise . . ."

Mouse sat back in the rickety chair, lit another Chesterfield, and thought it over. "In case something happens to you," the German meant. Like maybe a slug in the back of the head. And not from Spark's gun, either. But Kagen's idea started to sound good for a different reason. He wouldn't have to come back to London to get the money from Barclays. He could take it on the plane to Holland and make O'Brien fly him somewhere far from Jack's shithole, because he wouldn't have to fetch the money. He could dodge straight to some town on the coast and buy his way onto a ship to New York before Spark knew he was back. Then sail for home and tell his made-up story to Lansky about how all the money had been spent on guns and a plane and boats, but it was only him who had escaped.

"Okay. I'll take it out of the bank, like you want, but when we pop Spark, I'm not taking it with me. Joop's watching it for me." Joop was the only one he could count on. Rachael was too deep into Kagen, or him into her, and there Mouse smiled a bit. But Joop thought Kagen was a *groot pik*, a *Duitser* too. Joop didn't trust Kagen; no way would he let the German put his hands on Mouse's dough.

Mouse stuck his hand out across the table, leaning forward as he did, feeling the pressure of the Smith & Wesson against his stomach. Kagen reached out his. They shook on it, Mouse feeling the German put some muscle behind the handshake, Mouse returning the favor.

He smiled at the German, pretending to be stupid, pretending that it was all just fine now that they'd shook on it. But he'd be sleeping with one hand on the money, the other on the Smith & Wesson from now on.

Reka stood on the stoop of the house on Amsterdam's Utrechtsed-warsstraat, and knocked on the door. She glanced over her shoulder. No one. She knocked again, heard footsteps through the door. It opened. And Henrik stood there with his mouth hanging open and his eyes so large they wanted to jump from his head.

"Henrik," she said, craning her neck to see if anyone was behind him, but the corridor was empty. Henrik closed his mouth, opened it, closed it again. "Are you going to let me in? Or do you want the Gestapo to find me on your stoop?"

Dumb still, he stepped aside and Reka walked into the house. Henrik closed the door and shuffled into a small sitting room on the right. The furnishings were expensive, heavy upholstered damask chairs and a thick, pale green carpet over the wood floor. She had had things like these once, Reka remembered, she and David, Papa and Mama.

"What are you doing here?" He caught his breath, and Reka noticed the old man's leg trembled. He sat clumsily in a chair. "Do you know what you've done, coming here?"

Reka walked to Henrik's chair and stood over him. She wasn't much, but she thought she could frighten this man who frightened so easily.

"What I've done? You were the one who sent us to the Diemen-Nord. You're the informer, I think." If she bullied him like Johannes did, she might get to the truth.

He glanced up, his eyes bulging. He shook his head, back and forth, forth and back, like a rag doll's in a child's hand. "No, no, that's not true. I'm the one who hides you. I'm the one at risk for hiding you, little Jew."

Reka knelt, her dress hiking up, and she felt the rug under her bare knees. She put a hand on his arm. "What is Annje doing in your house?" she said quickly, hoping to take him by surprise.

"What do you mean? That girl has never been here. That would be mad, her coming here. She doesn't even know where I live. . . ." And his body sagged in the chair while his voice drained away.

"You understand, don't you? How I found you," Reka said, her voice now just a whisper. "I followed her here. I saw her come to this house five days ago. I saw the two of you in the window. I saw Annje touching you, old man. And the whore wore no clothes."

Henrik opened his mouth as if he was to say something, but he closed it. His leg, Reka saw, trembled the more.

"What does Annje want from you?" Reka asked.

Henrik wept, and that took her by surprise. She knew he was a nervous old man and easily bullied, but she had not expected this. But he cried like a woman, the tears streaming down both sides of his nose, his shoulders quaking as he softly sobbed. "Don't tell my wife, please don't tell my wife."

Reka stood, stepped over to another chair, and sat down. So Henrik feared his wife. "Annje sleeps with you," she said, a bit louder. The old man nodded, refusing to look at her. "Why does that whore sleep with you, Henrik?"

He looked up, his face confused behind the tears. "Why?" he asked, as if it was a stupid question.

"Yes, why does she fuck an old man like you?" Reka asked, using words she never thought she'd say. But she shoved aside her embarrassment and made her voice hard, knocking out the words. "She was Joop's girl. When he returns, he'll ask harder questions than me. He'll want to know why you fuck his girl."

Fear moved into Henrik's eyes. He had not known that Joop and Annje were lovers. She pushed harder. "Annje is after something besides your prick, old man," Reka said. "What else? Why does she come here?"

"Why?" he asked again, but his face told her he thought Annje came to his bed because she loved him. Reka wanted to laugh. The old man had fooled himself, and couldn't see how ridiculous it was.

"What have you told her?" She couldn't say what she suspected Annje of, but there was something about her behavior that felt wrong. She had followed her as recently as the day before yesterday, when Annje had taken a long walk for no reason and done nothing but buy a newspaper, read it in a café on Stadhouderskade, and then drop the paper into a waste bin down the street. So instead she had to fish.

The old man's tears had stopped, so had his sobbing. "I've told her nothing."

"You talk in bed after," Reka said. Absently, she touched the scar at her temple. "What do you say when you talk in bed? Or should I ask your wife? I could wait until she returns and ask her." Her voice was like nails.

"We don't talk," Henrik said slowly. Reka got up from her chair, knelt in front of him again, but this time she raised her hand and slapped him, hard, across the cheek.

"Don't lie," she said, hearing her voice sound a bit like Mama's when she had been angry. She struck Henrik on the other cheek with the back of her hand. The blows echoed in the room and Henrik put his hands in front of his face to shield himself. He began to weep again. "What have you told Annje?" She slapped his ear, very hard.

But he said nothing through his crying, only hunched his shoulders to pull his head out of her reach. Reka raised her hand to cuff him again, but a knock on the door, a soft knock, stayed her. Not the police, not with that knock. Too soft. Henrik looked up, his face wet with tears.

"Who's that? Is that your wife?" But Henrik shook his head.

"Annje," he said. Reka went to the window and, from behind the edge of the curtains, peeked to the stoop and saw Annje standing there, one hand on her hip. Reka thought for a moment she might confront Annje here, but that was stupid. She had nothing. Henrik had told Annje something, but she needed more if she was to convince Johannes. Johannes wouldn't believe her over Annje without proof. Especially if Johannes himself wanted up Annje's dress, as she suspected.

"The back door to the house, where is it? Henrik! The back door?"

The old man whispered, "The kitchen. There's a door to the garden."

"Get hold of yourself, old man," Reka said, towering over Henrik and his chair again. "Don't say anything of this." She waited until he looked at her. Annje knocked at the door again and Reka thought she heard the woman call Henrik's name. "If you say a word, I'll come back, Henrik, I swear. I'll tell your wife." The fear was back in his eyes. He was most afraid of his wife. "Breathe a word of this and I'll tell her everything."

Reka walked down the corridor, found the kitchen, and let herself out through the garden door. But by the time she'd made it through the small garden, down a narrow alley to the street, and back to the corner where she could see the stoop of Henrik's house, it was bare.

Reka wished Joop was here. The man was as hard as the rails he worked on. He would have gotten Henrik to talk.

She shook her head. She was all alone, as she'd been since that day on Westerbork's cold Appelplatz when the OD had shouted "Dekker" and taken Mama and Papa.

Reka stepped back around the corner and walked a different way home to the used clothing shop on Lindenstraat.

# *Nine*

Henrik wouldn't look at her. He had climbed down into the cellar and now stood beside Johannes, another piece of paper in his shaky hand. Reka glanced to Annje, but there was nothing there that told her Henrik had breathed a word.

"Another message from Joop," Johannes said as he read the slip of paper Henrik handed him. Johannes gave her the paper.

CHOSEN PARTY ARRIVES 0000 19 WESTEINDERPLASSEN
SOUTH 1KM CALSLAGEN BY AIR MAKE EL TO LIGHT LAND-
ING YASHER KOACH JOOP

*Yasher koach,* she read. It was the one Hebrew expression she'd taught Joop, but the words alone, "May you stay strong," were not everything. Now she knew why Joop had put "chosen party" in his messages; he was coming with Jews. "Chosen party," chosen people. The Hebrew told her it was so.

"Joop wants us to meet him at midnight, near the Westeinderplassen," said Johannes. "He's coming by airplane."

"Airplane?" Annje asked. "Are you sure? Joop, by airplane?"

"We're to signal with lights, in the shape of an L," Johannes said. "We'll need torches or lamps."

"Airplane? How can Joop come by airplane?" Annje asked.

Reka was stunned. Her heart beat—one-two, one-two—in her chest. Jews. Joop was bringing Jews to Holland. She shook her head. "I don't know," she said. But he could not come from Holland. France, perhaps, but how could he have found an airplane there? England? Had Joop run all the way to England?

"What does this mean, Reka?" Johannes asked, taking the paper from her. *"Yasher koach,"* he said. "What does that mean? Is it German? It sounds German."

Joop was bringing Jews. If Joop brought Jews, it meant they came for a Jewish reason. For revenge, perhaps. Shoot one of the *Sicherheitsdienst* or explode the evil building on the Euterpestraat. But more important, it meant she would no longer be alone.

In her excitement, Reka answered Johannes and said "Hebrew" before she could stop. As soon as the word escaped, she knew she'd done wrong. Johannes's eyes narrowed and recognition washed over his face as he said, "Ah," while looking at the paper again. He's figured out chosen party now too, Reka saw.

"What does it mean?" Annje asked.

"Nothing, it—" Reka began, but Johannes broke in.

"He's coming with Jews, is that it?" he asked Reka. "That's what 'chosen party' and this *yasher koach* mean. Is that right? Reka?"

"I don't know," she said, wary but too late. "Yes, I think so," she said finally. Johannes nodded. In the corner she heard the idiot Martin chant "Jews, Jews, Jews," in a low singsong.

"What do we need more Jews for?" Johannes asked.

The cellar was quiet. The one electric bulb cast sharp shadows and made the room seem even smaller, its ceiling even lower. In the corner Martin repeated "Jew" until Annje shushed him.

"We have to go," Reka said, realizing what the silence meant. "We must meet them. Joop's coming. He's one of us." Even though Jews are not, she told herself, reading Johannes's face.

After seconds that stretched as long as those when she'd crawled through Westerbork's wire, Johannes nodded his head. "Of course. We'll meet Joop and his airplane, wherever it comes from. And whoever it carries." More of Johannes's drama, Reka knew, meant to distract her. But she wouldn't forget the long, awkward quiet in the cellar.

Johannes rattled off orders, telling Henrik and Annje to find electric torches if they could, oil lamps if not, telling Reka to prepare their single gun. And there wasn't time to waste. The Westeinderplassen was twenty kilometers south, so they needed to leave quickly. The tram went only as far as Amstelveen, they'd have to walk the rest.

Reka wanted to say something as first Henrik then Annje climbed up the ladder and through the trap to the shop above to find torches or lamps. But what? Tell Johannes that Annje was an informer? She had no proof. The police hadn't come to the cellar, had they?

Johannes handed her the old automatic, a Luger from the Great War, and told her to clean and load it. Reka unwrapped the Luger from its cloth. She liked the heavy feel of it.

Absentminded, Reka touched the scar at her temple with the muzzle of the pistol.


P reuss put the black telephone back in its cradle and looked at the paper in front of him. *Westeinderplassen landing 1 km. s. Calslagen 0000 commandos aircraft JEWS.* That last he'd underlined so heavily that he'd ripped the paper. Incredible. Jews, and coming by air.

The Visser bitch had steered him wrong before, to the old woman flying from the window, in fact. This could be the same, this fantastic tale. He looked at his watch. Ten hours.

He had heard someone else over the connection when the woman

Visser called with her news, her words spilling out so fast that Preuss wondered if he missed some. It was a man's voice, that was all he could tell. And the line went dead.

He should call Giskes. Visser had said it was not just Jews, but also commandos, coming by aircraft. That could mean only one thing. England. Airplanes and commandos only came from England. He had neither the men nor the experience to deal with black-faced commandos with knives in their teeth. Preuss picked up the telephone and told the girl on the switchboard to ring the number Giskes had given him. Unbelievable. Jews arriving, not evacuating. This was new.

He must have these Jews, if Jews there really were—if Visser told the truth. Not for their numbers, there could be no more than a handful, but because if Jews came with commandos and dared step here, they must be up to something. Something to do with *his* Jews. Had to be. Jews took care of their own, and only their own.

The line buzzed, clicked, and a voice answered, "Giskes," in his ear.

"This is Preuss. We have a very special package coming from England tonight. I thought you would like to meet it with me." Jews ran, they didn't come, thought Preuss as he waited for Giskes to say something. But there it was. Extraordinary.

"I'm listening," Giskes's old voice said over the line.

They crouched in the alley off Whitechurch Lane, twenty yards up the street from Spark's butcher shop, tucked behind a big bin. Trash, it smelled like—spoiled fruit. Apples. Kagen had hold of a Sten and his knuckles were white as white can be. The German swallowed, spit, swallowed again. He looked green.

"What's wrong, you shoot those fourteen from behind?" Mouse asked in a small voice. "Takes bigger balls to look in a man's eyes when you shoot him." Kagen looked up, and with the one eye free of the black patch, fixed him with a hateful stare.

"I'll be fine, gangster," Kagen said. "I've looked into lots of eyes."

Mouse glanced at his watch. It was nearly five. "I'll take a look," he said, and slipped along the wall to the mouth of the alley. He didn't feel nervous, he'd done this too many times. But he couldn't stop thinking about Rachael and what he would have to do in a few hours.

Mouse put Rachael out of his mind only by thinking of Lansky. He wondered again if he should have cabled Lansky to ask permission to pop Spark. He'd even written on the pad in the office of Commercial Cable three days before, printing in block letters:

TROUBLE FROM JACK STOP HE WANTS TO END DEAL WITH MISTER UITHUIZEN STOP CAN I DROP HIM FROM OUR BUSI-NESS STOP YES OR NO

But he'd not handed the form to the clerk, instead had put it inside his pocket. He was afraid of Little Man's answer, tell the truth. So he'd made the decision all on his own. Mouse felt uneasy about it, but if he was going to get back to New York with Lansky's money, it was the right play. And once he explained everything to Lansky, with the pop already done, he was pretty sure Little Man would understand. At the worst, Lansky would just think him stupid, like usual.

Mouse stuck his head around the corner to see down and across Whitechurch toward JOHN MARLEY & SON, MEATS. The two chairs either side of the door were empty.

That was when the black four-door rolled by, left to right. Mouse tried to become smaller than small. The driver was on this side, but the man—Mouse saw it was Richie—didn't look his way. The car, a '38 Ford with the slanting nose that always reminded him of Jimmy Durante, pulled up beside the curb in front of the shop. Its brakes squeaked as it rolled to a stop.

"It's time," he said to Kagen. Mouse shifted the bulky Welrod to his left hand, wincing. His hand was now free of its bandage, but it still pained him. He put a bullet in the chamber by twisting the Welrod's knob, pulling back the bolt, pushing it back in, and twisting again.

He motioned Kagen ahead, and then followed. He sure as shit wasn't going to put his back to this crazy yid now. They walked, didn't run—

walking was best, he'd told Kagen—from the alley across Whitechurch to the back fender of the Ford. Kagen crouched down at the rear wheel and Mouse turned toward the front of the car. The car was idling hard. He'd counted on that after scouting the street the day before and the day before that; both days, between four and five, Richie drove up in the noisy car to collect Jack Spark. Richie would never hear them as long as the engine ran.

Mouse stooped down, raised the Welrod, holding the grip in his right, his still-tender left hand under the barrel to keep the weight level, and edged the one step from the fender to just even with the back line of the front door. The window was down.

There was reason enough for this, Mouse thought, the way Spark had treated him.

"How you doin', Richie?" he said, loud enough for the ganef to hear over the rough sound of the engine.

"Piss off," Richie said, but he said it before he turned his head, and when he saw who it was, his face went as white as the wide strip of tape still pasted on his busted nose.

"Meyer Lansky sends regards, you dumb fuck," Mouse said, the words a habit, but still true or he wouldn't have said them. In a roundabout way, Little Man had said to do this. DEAL NOT JACKS BUSINESS, he'd cabled.

Mouse stuck the Welrod into the car and pulled its trigger, and the gun spat in a small sound no louder than a guy coughing in a quiet room. The slug made a neat hole in Richie's right eyebrow and painted the inside of the windshield a fire-engine red as it came out the other side. Richie made just one quick noise, and he twitched in the seat enough to rock the car. Mouse smelled the hot smell of blood.

Mouse ducked, working the bolt of the Welrod as fast as he could— he'd practiced that the last few days, holding the barrel in his left as tightly as that hand let him and moving the bolt with his right. As he finished, the black car's horn honked once, then blared in a long note that didn't stop.

Richie was zotzed, he was dead-dead-dead, Mouse thought as he stood up, bringing up the barrel of the Welrod. But in the time it had taken him to duck down and reload, dead Richie had slumped forward, not sideways. His chest was pressed against the metal rim inside the steering wheel.

"Richie, shut the fokk up," a voice shouted from the doorway of the butcher shop. Mouse reached in a hand to pull Ritchie off the horn, and it went quiet.

He hoped Kagen would be smart enough to hold off. This wasn't going the way he'd planned, but there was still time to save the situation. He could still pop Hugh—that's who was now shouting across the car's roof—with the quiet Welrod, so he and Kagen could get to the doorway. They could still do it like he'd planned, step inside the butcher's shop, Kagen with his Sten, and Mouse with the Smith & Wesson still tucked in his pants, to let in daylight on Spark and anyone else in the place.

Mouse straightened and tried to bring up the Welrod, but his left hand was tired, and he wasn't fast enough. Hugh's mouth moved and Mouse only heard "kike" and Kagen lost it and the racket of the Sten, a long ba-ba-ba-ba-banging sound louder even than the car horn had been, filled the street and the slugs pounded Hugh's chest and flung the man against the brick wall. He lay there, his legs tangled and the front of his suit a red river.

The gunshots echoed up and down Whitechurch Lane as Kagen shot wild, everywhere, goofy, like a crazy man. The dirty plate-glass window of John Marley & Son, Meats lost its greasiness as the slugs punched holes in it. The window shattered, the pieces falling but making no noise on account of all the gunfire.

The fuckin' yid flopped it, Mouse thought, but he still figured he might save it all. There was Jack Spark, dim, just a few feet inside the door, but Mouse could see it was Spark, for the shadow was round in the body and round in the head. Too proud maybe to hide. Mouse raised the Welrod, his left hand trembling, and pressed the trigger. The big man backed up and disappeared into the gloom inside. He'd hit him maybe, maybe not, he wasn't sure. Mouse crouched down again to work the Welrod's action.

He was only halfway through the working when the glass of the car's windows came down around him. They were shooting back. Lots of guns, quick shots that tore through the air and smacked into the other side of the Ford. Mouse felt the car rock again.

Kagen had stopped shooting and was back against the rear wheel of the car for cover. Mouse's brain almost went blank—he'd never had someone shoot at him like this, never been so scared, not even when that schvartzer got off one barrel from his over-under Browning years ago and the second hammer fell on a bad primer and the shotgun hadn't fired, lucky-lucky-lucky. But Mouse had enough left in him to know they had to get the hell out of there.

He looked at Kagen, who looked back, his patchless eye gleaming, a grin on his face, meshuge for sure. Mouse held on to the Welrod with his left hand, stuck his right out and put out one finger, two fingers, three fingers to count, and he saw that Kagen understood. At three, Kagen took off for the alley and Mouse right behind him, hunched over like a man carrying a block of ice, trying to keep what was left of the car between him and those slugs zipping out of the busted plate glass window.

All he heard in his head was the slap-slap-slap of his shoes, and the slap-slap-slap as slugs ripped out pieces of brick when they got across Whitechurch Lane and cleared the corner and made it into the alley.

He ran full out, the Welrod almost too heavy for his left hand, but he didn't drop it, and he heard the sound of Kagen huffing alongside him in the narrow alley as they ran for Whitechapel High Street and the Morris with Schaap waiting for them.

And all that rolled though his mind was how this was the same as in front of Tootles's place on Canal. Except it wasn't.

The Morris roared up the A1 at fifty miles an hour, engine flat out yelling, and Mouse listened to the wind rip into the car through the open window at his side and whistle out through the pellet hole in the back window behind him. The sun was nearly gone, but there was still some light and as Schaap drove, Mouse watched the countryside he'd missed the time before, when he and Rachael drove up to Biggleswade in the dark.

Schaap said little, just smoked the Chesterfields Mouse gave him. He was out of uniform now, dressed in the old clothes Rachael had bought for him, a gray jacket with a hole in one elbow, brown pants, and a billed cap that looked like it had been in a closet for twenty years. Mouse scratched at the collar of his cheap white shirt, tugged at the thick cloth coat that smelled of mothballs. Rachael and little Joop had shopped secondhand stores for their clothes, and the Dutchman said they'd done a good job, considering. The clothes looked, more or less, like what Hollanders wore.

Kagen and Joop sat in the back seat, Rachael between them, all three packed in like sardines. No one bothered to talk. Fine by Mouse.

The cloth bag on the floor at his feet held the money, what was left of it. Fifteen thousand pounds, English, in worn-out twenties that looked too big and too plain. He'd exchanged Lansky's dollars for pounds early that day—Rachael had given him the name of a man who asked no questions, the banks would ask those questions exchanging so much, she'd said—but he'd taken a beating on the deal. Eighty cents on the dollar he got, that was all. Fifteen thousand and change, American, down the toilet.

Rachael said it was necessary, that Dutch fishermen would take pounds to hire their boats but not dollars. When Mouse said no, he was sticking with dollars, Kagen gave him the up and down, not saying anything, but the look said enough. Mouse wasn't afraid of the German—not as long as he kept an eye on him—but he'd done the deal to keep Kagen from wondering why he needed dollars when dollars would be no good, and maybe queering his plan. If Kagen thought too much, it might be tougher to surprise him and the others in Holland.

But twenty percent—Mouse had done the figuring—was a lot to give up. Even if he didn't give O'Brien another dime, he'd clear just a little over sixty grand, minus what it took to get home.

Whenever Mouse stopped looking at the villages and woods and fields they passed, he tried to think of that money. But every few seconds, the woman behind him interrupted. He'd thought if he found a reason to hate her, he could do it. But her sleeping with that fuck Kagen was not a big enough reason. And although her reason for this whole plan seemed so stupid—she was a sap, worrying about anyone but herself—that wasn't big enough either.

To make himself forget Rachael, Mouse thought of Kagen, knowing hate would follow and he could work himself up some anger. Mouse knew his plan hadn't been perfect—he should have waited until Spark climbed in the car and used a Sten like the German to pump it full of holes—but he blamed Kagen. The German had gone crazy and cost them surprise—like Dukey did that time when he'd had him help with that double pop in the Bronx—and Kagen's mistake had given Jack's boys a chance to start shooting. It was the deal with the farmer and his dog all over again, only more so.

The flopped pop only made things worse—unless Spark was stiff on a table somewhere, he was sure to come after them now. Mouse lit a Chesterfield, inhaled, and for the first time realized that his plan of doing what Meyer Lansky would do might not work. He was not nearly so smart as Little Man. Even if he thought hard, he couldn't make his brain think like Lansky's.

"There," he said to Schaap, pointing to the sign up ahead that read BIGGLESWADE 1 MILE. The Dutchman grunted. A minute later, the Morris bounced off the A1 and down a narrow road. Schaap slowed the car as they came into the village and pulled up behind a horse and cart. Mouse breathed a bit easier. Even if Spark had gotten here before them, which was unlikely, for it would take time to clean out Richie or get another car, he wouldn't risk shooting it up in daylight with people around. Then again . . . he put his hand on the Welrod.

"That's it ahead," he said to Schaap, pointing at the big wooden bird on the pole over the door of the Golden Pheasant. Two old guys stood outside the pub, but they looked like farmers, with muddy pants tucked into muddy boots. Mouse looked at his watch. Half-past seven; they were early by a half hour. "Keep going," he told Schaap. And he guided him to the next narrow street, then the next after that, until they had driven in a circle around and behind the pub. No black car. No cars at all, in fact. Just a woman in front of a small house, going at a patch of ground with a hoe, and a couple of kids, one on a rusted bicycle, the other trotting alongside.

"Here," he said to Schaap as he saw the back of the pub. Schaap steered the Morris to a stop. Mouse opened the door, not wanting to go, but he didn't trust the German and the Dutchmen had no idea, and although he sort of hoped Rachael would follow him in like before so he could somehow leave her in the pub and not have to do this, she didn't move. He got out and shut the Morris's door, leaned close enough to the window to say, "I'll check it out."

The two farmers were gone, but there was still no black car in sight. Mouse walked through the doorway and into the brighter light of the pub. No O'Brien. Just three men at the bar and the same fifty-some bald guy behind the bar. All turned to look, but he said nothing and sat at the same table as before, facing the door, the Welrod bulky under his coat where he held it there by pressing an arm against his side. After the bartender came and asked what he wanted, he laid the gun across his legs, under the table and out of sight. He'd cocked it, and when he drank the beer the bartender brought, he kept his right hand under the table and on the butt of the silenced pistol.

O'Brien walked through the doorway at ten to eight, saw Mouse, and sat down across the small square table, calm as could be. Mouse looked him over, trying to read the Irishman's face but having no luck. He couldn't tell if the mick was in with Spark or not. If he was, now that he was here, it would be because he was greedy, plain and simple, and wanted more to show than the thousand quid he already had.

"Lovely scratch there," O'Brien said, nodding to Mouse's stitched hand, the one around the glass of beer. O'Brien put both his hands on the table, folded one atop the other. He smiled enough to show his missing tooth there on the bottom.

Mouse ignored both O'Brien's words and his smile. "Where's the plane?"

"Oh, nearby, nearby. The money?"

"When you get us there, like we said."

"That's what we need to talk about," the mick said, smiling again.

"Yeah?" Even now, Mouse wasn't sure if Spark was coming. He'd expected the Irishman to squeeze him at the last minute no matter what.

"One thousan', four hundred is what we agreed," said O'Brien. "But I've been thinkin'. This is a much bigger job, more fierce, isn't it? All the way to 'Olland and back. I've had to spread some joy around, if you will, to cover me hole for bein' gone a lot longer than my usual excuse when I fly for Spark. I been thinkin' we need to discuss me fee before we leave."

130

"You been thinking a lot," Mouse said. The Irishman nodded, smiling still.

"That I have, Yank." O'Brien hesitated, like he wasn't sure how far to push this. "A number in me head," the mick said finally, "and that number is three thousan' pounds. Payable now, before the Lysander's wheels leave the ground."

It was then that Mouse knew for sure that Jack Spark had gotten to the Irishman, and that the East Ender would be here. The mick wanted his money before they left because he wanted it before Spark came and popped Mouse.

O'Brien finally moved a hand, his right, toward the edge of the table, but before he could drop it out of sight Mouse tapped the heavy, invisible barrel of the Welrod against the underside of the table.

"Hear that?" Mouse asked. O'Brien's hand froze a couple inches from the tabletop's edge. "That's a very big gun. And guess where it's pointing?"

"You wouldn't dare," O'Brien said softly. "Not here."

"Really? It's one of the Welrods you sold Jack. You know the Welrod, don't you, Harry? I've used it and guess what? It don't sound much like a gun. By the time they figure out it wasn't just you falling out of your chair, I'll be out the door." O'Brien said nothing and left his hands in sight. "I've done a lot of thinking, too, Irish. Want to know what I'm thinking?"

"You'll tell me, I suppose."

Mouse nodded. "When's Jack supposed to show, Irish? That's number one. And don't tell me he's not, I know he is. You tell him to come a bit late so you have time to squeeze me?" When O'Brien sat, stony like a Brownsville boy dragged down to the station house, Mouse tapped the Welrod up against the table again. The mick looked very, very unhappy, but he answered.

"Any minute now, Yank."

"Where's the plane, that's number two."

"Ten minutes from here, but we have to wait for full dark to take off. They'll throw me in the jail for sure if someone sees the plane fly from the field I put her in."

"No, I think we're leaving now."

"Me money?"

"Like we agreed. Fourteen hundred," Mouse said. He looked toward the doorway.

"Can't hurt to ask, can it, now?"

"Let's go, Irish." Mouse nodded toward the doorway.

"And if you shoot me, you won't have a pilot, will you?" The mick smiled, as if he had Mouse in a corner. O'Brien may have seen action, but he didn't know what he was doing. He must not have learned anything from Spark.

Mouse shook his head. "I'll find the plane. That's the important thing. I can always get another pilot," he lied, calling the mick's bluff. "But you. You're no cat, are you, Irish—you got just one life." And he tapped the table one last time with the Welrod, hard enough to make the beer glass jump.

O'Brien looked even more unhappy, but he stood. Mouse did the same, pulling the Welrod from under the table and letting it hang by his side. O'Brien caught a glimpse of it, but none of the others in the room did as much as look up.

They left the Golden Pheasant and went out into the twilight. Kagen leaned against the corner of the building, near a motorcycle on its stand, a leather helmet on its handlebars.

"Yours?" Mouse asked the Irishman, who nodded as they came to the machine. Kagen straightened and Mouse saw that the German had a Sten in his hands. Kagen had been watching, maybe worried he would try to give them the slip in the dark, Mouse thought. No trust from Kagen, he remembered. But soon it wouldn't matter.

"Can you ride this thing?" Mouse asked Kagen. If he couldn't, it was going to be a tight fit in the car with the six of them. But Kagen nodded. "We're leaving now," Mouse said. "Follow us on this."

The German slung the Sten over a shoulder, straddled the motorcycle, kicked its starter a time or two, and its engine buzzed. Kagen slipped the helmet over his head.

Mouse prodded O'Brien to the Morris with the Welrod and made him lean against the car while he patted him down. He found the revolver stuck in the belt of his pants, and made the mick get in the front seat, beside Schaap. He shoved into the back seat beside Rachael—not that he wanted to sit next to her and smell her, now of all times—but he had to be behind the Irishman. "Give us directions to the plane," he said over O'Brien's shoulder. "No fuckin' around. I bet this'll go through the seat just fine." And he tapped the barrel of the Welrod lightly on O'Brien's shoulder, then let the gun drop so it was in his lap, his right hand around the grip and finger on the trigger.

Schaap put the Morris in reverse, backed up and turned around, and when O'Brien pointed, ground into first gear. The little car rattled down the darkening, narrow street.

W here's Paul?" Rachael asked. Mouse turned to look back the way they'd come. The moon up above the trees was full, but now that the sun was down, even that wasn't enough to see if Kagen and his motorcycle were out there.

They stood around the Morris, now parked under a tree at the edge of this field. It was like a big fenced yard, with a black wall of trees along three sides.

O'Brien's airplane was big and fat and looked slow as Little Farvel's brain. Painted flat black, the Lysander was like a biplane missing its bottom wing; the one thick wing was mounted atop the fuselage. Fifty feet long from the radial engine at the front to the tall tail at the back, the plane stood on stocky struts for legs, the wheels nearly hidden in the grass. Between those struts was a long, dark tank.

O'Brien was already ducking under the engine cowling to the other side of the plane. "Make sure he doesn't leave without us," Mouse said to Joop, and the little guy nodded and followed. Less than a minute later, O'Brien's voice called down from the cockpit above him. "Climb aboard on that ladder port side. I had 'em remove the fuel tank between me and the gunner's spot and sling an external under to make more room inside. Cozy, but you'll fit."

Rachael climbed the ladder that led up into the fuselage at the back where the glass canopy was propped open. She took the two duffels and the two other bags that her brother pulled from the trunk of the Morris and handed up.

Where was Kagen? The last time he'd looked back and seen the motorcycle's narrow headlight was just a couple minutes before O'Brien pointed them to the dirt road that ended at this field.

A long echoing roll of gunfire was his answer. It was a Sten—Mouse never forgot a gun—and no sooner did its echo die than it started again. Underneath the chatter of the Sten, Mouse heard other guns, short pops for pistols.

O'Brien must have heard the shots, too, since he leaned out the window of the cockpit above Mouse's head and said, "Sounds like Mr. Spark hasn't forgotten you, Yank."

"Start it up, Irish," he said. O'Brien hesitated, and Mouse yelled through the canopy to where he knew Joop must be. "Shoot him. If the engine's not turning by the time you count to three, shoot him." All Mouse could see was a dark shape of something pushed against the back of O'Brien's neck.

"Your funeral, Yank," O'Brien said, and pulled his head back into the cockpit. In a second or two Mouse heard something whine from inside the airplane, the propeller inched around, and with a big cough, the radial caught and roared. The propeller spun until it was just a watery blur, its wash flattening the grass behind the plane.

More Sten gunfire just beyond the trees. Mouse ran to the Morris in the dark, felt on the back seat for the cloth bag with the fifteen thousand pounds, and the Welrod. He handed both to Schaap, who stood beside the plane at the bottom of the ladder.

"Get on!" Mouse yelled over the thunder of the Lysander's engine. "Take these and throw down a Sten!"

Schaap put his mouth close to Mouse's ear and shouted. "I'll do it, you get on." Mouse shook his head. At a long burst from a Sten, and one-two-three pistol shots came through the trees, he felt some of the same scare as in Whitechurch Lane when Spark's boys had shot, shot at *him*, he couldn't fuckin' believe it, shot at *me*. But Mouse stuffed the feeling into a corner. Spark was *his* problem. And Mouse always fixed his problems.

He shoved the Dutchman toward the ladder. Schaap monkeyed up with the Welrod and bag, and tossed down a Sten. A pair of magazines landed in the dark grass at his feet. He tried to remember what Kagen had showed him, but his fingers fumbled. He dropped a magazine twice, each time losing it in the grass, before he managed to shove it home where it belonged. Pull back the bolt, he told himself, and he did.

As he looked up from the Sten, a single headlight showed at the far end of the field, and as the motorcycle got closer, he thought he saw Kagen low over the handlebars. The motorcycle skidded on the road and into the field. It bounced through the grass, the headlight jumping, space between tires and ground for sure, but Kagen held on somehow. He was heading straight for Mouse.

Mouse raised the Sten and put his finger on the trigger. He could shoot now and save himself the trouble in Holland. But he didn't.

Not more than fifty yards behind Kagen and his circus trick was a pair of bigger headlights, and in the moonlight he recognized the Ford that had been Richie's coffin a couple hours before. Mouse stepped to the side to give himself a shot, and as soon as Kagen was clear, the motorcycle sliding on its side as the German finally lost control, Mouse pulled the trigger. The Sten pounded his shoulder, his left hand on fire as he held the gun, and he had no idea if he hit a damn thing.

But the magazine lasted long enough for Kagen to pull himself from under the motorcycle and get to the Lysander. Mouse glanced at the fat, dark plane behind him. The plane began to move.

Mouse felt in the grass for the second magazine, found it after one-two heartbeats, tore out the empty and slammed the new in place. He turned his back on the moving airplane now and faced Spark's black car one last time.

It slewed to a stop thirty yards away. The back door opened and Spark himself staggered out; he was impossible to mistake even in the moonlight with that big round ball of a head. Mouse pointed the Sten from his hip, no time for the shoulder. As if it mattered. He couldn't hit anything.

Jack Spark raised his arm, and even from thirty yards Mouse could see Spark had a pistol, and he imagined he could see the slide of the automatic slip back and a cartridge slowly jump out of the ejector and the slide work again and another empty cartridge case tumble through the air. Spark was shooting at him. At *him*.

The image was gone and Mouse pulled the Sten's trigger, trying to keep the gun from bucking its muzzle up, and he fired and fired and fired, hoping he put new holes in the Ford to match the old from those seconds on Whitechurch. He let loose the whole magazine.

The big man disappeared—falling or slipping or going to ground for cover, Mouse wasn't sure, but he was gone. Had he popped him? Mouse didn't know, not in the dark.

"Gangster!" someone called from behind, and he turned and saw the Lysander rolling away. He ran for the airplane, grabbed the ladder with one hand, his left, and the pain almost made him black out. Someone took the Sten from his right, reached out and gripped that hand and yanked him off his feet, up the last two rungs of the ladder and into the Lysander.

He landed on top of Kagen. The German still held his hand in a grip that felt like a vise turned two turns too far.

The Lysander rolled faster. Mouse could tell the plane was picking up speed from the yowl of the radial engine and the noise of the wind over the canopy still open, and in less time than it took for him to wonder where Schaap had put his money, the airplane jumped into the night.

Someone slammed down the canopy and the wind's sound shrank. From the front of the Lysander, Mouse could hear O'Brien yelling, but he couldn't make it out.

The plane leveled and Mouse looked at Kagen, who had let go his hand and was sitting with his back against the inside of the Lysander's fuselage. "What?" Mouse shouted over the noise of the engine. "What did he say?"

"He said," yelled back Kagen, "he said he thinks Spark's friends will be waiting when we come back." And Kagen started laughing.

"What the fuck's so funny?" Mouse shouted, leaning closer to Kagen so the German could hear him.

"You don't think any of us will make it back, do you?" And Kagen put his head back and laughed some more.

———

# PART TWO

# Amsterdam

. . . protect me from murderous enemies

who surround me . . .

PSALM 17:9

# Ten

Monday: April 19, 1943

Rachael, look! Home!" Schaap yelled and pointed down. Mouse pressed his face against the glass of the canopy. In the bright light of the nearly full moon, he had no trouble seeing where water met land. The white curves of the surf running up the beach below stretched as far as he could see.

As they crossed the coastline, a string of red beads climbed to pace them, lazy-like, but they were far off to the left. The airplane's nose tilted down.

"Tracers," Schaap shouted at him. "The Germans are shooting. Poor shots!" He shook his head. "But your pilot's taking us lower. The gunners have less time to aim."

Why not, thought Mouse. Everyone else had taken a shot.

"How much longer?" he yelled back.

"Soon, perhaps. I'm not sure."

Neither was Mouse. That was why Joop squatted behind O'Brien, holding a Webley on the mick. Maybe Joop could recognize the landing place, the big lake they'd picked out and radioed to Joop's friends in Amsterdam.

It was almost impossible to talk over the sound of the engine, so Mouse just watched as the plane dropped lower and lower still, until they waggled so low the roofs looked no farther than from a window in Manhattan. The plane bounced, shuddered, came level. Mouse closed his eyes. He hated planes.

"Here, take this!" Kagen yelled at him. Mouse opened his eyes and took the Sten. He laid it on the floor of the Lysander. The cloth bag with the money and the Welrod were in his lap; they were more important. Mouse touched the Welrod. He looked at Kagen, at Rachael and Schaap, them talking with heads together a couple feet away—they were jammed in here like pickles in a jar—and finally up the fuselage at Joop's back. One-two-three-four, he counted, thinking of Kagen and the fourteen he said he'd popped. One-two-three-four, he told himself again.

"There! The Westeinderplassen, there!" Schaap shouted. But Joop had already seen, and the Lysander banked to the right. Mouse looked over the edge of the glassed canopy and down into Holland. The moonlight gleamed off the long, narrow lake. It was as easy to see as a street sign at noon. The airplane slowed, dropped lower, and began to circle.

One minute, two minutes ticked by, and still the Lysander circled, O'Brien putting it in such a tight turn that Mouse worried he'd fall through the glass of the closed canopy.

"I see it!" Schaap yelled. Mouse followed his hand and saw three small lights in all the darkness. The lights blinked but stayed on. They'd be on the ground soon. Mouse, holding the Welrod and the money, crawled over and past Rachael and Schaap to behind Joop, tapped him on the shoulder, and pointed to the rear of the Lysander. Joop, obedient as ever, gave up his spot and wormed his way around Mouse and toward Kagen.

From here he could look over O'Brien's shoulder and see out the windshield. O'Brien took the Lysander over the three lights, just clearing the trees that bordered the field. The engine growled softer, the Lysander fell lower, the wheels hit and bounced, and when the plane touched again, it slowed, turned in a half-circle, and stopped.

O'Brien kept the propeller spinning, but throttled it back. "Safe and sound, just like you asked," he said, no need to yell now. "Me money."

Mouse glanced down the narrow circle of the Lysander's fuselage. Kagen was already pushing the canopy open, Joop and Rachael and Schaap crouched near him, each holding a Sten, bags piled at Kagen's feet. It was time to make his plan work. Time to pop her.

"Change of plans, Irish," he said quietly. "I'm getting out for a minute or two, then you're taking me back. I'll give you another thousand pounds."

O'Brien twisted in his seat to look over his shoulder. "You're more mad than the hatter, Yank. Give me me money."

Mouse looked again down the fuselage. Kagen was gone, Schaap too, and Joop had a leg over the edge, ready to climb down. Rachael was tossing out bags. And she looked his direction. There was no way she'd heard them talk, she was too far and the engine was too loud, but to Mouse, Rachael looked like she had smelled something. Maybe she had the same prickly feeling on the back of her neck that he sometimes got when things weren't right.

He pulled a small bundle of money from his coat, the thousand pounds he'd counted out before and tied with string. He tossed it over O'Brien's shoulder to put it in his lap. "A thousand quid now. Another two when we get home. Wait for me. You take off and that's all you'll see." He left the bag with the money on the floor of the fuselage—it was too dark back there for O'Brien to see—and holding the Welrod in his right hand, Mouse crawled to the canopy, put a leg over the lip, set a foot on the ladder, and looked back toward the cockpit. O'Brien's head was just a shadow. "Don't leave me, Irish," he yelled. And he slid down the short ladder and stood in the grass as the propeller's wind pressed his coat against his back.

The four of them had run for the nearest cover, a stand of brush twenty yards away, waiting there before dashing off the field soon as the Dutch who had held the lights got here. He only had a few seconds. Mouse tightened his hand around the grip of the Welrod and sprinted for them. He held the gun along his leg, it heavy in his hand.

When he got close, all four of them crouching next to the brush four feet tall, he put his aching left hand under the barrel of the Welrod to bring up the gun. Twist, pull, push, twist, he told himself. If he did it fast enough he could pop them one-two-three-four before they figured out that each *phfft* was a shot and realized what was happening.

He led with the Welrod, its muzzle on Kagen. Him first. He was most dangerous, and easiest. Rachael he would save for last, figuring to build to her, that by the time he'd popped the third, his hands would do his thinking.

But as he spread his legs to give him a better shooting stance, the Welrod aimed at the back of Kagen's head five feet away, a shadow moved and stepped from beside the brush, close enough to touch almost. And the shadow spoiled it all.

The broad moon put out enough light for him to see it was a woman, long hair dark, and with a woman's build even under the coat. Another woman. He shifted the Welrod from Kagen to her and he saw her eyes in the moonlight. She was looking at the Welrod, looking at its fat prick of a barrel.

He heard Rachael's voice, behind this woman and beyond Kagen's back. Mouse looked up and Rachael was staring at him too, or at the Welrod, he couldn't tell because her eyes were just dark pools. "Put the gun down, Mr. Weiss, we're safe," she said. There wasn't any nervousness in her voice, but he thought it sounded like she knew what was in his head.

His finger, already on the trigger, caressed it, but he didn't pull to make the Welrod cough. He couldn't. He'd worked himself up to this moment, thinking he had a small enough bit of hate in his heart for Rachael, but it had taken him days. He couldn't find enough for this second woman, not in just the time it took for her to blink. This was just like Tootles, except it wasn't, not at all.

That was when all hell broke loose.

Preuss was busy brushing insects from his face when the aircraft thundered overhead, a black shape that clipped the moonlight. But rather than land in the field in front of them, it disappeared over the tree line sixty meters away.

They'd waited here beside this stagnant, stinking ditch for over an hour, after another hour of creeping up on the partisans, after yet another fumbling in the darkness looking for them among the countless fields of grass and clover. But the English overshot the landing field and spoiled it all.

The partisans had turned off their torches. But the moonlight was strong and the four were easy to spot as they ran for the far end of the field.

Giskes, until a moment ago swearing at the gnats that plagued this place, recovered first, and hissed orders to the man beside him. He was Giskes's, like all but the three SS Preuss had brought from the office on Euterpestraat. "We'll flank them using the ditches. You and I, we'll take up position in the trees ahead," Giskes whispered. "I'm sending four to circle behind that field. We want my English, and your Jews in one piece."

And Giskes slinked off into the dark. Preuss held tight his Walther, the Bakelite grip long ago slick. He followed the Abwehr officer, motioning to the three SS beside him to come along.

Christ," Johannes shouted, far behind her as the black aircraft refused to touch down on this polder but instead clipped the trees at the far end with its wheels and hopped into the next. Reka switched off her electric torch, Annje did the same, and Martin followed. It took her eyes a moment to adjust to the moonlight.

She was closest to those trees and the first to start running through the grass. The ancient Luger was an anvil in her hand. Jews, she kept telling herself. I'm not alone. And she ran faster.

In the minutes it took them to reach the tree line, Preuss fell twice into ditches. One trouser leg was soaked to the knee, and that boot made water noises when he walked. He hated the Dutch and their damned sodden country.

Preuss kept close to Giskes. He was no better with directions than with this pistol, and the last thing he wanted to do was wander into the line of fire. They crept through a thin band of silent poplars and knelt down where the trees ended and the grass began.

The aircraft, a bulbous single-engine monoplane, squatted at the far end of this field a hundred meters away, like a dragonfly gone to fat. The sound of its engine, once loud enough, he had thought, to be heard in Amsterdam, was now muted.

"It's a Lysander," Giskes said. "That's SOE. How did I miss this one?" The four partisans were not yet halfway to the aircraft.

The Abwehr man made no sense to Preuss, but instead of asking questions, he simply watched. Two small figures stood beside this Lysander, almost plain as day in the moonlight. A third climbed out, then a fourth. They ran past its tail and disappeared.

But the aircraft's engine didn't grow louder. It sat there, the propeller a silver coin in the moonlight. A fifth dropped out of the aircraft and ran after the others.

"What now?" he asked Giskes. This was new, scrambling in the dark after partisans and commandos who had guns. He wished for his lists and his quotas.

Giskes didn't answer. Instead, a single shot rang from the left and far ahead. Without hesitation, the four men on the far side of Giskes joined in, their machine pistols chattering at the aircraft. The three SS to Preuss's right decided this was the time as well, and they ran through their magazines in one long sound, like cloth rent by a dozen hands.

Preuss only ducked at first, but as the partisans and commandos answered back, muzzles blinking like summer fireflies, he groveled, snaking himself flat into the grass, putting his hands over his head. As he peeked out from under their protection, he felt himself piss down his one dry leg.

At first Mouse thought he'd stepped into a nest of bees, because the sounds all around were like insects, *zips* and *zoops* that brushed air against his face. *Slugs*, his brain finally said, running slow.

He doubled back for the Lysander through the bees. His money was in the plane, but more important, so was his only way home.

Mouse reached the Lysander, its wheels still stuck to their spots in the grass, got up the ladder faster than he thought his hand would let him, and tumbled into the fuselage, the Welrod clattering to the floor. Slugs pinged off the metal wing.

He was screwed. His plan was gone as if it had never been dreamed, and Lansky the least of his problems. The important thing now was to get away. He had to get out of here.

Mouse grabbed for the gun and crawled up to the cockpit and behind O'Brien. When he raised his head to look over O'Brien's shoulder and through the windshield, he first noticed the small lights winking in the black tree line a hundred yards away. Only then did he see the three round holes in the windshield, each as big as his thumb, spider lines cracking the glass from each circle.

Mouse put the barrel of the Welrod against O'Brien's neck and shouted, "Get this thing off the ground!" But although the engine roared louder, the airplane didn't move. "Go! Get the fuck going!"

Mouse smelled blood in the cockpit then, the same smell as in Spark's Ford, and frantically he looked down, expecting to see blood staining his secondhand clothes. But he was clean and then he knew that it was the Irishman who had been hit. O'Brien said nothing, but Mouse could see his hand move clumsily on the control stick between his legs. The airplane started to roll forward.

The hand on his shoulder almost made him drop the Welrod from its spot at O'Brien's neck. He turned to face the woman who'd stepped out of the shadows and flopped the plan that had been wrong from the start. There was a scar at the side of her face from eye back to ear, something he'd not noticed before because she'd had her head turned, the white scar like a line on a road, white enough to show in the moonlight coming through the canopy.

"You can't stay!" she yelled over the noise of the engine and tugged at the shoulder of his coat. That's what he thought, too, but his meaning was different from hers. More slugs rattled against the wing of the Lysander, and the plane, still rolling slowly, lurched left. "Now!" she shouted.

Mouse looked at her face, a plain face really, but her eyes, ice ponds like Lansky's, grabbed him. He pulled the hand holding the Welrod away from O'Brien.

"There's no time," she said, and she yanked at his arm as she started to back down the fuselage. The Lysander's engine skipped a beat; black smoke filled the cockpit and oil coated the windshield.

This was no place for a boy from Brownsville, Mouse decided, and crabbed after the girl, who shoved him to the edge of the canopy and pointed at the ladder. He fumbled in the dark on the floor for the cloth bag, and after another lurch of the Lysander, found it. One hand holding the Welrod, the other gripping the bag, Mouse lifted himself over the side and put his foot on the first rung of the ladder. The Lysander jerked forward, and the girl shoved him. He fell off the ladder and landed in the grass, wind knocked out of him, and she fell on him and pushed what was left from his lungs. The Lysander rolled toward the sparks in the tree line.

"Use this!" the girl shouted in his ear and shoved a Sten at him. She must have picked it up off the metal floor of the plane. She was on one knee and firing a pistol at the trees. If he could catch a breath, Mouse would have told her she was too far away. "Shoot, shoot back!" she yelled. The bees were thick as raindrops in a summer thunderstorm.

Mouse saw the airplane from where he lay, its black paint almost washed gray by the moonlight, and the fat bird picked up speed. The mick was going to get away.

Or not, because another volley from the trees hammered at the plane. Sparks flicked off the engine cowling, and the engine went to flame. The Lysander bounced once—Maybe he's gonna make it, Mouse thought for a second, he's gonna make it—bounced again, and with the fire licking over the top of the windshield, the plane slammed into the trees.

It sounded like a car wreck, metal bending and screeching, with a final hollow thump and bang as a big part smacked into something solid. The flames found the gas tank between its stocky wheels and the Lysander blossomed into an orange and yellow and red ball that ate its way through the trees and ballooned into the sky. For a moment the field was lit like noon. Then it went inky dark and all Mouse could see was yellow spots.

"Get up, get up," the girl said. The bees had stopped, as if everyone with a gun were watching the burning plane. Mouse struggled to one knee, wanting to puke from the empty feeling in his lungs, but he finally got some air and sucked it down deep and he was okay. The girl grabbed the cloth bag from his aching left hand and ran off into the dark.

Mouse kept the Welrod in his right hand and picked up the Sten with his left. The girl was sprinting for the far end of the field. Either follow her and the money, or die here, a long long way from Brownsville, Brooklyn.

R eka was out of breath by the time she reached the shallow ditch at the far corner of the polder, and she hadn't the strength left to leap the ribbon of water. She waded through it and flopped down on the grass, knowing she must keep going, but she had to rest, if only for a moment.

Strangely enough, she had felt a calm ever since the ambush shocked her into running after the man who had pointed the big gun at her. But she had kept her head, even as she raced past Martin, who was down in a heap near the aircraft's tail.

After that, chaos. The man scampered up the ladder and the aircraft lumbered through the grass while the gunfire grew and grew and grew. She knew for a fact that the aircraft would never make it off the polder. And so she put the Luger in her pocket and climbed up, and crawled into its nose to save this one.

The man splashed through the ditch and tumbled into the grass beside her. His breathing was ragged. She had wanted to reach out and touch his face there that first moment she had seen him, but now she stayed her hand. He had put his huge gun on her, its barrel as big as an eel hauled out of Markermeer waters. What had he been thinking?

He said something she didn't understand—her English wasn't perfect. Then he hoarsely whispered something in a language she knew. *Oysgeshpilt.* It was Yiddish. He was played out, he said, exhausted.

And so he was Jew. Her days and nights of solitary were over. She decided there and then he must have been afraid and confused that first moment; that was why he had pointed the gun at the others, and at her. Afraid like he'd been afraid a few minutes ago there in the grass, when he'd refused to pick up the machine pistol and return the Germans' fire.

"We must go," Reka said quietly. But she heard German voices beyond the ditch and quickly put her fingers to his lips to keep him quiet.

She pulled her fingers away from his lips, embarrassed, but she tugged at his coat sleeve so he'd follow as she crawled away through the grass. It was a long eight kilometers to Amstelveen and the closest tram to Amsterdam. They had to be at the tram by daylight when it started its run, to blend in with the crowds traveling to work.

Reka reeled in her beautiful Jew and took him home.

This was your fault," Preuss said, trying to keep his voice level. He stood a hundred meters from the aircraft burning still, its flames smaller now than those that had consumed the machine. To the east, the sky was pinking. He needed to return to the city soon; he had another column to snake through the streets from the *Joodsche Schouwburg* to Muiderpoort station, where a train waited to take the one thousand and fifty-three to Westerbork.

"No, no, it wasn't," Giskes said.

"Your men let them get away."

"Calm yourself. Of course it was my men. Yours got themselves killed, didn't they?"

"And whose fault is that?" Preuss sputtered.

"We have two for our trouble," Giskes said, as if that made a difference.

"But both dead," said Preuss, looking now to the boy on the ground a few meters away. They'd rolled him over and found the new round eye in his skull, but no papers. The other was crisped in the melted fabric and warped metal of the plane caught in the trees, a shrunken, blackened corpse no bigger than a child in the ruins of the cockpit. "Four if you count mine," he said, trying to sound aggrieved, but not even convincing himself. They weren't really his, only two Unterscharführers he'd grabbed from the duty room at Euterpestraat. He'd already forgotten their names. The third, a young Rottenführer, had escaped death, but was badly burned on his face and arms. Marta must have been watching over me, Preuss thought, to keep me from harm. The aircraft had slid into the trees near enough to feel its flames like a hot Russian summer sun.

Three shapes shoved through a band of thin brush to their left. Two of Giskes's men with machine pistols slung over shoulders, and between them a short man with small spectacles askew and ready to slip off his bloodied face. The two on either side released his arms and the little man collapsed into the grass, his legs folding under him. Giskes walked to the pair, paying little attention to the one on the ground, and Preuss heard Giskes and his men exchange words.

Giskes returned. "One of the commandos," he said.

"He looks like a farmer," said Preuss. The little man's trousers were patched in places and his coat was missing a pocket. Where was the blackened face and the sawtoothed knife?

"No," said Giskes. He went to his men and returned with a strange machine pistol. "He had this British Sten," and Giskes handed him the weapon, but Preuss had no idea what to do with it and so gave it back. "And this." Giskes passed Preuss a slip of paper. It was a banknote. English. At the bottom left, there was the mark "£20," and even Preuss knew what that meant. "He's from the SOE, no doubt about that, but not very smart to have that in his pocket. Come to raise hell for Churchill, have you?" Giskes asked the one on the ground, his Dutch sloppy but understandable. The little man looked up and shook his head.

"What about the others?" Preuss asked. "Is he the only one?"

"My men followed them as far as Kudelstaart but lost them there. They may have taken a boat across the Westeinderplassen, or perhaps bicycles into Aalsmeer or even Uithoorn. But we'll find them. He'll tell us."

Preuss stared at the little man again. *"Bent jij een jood?"* he asked.

The man stood up slowly.

*"Waarom ben je hier, jood? Wat doe je hier?"* asked Preuss.

The little man opened his mouth. He was going to say something. He was going to explain why Jews had come here.

But the Dutchman only hawked and spit, the spittle striking Preuss on the cheek. Preuss wiped it away with the edge of his tunic sleeve and slapped the little man hard on the mouth, drew fresh blood. The man glared at him still, and Preuss was ready to strike again when Giskes touched his arm.

"Don't waste your time. We'll find out what he knows in more civilized surroundings. Unless you want to pull down his pants here to see if he's Jewish?" Giskes was taunting him again. Preuss seethed, but let his arm drop to his side.

"He's no Jew. Jews wouldn't dare do what he just did," he said. *"Jij zal spoedig in de hel zijn, mijn vriend,"* Preuss said. The Dutchman swayed, and closed his eyes as if against the hell that Preuss had just promised him.

# Eleven

"Call me Mouse," he said to the girl who had flopped his plan. She pulled her hair from behind her ear to hide the scar.

"Mouse," she said, unsure, as if trying it out.

"Yeah. Everyone calls me Mouse."

This Reka was the one that Joop had told him of back in London—the girl who had a lot of hate in her heart. She didn't look the part.

Joop. The little guy was missing. No one had seen him after the plane exploded. And one of this bunch, the one Joop said was backward, he was gone, too. Reka saw him on the ground near the Lysander, she'd said, but there wasn't time to see if he was dead or only wounded. Everyone else had made it. Some, like Kagen and the gentile Annje, were here when he and Reka dropped into the cellar. Schaap had come later with his sister, Rachael, the gentile Johannes guiding them back. There were seven crammed into this cellar with the too-low ceiling and the one bulb hanging from a cord and the smell of a backed-up toilet.

"What kind of name is Mouse?" Reka asked. Her smile was a wicked one, and it didn't do her plain face any good. Her nose was a bit too long, her lips a bit too thin. She had brown hair, almost black, that hung to her shoulders and framed her face. But her eyes. In the better light of the cellar, her dark eyes looked even more like Lansky's, not the color but the way they looked through you. "Because you are shy like a mouse? Or take fright like one?" she asked.

He ignored her crack and returned the favor. "Thanks for yesterday," he said. But she didn't get that he meant just the opposite.

Not that it would have mattered in the end, whether she'd been on that field or not. He had put his mind to it after they'd reached the cellar and figured that even if this Reka hadn't shown up and he had popped the four, Rachael included, there was no way he would have made it back to the Lysander before the Germans opened up. It was fucked even before the plane landed. Someone had spilled that they were coming.

"Yes?" she asked. She wasn't going to make this easy for him.

"Thanks for pulling me out of the plane," he said, meaning it straight this time.

"Mouse," she said, chewing on the word. "A mouse hides in the grass, yes?"

He looked in those ice-pond eyes, which were easier to look into than Lansky's, ice or not. He'd heard her say the Shema this morning after they woke and last night before they went to sleep. *"Sh'ma Yisrael Adonai Elohaynu Adonai Echad,"* she had begun both times, saying the prayer in the Hebrew, though he recognized the prayer from its first word, *Sh'ma.* "Hear, Israel, the Lord is our God, the Lord is One," he knew it meant in English, something his muter had drummed into him when he was little. So he tried to give her a smile.

She smiled back and this smile was not as wicked, her face not as pinched. If she cleaned up, she might look okay.

"Why are you called Mouse?" He thought she wasn't mocking him this time.

*"Moyz.* You know the word? It means 'mouse' in Yiddish—you know Yiddish, don't you?"

"Some, yes."

"It also means 'ace,' *moyz* does. In America, 'ace' means good, like great. The best. The people I work for in America, they said I was a natural. An 'ace.' *Moyz.* Mouse. See?"

She looked confused. As he stared into those Lansky eyes of hers, he told himself she wasn't the rat. So he asked her.

"Someone told them about us coming, didn't they? How else did they know we were coming? The Germans, I mean." The day before, the same questions had been asked by Kagen and Schaap, but Johannes's answers hadn't satisfied Mouse.

Her eyes darted to the side and past him. She wasn't practiced at telling tales and gave it away. Mouse turned to look where her eyes had been, and there were Johannes and Annje, her two pals, although maybe not.

"I don't know . . . Mr. Weiss," she said, not able, it seemed, to say his name. Like Lansky, he thought.

But he had more now than yesterday, when all Johannes told them was that an informer hid somewhere in the Resistance. They'd had troubles two weeks before, he said, only saying that a meeting had gone bad, and they suspected the Germans knew somehow of the messages passed from Schaap in England to them in Amsterdam.

Mouse thought she was going to say something else, but that was when Kagen made a racket dragging a wooden box to the middle of the cellar. He unfolded a map and laid it on the crate.

"Gather round," he said, and Mouse helped Reka to her feet, liking the feel of her hand in his, remembering how she'd pressed her fingers to his mouth there near the ditch. They moved to the center of the cellar to sit on the rough floor. Kagen faced them, standing with hands behind his back, but he looked most at Johannes and Annje, the girl red-eyed from crying over her missing brother. "We are here to seize a Jewish transport. We will take one of the trains and see its Jews to England on boats." He paused, still looking at Johannes and Annje. "We would like your help." Schaap translated as Kagen talked in English.

Mouse felt Reka's hand on his sleeve, first a touch, then more as her fingers tightened on his wrist. He watched, but her eyes stayed on Kagen and didn't glide to Annje or Johannes.

It was Johannes who spoke up. There was anger, and something else, in his voice. "That's impossible," he said in English.

Not a good start. But he thought the same as the Dutchman, didn't he?

He had two raw wounds on the back of his hand, their red edges crossed by white thread that stitched them together. Like railroad tracks. Reka touched the scar on her own face. Perhaps it was a sign.

Only two Jews had come from England to chase her loneliness. She had expected more. But this one from America who called himself a mouse was beautiful enough to make her forget her disappointment. He was tall, with dark hair that outlined his face, the face with a strong chin and pink cheeks. His eyes, gray like smoke now, though they had seemed darker before, looked from under heavy eyelids. But he was afraid, this beautiful man. He had run out of the aircraft with a gun in his hand, pointed it at the other Jew, the German, then at her, still another Jew, and hesitated. There had been fright on his face and he'd run back to the aircraft, hoping to flee, she thought.

Her second Jew was the German, and his accent sounded hard in her ears. He was not so handsome, shorter, with that one fierce blue eye bright against his darker, sun-touched face. But this Paul Kagen began to talk and Reka forgot his eye and listened instead. Kagen said they would steal a train from the Germans, a train full of Jews, and Reka felt a heat come over her. Partly relief, she knew, that she might avenge Mama and Papa in a small way, but in the same moment, anger. Where were you, Paul Kagen, six months ago?

". . . not tell us when you will do this?" Johannes asked. Reka had come into the middle.

Kagen shook his head. "No details. Not now. If you agree to help, then yes." The tall blond one, Kristiaan, translated for Annje.

"You don't trust us," Annje said. Kristiaan turned the Dutch into English so the German and Mr. Weiss could understand.

"No," said Kagen.

Good. Kagen should not trust them. Especially Annje. Perhaps Johannes was right yesterday, that above them the Resistance was a sieve and that was how the police surprised them on the polder, had found out about the aircraft and its passengers. Or perhaps it was closer, this betrayal. But she didn't have anything as proof.

"Cart off a train full of Jews?" Johannes asked. "To what purpose? No, it is madness."

And Kagen told them a story about what really happened in the East, his sentences broken into small pieces so the tall Kristiaan could translate. It was a tale even more fantastic than Mama's bedtime stories of the Golem.

But Reka believed every word of this story. She couldn't do anything but believe, not with the way it rang with the truth she'd felt the moment she'd seen her first selection in Westerbork. She'd heard the words of a young SS in gray uniform, his voice ringing out over the Appelplatz. Resettlement and labor and evacuation and safe and life, those were all words he had called out. Germans lied, she knew even then— she'd been a Jew in Amsterdam, hadn't she?—and the more they said one thing, the less it was true. The furthest truth from the words meant death, not the lie of life.

Almost everyone else had thought different. They refused to believe in the worst, wanting to think of the best. Like her brother, David.

Kagen's story proved her right, not that it made a difference to Mama and Papa now. He said that Holland's Jews were not resettled in the East or sent to labor camps to make cooking pots for the Wehrmacht or put to work building roads across the cornfields of the Ukraine. They were murdered in the East, killed each and every one, in strange-sounding places hard in the mouth, Sobibor, Treblinka, Belzec. They were poisoned with gas and their bodies burned to end as smoke.

Smoke. She had never expected lives erased so completely, and it took her by surprise. Reka looked at her hand. She felt the ghost of Mama's hand there, that hand trembling in hers as they had stood on the Appelplatz. Mama. Papa. She had told herself every night, every dawn, that they were truly gone, always after saying Shema. But smoke. Smoke.

Not even a grave to weep over. And for that Reka began to cry.

---

Mouse was surprised. Reka was tough—she'd shot back while he stuck his face in the grass—and so when she sobbed he didn't know what to do.

Rachael came to the girl, sat beside her and put her arms around her. They rocked, Reka crying and Rachael talking to her softly in Dutch. And when their eyes met, his and Rachael's, she looked at him like she knew what he'd been up to on that field by the Lysander. Mouse swallowed. If she knew, so did Kagen, or would.

Johannes said something in Dutch. Mouse couldn't make out the specifics, his German was too different from the Dutch, but the meaning was plain. Johannes spit his words from a red face, and when Schaap talked back in Dutch, he got loud too. It wasn't hard to figure it out. Johannes had heard Kagen's story and their plan, and he knew it was cracked.

Mouse had his own problems. It was still a shock, him here. The only thing left of his plan was the fourteen thousand pounds and change, a thousand quid shorter than when he left London, that thousand burnt in the Lysander on O'Brien's lap.

England was a long way away, Brooklyn even further. And there was only one way out, as far as he could see. This had to work. The only way home led through that train, and he sure as shit wasn't going to let any of these idiots fuck it up.

"This is madness," Johannes said, now in English as he looked at Kagen. "I feel pity for the Jews, I do not say I do not, but to say they are all murdered. No. Even the Germans are not so mad. I am a patriot, but risk everything to save Jews from a little work? No."

Mouse took a breath. He was ready to say something, ready to pull English money out of the cloth bag and toss it at Johannes and Annje to get them to help, but he happened to look again at Reka.

And he kept his mouth shut and his money to himself. If those two had spilled, ratted them out, no amount of talk or money was going to change things. Once a rat, always. That was one thing he'd learned from Lansky, and why Kid Twist had ended up flying from that hotel window.

———

$P$reuss kept his eyes on the screaming Dutchman. The Gestapo, the one with the tiny ears, his sleeves rolled up over his elbows, touched a thin steel rod to the little man's hand. It was just a caress, but the Dutchman screamed again, high and forever.

The Dutchman sat in a chair shoved up tight against the table, his arms stretched out across that table, his hands pinned with manacles screwed into the wood. There was a rose splayed around each hand, some of the blood still wet enough to glisten under the light, some of it turned dirt brown as it had dried. His small spectacles, long smashed, glinted in the corner of the tight cellar room.

Giskes stepped close to the Dutchman. Preuss stayed near the stout door, farthest from the blood.

"What now, Joop van der Werf?" Giskes asked quietly. The only other sound in the room was the metronome tapping of the Gestapo's steel rod. He rapped the table a centimeter from the Dutchman's left hand, the one missing a joint on its middle finger. The hand looked like a chop left in the sun too long, then attacked with a hammer. The Dutchman didn't answer. Giskes pulled the man's hair to lift up his head.

"Is he—" Preuss started.

"No, he's asleep," said Giskes, and let the Dutchman's head fall to the table.

"Asleep . . ."

"Out. He's passed out." Giskes straightened and looked over at the Gestapo man. "Wake him." The Gestapo looked toward Preuss, who nodded to tell him to do what Giskes asked. The Gestapo fetched the pail of water from the corner and poured some over the Dutchman. He sputtered, tried to raise his head from the tabletop but failed, and groaned, a long sound that made the small hairs on Preuss's arms uncurl. He'd not heard a sound like that since Russia and his days in the Sonderkommando.

"Little one," Giskes said, stepping over the puddle of water on the concrete. "Tell me of your friends from England. Are they from Churchill? From the SOE? Commandos? What are they doing here, Joop? Tell me something and I'll let you sleep. I'll make him put away the rod." His Dutch was awkward, but he got his words across.

The Dutchman mumbled something and Preuss strained to hear. But the words were unintelligible.

"Sleep. You can sleep if you tell me what you came for." Giskes's mouth was just a few centimeters from the Dutchman's ear, lover's close.

*"De jood,"* whispered the Dutchman. *"We komen voor de jodin. We komen voor haar."* Giskes looked at Preuss.

One Jew—no, a Jewess. He'd said they came for *her.* They come for only one Jewess?

"We know that, little one. We know all about Jews. Tell me something I don't know and I'll have someone see to your hands," Giskes said.

The Dutchman moaned again, that terrible sound, and he whispered again. *"Ga je moeder neuken."* Giskes looked up at Preuss, confused.

"'Go fuck yourself,' he says," Preuss translated. Giskes knew his Dutch, it seemed, but not well enough.

Giskes laughed, a tight laugh. "You won't be so quick later, little one, to say things like that," said Giskes, now in German. He glanced to the Gestapo with the steel rod. "Take him back to his cell. Don't let him sleep. And nothing to eat. But before you do, another five with that. Make him wish he was dead this time. You know how to do that, don't you?"

The Gestapo looked weary. "Yes. Of course I know, Herr Oberst."

Preuss couldn't stand the small room any longer, yanked open the door and stepped into the corridor with its fresher air. He had let Giskes bring the Dutchman to the cellar, had even cajoled the Gestapo interrogator from the man's superior and put him at Giskes's disposal, which was, strictly speaking, not allowed. He had little choice, he thought, I have no experience at this. There is no talking in what I do with the Jews.

He lit a Nil, put the blue tin back in his tunic pocket. Marta, what was Marta doing this moment, he made himself think. But he couldn't concentrate with the sound of the Dutchman taking the rod on those broken hands again. Giskes joined him a moment later, closed the thick door, and the sounds were swallowed.

"He'll tell us something soon," Giskes said.

Preuss wasn't so sure. The little Dutchman had only told them his name since yesterday, and just now that he came for a Jewess. But they'd already known this involved Jews.

"You should bring in that blond I gave you, ask her what she knows," Giskes said. The old Abwehr twisted his neck and Preuss heard it pop. "I must have slept on it wrong," he explained, rubbing at his neck.

Preuss lit another cigarette from the half-smoked one already in his hand. "Preuss, the girl?" Giskes asked. "Preuss?"

He looked from the end of the Nil and into the Abwehr officer's eyes. "I don't know where she is," he said.

"What? You don't know—"

"That's what I said, wasn't it?" Preuss snapped, not bothering to hide his anger. "She's disappeared. I went to Van Breestraat yesterday after-noon after I finished taking Jews to my Monday transport, and she's not there. Only her mother. She doesn't know where the girl and her brother are. The mother claims they've not been at her house for weeks."

"She's afraid after betraying those last week, and then the comman-dos from England," Giskes said. "Perhaps that's why she's hiding."

Preuss nodded. Yes, that made sense. "But I think she'll show. She's frightened enough. She gave me those Jews, remember."

"Ah, yes, the famous *Aktion*," Giskes said, smiling. "All of two, wasn't it?"

Preuss ignored him. "I gave the old woman a good scare, told her I'll bring her here if the daughter disappoints me." He smoked some more. "I'll give her a day or two."

Giskes shrugged. "It doesn't matter, I suppose. He's the one who will tell us why he came." He jerked a thumb at the closed door. "Although I wonder if this is really SOE work. Somehow it doesn't have the feel. . . ." Giskes looked up.

Preuss remembered what Naumann had told him. "Churchill's gang of criminals," Naumann had said of the Englanders' Special Operations Executive. Spies and saboteurs, Naumann had said.

The Abwehr man slapped a hand on his shoulder. "No matter. I'll get to the bottom of this, I promise you."

Preuss slipped out from under the hand. He was losing interest in the screaming Dutchman. He was no Jew. Nor was the boy shot through the head and left on the landing field. Perhaps none on the aircraft had been Jews. Perhaps the Visser woman had dreamed up these incredible Jews to give herself time to disappear. After all, the little one behind the thick cellar door said that they came for a Jewess. Just one. He didn't say there had been Jews on the aircraft from England. Visser got it wrong or misled them on purpose.

In any case, he had more pressing business. He put his hand into his pocket and fingered the piece of paper there. It had chattered off the tele-type from The Hague yesterday. He'd had it long enough to memorize its words.

Hstuf. H. Preuss

As part of the process of the solution of the European Jewish question, and acting on behalf Ostubaf. A. Eichmann, Amt IV B-4, I today order that of those Jews remaining in Amsterdam:

April // 5.800 are to be dispatched for labor deportation, Sobibor
May // 9.250 are to be dispatched for labor deportation, Sobibor
June // 17.600 are to be dispatched for work assignment, Auschwitz

Additional special action transports will be arranged by RSHA IV B-4-a, Hstuf. F. Novak. Two (2) weekly May, four (4) weekly June. Advise immediately if unable to comply so I may inform RHSA IV B-4 and RFSS Himmler.

*(signed) Stubaf. Wilhelm Zoepf* 19.4.43

Naumann had been right. The quotas were enormous. Impossible. But there they were. Preuss glanced at his watch. De Groot and his Amsterdam policemen were waiting for him. Another *Aktion*.

The one beyond the door was not going to lead him to more Jews.

Nor, it seemed, were the commandos here to interfere with his Jews, if indeed they were commandos. They came for just the one Jewess.

This was Giskes's area of expertise, not his. "Let me know what you get out of him," he said, then turned and walked for the stairway. He was glad to have the last word for once.

"Good luck with your Jews, Hauptsturmführer," Giskes called to his back. And for a moment Preuss thought the Abwehr man was laughing.

R eka looked at the tulips. Hundreds of tulips, all yellows and reds, thick in the boxes at every window of the houses across Wijtten-bachstraat.

The four of them faced the house of Kristiaan Schaap's Jewish in-laws. Kristiaan held his cap in his hands, worrying it into a twist. Rachael was beside her brother, her hand on his arm. Mr. Weiss was on her other side, calmer. He seemed like the kind who was used to watching and waiting.

The spring sun felt good on her face, and after the stink of the cellar, the air smelled like sugar. But the sights and smell and fine spring day were forgotten as soon as she heard the chuff of a train and its long whistle. She started to tremble, just the slightest, even though she knew it wasn't a transport leaving for Westerbork. Transports left only on Mondays.

A few streets to the east was Muiderpoort, the station where she and David, Mama and Papa, had been marched to board the train to Westerbork. How strange, she thought, that Jews would live so close to the thing that took them to their deaths. But how could Kristiaan's wife and her family have known?

Reka tried to ignore the train. "Are you going to knock at the door, or should I?" she asked Kristiaan. He didn't hear her, only looked at the house all the harder. She asked Rachael the same question, but the woman had a look on her face that pained Reka to see.

Two hours before, Kristiaan had argued with Kagen in the cellar, their voices getting so loud and angry Reka thought they might come to blows. Kristiaan had said he was out to find his wife, Vreesje, who was now in Westerbork by all accounts, but he at least wanted to see her father's house and talk to her neighbors to see what they knew. Kagen forbade it. The German admitted he had agreed earlier, looking to the Dutchwoman Rachael for several quiet moments, but now he ticked objections off one finger at a time: they had no papers; the police, whom they'd evaded at the landing field, would be looking for them; they must concentrate on their job. None impressed Kristiaan. He had deserted his post in the commando to do this, he said. It was why he had put weeks into these plans after Joop turned up at his sister's door in London. It was why he had searched out Kagen's friend in New York, who had in turn found the money that Mr. Weiss brought. Without him, there would be no job, Kristiaan shouted.

Kagen only relented when Rachael had put her head close to his and whispered to him, tears shining in her eyes. The way they whispered, her mouth so near his ear that he must feel her moist breath, made Reka think they were lovers. And when Kagen finally agreed, she knew it was so.

That was when she volunteered to go with Kristiaan and Rachael— she knew today's Amsterdam—and when Mr. Weiss said he would go, too. It would be better if they walked through Amsterdam as couples, she told Kagen, less chance the police would stop them and demand identity cards.

"Kristiaan, did you hear what I said?" Reka asked now, her mind back on the street and the house across. He looked at her, blank-faced for a moment, but he nodded and life returned to his eyes.

"I know she's not there . . ." He stopped, choking off the words.

"Go," she said. "Go ask your questions." And she gently pushed him from the curb. He walked across the street, Rachael right behind him, up the narrow steps, and to the green-painted door. Kristiaan rapped on it, looking at his sister before turning as the door opened.

Of course it was not Vreesje. Reka had seen the curled photograph Kristiaan had pulled from his pocket yesterday, and this was not her. The woman in the doorway was in her thirties, and three small children peeked from behind her dress as she stepped onto the stoop. She was shaking her head.

A tram came, its blue bulk screeching over the rails set in the middle of Wijttenbachstraat, and by the time it passed and Reka reached the stoop, Kristiaan and Rachael were coming down the stairs.

His face said nothing—he tried to stay strong—but Rachael's face told her everything. Reka stayed quiet, and the brother and sister went first to the door of the house to the left, next to the red door of the house to the left of that, knocking on each. She and Mr. Weiss followed at a distance. No one answered the first, and at the second, Rachael talked for several minutes to an elderly man, bow-backed with white hair, who smiled first, then shook his head.

"What's the news?" Mr. Weiss whispered to her in English, but she glared at him and put a finger to her lips. Wijttenbachstraat was busy and there were people around. The last thing they needed was someone to wonder why they spoke English.

Kristiaan stood at the bottom of the old man's stoop—the door was closed again—and Rachael sat down slowly on a step.

"Rachael," Reka said. "Kristiaan?"

He shook his head. Rachael looked up, tears hanging in the corners of her eyes.

"Mr. Dijkstra said the same thing Joop told us," Rachael said quietly. "It was February, the sixteenth, perhaps the day after. He doesn't remember exactly, when Vreesje, her little brother Autje, her *mother, father* too . . . they were all ordered to report to the *Hollandsche Schouwburg* for deportation." No one had called it the *Hollandsche Schouwburg* for a year—now it was named for the Jews who were marched there.

"She may not have gone East, not yet," Reka reminded them. She told them of how her mama and papa had spent four long months in Westerbork before their turn came. It was only two since the train took Vreesje and her family. "She's probably still in the camp."

Rachael looked up, their eyes met for a moment, and she nodded.

She wants to believe, thought Reka, and for a moment she regretted giving Rachael this hope. She could be wrong. Sometimes people were pushed East faster. She watched as Rachael wiped away her tears with the back of her hand.

"I want to see this place where Vreesje was taken," Kristiaan said. His voice shivered. "This theater."

"No, Kristiaan," his sister said softly, wiping again at her face. "We know she's gone. What good will that do?"

"I want to remember the place."

Reka gave in, not because of Rachael's tears—there were plenty of tears these days—but because they both looked like they didn't understand how this could happen. They should understand everything, she thought. "It's not far," she said to Kristiaan in a small voice. "I'll take you there."

But it took her several seconds to work up the courage to move her feet. The only thing she feared more than trains, she decided, was facing hard memories.

A msterdam was as different from London as London was from Brooklyn. There was none of the war here like in the East End, no shells of buildings or piles of burnt bricks. Every street had its canal, every canal a dozen tiny bridges. The place was cleaner, the people only a little thinner, and the air smelled fresher by far. And the flowers . . . everywhere he looked there were flowers sold from carts, in pots and boxes at windows, and thick wherever there was a patch of dirt. He breathed deeply.

The pretty scenery didn't change what had happened. Schaap's wife, Rachael's sister-in-law, was really gone. Reka chatted with them both in Dutch on the steps of this house with the red door, people walking by glancing their way, but Mouse had no way to understand the details of the conversation. The big picture, well, he had that. The way Rachael looked, tears in her eyes and on her face like that time in the kitchen of the house on Argyle Street, said everything.

When they started walking, he fell in next to Reka, the two Schaaps behind them. They took a right at a wider street, walked across a narrow bridge over a broad canal, and after a quarter hour, they came to a park. That was where they found the Jews.

He didn't ask Reka what was happening—she'd just shush him like before, glare at him with those eyes again. Besides, he could see for himself.

Two cops, they had to be cops, blocked the street and their way. They

wore cop blue but had odd hats that were too tall and stiff. A tram rumbled on rails off to their right. Beyond the cops was a crowd of people
in a long column that stretched ahead a block or more. Old folks
and women with children, men wearing hats walking alongside fami-
lies, younger men and boys, and girls who looked Reka's age. When any
of them turned, he saw the yellow stars. With suitcases and satchels
and cloth bags and bedrolls tied over shoulders and blankets bundled and
bound with rope, they walked slowly, looking nervous and angry and
frightened and witless. They were well dressed, almost every one. Most
of the men wore overcoats and sharp hats, while many of the women
walked in heels, smart dresses, and stockings. Even the children were
turned out, boys in short pants and crushed caps, girls in colorful dresses
and bright coats. Take away the bags and suitcases and yellow stars and
they looked like Brownsville's Jews heading to synagogue, like the one
time he remembered best doing that, when he'd walked alongside foter,
his muter a half-step behind, to his Bar Mitzvah. All three of them had
been dressed to the nines, like these.

"*Razzia*," Reka said under her breath as they walked around and past
the cops at the end of the column, moving in the same direction as the
worm of marching Jews. They stopped, almost at the head of the line,
where a knot of plugs pressed close together, gawking. "A roundup,"
Reka whispered, this time English.

Even the whisper sounded loud. The only sounds were shoes on cobblestones. Even the cops were quiet, and the watching Dutch, too. All
he heard was some quiet Dutch as children called to family.

More cops herded the Jews toward a building on the left. It was three
stories tall, fancy with wide pillars across the front on the second floor
and made of white stone, like the big houses off Fifth Avenue.

He heard German then and stood on his toes. First nothing more than
"*Los!*" and then something longer and clearer. "*Hoch mit dir, du alte Kuh, geb'
rein!*" and he pushed ahead to see, pulling Reka with him through the
crowd, leaving the Schaaps, the brother looking at nothing but now
matching tears with his sister.

Mouse and Reka stood with only a cop between them and the Jews.
An old woman had fallen, or been pushed, and she was stretched out on

the cobbles. A German dressed in a gray uniform and gray cap beat the old woman with the butt of his rifle. She had a hand over her gray hair trying to shield herself.

Jews close by pushed to get out of the way, scrambling some of them, and the noise got louder as some shouted and yelled. The space between the old woman and the others got wider, fathers shoving their sons to move faster, mothers pushing their daughters toward the doors of the white stone building. The German with the rifle was getting tired, the time between his blows longer. He stopped and wiped sweat from his forehead. Not a Jew had lifted a finger while the old lady got her brains beat in.

Mouse noticed another German, this one taller and younger with a face that looked flabby under the eyes and along the chin. The German watched the Jews but didn't really watch, that was how Mouse saw it. Beside this German was a fat Dutchman, dressed in a dark blue suit. He looked like a cop to Mouse, like a plainclothes dick the way he stood. The fat man turned away from the beating, his face pinched as if he'd seen this all before and didn't need to look.

Mouse wished he had the Welrod or at least the Smith & Wesson. He'd start with him, that German. But there was no gun inside his coat. Reka made him leave them in the cellar, telling him if the police found a gun they would know he was Resistance, and straight to the Gestapo he'd go. Without a gun, he had a chance, she said, if they were stopped.

The crowd had slowed after the first panic, and now moved more deliberately toward the white building. They left behind the empty circle with the still, old woman in its middle. Mouse counted cops. Eight Dutch in blue, nine counting the dick in plainclothes, and three Germans in gray. There must be hundreds here, the column stretching back at least a block. At least a hundred men and boys. But not a one tried to save the old woman. Or themselves. Why weren't they putting up a fight? Why didn't they rush the cops?

Mouse's tiny breakfast of bread and jam tried to climb out, but he choked it back. These weren't Jews, they couldn't be. Not like he knew Jews, like Little Farvel and Dukey and Meyer Lansky and Lepke Buchalter and even his muter—short, round Ruth Weiss.

But yellow stars said they were. It made him ashamed that he'd been made to see them this way. But at the same time he felt a kind of pride, proud he at least was a real Jew, not like these.

Words came to him suddenly and out of nowhere, maybe because of what he'd been thinking earlier about that Sabbath so long ago when he'd stood up and recited the memorized Hebrew that had made his muter most proud. *"Ve'atem teluktu le'achad echad b'nai Yisrael,"* he still remembered from his Bar Mitzvah. "And you will be gathered one by one, O you children of Israel."

The old woman's hand moved and her leg twitched and Mouse saw blood on the stones. Was she invisible? He took half a step forward, but got only that far before Reka's hand clawed into his arm and held on tight. She leaned toward him, her breath hot in his ear. "You can't."

If one of the Jews had been closer, Mouse might have punched him good instead, shouted at him to do something, but there were cops between him and them. So he shrugged off Reka's hand and stepped the two steps to the nearest cop, the man's back to him, grabbed the collar of his blue jacket and spun him around, made his hand a fist and punched the cop just once, bang, right under the eye, and the cop, the first cop he'd ever laid hands on, went spinning to the ground. He'd show all these fuckers what a Jew was.

And the street went oh-so-quiet, quiet like his old neighborhood Saturdays, but that might have just been his imagination, and then he heard Reka's voice, not hot in his ear now, but yelling, her hand tugging at his coat again.

He caught the eye of the soft-faced German, the one dressed in a spotless gray uniform, the two letters "S" and "D" stitched on his left elbow in a black diamond patch. The German stared at him like he was the first Jew he'd ever seen.

R eka worried she'd be sick and draw attention. She had watched the SS man beat the old woman with his rifle, and in a faraway kind of way, thought she'd seen this woman before. And she remembered. That was the *oma*, the grandmother she'd knocked down on the street when she followed Annje to Henrik's house. The *oma* had nothing to press to her chest to hide her star now, just a sad-looking satchel on the cobbles beside her.

Her eyes went searching for the man who commanded this *razzia* and did this murder, and she found him only ten meters away, dressed in gray with one of the peaked caps showing the death's head on a small metal badge at its front. The round face, thick under the eyes so that they looked like small holes, the wide mouth: it was the Sicherheitsdienst who had shot at her the day Gerrit had died. Her hand went up and her fingers felt the line of her scar. But she wasn't afraid. Perhaps it was because she still held Mr. Weiss's arm.

But Mr. Weiss went mad that moment, and struck the policeman and knocked him to the ground. She shouted at him to stop, not knowing if it was Dutch or English she yelled. From the corner of her eye she saw the SD man turn, and her eyes met his for a moment and she stretched out a hand and pulled Mr. Weiss back into the small safety of the crowd, past Kristiaan and Rachael, their mouths open.

Pulling him along, she fled.


Preuss watched as the Scharführer stepped away from the old woman and pushed the Jews with his rifle stock toward the doors of the theater. Preuss was thinking of Marta, then of the cellars in the old school building on Euterpestraat where he'd left Giskes, then of Marta again.

Another two hundred nineteen this afternoon. No, only two hundred eighteen now, he thought, glancing at the Jewess on the street. Atop the one hundred eighty-two this morning, it had been a good day.

Even the old woman on the ground didn't bother him. By rights he should be furious at the careless Scharführer for killing her before she'd been put in his ledger. But he felt generous.

"Another fruitful *Aktion*, Detective-Sergeant," Preuss said to de Groot, who wore the same blue suit as always, too tight around his middle, as always. The policeman grunted. De Groot had turned his face from the mess on the street; he'd not wanted to look at the old woman. Preuss knew he would have to speak to de Groot's superior soon; the Dutchman got more insolent by the day. Ever since that old woman had flown from her window, de Groot had lost his stomach. Not literally, Preuss thought as he looked at the big-bellied policeman. But the Dutchman's enthusiasm, never great, seemed gone entirely.

Preuss followed de Groot's gaze and saw movement in the crowd of onlookers. There, beyond the thin line of policemen, a Dutchman with very pink cheeks and a strong chin stared at the motionless yid on the street. Even from ten meters' distance, Preuss saw the unusual fury in the man's face. If they were bothered by the way Jews were treated, the Dutch rarely showed it. The man took a step forward, toward the nearest of de Groot's men, and for a split second Preuss had the absurd idea that the man was going to strike the policeman.

And that was exactly what happened. The policeman fell backward to the cobbles from the single blow of the Dutchman. He heard a woman shout, not Dutch, one short word said twice, and saw the woman lean from the crowd and grab her man by the arm.

As she did, her head turned his way and showed him her scar.

The Muiderstraat almost three weeks ago. The NSB man, clothes afire, hanging out of the shattered Renault. The dead boy on the walk. And this woman, the one with the scar, today white but that day a red and fresh wound from the fragments of the grenade. This was the young woman he had shot at as she'd run away.

The man beside the woman with the scar looked up and his eyes met Preuss's for a moment. The pink-cheeked man's eyes were dark. Preuss was startled by the hate in them.

He groped at the holster on his belt, pulled at the flap, and reached for the pistol within. At the same time, he took a step toward the line of policemen and the crowd beyond it.

"Come here, girl!" he shouted. Even the plodding of Jewish feet on cobblestones had stopped. He had the pistol free from its holster and raised as the woman, her hand still clutching the coat of her man, turned away. But he had forgotten the safety, and when he pulled the trigger, nothing happened.

Preuss looked down and thumbed the safety on the left side of the Walther. When he raised his head, both the woman and her man were gone.

Preuss brushed past a policeman and shoved at the Dutch who blocked his way. They moved aside too slowly, and by the time he had bullied his way through them, the woman with the scar and the man with the dark eyes were nowhere to be seen.

# *Twelve*

I don't trust them," Kagen said, meaning Johannes and Annje, the two they'd left down in the stinking cellar. "We don't have much time," he said, talking to Reka. "And short of hands as it is. But I don't trust those two. We'll have to do without their help."

It was the first time Mouse thought Kagen was right on target. He'd seen how Reka had looked at those two yesterday.

Kagen spelled out the plan to Reka, showing her the hand-drawn map that Schaap had made from memory in the cellar after Joop had disappeared. He explained how they must steal aboard the transport from Amsterdam on Monday—Joop had said that transports left Amsterdam for Westerbork every Monday from Muiderpoort station, and Reka nodded—to get inside Westerbork. That was why they needed identity cards, so they all could pose as Jews, even Rachael and Schaap.

They would lie low in the camp for one night, giving them a little time to sniff around for their Vreesje, and there Kagen looked to the stony-faced Schaap and his sad-eyed sister. The next day they must find a way aboard the train to the East—didn't the transports always leave on Tuesdays?

Reka nodded again.

Then they'd shoot their way out of the railway car before it reached the outskirts of a town called Assen. "Joop said the train must slow there, slow enough for us to run alongside and reach the locomotive," said Kagen. "We deal with the rest of the guards once we've stopped the train. Here." He thumped a finger at a spot on the map where Joop had said a spur went off the main line, south of Groningen. "We can shunt the train off the main line here, Joop said, and not worry about anyone seeing."

Because Joop was gone, he said, they must force the engineer to guide the train through Groningen and onto the tracks north. "The second spur, the one from Uithuizen," Kagen said, "goes right to the coast. Joop said there was a dock there once for a cannery. We can load from the dock." He told her the times they'd figured from their charts and tide tables in London; half-past ten, that was when the tide would be rising. "We need to be at the coast by then."

Kagen explained, too, why this had to happen next week. They must finish before an important conference ended. They were doing this to make the world take notice that Jews were in mortal danger, he said, to show that Jews could be saved.

It sounded almost possible when Kagen laid it out like this. Reka took it all in, smiling in a way that turned her plain face pretty.

Kagen asked Reka questions: the route Jews were taken to the train station here for the trip to Westerbork, how many were in a transport, what time of day Jews left the camp each Tuesday. When she was done answering, he nodded.

"We need boats," Kagen said. "And identity papers. We must reconnoiter this Muiderpoort station so we can find a way to get on that train. And scout the rail line in the north if we have time. But the boats are most important. Without them we have nothing."

"What kind of boats?" Reka asked.

"Fishing boats," said Schaap. The Dutchman hadn't gotten over yesterday, Mouse thought, seeing the pain in Schaap's face. "That's what Joop said we would do—he came to England on a fishing boat, he said."

"And I'll be paying for them," Mouse said. It was automatic, what he said—part of him still counted on getting home with as much money as he could—but the words sounded hollow in his head.

"Joop told us the name of the boat that brought him to England," said Schaap. "*Nes*, Joop said the boat was named, out of Amsterdam. Its captain helps people escape, for a price, that's what Joop said."

Reka's smile was gone now. "We're forgetting something," she said. "What of Joop? What if he's alive and the police have him? What if he talks? Everyone talks, sooner or later."

Mouse hadn't thought of that, and from Kagen's look, neither had he. It was quiet in the room. Mouse was the one who broke the silence. "Then we're"—and he tried to think of a different word because Reka was here—"sunk," he said.

Kagen looked his way. "We can't change the date. It must be next week. We have to take the chance that he's . . . that Joop's dead. I'm sorry," Kagen said, "but that's all we can do."

"I think she's saying we shouldn't use Joop's boat," Mouse said slowly, thinking this through. "In case he's alive and spills. Talks." Reka nodded.

"We should go outside Amsterdam for boats—" she said, and Mouse knew she'd stopped because she was probably hoping Joop was dead, and didn't like herself for that. "Ijmuiden, lots of fishing from Ijmuiden, that's far enough away."

Kagen glanced at her. "Joop was to find us the boats, but now . . . Weiss and I, we'll see to the boats." He looked at Mouse, and Mouse stared back.

"What do you think I'll do, run? Where would I run?" he asked Kagen, figuring the German meant to come along to watch him and his money.

Kagen smiled. "That's the good thing about Holland, isn't it? You don't have any of your gangster friends here for me to worry about, do you? I—"

Reka interrupted Kagen. "Someone must speak Dutch, yes? You and

Mr. Weiss, neither of you do. I should be the one who talks to the fishermen. Besides, someone needs to find identity cards. And find a way into Muiderpoort. Yes?"

Kagen chewed on that awhile. Finally he nodded, the black patch going up and down. "Yes. Schaap and I, perhaps we should stay and scout the route to the station. We counted on their help getting identity papers, but . . ." Kagen pointed to the shut trapdoor under which Johannes and Annje sat in the cellar, and he shrugged. "But Rachael says she knows a man who may be able to find us cards."

He turned back to the handmade map and pointed out Uithuizen, the village Joop said was closest to the water. The boats must meet them there, at the old cannery five kilometers, maybe six, north of Uithuizen, after dark on the 27th when the tide had turned. Half-past ten, remember that, he said.

When Kagen was through, Reka turned to Mouse. "I'll go to Ijmuiden to find boats, but I'll need money to pay the captains." Maybe she was giving him an out. Maybe she was afraid he'd let her down, like in the field, or lose it, like on the street. Mouse didn't like either thought.

He looked first at Rachael, who stood closer to Kagen than usual, the front of her right shoulder almost touching the back of his left. Then at Reka. If he had a choice between sitting in the cellar with Rachael and those eyes of hers that looked inside his head, or walking streets with Reka, it was easy. "No. I handle the money. I'll go."

There was something about this Reka, Mouse told himself.


R eka made everything clear with small movements of her hands. Walk with me, her hands said, and they walked the fifteen minutes from the store to the station. Get on the train, her hands told him, and he sat with her in a compartment with four other women. Even before the train pulled out of the station, Reka put her hand on his and he felt it tremble. He opened his hand and she slid hers in his, their fingers locking.

Mouse pretended to sleep as Reka talked softly with the women. But when the conductor opened the door of the compartment, Reka just handed over the tickets she'd bought from two different clerks and that was that. No check for papers, like he'd worried.

Get off the train, her hands said as she took her fingers from his. The train slowed and pulled into a station with the sign DREIHUIS large and in red. He stood when she did and stepped out of the compartment and off the train and onto the platform.

Only when they walked from the station, now on narrow streets past stout brick houses on the right, swamp and sand dunes to the left, did they talk with their mouths.

"Thanks for yesterday," he said. A horse and cart jogged by them, milk cans bouncing in the back. "Thanks again."

She didn't look at him as she answered. "That German knew me. He knows me from this." And she brushed her hair back from where it hung loose and pointed to the scar.

"I would have killed him," Mouse said. "But I didn't have a gun."

She stopped, so he did too. "You cannot kill here, not Germans, without . . . what is the word? An outcome. I know this. I have seen it."

"Consequences," Mouse said, gently correcting her.

"Reprisals," she said, coming up with the word. She started walking again, and he hurried to catch up. "Rachael told me what you do in America," she said after a long silent slice of time, half a mile or more, the sign along the road now reading IJMUIDEN. "What you did in England. You killed men there, she said." Mouse put out his hand, touched her arm, and she stopped again.

"I only pop guys for good reason," he said.

"Pop?"

Softer. "Shoot." She made like she was going to walk, and he left his hand on her arm. "And I've never killed a woman," Mouse said, thinking not of the old woman who had her brains beat in, but of Rachael and Reka there in the dark on the field. "Ever."

She nodded. "You only murder those *you* think should die? That sounds like how the Germans think, Mr. Weiss."

"Call me Mouse."

"I'm not saying you're wrong. Sometimes people deserve . . . sometimes they are even women who . . ." But again she clammed up.

He waited until two young Dutch girls, no older than twelve or thirteen, laughing and holding hands, moved out of earshot. "If you have something to tell me, spit it out."

"Spit it out?"

"Tell me, that's what it means. I get the feeling you want to tell me something."

They stood there in the road, looking at each other, and just when he couldn't hold her stare anymore, she said, "Annje," in a small voice.

"What about her?"

"I think she's the one who betrayed us on the polder," Reka said. There was some doubt on her face, Mouse saw, but not much. "Before you came, Annje was arrested. She was released a few hours later and said the police told her it was all a mistake. I'm not so sure, Mr. Weiss. Perhaps she told the police about us, about you coming from England."

"She's the rat?" he asked but got no answer. "The one who talked, I mean. You're sure?"

She shook her head. "No, I'm not sure."

"You've seen her spill to the Germans?" he asked.

"Spill?"

"Tell, talk." A rat, Mouse thought. Like Kid Twist. But there was no hotel room to pitch this Annje from.

Again she shook her head. "No. I've followed her, but no." A group of Dutch children came on them from behind and she touched his arm with her hand again to get them walking. The road quickly became a street, the separated houses became row houses and stores, and the occasional Dutchman and the occasional horse and cart became small crowds and flocks of bicycles. Another fifteen minutes and the smell of fish and salt air got stronger, and after Reka asked directions once of an old man, they wandered through a warehouse district, large cranes looming in the distance, and rounded a final corner. Fishing boats were roped to the one long concrete dock in ranks, like parked cars.

Reka walked slow, looking carefully at each of the boats. The dock was busy, with men on the decks of most of the boats, men with carts wheeling big wooden boxes of fish and mussels and clams. Mouse noticed that most gave Reka the up and down, some smiling as she passed.

The wind was brisk and her dress sometimes caught the breeze and came up over her knees. She had nice-looking legs.

"Here," she said after they'd walked all the way up the dock, then turned and come halfway back. ROOSJE was the name painted on the front of this boat, black letters outlined in faded orange. Dark nets hung from the mast, a small boxlike cabin near the back. It was small, thirty or thirty-five feet, tops. "The orange paint, you see that?" she asked. "That's a sign. Orange is Holland's color. It means he's a patriot, or thinks he is. Perhaps he'll take your money."

A man, his thick beard gone to gray, sat near the front of the boat on a hatch, a cigarette dangling from the corner of his mouth. He was big, even sitting down, and his green jacket stretched tight across his chest and shoulders. He was working on a net folded over his feet.

Reka walked to the edge of the dock and called softly in Dutch. The man looked up, stood up, his face blank, but Reka talked more Dutch, a quiet voice. Mouse made out only "geld"—which meant the same, he supposed, in Dutch and German: money. A magic word. At that, the big man smiled warily through his beard. He tossed his cigarette into the water, stepped onto the pier, took hold of Reka's two hands in one paw, the two of them talking fast now and stepping onto the boat. Mouse followed them to the cabin at the back.

Inside the tiny room, barely enough space to keep his hip away from the wheel, Mouse tried to get a feel for the fisherman. The Dutchman had fifty pounds on him easy, and his hands were rough and the crow's-feet at the corners of his eyes were long and deep. The guy had a habit of looking away just as you put eyes to his, and it made Mouse edgy.

They talked, Reka and the fisherman, Reka using her hands to give some words extra weight, talking soft, then louder, then soft again. Mouse thought he heard words for places, like "Waddenzee" and "Uithuizen." The big fisherman nodded, kept sliding his eyes around the cabin.

"*En hoeveel gaan jullie mij hiervoor betalen?*" the big man said, Mouse hearing how he said the words, but not knowing what they meant. That was when Reka finally leaned to him and switched to English as she whispered in his ear.

"I told him you are an English flier who parachuted from his bomber.

You want to go home, I told him. And I said that others, a lot of others, want to go to England, too, Dutchmen who want to escape labor service, and those who want to join the British. It's a poor story, I know, but I couldn't tell him he would be taking . . ." and there she paused. "I don't know how he feels about that. He wants to know how much we'll pay. He'll do it, I think, for enough money. What do I tell him?"

"We can't get them all on this boat. You said there might be a thousand. How we going to get a thousand on this tiny boat?"

"There is room below deck, and they can stand. Mr. Boersma has another boat. I think we need three more besides. Perhaps he knows other captains. But my question, Mr. Weiss, is how much do we pay?"

"Does he speak English?" Mouse asked.

Reka put the question to the captain in Dutch. "Some. A little," she said.

Mouse dipped a hand in the pocket of his brown cloth coat for one of the two bundles of British pounds. There was a small table screwed to the wall that had been putting a crease in his back, and atop the chart that was spread over that table, he made five stacks of twenty-pound notes. He made each stack twenty notes deep. Four hundred pounds each. Eight grand American altogether.

Mouse looked at the big man's face, trying to see if it was enough, but the fisherman gave him no clue.

"For each boat. Boats, you understand? Five." Mouse held up a hand and showed all five fingers. "Half now, another half when we get to England. You understand?"

The fisherman shook his head. "More," Boersma said, his voice heavy. His accent was even thicker than Joop's. "Three boats, more."

"No, not three." He held up three fingers and shook his head. "Five." Again he spread his hand.

Boersma looked long at the money, not letting his eyes slide off that, Mouse saw. The fisherman held up four fingers.

Four, five, one. A day ago, it wouldn't have mattered. All he needed was the one boat that would take *him* back. But the old woman dead on the street came to him like it was another of Bergson's pictures. And Reka watched him.

"Five," he said again, holding up fingers. He pointed to the five stacks of British banknotes. "That's a lot of money, *geld,* right there. But five boats. Five," and he said it loud, like that would make the Dutchman understand.

Boersma shrugged at first, nodded second. Five it was. "Not England," the Dutchman said. "The *Duitsers* . . . Germans . . . have boats." And he made a noise with his lips, like a raspberry, and Mouse got it. Motorboats. Patrol boats, like Schaap had said back in London.

Mouse put five more bills on each stack. He looked at Boersma, but the fisherman, with a sorry expression on his face, shook his head again.

"Diesel" was all Boersma said.

"What?"

"Diesel. Petrol, yes? For boats." And he looked impatient, and flapped his lips at Reka in Dutch.

"They need fuel, he says," Reka said. "Diesel they'll have to buy on the black market. Their petrol ration isn't enough to sail to Friesland, on to England, and back. He's right about this."

Mouse sighed, and counted out the last notes in this bundle, five more for each stack. Mouse looked up from the five piles, six hundred pounds each. Twelve grand on the table, Mouse figured, adding the numbers in his head, it taking a bit of time. That would drop what he had left to under fifty. How had Lansky's money disappeared so fast?

Boersma looked sad again. "More."

"That's a fortune," Reka said, not to the Dutchman but to him.

Mouse gave Boersma the up and down, locked looks with the fisherman for just a blink, and took his cue from the girl. "No. That's all." And he showed his empty hands, palms up. There was another bundle in his waistband, but this was all he was going to pay.

He leaned to Reka. "What if he doesn't go for it? There are other boats with the orange paint, right?"

"I don't know," she said back to him quietly, not taking her eyes off Boersma, who had moved to the chart table and was looking at the five stacks. "The more people we talk to, the better the chance someone will go to the Germans. Especially if they've not been paid to stay silent."

Boersma turned to them. "Okay," he said in his accented English, and picked one stack and counted quickly. Now he smiled through his beard, and spoke quick Dutch to Reka. Mouse thought they had a deal, but Reka wasn't translating, instead talking back to Boersma, pointing to Mouse's empty hand and shaking her head. She did something Mouse would never have expected: Reka reached for the notes in Boersma's hand and gently tugged out one. Twenty pounds, eighty bucks. She took one from each of the four stacks still on the chart table. A hundred pounds, four hundred American.

Reka talked again, a string of Dutch, and at the end, Boersma wasn't smiling. But they had a deal. Boersma stuck out his hand to Mouse, and when they shook on it, the fisherman crushed his with a grip like iron hoops.

Boersma scooped up the money and stuck it in his pocket. He pulled a chart from a drawer, pointed to it, gunned Dutch rapid-fire to Reka. He grabbed a thin book, paged through it, ran his fingers down a list of numbers, talked some more in Dutch. Reka nodded and talked.

"What's he saying now?" Mouse asked.

"We're talking about the tides and times. Be quiet," she said. After Boersma gave her paper and pencil, she wrote, listened, and wrote again. She put the folded paper in the pocket at the front of her dress.

They were finished. Like those times he sat in Lansky's room at the back of Ratner's, Mouse could tell when a conversation was over.

"What did you tell him at the end, when you took the money back?" he asked.

Reka looked up, pulled her hair down to hide her scar. "We have a saying in my family, I told him," she said. "'Never pay so much that the other man smiles.'" She handed him the pounds she'd pulled from Boersma. "Take your money."

This girl knew how to drive a deal. He liked that. He didn't like the way she said "your money," as if it was dirty. But he was beginning to really like her.

Boersma started to squeeze past him for the door, but Mouse put a hand on the man's green jacket. It smelled like old fish, and this close, the guy was enormous.

"You be there, won't you?" he asked the Dutchman. Boersma still looked slippery-eyed. Spark and O'Brien he could read, but this one, he wasn't sure. "Look at me when I'm talkin'," Mouse said. He put a finger on the second button of the green coat but didn't push, just lightly let his finger touch the button. "Don't get lost, or forget." Reka translated.

"*Maak je geen zorgen, ik zal er zijn,*" Boersma said back.

"He'll be there, he says," said Reka.

"Ask him if he's got kids," Mouse said. "Children." The Dutch went from her to Boersma and back. The fisherman looked down at Mouse's finger and nodded.

Mouse pulled his finger from the Dutchman's button. "You get lost or forget about us, and I'll come back here and feed your kids to those fish of yours. Not you, your kids. You understand?" But Boersma didn't, that was plain. "Tell him that." Reka hesitated, but she did what he asked.

He looked up at the fisherman. "I'm no British pilot, you know that." Boersma nodded. "You do what I paid for, that's all I'm saying." Reka talked again, but Mouse figured the fisherman had gotten the idea. Boersma now looked him in the eyes. Whether that meant he was scared or just understood, Mouse couldn't tell.

They stepped out onto the deck of the *Roosje,* and onto the dock. There, Reka turned to face him.

"Just what kind of man are you, Mr. Weiss?" she asked.

"Call me Mouse, why don't you?" he said.


The walk back to the station was the same, just backward, and because the chalkboard said they had over an hour until the next train, Reka stepped into the small café beside the platform and went to a corner table, a good spot. No one was near and they could watch the door.

The waiter, wiping dirty hands on an even dirtier apron as he walked up, listened to Reka, said to her, "*Twee koffie. Jahoor, mevrouw, het komt er gelijk aan,*" and ambled away. Mouse pulled out a Chesterfield, lit it, and drew deep, blowing the smoke out through his nose.

She sniffed the air and her face got angry, those eyes like Lansky's drilling him through. "Put that out, you fool," she hissed. "Do you want them to know who you are?"

He didn't understand.

"The tobacco. It's real tobacco. No one but the Germans have real tobacco. Put it out."

He dropped the Chesterfield to the floor, ground it under a boot, and there was the waiter with two small cups of coffee. He sniffed, looked at Mouse, and his eyes went wide. He muttered, "*Gestapo,*" and scurried away.

Reka looked over the rim of her coffee. When she lowered the cup, Mouse saw her smiling, maybe a little sheepish. "He smelled your cigarette, Mr. Weiss, and he thinks you're Gestapo. Germans get the best of everything, but the Gestapo, it seems they get the best of that." She laughed softly. "He won't bother us, I think."

The silence between them was comfortable. He drank the strong coffee, which didn't really taste like coffee, more like nuts, he thought, and looked at her. She had a habit of turning her head to hide the scar.

She was so different from the girls his muter kept aiming at him. She didn't care if she called him a fool, or worse. So he talked to her, curious.

Her father had been a publisher of books, her mother had been, well, a mother. Reka spoke of both like they were dead. She had been in school when the Germans came, but she was also working for her father, typing and keeping accounts—she had a head for numbers, something he already knew after seeing her deal with the fisherman.

At first, life after the Germans came wasn't much different. But as the months rolled by, new laws came fast. Her father had to register his business at the end of '40, the whole family had to register soon after—she remembered them all trooping down to the police station on a bright, chilly day in January. By summer '41, their identity cards showed large letter Js. Her mother had cried, Reka said, saying that this was the end. She had told her that was nonsense. And there Reka stared into space for a long time. Mouse didn't interrupt but drank his strange-tasting coffee, now almost cold. She had been right, the waiter didn't come back.

By August, her one brother was turned out of his last year of technical school and her father's bank accounts were blocked. They could draw only two hundred fifty guilders each month, a pittance compared to what they'd had before. Twenty-five pounds, Mr. Weiss, she told him, and

Mouse did the arithmetic. He'd just given the fisherman two years' worth for each of the five boats. She'd been right, it had been a fortune.

Reka's voice got louder, and he leaned forward until she looked at him, and she whispered again. That was not the worst, she said. Next came the yellow star with its printed *Jood*. That was almost a year ago. Her father's business was seized by the Germans, its Jewish employees dismissed. Curfews next, and they could not ride the trams and trains, and the police came to the door and took the radio and the telephone, she said, angrier at that than the star, it seemed to Mouse. And two months later, July last year, policemen pounded on the door of their house on Botticellistraat and told them they must come in an hour to the Jewish Theater, that theater where the old woman was killed. They could bring but a bag each, just one. Reka had helped her mother pack, she said, made sure that she took warm clothes and left behind the things that must be left, like a painting of her mother and father that she herself had made when she was younger. And we walked through the streets, just like those people we saw yesterday, Reka said. The woman who was killed, that could have been my mother.

The train took them to Westerbork, a place so foreign it seemed out of those dark German fairy tales where witches eat children. Four months there, trying not to starve, trying to hope. And last November—it was a Monday afternoon, the day before she was to turn twenty, of all days— her name and the names of her mama and papa were called from the list.

She crept out through a hole she cut in the wire fence around the camp, she said. Found a woman who hid her, and . . . Reka looked up, her eyes all shiny.

"When I was a little girl I wanted to be a painter. Portraits. I was going to paint until I was thirty, then I would find a good man and have a family." Mouse stayed quiet, afraid if he said something she'd stop talking.

"How old are you, Mr. Weiss? Are you thirty?"

"Thirty-one this December."

She went quiet for a while. "You can remember a time before the Nazis, can't you? I can't. They have always been. Even before they came to power in Germany, Mama and Papa talked of them to scare me into minding. And on my fifteenth birthday, I read about them burning synagogues in Germany. That was when I decided I could not become a painter until they were gone. How could I paint portraits of smiling faces when God allowed such things?

"And when the Nazis came to Holland, they took my mama and papa to the East and killed them. . . ." Her voice was barely a whisper, hard to hear now over the train rolling in and blowing off steam just thirty yards outside the café. Mouse was amazed. Listening to her was like listening to Lansky. Like Little Man's, Reka's words sounded the same as other people's, but her meanings were different.

Reka reached across the table, took his hand in hers, just like on the train ride here. Her grip was too tight on his left hand. She looked at that hand.

"The world has enough painters already, yes?" Reka's eyes were hard now, twice-frozen, he thought.

"Call me Mouse," he said, holding her hand, feeling it warm in his. The last whoosh of steam from the engine outside, and her hand trembled.

She shook her head. "What is your *voornaam* . . . your first name? The real one?"

Only his muter and Lansky and Tootles called him by that name, but he didn't hesitate. "Leonard. It's Leonard."

"Then I'll call you Leonard," she said. It was something, Mouse thought. And her smile was like his muter's in the old pictures on the mantel, from when she had been young and pretty.

T he five of them whispered in the corner, keeping voices down because Johannes and Annje were across the small cellar.

Mouse and Reka had done their part. Kagen and Schaap said they'd found a place between the theater and the station, an alley where they could hide until the Jews walked past, then slip into the crowd. And Rachael had found an old friend who said he could help them with identity cards, for the right price. He was afraid to let them come to his house, she said, and would instead bring his camera to the shop tomorrow to take their pictures. He needed to make pictures to replace the photographs of real Jews on real cards he had in his possession. Things were shaping up, it seemed, and Mouse felt better for it.

Whenever Mouse checked out Annje, she pretended like she wasn't paying attention. The one time their eyes met, her blue ones were empty and her stare as blank as doll's eyes. Rat, Mouse thought, and Kid Twist's face came to him.

Above them, something scraped the ceiling of the cellar and they all went quiet. Mouse heard Reka breathing beside him. The trapdoor opened and Mouse went to his corner of the cellar and picked up the Welrod, pulled out the bolt to check that a cartridge was in the chamber.

It was only Henrik, who owned the store. Mouse didn't trust this one either. The old man climbed down into the glare of the cellar's single light. His eyes darted between Annje and Reka, and he licked his lips.

Henrik said something in Dutch to Johannes and handed him a bag. Johannes opened it and pulled out bread, a small chunk of cheese, an even smaller chunk of butter, and some apples. The old man went to Annje and they talked in quiet Dutch, Henrik sweating bad. He wiped it from his forehead, looked at Annje again. He's schtupping that girl, it was as plain as the sweat on his face—good thing Joop wasn't here to see that look. Then Henrik turned to Johannes and the two of them talked some more in Dutch.

"Henrik has a message from Annje's mother," Johannes said. "He telephoned to see how she was, he does that once a week, for my brothers, too. Annje's mother said she must see her." Johannes looked at Kagen, like he was the one in charge and was the one who would decide. "Her mother's old, she needs to go to her."

Mouse turned and saw Reka looking at Annje, counting her bruises it seemed. Reka gave her the up and down long and longer. Henrik wanted to get Annje out of the cellar so he could schtup her, Mouse thought. This story of a mother was bullshit.

Kagen looked at Rachael, and she nodded. A soft touch, Mouse thought. Kagen waved his hand as if telling the old man and Annje to go, go on, not smart enough to not trust them. Henrik climbed quickly up the ladder, Annje following him, her legs under her dress the last thing to leave. Reka went right to the spot near the cellar wall where she had her blankets spread on the floor. She rummaged under them and reached for her big handbag. Mouse couldn't see what she found there in the blankets—her back blocked the view—but from the way she moved, he knew she was dropping it in the bag. She made for the ladder and the store above.

Johannes asked Reka something in Dutch, and she answered. Her voice was steady, but Mouse knew she was angry. He had seen her angry look, and this was right up there with the one he'd got when he'd lit the Chesterfield in the café. Johannes shut up, and Reka reached for the ladder and started to climb.

"Where are you going?" Kagen called, but Reka didn't answer and her legs disappeared up the ladder like Annje's. Mouse reached for his brown coat, jammed the Welrod in his waistband, and pulled the coat over its butt.

"And you, where do you think—" Kagen started as Mouse stepped on the first rung of the ladder.

"With her," he said.

"Weiss, don't be stupid," Kagen said. "You were nearly caught yesterday. You don't know what you're doing."

"You're the one who don't know what he's doing," Mouse said, and climbed out of the cellar. He tipped the trapdoor so it slammed—bang!—like a clap of thunder in the distance, and hurried to the front of the store and after Reka.

Reka stood just outside the door, looking to her right up the street. When he looked that way too, he saw Henrik a block away, Annje facing him, the old man's hands moving but the woman with hers on her hips.

"I could hear you talking in English from here," she said as he stood alongside her. "Remember where you are." She didn't sound angry this time, just matter-of-fact.

"What's going on?" He watched Henrik and Annje.

"Arguing."

"I can see that. About what?"

He waited for her to answer. And waited. Henrik was now in Annje's face, shaking his finger in front of her nose. "I don't know," Reka said.

"He wants to sleep with her."

She turned to face him, and her face flushed. She was embarrassed. It was easy to forget she was so young, just . . . what, twenty . . . when she talked so tough sometimes.

"You could see it the way he looked at her down there," he said.

She said nothing, just touched his arm, and he looked down the street. Annje walked away from the old man, Henrik standing there like a dog so dumb it didn't know when it was kicked. Reka walked that way too and Mouse followed.

Reka didn't break stride when they passed Henrik, the old man looking broken, his face turned to watch Annje up the street. Mouse saw the look he gave Annje; she'd told him to get lost. Past Henrik now, he caught Reka's arm and turned her to him. "Where are we going?"

"If I knew, I'd tell you."

He glanced up the street, made sure that Annje was still in sight. Following was his kind of work.

"We better not let her get away, then," he said quietly, and took over the lead, watching Annje's blue scarf. He kept pace a block back, stopping when Annje stopped, guiding Reka into a doorway when it seemed like Annje might turn around.

They walked for half an hour south, then waited at a corner when Annje knocked at the door of a house, and disappeared inside after an older woman answered. The woman was in her late forties, thick around the arms and waist, blond hair gone brown and gray, looking like Annje would someday. Her mother's house, Reka whispered.

"Maybe this is all there is to it," Mouse said, but Reka touched his arm and shook her head. Even so, a passing woman looked at them odd, as if she'd heard his English.

Annje was in the house three-quarters of an hour by Mouse's watch. When she came out her face was pale and they had to hurry to keep up with her, she walked so fast. She headed east and north this time, across a big canal and into the old city. Twenty minutes walking, and with the sun close to setting, Annje finally stepped into a café on the corner of a street with a sign that read NOORDERSTRAAT. Mouse steered Reka under an awning across. And they watched.

Reka said something right away in Dutch, her words hissing like the steam from that train. Through the plate-glass window—cleaner even than Tootles's—Mouse saw Annje at a table up front. A big man—a fat man, dark blue suit, he looked familiar under his hat—was at the table too. Mouse studied his face through the glass. It was the Dutch dick, the plainclothes cop who yesterday stood by while the old woman got her brains beat in.

He and Annje talked. And then from the rear of the café, another man in a dark suit came to the table and sat between the Dutch dick and Annje.

"Sicherheitsdienst," said Reka, the word long and nasty sounding. "Do you recognize him? Look at his face." Mouse looked. The man's brown hair was cut short. Nothing.

"Put a gray uniform on him and a cap," Reka said. "Put a pistol in his hand." Sure. It was the German from yesterday, the one who pulled out a black automatic and pointed it through the crowd at them.

"Oh, fuck," he whispered, forgetting his manners in front of her for once.

"Yes, the SD," Reka said. And she put a hand in her big cloth hand-bag, the bag balanced on her knee. Before her hand cleared the bag, he saw the butt of a gun and the trigger guard, her finger already in it, finally the barrel of a gun. It was a Luger so old that its bluing was worn to black.

"No," he said and put his hand over hers, like on the train, but her hand was rock-steady now. "Don't be stupid. Put that away." Her hand tried to escape, and Mouse stepped so his back was to the plate-glass window across the street, so that he was between her and the rat bitch Annje and the Dutch dick and the German policeman who rounded up Jews.

"Get out of the way, Leonard," she said quietly, looking at him with those eyes of hers.

"No, put the gun away. Not here. Not now."

"She's betrayed us," she said, still giving him her eyes. "If she hasn't yet, she's about to."

Mouse nodded. "She'll get what's coming, Reka. But not here. This we need to think through." It was the first time he'd said her name out loud and it sounded odd, but a good odd. The seconds dragged by, one after the other, but she finally put her hand back in the bag and when it showed again, the gun was gone.

"We've seen everything we need to see, right?" he asked. She nodded. But she didn't want to leave. He touched her hand. "Unless you want to walk in there to hear what they say, we need to leave now. We need to get back to the store. We need to find a new place to hide." As he watched the café again, a waiter showed at the window and pulled its curtains closed.

"Yes," she said after more seconds. She pulled at the strap of her bag to set it on her shoulder, looked him straight, and said, "Thank you, Leonard." But the dark coldness in her eyes was still there, so he didn't know quite what to think.

In this old brown suit, Preuss felt less like the Hauptsturmführer of the SS and SD that he was, more like the postal inspector he'd once been. But his voice was still SS and SD. "Where have you been? And where are my Jews?" he asked. The Visser woman, her blond hair not long enough to hide the bruises, flinched as he squeezed between her and de Groot.

But she had some courage. "Not until you tell me what's happened to my brother. Is Martin alive? Or did you kill him back at the Westein- derplassen?" she asked softly.

He had no idea what she meant. "Your brother?"

"Yes, my brother. Martin. Is he alive?"

It came to him: the big one they'd found on the landing field with the bullet through his head had been her brother.

"You were there?" he asked.

She nodded.

What an idiot he was—he had taken her for an informer like every other, who put distance between themselves and those they betrayed, not for an actor in this drama. That she had been on the polder that night had never crossed his mind.

I'm used to simpler methods, he told himself—orderly *Aktionen*, ad- dresses of Jews typed on paper, and sometimes the Dutch who betrayed their neighbors for the fifty guilders and ten packages of cigarettes. But Preuss got his wits about him quickly and lied. "Your brother, yes. He's alive. He was injured, true, but we have him in hospital. He will live. If . . ."

"If—" she said, her face brighter now with hope.

"What are these commandos up to? You vanish for two days, then telephone only after I go to your home. To talk to your mother," and he let his voice drop there. She shivered, a bit like when she had sat in the chair in the corner of the cell under Euterpestraat. "You said you had something important to tell me."

"Commandos?" she asked quietly, confused. "No, they're not soldiers."

"Why are they here?" he asked.

"I don't know. They won't tell us anything. Only Reka, she's the only one they tell. Because she's a Jew. The Jews keep their secrets," she said. A sly smile flicked across her once-pretty face. "You know how they are."

Not commandos? Jews, every one? That made them less dangerous, didn't it, and set his mind turning. "Your brother, should he take a turn for the worse . . ." He left the threat hanging in the air. "They must have said something."

"Trains," she said finally, her hands clenched together on the table. "They say they are here to take a train of Jews." She looked at Preuss and tears crept down her discolored cheek. "My brother, please don't hurt him, please."

Preuss was stunned; her words made no sense. In his six years in the SD, Jews had never raised a hand to help themselves. They went to the slaughterhouse like lambs led by a Judas goat.

"And they need boats," Visser said. "They must have boats to take the Jews to England." She looked at him first, then at the fat detective-sergeant in the chair beside him.

"Boats?" Preuss asked dully. First trains, now boats. How fantastic. He wanted to laugh at this farce, but he could see she was telling the truth. The way she begged for her brother told him that.

And the dangerous pieces fell into place in his head. He had a transport for Westerbork scheduled Monday of next week. These Jews were after *his* Jews. If they took his train, he would have to replace the missing to balance his ledger, which already looked like it would come up short again this month. No, it would be worse than that, Preuss realized. Everything would come crashing down. Zoepf's quotas would be the least of his problems. He had heard the talk, everyone had heard the talk, of how the Jewish ghetto in Warsaw was being razed this very week, but that its Jews fought back—that they had, in fact, beat back the first assault by the SS day before last. Heads would roll, everyone in his office had agreed, glad not to be in Warsaw now and forever. Preuss knew his head would roll too, if he was the first man to lose a transport.

He would face not only the wrath of Zoepf, but of Eichmann, that thin-lipped, thin-necked clerk in Berlin. No, not just Eichmann. This would go much higher, much much higher. Müller, head of Gestapo, and Kaltenbrunner, chief of Reich Security Main Office, would hear of the disaster. Preuss remembered the memorandum Naumann had showed him. Even the Reichsführer, Himmler himself, would surely hear.

Marta and Vienna would be but a memory. He'd be lucky if all that happened were orders to Yugoslavia to chase partisans. More likely a visit to the cellars on Prinz-Albrechtstrasse in Berlin, where Müller's men plied their trade.

Preuss leaned closer to the girl, spoke softly in his Dutch. He tried to put calm back in his voice. "Where will this happen? And when? You must tell me when they mean to do this."

Visser shook her head. "I don't know, I told you. Only Reka knows."

He grabbed her arm and squeezed tight.

"They've told us nothing of the time or place, I swear," she said. "You're hurting me!"

"Your brother—" he began.

"I swear, I swear. Don't hurt him, please. He's *achterlijk*," she said, but Preuss didn't know the word. "He wouldn't hurt anyone, please. If I knew, don't you think I'd tell you?" Her face, puffy now from tears as well as her days-old bruises, was set in a mask of fright.

"I think she's telling the truth," de Groot said in his pathetic German. Preuss glared at the detective-sergeant.

"Tell me," Preuss said to Visser, still clutching her arm, his voice now loud. He leaned forward, his hand raised, ready to strike her, and she cried out, expecting a blow. The café went as quiet as a Russian woods.

"Please," de Groot pleaded.

"I swear to you, on my brother's life," she said. "I know nothing more, I swear. They need identity cards, that's all. I heard them talk of getting papers."

"For what?"

"I don't know, I don't know."

Everyone needed identity cards, they would need them even if all they were going to do was sit on their arses. He asked, "How many? How many of these Jews?"

Between soft sobs, she told him there were five: two Dutch, an American, one German, and this woman she'd named, Reka. A waiter stepped between their table and the window to pull closed the blackout curtains. Preuss thought while he waited for the man to move away. A German? An American? That was just like Jews, them and their conspiracies.

"That's all? Only five? And where are they now?" he asked. "Where are they hiding?"

Visser's hands dropped from her face and her crying slowed more, then finally hiccupped to a halt. "You'll leave us alone, my brother, my mother, if I tell you? I'll take you to them, but then you'll leave me alone. You'll swear, won't you?"

If the visions of trains and boats and Yugoslavia and Prinz-Albrecht-strasse hadn't made this so very serious, he would have laughed at her. "Yes, of course," he said easily. "Tell me and I swear." De Groot made a low sound behind him, which he ignored.

Visser took a long moment, then nodded just the slightest. "A clothing shop on Lindenstraat. No. 28 Lindenstraat. In the Jordaan. That's where we're hiding."

Preuss knew the neighborhood, just beyond the Prinsengracht to the north and west of the Dam. Two kilometers from here, no more.

He had them. He would round up these five Jews just as if they were five on his lists. He would write a report and send it to Zoepf in The Hague and Eichmann in Berlin and Naumann, too. The report would tell how he had crushed this plan to steal Jews from the SD. He would become a legend in the small world of the Sicherheitsdienst, and no one would mention he'd not met the quota for this month, or next, or even the month after that. He would be the man who had saved the Jews.

He looked at his watch. Nearly eight. He would knock down their door just before first light, as always. He'd do this without Giskes, to hell with his promise. There were only five, and they weren't commandos with knives and blackened faces. He might have pissed himself there on the polder, but he knew how to run an *Aktion*. And the credit would be his alone.

Preuss turned to de Groot and switched to German. "Take her to this shop. Post men to watch it, front and back. You yourself, I want you to be there to watch this shop. All night. I'll call the Euterpestraat for another car."

"I'll see to it," de Groot said, clearly unhappy at the prospect of missing a night's sleep, but he put a sloppy salute to the brim of his fedora.

"Not a word of this," Preuss said to Visser.

"Yes," she said in a small voice. De Groot took her by the arm and walked her out.

Preuss was in no hurry to leave now. He waved a hand at the waiter. He wanted more bitter ersatz coffee. He wanted to smoke a Nil or two or three and think of how he would write his report. He glanced at his watch again. Marta was finishing her dinner.

Soon they'd be together. But for now he was content to sit alone and think of how all his shame would be erased.

# Thirteen

No one had stopped him when he grabbed Annje by the front of her dress, no one in the room said anything, either. Not even Johannes, who had edged forward a bit but backed away. Mouse pulled back his hand, intending to punch her, bang, right on her biggest bruise. But he hesitated, looking in those eyes of hers, now wider than wide, their blue like glass almost. He'd never hit a woman, rat or not.

She started crying very quietly.

Mouse let his hand drop to his side. And that made him madder still, almost as mad at himself for not being able to punch her as he was at her for what she'd done. He shoved her to the floor, where she ended up in a curl against the papered wall.

He turned to face the others. Kagen glared at Annje with his one good eye, Schaap beside him all angry and red under his blond hair; even Rachael, standing so close to Kagen that their shoulders touched, had made her face like stone. They all remembered little Joop, who had disappeared because this girl ratted them out.

Reka was harder to read. Her dark eyes drilled holes in the girl on the floor.

Ever since he and Reka got back to Henrik's store, her eyes had been like that. The two of them had told the others of the scene behind the café glass, and Reka had shouted at Johannes in their Dutch until she lost her temper and slapped him, like a woman would.

Then they'd all waited in the dark across the street, not in that shithouse cellar in case Annje came with the cops. But when she showed just before ten, she was alone. Kagen and Mouse followed her into the store, the German grabbed her by the arms and Mouse jammed a piece of a shirt in her mouth. And with Annje held tight between Kagen and Schaap, Reka led them through the dark to Henrik's house. The walk had been dicey because it was past curfew and they could be shot for that, but they made it. Only once, right after they came out of the store, did Mouse wonder if someone watched them. Between two buildings across the way, in the deeper shadows where the moonlight didn't reach, Mouse thought he saw a big silhouette. But when it didn't move even after he stared at it for five, ten seconds, he took the shape for shadows, that's all.

Mouse looked at Henrik, who sat in a chair in the far corner of this room—his dining room, with a large table and four chairs still empty. He was hunched over, his head in his hands, those hands almost on his thighs. An old woman sat next to Henrik, where Schaap had thumped a chair on the wood floor. Even though her gray hair was this way and that and she held a green dressing gown closed tight at her throat, she glared at them one at a time with steady eyes that hardly blinked. If there was a hard case in this room, it was Henrik's wife, not Henrik. This house, Henrik's house, has been the only hiding place Reka could come up with, and the old man's old wife hated them for thinking of it.

"What about her?" Kagen asked, nodding to Annje. No one, not even Johannes, had gone across the room.

Reka kept her eyes on the girl. "We must find out what she's told the SD. We must know what she's told him about our plan."

Johannes moved toward Annje, like he'd finally worked up enough nerve. But Reka grabbed his wrist and when he twisted away, she let him have it all over again, like in the clothing shop. Mouse made out "Joop" and "Martin," the names all he understood. Her voice was hard, but this time she didn't slap him. Johannes backed away. He wasn't much of a man, Mouse thought, to let a girl he liked get the treatment.

"Take her where it's quiet," Reka said, looking not at Kagen but at Mouse. He understood what she meant.

Kagen might think he was in charge, and maybe Mouse was in charge of the money, but Reka, she was running things now. She could have been Meyer Lansky's daughter, if he had a daughter, which he didn't. But if he had, Reka would have been it.

P reuss looked at his watch. Nearly five; Marta would be sleeping yet. The light was still gray, half an hour until sunrise, but enough to see by. He looked to his right, up Lindenstraat toward Noorderkerkstraat and beyond that, the shadow he knew was the high crown of the Noorderkerk, the big Protestant church around the corner. One of the trucks he used to transport Jews too old or crippled to march to the theater or the station blocked the intersection. Two Rottenführers stood behind the Opel-Blitz, rifles perched over its high green hood.

He looked left. De Groot's blue-jackets stood twenty meters down the street, just dark shapes against the growing light. The fat Dutchman was beside him.

He nodded to the Scharführer, Krempel was his name, and the man motioned to the others. Eight in all, three of the Kriminalpolizei—Kripo—and five SS, all that Naumann had sent him from The Hague. The men moved quickly across the street, but he stayed where he was; he could watch the door from here.

Krempel sprinted to the doorway of the shop with two others close behind. And while those two pointed machine pistols, Krempel gave the latch one kick, and the glass in the upper half of the door shattered and the door swung open. The three ducked out of sight into the shop, the other five on their heels. Preuss waited . . . and waited . . . listening to the sounds of sixteen hands tipping things to the floor, but there were no shots.

"Hauptsturmführer," one called from the darker doorway across Lindenstraat.

Preuss walked to the shop—de Groot close behind him—and through its smashed door, but there were only his men, their electric torches playing games on the wall and floor. He was confused.

"Here, Hauptsturmführer," another voice called, this time from behind the blinding glare of a torch. Preuss stepped carefully over the toppled racks of clothes, followed the torch beam through a doorway and into a small room. Someone had pulled a bureau from the wall and exposed a trap in the floor. It was open and a column of light rose from it like a pillar.

"Down here, Hauptsturmführer." Yet a third voice, this one hollow from the cellar. Preuss backed down the ladder, de Groot nearly stepping on his hands as the detective followed him.

Preuss turned and looked around the shabby space with the concrete floor and the one electric bulb dangling from a wire. The low ceiling made him think of the rooms under Euterpestraat. The cellar was a shambles, with discarded clothes and empty food tins in the corners and filthy bedding along the walls. And it stank like an outhouse.

"Herr Hauptsturmführer," and Preuss knew it was Krempel. The Scharführer's voice was the only one he recognized. "What do you make of this?"

Krempel pointed to the whitewashed wall near a corner and pinned the words in the circle of his torch.

MEYER LANSKY SENDS REGARDS, YOU FUCK

English, Preuss concluded—but he knew not a word of that language.

Krempel picked up a rag, stained dark, from the floor below the words. He lifted it to his nose, sniffed, and brought it to Preuss, who caught the odor before he touched it and so kept his fingers clean. It had the stink of shit, and was, Preuss understood, what they'd used to write their words on the wall. Krempel pointed his torch into the far corner, where a

blanket strung on a rope had been pulled aside. There was a bucket behind the blanket, a latrine.

"Anyone know English?" he called in the cellar, and a Kripo, stout
and thick-necked, stepped forward and said, "Yes, Hauptsturmführer,"
and Preuss told him to translate.

The Kripo hesitated. Preuss said softly, "I won't shoot the messenger."

The Kripo cleared his throat, said, "I think the first is a name, 'Meyer
Lansky,' Hauptsturmführer."

"Yes?"

"It says that this Lansky sends his respects . . ."

"Yes?" That wasn't all, Preuss knew that much.

". . . and it says you can . . . you can fuck yourself. Herr Hauptsturmführer." Beside him, de Groot grunted, and someone in a darker corner
of the cellar sniggered.

"Shut up!" Preuss yelled, so loud it echoed back and forth from concrete floor to wood ceiling, wall to wall. "Shut up this instant or you'll
be washing out this shithole with your tongue!" He was shouting the
words, he knew. Preuss pinched the bridge of his nose against the migraine he worried would come.


Y ou let them slip away," Preuss said quietly to Detective-Sergeant de
Groot. They were back on Lindenstraat, out of the stinking cellar
and far from the rank words smeared on the wall. Preuss's headache still
pounded at his temples, but he kept his voice low.

"No, I did not." De Groot had one hand hooked under a suspender,
his bulk of a belly stretching the brace until it looked like it might snap.

"I told you to make sure they didn't escape. And you failed to carry
out my order." Preuss moved closer to de Groot. The early-morning sun
cast long shadows over the Dutchman's face.

"No, I did as you said. I was here all night. I let the girl out of the car,
watched her go inside, then drove to a telephone box and phoned my
office. My men were here within the half hour."

"How do you explain their disappearance?" Preuss asked.

De Groot smiled for just a moment. "Perhaps they went out the back door?"

"There is no back door," Preuss said, his voice growing.

"A window perhaps," said de Groot. Preuss noticed that four of de Groot's policemen edged nearer. He glanced behind him. Krempel and his men were still in the clothing shop, turning it inside out, looking for the name of its owner. He was the lone German on the street.

"There is no window." Preuss gathered his thoughts for a moment before staring again at the Dutch detective. "You looked the other way—" he started.

"I haven't lifted a finger for a Jew."

Preuss felt the blue-jackets close their ring. Was this his imagination?

"You—" he began, but again de Groot interrupted.

"It's unfortunate they escaped. I'm sorry for it. But there are explanations. Perhaps they fled while we talked with Visser. Or she's playing both ends, and she told them to run before she came to meet with us. She hid from us before, correct?" All this was possible, Preuss knew.

He wondered if his Walther might get to a truth, but the four Amsterdam policemen were close now and armed, and he was alone, with no SD or SS or Kripo or even Wehrmacht uniforms to cocoon him.

"If you're lying to me, Detective-Sergeant—"

"I've done everything you asked," de Groot said. The Dutchman met his gaze. "We'll catch these Jews," said de Groot. "We always do, don't we?"

M ouse smoked a Chesterfield and watched Reka squeeze Annje. A half hour ago, Reka had started gentle. The conversation was soft and quiet—Mouse couldn't understand the words—but it went nowhere. Annje only cried great crocodile tears.

But now Reka put on the pressure. She bent near Annje's face, kneeled on the floor beside her, said something to her, pointed to Mouse, said something else. He recognized the game, though Reka wouldn't know it. That meant she was a natural, he decided.

Reka asked another question, still patient, and the girl cried bigger tears than ever, looked at Mouse, and finally nodded. Another question, another nod. A third question. The girl cried, quieter now, but said nothing.

Reka slapped her. Even the sound stung. Annje looked surprised. Reka asked again. Slap. Annje shouted and tried to guard her face, but Reka just grabbed Annje's hands with one of hers and pinned them to Annje's chest. Another question. Slap. And slap.

But Annje wouldn't talk, even though her nose had been bloodied. Maybe the Nazis had beat her harder when they had made her tell them things.

Reka's face was flushed and she stormed out of the small room, slamming the door open. Mouse watched Annje cry there on the floor until Reka returned. She had the ancient Luger in one hand now, that hand by her side and shaking. She shouted in Dutch at Annje, and when Annje didn't answer, Mouse expected Reka to point the Luger and pull the trigger, but she didn't. Instead, she went to Annje, and held the gun up to the girl's face, made her look at it by grabbing and turning her chin. She shouted again, and this time Mouse understood one word in the Dutch—*moeder*—because it was so close to muter. Reka yelled again, that word *moeder* in the shouting again, and Annje screamed.

Mouse heard a noise behind him, and there was Johannes in the doorway, his eyes so big they looked like they'd blend together in just a moment. Mouse grabbed the edge of the door and slammed it shut. Johannes yelled through the door. Mouse turned the key in the lock.

Annje talked now, whispering some words, crying others, all the while staring at the floor, not the Luger. She talked and talked and talked. Reka listened, still crouched down by Annje, her hand holding the gun again by her side and out of Annje's sight. But that hand still shook.

Reka was tough, tougher than any woman he'd ever met. She was a beauty, but she could be mean as a snake when she had to.

Reka straightened and came to Mouse. She looked down at the gun as if seeing it for the first time. Mouse gently pried it from her grip.

She talked, now in English, just loud enough for him to hear her over the blubbering of the girl on the floor. She said that Annje had not told about this place they were hiding in, or about Henrik, she was almost sure of that. Nor had Annje given the SD any details of their plan, but only because she had not known them. She had told him, Reka said, that they were here to steal a train and that they planned to get away in boats, but not the when or where.

It had been Annje who had betrayed them that night near the Westeinderplassen. And Annje had given the SD the name of at least one other Resistance group; Henrik had told her of it after they'd made love once, Reka said. Martin was alive, Annje swore. She did this for him, and for her mother.

Reka looked up at Mouse. "I think we're safe here, but I'm not sure."

"You did good," Mouse said to her. He wanted to pull her close, but something told him that he shouldn't, and he didn't.

"Never again," Reka said, looking at the floor, and when Mouse's eyes followed hers, he saw blood there. Annje's blood had gotten on Reka's hand, and some had dripped to the floor. Mouse thought Reka meant she would never do this again.

"When the Germans took my father, he said some words from the Tanach. I remembered them, and I found them whole in Mrs. van Mieps's Old Testament. 'They hunt our steps that we cannot go in our streets. Our end is near, our days are fulfilled, for our end has come.' Those were my papa's words." She drew a breath. "I will not let them do this."

Mouse looked again at the blood on Reka's hand.

She turned the key in the lock, opened the door, and walked from the room. The door slammed behind her.

R eka leaned against the wallpaper of the dark corridor and closed her eyes. Her heart hammered in her breast.

She had stared into Annje's wild eyes and seen something she'd never expected. Annje was afraid of her. But the thought only dragged its way through her head.

Mama and Papa dead by now, perhaps David too. Thousands of names said on the Appelplatz of Westerbork, each one dead. If it took cruelty to stop this, then so be it.

But why must I be the one? Leonard, he is the killer among us. I should be painting, or falling in love.

She wanted to be strong, mostly for herself, and some for Mama and Papa, and what little remained for Leonard. But she had not even been able to throw the grenade into the NSB car that day on Muiderstraat. Gerrit had had to do that, and had died for it.

But if they were not willing to fight—with all that meant, Reka thought, remembering the way Annje had looked when she'd promised to kill her mother—they would all die, just as surely as had those whose names had been called.

"Please, Mama," Reka whispered, wanting someone to tell her what to do.

*Fourteen*

Friday: April 23, 1943

Nothing more, Hauptsturmführer, but I'm still looking," said the Kripo, Munkhart.

Preuss placed the handset in its cradle and rubbed his forehead; the skin under his fingers felt raw.

He looked at the thin file folder of papers, all that they'd found in the shop on Lindenstraat worth taking. The owner had been a careful man or a frightened man or both. There was nothing in these papers to say who he was.

So Preuss had had his men drag Visser's mother from her house on Van Breestraat, but she screamed she knew nothing all the way to Euterpe-straat, where they'd clapped her in a cell. Then he'd sent them banging on every door on Lindenstraat asking who owned the shop, and when they came back with nothing, he'd made them go back with better man-ners and rewards, two hundred guilders and five cartons of cigarettes for information. At least then they brought him a name: Henrik Keuning.

But no one knew where Keuning lived, no such name was in the Gestapo Department C's Jewish card file kept at the far end of the former schoolhouse, and when he telephoned the Kripo office on Marnix-straat to tell them to search their identity index, he had only heard excuses about how they were short of clerks. So Preuss sent his own Kripo, Munkhart, the thick-necked one who had read him the shit-scrawled message from the cellar wall, to Marnixstraat to look through the files.

Munkhart had found evidence of a Henrik Keuning who lived in the shop on Lindenstraat, but by the phone call just now, there the trail went cold. Keuning must have a forged identity card, counterfeit papers. The Resistance made them by the score, Preuss had seen enough pulled from Jewish pockets to know.

He picked up the telephone's handset, thought better of it, put it back, but reconsidered and reached again. He heard the connection click to the switchboard. "Ring Sturmbannführer Zoepf, The Hague," he told the girl.

Ever since the Jews disappeared on him from the shop on Lindenstraat, he'd wrestled with this decision. Telephone Zoepf to tell him of his secret, but to say what? That I've uncovered a plot to steal a trainload of my Jews, but I'm sorry, Sturmbannführer, they've slipped through my fingers? And because I have spent so much time chasing these, I won't meet this month's quota? And that next month's is simply out of the question? Preuss shook his head and said, "Cancel the call," and returned the handset to its place.

Giskes was there when he looked up, and the surprise made him flinch. The Abwehr officer was in uniform this visit, his gray tunic showing an Iron Cross Second Class ribbon through a buttonhole and the Winter War shield on its left pocket. Preuss reached for a cigarette, lit it, inhaled, and waved Giskes to the empty chair.

Giskes refused the seat, instead removed his hat, brushed back his gray hair, and tossed the cap onto Preuss's desk. It came to rest on the open file folder.

"I have news from our friend the Dutchman," he said. "Joop van der Werf. You remember Joop."

Preuss waited for this news while his mind replayed the sound of the steel rod.

"He's said a thing or two. Our commandos, it seems, are after a train. What kind of train might they be after, Preuss?" Giskes folded his arms over his chest. He knows, Preuss thought, he just wants me to say it.

"What else did van der Werf say?"

Giskes shrugged. "Nothing else. He's near his rope's end. Either he'll tell us everything soon or . . ." Preuss imagined the little Dutchman's screams coming through the floor from the cellar. "What kind of train?" Giskes asked again.

Preuss glanced at his watch, eleven o'clock, and thought of how Vienna looked in the mornings. He crushed the half-smoked cigarette in the tray on his desk. "A transport. That's what the Dutchman said they want to steal. A transport of my Jews. Isn't that what he said?"

Giskes shook his head. "No, the Dutchman said nothing about it being a transport, only that it was a train. I just assumed, since it's been about Jews all along, hasn't it?" The start of a smile was on his lips.

"Stop it," Preuss said, irritated. Giskes enjoyed baiting him like this.

Giskes's smile disappeared. "Where's the Visser girl now, Preuss? Not in the shop on Lindenstraat. Someone's turned that place upside down."

"Lindenstraat, what do you mean?" Preuss asked, trying to keep the surprise from his voice.

"We had an agreement. You were to call me if you found anything. That was our understanding, wasn't it?" Giskes's jaw was tight.

How did Giskes know of Lindenstraat and the shop there? Preuss shrugged. There could be any number of explanations. The Abwehr had its sources, he knew, just as did the SD. Any of dozens, Dutch police or the men loaned from The Hague, even the neighbors on Lindenstraat, could have told Giskes of the raid. De Groot, for all he knew.

Preuss looked Giskes in the eyes. He didn't need to explain himself. Unless Giskes had suddenly taken up with the Reich Security Main Office, he didn't need to explain anything.

"You know, Preuss, we could both benefit from this," Giskes said, his voice softer, although his jaw was still set. Preuss lit another Nil and listened.

"You get the honor of stopping a plot to spirit away your precious Jews. Bands play, flags wave, the Reichsführer himself pinches your cheek. I get the credit for running down British commandos, a much more dangerous breed than ill-mannered Dutchmen out to scatter leaflets or steal ration cards." Preuss didn't bother correcting Giskes; these were not commandos.

Preuss inhaled, blew the smoke toward Giskes. He had never seen the man smoke, and he never really trusted anyone who didn't.

"We would both be heroes, Preuss," said Giskes. "But we must trust each other. And work together. On his own, each will fail, but together, think what we would accomplish."

Preuss did think. He was getting nowhere. The Kripo's index, the Lindenstraat neighbors, the traitor's screaming mother, the papers from the shop. Nowhere. Sharing meant diluting the glory, but half was better than nothing. And if the Jews took his train, he was in a very deep well of trouble.

"Before she disappeared, Visser said they needed boats," Preuss said. "They mean to pilfer my transport and take the Jews to boats. To England."

Giskes said nothing for a bit. "Boats, how ingenious. And here I thought it was something crude." And Giskes told him a story of how three nights earlier, just across the border in Belgium, men tricked a transport into stopping and opened the door of one cattle wagon. A hundred had scampered into the dark. Three dozen were still unaccounted for. "First the ghetto in Warsaw," Giskes said—and so the Abwehr knows of the ghetto too, thought Preuss—"and this in Belgium. Now commandos in Holland want to steal your Jews. All within a few days. Perhaps it's the beginning of something bigger."

Preuss felt his mouth open in astonishment.

"It seems too much a coincidence, don't you think? Jews fight back in Warsaw, Jews freed in Belgium, more Jews spirited away here," Giskes said, "on trains and boats, of all things. Perhaps there's a deeper reason for these events."

"It sounds far-fetched," Preuss said.

"So do Jews who thump the SS," Giskes said, grinning.

Conspiracy. If true, this was an even bigger prize, this secret he shared with Giskes. So Preuss told Giskes of his unsuccessful search for Henrik Keuning; how the Visser girl claimed there were but five; how he had names for two, a woman called Reka and a man, Meyer Lansky.

"Not commandos, you're sure?" Giskes asked. Preuss nodded. "How remarkable." The Abwehr officer thought for a moment. "You'll want to reinforce the guard on your trains. And at the station."

"I'm taking care of that," Preuss said. "But perhaps I should postpone Monday's train."

Giskes shook his head. "Certainly not. The longer this plays, the more chance our secret's out. These Jews will make a mistake and others will stick their noses in our business. We don't want that, do we?"

Preuss nodded. No, certainly not. This was his chance for fame, and an insurance against future deficits in his quotas.

"If we can't find them, they'll come to us," Giskes said. "The train is our bait. Run the train as usual, and we'll snare them at the station here in Amsterdam. I can bring my eleven men to help."

"I have eight, and the police, of course, and the Marechaussee. Another thirty or forty, say."

"Good, good. I'll get my informers asking about this Keuning and sniffing for anything out of the ordinary. Perhaps they'll misstep and show themselves. I'll poke around the docks for talk of hired boats. And perhaps I can flush them out other ways." Giskes winked, and Preuss remembered the Brigadeführer's explanation of Nightingale, the turncoat operation Giskes ran in Holland. That gave him an idea.

Giskes leaned forward. "But we should keep this to ourselves, agreed?"

Preuss nodded, not so much at Giskes's question as at the wonderful new idea forming in his head. He would accept Giskes's help, yes, and why not? But when they were done and this conspiracy was broken, he could denounce the Abwehr officer as a traitor to Naumann. He would paint Giskes with the black brush, make up some story. Naumann would believe him, he knew he would—hadn't he said the Abwehr was thick with traitors?

Preuss reached into the wooden file cabinet where he kept the Pierre Ferrand, pulled out the bottle and two glasses. He poured a finger's worth into each, shaking the bottle to bring out the last drops of cognac. He handed one glass to Giskes.

"To a profitable partnership," the Abwehr officer said, reaching over the desk and clinking his glass to Preuss's. "To fame."

No, we do not have identity cards yet," Kagen said, his voice low and threatening as he answered Leonard's question.

Reka looked away from the two men, wishing Rachael were here to keep her *Duitser* calm. But Rachael was in that back room, her turn to watch Annje. Johannes was there too, as were Henrik and his evil-eyed wife, none of them trusted now. At least there was some justice in the world, she thought: Henrik had to share that room with not only his furious wife, but his mistress, too.

"They check identity cards when the trains from Amsterdam reach Westerbork, right?" Leonard asked. "Reka, isn't that right?"

He was talking to her. "Yes, that's right. When we reached Westerbork, they took our cards at registration and made us new identity cards for the camp."

"See?" he asked everyone, his voice becoming angry. "How you plan to get through that without cards?"

Leonard was right. Rachael's friend was to have come to Lindenstraat to take their photographs and put them on Jewish cards. But that was yesterday. Even if he hadn't been caught by the police, he would have dived deep when he found the shop deserted. They'd never find him, even if they could risk going out.

"I don't know," said Kagen. "But we must find a way onto that train."

"We show up at Westerbork without cards and they'll grab us at this registration place," said Leonard. "We'll never get into the camp."

"Why would they care if they have a few extra Jews?" asked Kagen. "They worry about not enough Jews, not too many."

Reka shook her head. He was so thick sometimes.

"Annje's told them we're here to take one of their trains, you dumb yid," said Leonard, and the *Duitser* tugged at his patch. "They'll be giving everything the eye. They're not stupid."

"So we take what we need," said Kagen, his one good eye locked on Leonard. "When we get on the train here, we take identity cards from five Jews."

"They'll be punished," Reka said softly, but no one looked at her. "No, those five would be punished for losing their cards."

"If that's what it takes—" started Kagen, but he went silent when she looked at him.

"No, " said Leonard, who was losing his patience. "They'll tell the Germans someone took their cards on the train and they'll finger us. Or they'll give them their names and then the Germans will line us up and look at our cards and find us."

"Oh, I doubt that they'll go to all that trouble," said Kagen.

Leonard laughed, the first time she'd heard him laugh. "You don't know cops, do you? These Germans are like cops. They'll keep asking questions until they find us if they think we're in the camp."

Kagen played with his patch. "What's your idea, then, gangster?"

And for the first time in minutes, Leonard was silent.

"I thought so," Kagen said.

# *Fifteen*

Mouse had pulled a chair into the hallway so he could watch the front door. The Welrod was in his lap, a Sten on the floor beside him, and in the coat he wore were the six bundles of English pounds. He'd found thread and needle and slowly stitched the twelve thousand pounds, nearly fifty grand American, into the lining.

But he wasn't thinking so much about the door or the guns or the money, but about Reka. He couldn't stop thinking about her.

His muter was always playing matchmaker, telling him about this girl, that girl, wasn't it time to settle down? Pretty, some of them, but they bored him. All they did was talk about their silly girlfriends and whine how their stupid fathers were too strict and how they wanted to have some fun, but only with the right man, if you get my meaning.

But this Reka, she was different. She was serious. Tough and strong, not weak and shrill. Not taking crap from anyone. Hard, from the life she'd already lived. And there was the way her hand had felt in his on the train. He had liked that.

He heard a noise from the rear of the house and she stayed in his mind because she was back there. Just a bump, like someone knocking their knee against a piece of furniture. A shout next, not loud, and Mouse was out of his chair, holding the Welrod. Another bump, louder, and footsteps, slap-slap-slap, on the floor back there, and a door busting open. Reka's voice, yelling something in Dutch.

Mouse sprinted down the hallway with his hand wrapped around the Welrod.

Annje's gone!" Reka said as she leaned in the doorway. Mouse put his hand on her shoulder to steady her. "Johannes knocked me down from behind," she said. Her voice was angry. "Annje said she had more to tell me and when I turned my back on him . . . I didn't think, I'm sorry, Leonard."

Boots on the stairs and in the hallway behind them, and there were Schaap and Kagen both.

"He took the Luger," Reka said.

Mouse ignored Kagen's look and made for the kitchen, shoving open the door already busted. Once outside and through the garden, then into the alley behind the house, he stopped and listened for footsteps. "I'm coming, too," she said, at his shoulder. She had no gun, but that didn't matter. He had the Welrod.

"We'll never find them," Mouse said.

"They can't be far," Reka said. "Annje's legs will give her trouble until the blood comes back." He must have looked confused. "She's been tied for hours."

He heard the bells of the tram and they looked at each other. The tram ran on the street up the block, he'd heard those tinkling bells since they moved in here.

Mouse ran for the end of the alley, turned left, almost knocking a mother and her two kids to the pavement, and with Reka behind him, sprinted for the tram fifty yards ahead. It was at a stop, taking on and letting off. Mouse kept the Welrod in his right hand, the foot-long barrel tight against his leg. It was a shape so wrong for a gun that it might not be noticed for what it was, especially at just a glance.

They made it to the blue-painted tram just in time. As Mouse put his foot on the lowest step and hoisted himself in, his left hand hurting, its bells rang again. Reka was right behind him. They stood in the packed aisle, both panting. It was so crowded, no one would be able to see the Welrod beside his leg. Mouse felt the sweat run down his sides under his coat. He wiped his face and looked the length of the tram. Mouse gave each head in the aisle and each one in a seat the up and down. The two of them might not be together. They might be smart enough for that.

But Reka found them on her side. She nudged Mouse's arm and twitched her head to point the way, then held up five fingers. Mouse counted the rows from where they were, five, but saw only an old couple, so he counted five from the front of the car and saw Annje first then Johannes beside her. They weren't so smart after all.

A Dutchman was suddenly in Mouse's face. He held up a pad of tickets and asked his Dutch question again. Reka rescued him with a couple of coins she pressed into the conductor's palm, and the old man tore tickets off his pad and handed them over.

They couldn't stay much longer like this. Someone would notice the Welrod, even in this crush.

The conductor squeezed by as he retraced his steps after making the trip through the tram collecting tickets. The tram began to slow, its brakes noisy, and beyond the conductor Mouse saw Johannes, then Annje, stand and push toward the front. Annje and Johannes got off at the front, Mouse and Reka stepping off the back. Johannes held Annje's arm, and they slowly walked up the street, Annje limping. Her legs were not back yet.

As they walked, Mouse shrugged his arms out of his coat, switching the Welrod from one hand to the other as he did. He folded the coat overtop the Welrod, which he held in both hands. They followed Johannes and Annje, keeping close—forty, fifty feet, no more—as they turned left at a corner and walked alongside a canal. This street was busier, so that Mouse's shoulders brushed strangers constantly, and there was a steady stream of bicycles on the cobbles.

Ten minutes walking, fifteen, and then Reka whispered, "Politie." He knew what she meant—a cop by any name was still a cop. Ahead of Johannes and Annje and across the street was a policeman, dressed in the same blue jacket as those who had marched the Jews to the theater. Johannes guided Annje by the arm toward the cop, angled off the curb and onto the street, and stopped to wait for a break in the bicycle traffic. They were going to spill.

He had only a heartbeat to decide. Reka whispered a single word, *"schiet,"* which was Dutch, but this word was also easy to understand in the moment. But shoot who? He had never shot a cop and he wasn't about to start. Nothing good ever came from killing a cop. Then he saw that the Dutch policeman had no gun, which made the decision even easier.

Reka lifted the coat from his hands, and Mouse stepped off the curb and into the street, raised the gun, good right hand holding the grip, the weaker left under the barrel, and pulled the trigger. The soft *phfft* sound was loud in Mouse's ears, but only a few Dutch nearby turned their heads. The slug caught Johannes high on the back, not a lung shot but maybe enough to kill him after a few days lingering. It shoved him into a bicycle, sending it and its rider clattering to the cobbles.

Mouse kept walking while his fingers worked the Welrod's clumsy action. "Hurry," Reka said in English. He was. Twist, pull, push, twist, and the empty cartridge case clinked to the street. Annje stared at Johannes and the wet circle on his back as he lay there in the street. Then she looked up and saw them. She was just twenty feet away, an easy shot, but a bicycle cut between them, another and another, and all Mouse could do was watch while Annje bent down and pulled something from Johannes's hand. She limped to the curb, pushed open a store door, and disappeared inside.

Mouse dropped the Welrod to his side again and, walking as quickly as he could without breaking into a trot, made it to the curb. There was the young Dutch cop, still not sure what had happened, but he made to stand in the way, so Mouse hit him against the temple with the barrel of the heavy gun. The cop went down, blood on his face, and the plugs around started screaming. Mouse stepped over the cop and shoved open the door of the store, feeling Reka's shoulder brushing against his arm. A bell above the door tinkled.

It was a bookstore, old books by the smell, and that made him think of Little Man's office back of Ratner's. Four or five plugs in the store, all women but one, stared.

*"Waar is ze heen gegaan,"* Reka asked them. Mouse closed the door and the bell jingled again.

None of the Dutch answered. Mouse walked for the rear of the store, down aisles past shelves of books that rose a good dozen feet, which reminded him of Manhattan streets, dim and cool. From the darkness ahead came the sound of books falling to the floor and a creak of hinges that needed oil. He followed the sound through a half-open door. The room was dim, lit only by a small window set high. Something moved in the shadows and a gunshot filled the space and the pressure beat on his eardrums and a slug smacked into the frame of the door.

Mouse didn't duck, didn't hesitate, but raised the Welrod and aimed where the bright muzzle flash still burned the back of his eyes. *Phfft,* went the pistol, and someone moaned, then the sound of something falling, not books this time.

Twist, pull, push, twist. He led with the Welrod, stepped deeper into the room, and saw Annje crumpled against the wall. The Luger was on the floor, and he pushed it away with his foot.

"Is she dead?" Reka asked from behind his shoulder.

Mouse bent down. She wasn't. The .32 slug from the Welrod had punched a hole in her arm. Annje was alive, breathing hard, and in the light from the window, he saw her eyes. Wild-like, hating him. Fuck her.

Mouse stood up and pointed the Welrod, sure this time he could put a slug in a woman because he wasn't going to listen to any crying. But Reka put a hand on the Welrod's thick barrel.

"No," she said.

He got ready to argue with her, even though he could hear a whistle from the street coming through the bookstore and back to this room.

She was going to let Annje be. But when she took the gun from his hands, she put it on Annje herself.

"*Reka, nee,*" Annje said, a palm up against Reka. "*Reka, het spijt me.*" Even though he didn't understand the words, Annje was begging. He'd heard begging before.

Cold, she was so cold, Mouse thought as he watched Reka instead of the girl on the floor. Her face was cold, a dropper's face, and Mouse saw in it no pity, not a pinch of it.

But the Welrod wavered. Reka asked, "How do I do it?" and her voice sounded like a girl's for the very first time, high and with a quiver. "I don't know how to do it." The Welrod sniffed for the floor now.

"Give me the gun," he said and held out his hand.

"No," and she raised the Welrod again at Annje. "Just tell me what to do. You've done this, you know what to do."

"*Het spijt me, Reka, het spijt me,*" said Annje.

"Leonard, please," Reka said. She begged too, it sounded to him. "Tell me. Or I can't—"

"You just do it," he whispered. "You don't close your eyes and you just do it." He moved to stand beside her so their shoulders almost touched.

"Leonard—"

"You'll think about it later, Reka, don't worry. But now, now you don't."

He heard a sigh and the Welrod went *phfft* and Annje's head recoiled and she slumped to the side. That hot smell again, like in Richie's car. Reka didn't drop the gun, but only looked at it as if it were a snake or spider she'd picked up by mistake. He'd done that his first time, too.

But she surprised him. "How do you shoot again?" she asked, her voice flat. Cold, cold, cold.

"She's dead," he answered. The star of blood on the wall behind Annje's head was plain proof of that.

Mouse reached inside his coat, ripped open the lining, and freed a twenty-pound note. He folded the note, squatted down, and shoved it in the dead girl's mouth. Half showed, like a cigarette the way it dangled from her lips. He found the Luger on the floor and slipped it into the pocket of his coat.

Mouse took the Welrod from Reka; she gave it up easily. The bell at the front of the store jingled finally, and in the gloom he picked out another door at the back of the room, beyond the dead girl.

He touched Reka's shoulder and as she leaned into him, Mouse put his arm around her waist and pulled her to that door.


P reuss turned off the ignition and the BMW stuttered to quiet. Krempel got out the passenger side, the thick-necked Kripo Munkhart climbed from the back seat.

When Giskes had reached him by messenger, he had been at a pitiful *Aktion* near Sarphatipark, a pathetic eighty-seven Jews. The message had been cryptic, but he'd raced here in the BMW, leaving de Groot to finish things.

COME IMMEDIATELY NO. 483 HERENGRACHT—GISKES

Preuss stood beside the car, looked at the half-dozen blue-jackets holding arms out whenever a Dutchman came near. There was a wide pond of still-wet blood on the cobblestones, and when he moved around the front of the car, he saw another on the concrete walk, this one smaller. But no bodies.

He had parked behind Giskes's gray Kübelwagen, directly opposite a shop with a sign saying BOEKHANDELAAR DE VRIES. A Dutch policeman stood in front of the shop. Preuss brushed by him and inside, and as he pushed open the door, a bell chimed. Four Dutch, three of them women, stood against a high shelf of books, a policeman talking to them and writing in a notebook.

Preuss followed the sounds coming from the rear of the shop, and found Giskes in a small room at its end.

"Preuss," Giskes said pleasantly as he stood up from his crouch beside a dead woman slumped against the wall. Her dress had ridden up above her knees. Giskes was in uniform again, but the two men with him were turned out in suits and well-shined shoes.

"Do you recognize her?" Giskes asked. Preuss looked at her face. The light from the open door was bright, but it still took him a moment because of the blood.

"Visser." Preuss couldn't keep the bitterness from his voice. So much for his informer.

"Good news," Giskes said.

"Good?" The headache was trying to beat its way through his temples.

"It means that our friends are still in Amsterdam," Giskes answered. The Abwehr man paused, wiped one hand with the other as he came closer. "And I know where they are."

Preuss looked from the girl Visser to Giskes, trying to think through the pounding. He had missed something.

"They shot a friend of hers, too," Giskes said. "The police found him in the street, badly wounded, but before they took him to hospital, I spoke to him." Giskes paused again, drawing it out.

"Where are they?" Preuss asked, detesting Giskes for his dramatics.

"They're in a house on Utrechtsedwarsstraat. Less than a kilometer from here."

"How did you know—" Preuss began.

"How did I hear of this? I have men in the Amsterdam police, too, Preuss, just like you. Anything that involves a gun, I hear about."

Preuss nodded. "Yes, of course you do," he said.

"Witnesses said it was very quiet, this gun that shot the one in the street, and your girl too, I'd wager," said Giskes. "It didn't sound at all like a gun, in fact. More like *shuu*." Giskes made a sound like a quickly passing car. "It was a silenced pistol. Only the SOE makes guns like that. These are our commandos, Jews or not. Absolutely no question. And we have them." He was grinning, like a cat carrying a rabbit in her mouth.

"But I thought you might shed light on one mystery," Giskes went on. And he squatted beside the dead Visser woman and pointed with a thin finger. "See that in her mouth?"

It looked like a rolled cigarette. Odd. Giskes gently tugged it from the dead girl's lips, unfolded it, and handed it to Preuss. It was a banknote. Giskes already knows that, he's pulled it out and returned it to her mouth. He enjoys these lessons.

"It's English," said Giskes. Preuss could see that. The blue and white banknote showed "£20" in the bottom corner on the left, and the word "England" in the script across the top.

"What does this mean?" asked Giskes. "Joop had one on him, too, remember? It's a message, of course. But of what? I thought it might be Jewish, something I don't know. A tradition of theirs?"

Preuss shook his head and that made the hurt worse. "No, I've never heard of such a thing." He looked at the banknote again and shrugged. "I have no idea." But he put the note in his tunic breast pocket.

Giskes stood up. "No matter. We have them now. Let's pay a visit." Giskes's grin was broader than ever.

R eka led the way, Mouse behind her, Kagen and Rachael after him, Schaap last. They'd stuffed everything in four cloth-covered satchels they'd found in Henrik's house, split the loads of Stens and revolvers and ammunition among them, but even so, his bag was heavy. His right shoulder ached—he couldn't carry the satchel for more than a moment in his left hand.

Henrik and his wife they'd left in the back room of the house, bound with strips of cloth, more cloth stuffed in their mouths. They couldn't take them along, not in the daylight an hour before sundown. And Reka had refused to let anyone pop the two, saying she owed Henrik something for hiding her in his shop all these months. They knew nothing of where they were going in any case, she said. And the Gestapo will do more harm to them than we ever would. She'd sold him on it, but Mouse thought she really wanted them to live because so little time had passed since she'd popped Annje.

No one stopped them on their walk to the street with the strange name—Wijttenbachstraat—where Rachael went to the same red door as four days before and talked to the same old man who came out onto the stoop. She and the old man talked . . . one minute, two . . . but finally she waved them up the steps and into the narrow hallway just inside the door.

When Mouse stepped out of the day and into the dim house, he'd given Rachael the up and down, and she'd told him that Mr. Dijkstra, the old man, was happy to help them for his friends, the Ikkersheims. Mouse put the two and two together and figured out that Ikkersheim was the name of Rachael's best of friends, Vreesje, before she had married her brother.

The old man lived alone and showed them to a third-floor attic. A glassed window in the ceiling tilted up and gave them a way out over the roof if they needed it. He brought them cheese and boiled eggs and bread and beer, and showed them the bathroom with running water, hot even, and a tub.

Mouse claimed first for the bath. He washed, he shaved with a sharp razor the old man brought up, and when he was done, standing in front of the mirror, the glass hazed over from the steam, he looked like he should look. He rubbed a hand over his cheeks, feeling how smooth they were again. He'd never gone this long between shaves.

"I saved you some cheese and an egg," Reka said when he sat down beside her. She reached out and touched his shaved cheek. "How pink," she said, and he felt embarrassed. "I think they call you 'Mouse' because of this, Leonard," she said. "Pink, like a mouse's ears." Her voice was soft, the touch of her fingers on his cheek even softer, but her ice-pond eyes were odd.

But before he could say anything back, she stood, her hands on the back of her dress, up high at her neck, unbuttoning the top button as she disappeared into the hallway. Toward the bath. Mouse chewed the thick slice of cheese and cracked open the boiled egg. The beer was flat but made him feel fat and happy.

By the time Reka, fresh from the bath, sat down beside him with her back to the wall like him, it was full dark through the window in the ceiling and the window that looked down to the street. There were no curtains in the attic, so they couldn't light a lamp. She was next to him, invisible in the darkness. All that told him she was there was her smell, not just soap, but her. Like the smell of Rachael there in the Morris that time on the way to Biggleswade, but better.

"Do you want to talk about it?" he asked. She said nothing, smelling good but that was all.

Mouse remembered his first pop. Twelve years ago, December, it snowed all day that day, the chink who dared to make a play for Little Man's action. He remembered how he had felt that first time, you didn't forget, ever, that first one. The second and third, well, those you might be able to forget. But the first, no. He'd thrown up after and had to listen to Mendy, who had showed him the ropes, laugh about that for days, though he found out later it was almost usual. But what he remembered most was the way the chink's mouth made that perfect "O" when he'd pointed the .38, and the way the snow caught on the chink's eyelashes, and how the seconds didn't stop, like he thought they might, but sped up so that it was all over and done before he knew he'd pulled on the .38's trigger.

Reka slid closer and slowly laid her head in his lap. Mouse didn't know what to do. No girl had ever done that. Awkwardly, he put a hand on her shoulder.

And from the train station a couple blocks away came a short whistle. Reka's hand trembled on his leg and he took hold of hers with his left, gently because it still hurt. The train whistled once more, and Reka's hand tightened on his but he chewed his lip against the pain. Under his other hand he felt her shoulder start to shake.

"It's gonna be okay," he said quietly while he touched her dark hair with the fingers of his right hand. "Don't worry, it's gonna be fine." Mouse pulled his coat from the floor next to him and covered Reka with it, money and all.

But it wasn't her soft crying or her shaking, trembling hand that worried Mouse. She'd not said the Shema, the prayer she'd said every night he'd known her. And here it was the Sabbath and everything.

N othing," Giskes said. "Not a thing but those two. And one dead. Shit."

Preuss leaned against the hood of the BMW. As he smoked the Nil, his only satisfaction was that Giskes had come up as empty-handed as he had two nights before. He wasn't the only one these Jews eluded.

They had stormed the house with a dozen men, but it was empty except for an old woman—who screamed in Dutch about how she was going to kill her husband for fucking that *boer*—and the husband, dead, it seemed, from choking on the cloth stuffed into his mouth to keep him quiet. Henrik Keuning, they guessed.

Preuss looked at his watch; nearly half-past seven. Vienna would be dark by now. Marta would be home. No, she would be out. It was Saturday, he'd forgotten it was Saturday—she'd be with friends.

"They're clever," Giskes said. "Always one step in front of us. This isn't usual, is it? They have some brains. Balls, too, I think." Giskes paused, pulled off his cap, brushed back his gray hair.

He nodded. Giskes's words were heresy, but he had to agree.

Preuss thought then about the stories he'd heard of how partisans in Yugoslavia collected German ears and wore them on strings around their necks. Of other stories, too, ones that swore the screaming from Prinz-Albrechtstrasse could be heard through its thick, gray walls. He felt nauseous, and the sudden, clammy fear made his heart pound, as if someone were knocking on the hood of the BMW with the flat of a hand.

He massaged his temples to make the pain go away.

# *Sixteen*

They spent the day cleaning weapons in that third-floor attic. Those guns that still had the Cosmoline coating they wiped with rags soaked in a pan of boiling water brought up from the kitchen. Reka and Rachael loaded magazines, Schaap and Kagen pulled the Stens into pieces and wrapped each in cloth. Mouse took care of the revolvers himself. It was mindless work, which suited him. Every minute he looked at his watch was one closer to midnight, when it would be the day they'd walk to the station and get on the train that would take them to Westerbork.

Mouse was used to waiting, but not like this. This was one long drawn-out wait, like a pop that had no end. Jobs back home, a day or two, three or four at the most, to watch and figure out the bum's moves, that was how he knew waiting.

He wondered if that meant he was afraid. He wasn't sure. He'd never been scared as a dropper, but this, well, this was different. If things went wrong here, he couldn't just hoof it to a waiting car. The memory of Bergson's photograph, the black smoke above trees, came to him. Smoke.

The only thing that pushed away the photograph was looking across the room at Reka. He watched her, stealing a glance here, another there. She had paper in her lap and a pencil in her hand. Writing something. She caught him looking and half-turned away.

Reka had slept against him through the night. Once, when he had dozed off too, he had dreamed of his muter's kitchen, and Reka was there talking to the old woman across the oilskin-covered table as if they'd known each other all their lives, as if she had grown up just around the corner and Mouse had brought her home to meet Ruth Weiss.

He couldn't stop thinking of her and how her hand felt in his and how he had touched her hair while she slept and how she smelled fresh out of the bath. Or how she'd looked there in the back room of the bookstore with the begging Annje.

"Leonard," said Reka, who was suddenly kneeling in front of him. This was wrong, this daydreaming. This could get him killed.

She held a piece of paper in one hand and a pencil in the other. "The old man found these for me," Reka said. "I . . . ," she started, but couldn't finish.

"What you been writing over there?" he asked.

Her glance rested on his, slid away, came back again. "Not writing. Drawing." And she held up the brown pencil.

He was slow sometimes, Mouse knew, but he figured this out. "You painting again, Reka?" he asked her. She looked up and this time didn't look away.

"No. No paints. See, just a pencil," and she twirled the pencil a bit. She smiled one of the smiles that made her pretty and even laughed a little laugh that he'd never heard. It sounded so good.

"Can I look?" He held out his hand.

She gave him the paper, and for a moment Mouse thought she was going to leave, but she just moved to sit, her legs under her, the hem of her plain dress covering her knees.

It was good, the drawing. Mouse knew what he looked like—he'd spent enough time staring into mirrors—and the likeness was good. She had drawn him with a strong chin, and caught him with a look as if he was paying attention to something in his hands. But as he looked more at the drawing, he saw she had drawn him sad. In the eyes and around the mouth, the drawing was sad. Did he look like that, did he really?

"I like it," he said, glancing over the edge of the paper and into her eyes. "A lot. Thanks."

"You're welcome," she said, not able to look at him again. Mouse reminded himself that she was just twenty, only a girl. He'd embarrassed her. "Can I have it back?" she said, still not meeting his eyes. "It's not finished."

"Thank you, Reka," Mouse said, and he gave her back the drawing and leaned to her and kissed her soft on the cheek and while kissing her, smelled her soap smell. For that moment, he forgot all about smoke.

Mr. Weiss," said Rachael. She fooled with the crucifix, no longer around her neck but in her hands.

"Yeah?" Mouse said, putting down the Webley and the cartridge he'd been ready to shove into its cylinder. She sat down beside him, making sure her dress didn't climb. Leaning against the wall, she crossed her legs at the ankles and put the crucifix on the floor between them. Mouse looked over toward Reka, but she was sleeping there in the corner, curled up with her head on her arms.

"I need your coat," Rachael said, and she pulled thread and needle and a yellow, six-pointed star from the pocket at the front of her dress.

He reached for the coat, lumpy with the British banknotes, and gave it to her. She laid it across her lap and began sewing the star to the coat. She'd made the stars, one for each of the five of them, from a yellow sheet the old man brought them. The *Jood* was drawn with ink and a narrow brush.

"We won't have a chance to talk once we're on the train," Rachael said as her fingers moved and the needle went back and forth through the cloth of the coat. Like when she'd stitched up his hand, only faster.

"Yeah," Mouse said.

She looked up from the star and her sewing. "I wanted to thank you," she said. "For what you've done."

He didn't say anything because he didn't know how to answer. Taking thanks for what he'd thought when he'd climbed out of the Lysander felt wrong.

Rachael brushed her blond hair off her check and he remembered the drive up to Biggleswade that first time. Her eyes flicked to the star, then back to him. "You're such a funny man, Mr. Weiss." She took in a breath. "That night, on the polder, behind the Irishman's aircraft."

Whatever he said would be wrong, whether he admitted what she suspected or lied about what he'd planned to do, and so he kept quiet.

"I had the feeling that night that you meant to do something with that pistol of yours," Rachael said.

There, it was out. She knew. He met her gaze.

"Something in the way you looked at me."

Keep your mouth shut, Mouse, he told himself. Breathe a word and this will come apart. He knew that.

"But I was wrong," she said. Kagen walked past just then, coming from the bathroom down the hall, and she fell silent. There was a bit of blood on his neck where he'd nicked himself shaving. Rachael hadn't told him, Mouse knew. She may have been wise to him, but not sure enough to tell her man.

"That night, I thought you would shoot me, but now I know I was wrong. You've done so much for us. For me. Vreesje will live because of you, I know she will."

She sewed another stitch before looking up again. "But I was right about one thing. Remember the kitchen at Argyle Street? When you asked me why I loved Paul?" Her voice dropped to just above a whisper. "I was right then. You're not nearly as black-and-white as you think, Mr. Weiss. Or as I thought."

He dared one word, which felt right as soon as he'd said it. "Thanks."

"I'm sorry, Mr. Weiss," she said, back to the star and her needle and thread. "I know what you've sacrificed for this." She paused, looked up, and he wondered again if she could see inside his head, or maybe through the lining of the coat she held. "And I'm sorry for the thoughts I had. You being a gangster, like Paul said. Not to be trusted." She pulled one last time on the thread, tied a quick knot, bit it off near the coat's cloth, and patted the star. "There, finished." She handed him the coat.

"Thanks."

"Now we're all . . . yids, aren't we, Mr. Weiss?" Rachael smiled. "I know more than one Jew now, don't I?" She smiled still.

She stood up, her knees popping softly, and she smoothed her dress over her hips and walked across the attic to Kagen. Mouse glanced down and saw the crucifix still on the floor. He thought for a minute to pick it up and call to her, but he didn't. He might not be smart like Lansky, Mouse thought, but he was smart enough.

As he fingered the crucifix, Mouse raised his head to rest it against the wall and noticed Reka looking his way. He wondered how long she'd been awake and how much she'd heard.

Preuss glanced again at the sheet of notebook paper, its white marred by three specks he thought might be blood. The Gestapo armed with the steel rod had gotten the names on it from the Dutchman Joop today.

| | |
|---|---|
| ~~Annje~~ | (K?) Schaap |
| ~~Martin Visser~~ | Koster |
| Kagen | ~~Keuning~~ |
| Groeneweg | Dekker |
| Rachael | Mouse |
| | Vreesje |

Hours before, Preuss had scratched out "Annje" and "Martin Visser," the informer and her brother, the one with the hole in his head that his lie had put in hospital, and "Keuning," too. All dead.

He picked up the thick stack of file cards and flipped through them. He had no idea Amsterdam had once held so many Jews named Dekker or Schaap or Koster. Department C had pulled cards from its index for everyone with a last name left on Joop's list. But not a "Kagen" or "Groene-weg" or "Mouse" or "Vreesje" in the deck.

He glanced at one card, another, a third. Each was stamped ASSIGNED LABOR in blue ink, with a handwritten date beside the stamp. "13.8.42" the first card read, "19.11.42" the second, "28.1.43" on the third. East, East, and East again.

At least today's *Aktion* had been productive. Two hundred eighty-two culled this morning from the Jodenbreestraat, the Jewish quarter. The Dutch police preferred to let the Jews be on Sundays—they wanted to rest on their own Sabbath, if not on that of the Jews—but he had his train tomorrow and space unfilled. At least he had not had to argue with de Groot for once. De Groot's demeanor had improved since that night on the Lindenstraat. The ass-stinging had done some good, Preuss thought.

The telephone's bell rang and he picked up the heavy black handset. "Preuss here."

"Any luck with your cards?" It was Giskes.

"No," he said, still glancing at names and turning cards. "It's hopeless. We don't know if the names are even real." There was a long quiet on the line. "Giskes, are you there?" He flipped a card and the name "Dekker, Jacob" appeared. ASSIGNED LABOR, the stamped ink on the card read. Preuss turned Jacob Dekker facedown.

"Yes. Just thinking," Giskes said.

"Did your men find anything on the docks?" Preuss asked, cradling the handset between ear and shoulder so he could pull a Nil from the tin on the desk and light the cigarette while he continued to look through the cards.

"Hundreds of boats, that's what they found," Giskes said. "We'd have better luck locking up the port than finding one boat in that pigpile."

Preuss said nothing. Even Naumann couldn't do that. "The man you found yesterday?"

"Dead. Before he died in hospital, all he gave my man was his name. Johannes Koster." Preuss glanced at the list on his desk. He picked up a pencil and scratched through the name "Koster" on the stained paper.

"So . . . ," said Preuss.

"So we have nothing."

And the name jumped off the card in his hand. "Dekker, Reka." Reka, the name Visser had said. "31 Botticellistraat, Oud Zuid, Amsterdam." Stamped across the top of the card was ASSIGNED LABOR with the date penned in: "9.7.42." Handwritten under that, as on nearly all the other cards of deported Jews, was another date and notation: "13.7.42   Dulag. Westerbork." Preuss counted months backward; this one had gone to Westerbork nine months ago. Outside of a miracle, she had long gone East, disappeared in a pit, or if he had heard the rumors right, become smoke and a handful of ash.

But if this Reka Dekker was dead, who was the one on his list? He penciled in "Reka" after the name "Dekker" on Joop's confessional, put a "J" for Jew at its end.

"Let me get back to you," Preuss said. "I may have something." And with half an ear hearing Giskes's voice still chattering, he set the handset in its cradle.

It was nearly eight when the telephone woke Preuss from his dream of Marta and Vienna sunshine. He lifted his head from his desk, his neck in a pinch, reached for the handset, and heard the line crackle and pop. Long distance.

"Herr Hauptsturmführer?" the voice asked. "This is Brumm, Obersturmführer Gemmeker's adjutant? From Westerbork. About your call earlier . . ."

"Yes? What have you got?" Preuss asked, rubbing the final bit of sleep from his eyes.

"The Jewess Dekker," the man's voice said. "Reka Dekker."

"Yes, where is she? Is she still in the camp, or gone East?"

A long pause. "It seems neither, Hauptsturmführer. We went through the lists and found her name on the November tenth transport of last year. A mother and father, too. Jacob and Meijer." Dekker, Jacob. He'd seen that card.

"Yes?" Preuss rubbed his neck. He wasn't clear what Brumm was saying.

"She was not aboard the transport," Brumm said. His words came fast.

"We have her as missing. An escape the night of November ninth. According to our records, we notified the Marechaussee the next day, and filed a card with the Sicherheitsdienst and the Kriminalpolizei in The Hague the day after that. Of course, we deported ten others when she went missing . . ."

And finally he understood. This Reka Dekker had run from Westerbork. "But what became of her? Why wasn't I informed? She's from Amsterdam. She might have returned here, correct?"

The static on the line grew louder, then faded. "You must take that up with The Hague, Hauptsturmführer."

"But you were the ones who let her escape," Preuss said into the phone, now wide awake and feeling the headache coming. Incompetence, or something else. The man spoke in a slurry. Perhaps he was drunk.

"I am sorry, Hauptsturmführer. But she is, after all, just one—"

Preuss was about to yell into the handset but instead took a deep breath. That would get him nowhere. "Thank you, Brumm. Thank the Obersturmführer as well. But I must have her identity card. This is urgent, very urgent. Have someone drive it here immediately."

"Hauptsturmführer?" The stupid man didn't understand.

"I need her photograph from the card you made at your Dulag. Our cards here don't include photographs." Preuss tried to keep his voice level and calm.

"The Hague has such cards, does it not? The Hague is so much closer."

Preuss was not about to ask Zoepf for this woman's photograph, nor beg Naumann for help in getting it, not when he'd hidden so much from them both already. "The photograph you took would be that much newer, would it not?"

"Yes, I suppose it would," Brumm said. "But we're shorthanded here, I don't know if we can spare—"

"Untersturmführer," Preuss said, putting ice in his voice, standing up to talk louder into the telephone. "This is not just another Jew. Unless you want to answer to Brigadeführer Naumann about why you refused to cooperate with the Department of Jewish Affairs, I suggest that you—"

"Yes, yes, Herr Hauptsturmführer," the voice said so quickly. "I'll have my man on a motorcycle within the quarter hour. To your office on the—"

"Euterpestraat," Preuss said. "Thank you for your assistance." And without waiting for the man to answer or say anything that would just make his headache all the more painful, he slammed the handset in its cradle.

With a photograph, he could post reward leaflets. And with reward leaflets, someone would betray this Reka Dekker, her comrades, and their scheme to steal Jews.

The attic was long dark, but Mouse knew Reka was awake because she shifted on the floor beside him. They'd taken a spot farthest from the window.

"When this is over, will you go home?" she asked. In the close black of their place on the floor, her mouth seemed very near his ear. It was a question a woman would ask, Mouse thought, to avoid the other things they could have talked about: Annje or what they'd do tomorrow or what the hell he'd been thinking when he pointed that big pistol at her near the Lysander.

But he answered anyway. "Yeah, I'll go home. I have to take care of my muter. And I have a job."

"Your gangster job," she said.

"Yeah, my gangster job." He wanted to tell Reka what he'd been set to do on that field, in case she'd heard what Rachael had whispered to him earlier, but in this dark place and with the train tomorrow, he couldn't make himself tell her. He was selfish, he knew, because if he blurted it out she'd turn on him in a heartbeat and he didn't want that, now of all times.

"Come," Reka whispered, and he felt her hand first on his arm, then on his face. "Hold me. Please."

He put his arms around her and she laid her head on his chest. A few streets away, toward the Muiderpoort station, a long, low whistle blew.

Krempel stood at the door of his office, empty-handed.

"Nothing at Botticellistraat, Hauptsturmführer. We tossed the house at Number Thirty-one, and the ones on both sides of it, as you ordered. Nothing. No one's seen these Dekkers for months."

Preuss nodded, and fingered the photograph delivered just minutes before by the rain-soaked SS man on a motorcycle from Westerbork. He knew this one.

It had taken a moment to pull her face from his memory, probably because the photograph didn't show the scar. But this was the woman who had stared at him across the burning wreckage of the Renault more than three weeks ago, the same he'd seen just days before with that pink-cheeked man on the Plantage Middenlaan. He looked at the face again, the plain face and dark hair and darker eyes, the thin mouth and the Jewish nose.

There was not enough time to duplicate the photograph and print it on leaflets before his transport left the next morning. Less than eleven hours now.

"Anything else tonight, Hauptsturmführer?"

Preuss picked up the deck of cards from Department C and flipped through them. Three hundred easily. He'd been through them once already.

"Hauptsturmführer?" asked Krempel. Preuss looked up. The Scharführer's eyes were underlined by blue-black shadows.

"Find some coffee for yourself, and bring me a cup, too." Krempel nodded and turned to leave. "And keep the men nearby. I may need them." Preuss went back to the cards.

Hours later, on his third trip through the deck, he found what he had missed: "Schaap, Vreesje (born Ikkersheim)." This Vreesje on Joop's list had not been a last name, as he'd assumed. She was married, the card said, and not to a Jew, but to a gentile, which was why he wasn't in the yid index. "Schaap, Kristiaan," of the Dutch army, her card said, was her husband. He had disappeared in May of '40, said the card. Or fled, Preuss thought, looking at the list again and seeing the "K" with the question mark beside "Schaap." Some of the Dutch ran away to continue their war from England.

But this Vreesje Schaap/Ikkersheim or whatever she called herself had been deported. Like the other Jewess, this one's card said ASSIGNED LABOR and a date, "17.2.43," and under that, "22.2.43   Dulag. Westerbork." Two months there. She might still be in the camp.

The card held an address of this Schaap/Ikkersheim: "365 Wijtten-bachstraat, Watergraafsmeer, Amsterdam." That was close to the Muider-poort station, he knew. Within sight, in fact.

The pieces stacked one atop another in his head. The nearness of this house to the station where he loaded trains. The husband who just might have fled to England. And England, home of the SOE, and if Giskes was right, the home of the aircraft that had brought these Jews. This Vreesje could just as well have escaped Westerbork, like his Dekker. He put Dekker's photograph in his tunic pocket.

There wasn't time to call Westerbork and roust Brumm. The drunk would take hours with news whether this Vreesje was still in the camp. "Go get the men," he said to Krempel, who had sat in the chair across his desk all this time, dozing when it suited him. "I'm coming too. You'll drive my car." Preuss glanced at his watch. Only seven hours until the next transport pulled out of Muiderpoort.

W ake up," someone was telling her, and Reka came awake in one long moment in the dark. "I heard something," Leonard said, and put a revolver in her hands. She listened, and through the open-glassed window in the ceiling came the faint sound of a slamming door and boots on the cobblestones three floors below. Leonard got to his feet and padded to the window that looked onto Wijttenbachstraat. He held the gun that had killed Annje.

"Schaap, wake up," his silhouette hissed. With a grunt, Kristiaan rolled off his blankets and picked up his machine pistol. Reka joined them to look into the street. The moonlight was enough to show a canvas-covered truck and a smaller shape, a car. Two men stood at the car while others, Germans from the cut of their helmets, dropped from the truck.

"They're looking for us," Leonard said.

"Us, no. They don't know we're here, they can't know," Kristiaan said.

"Where's Paul?" Rachael asked behind her. "He's not here," she called from the place where she and Kagen had fallen asleep.

"Shut up," Leonard said.

Reka heard it too. The flat pounding of hands on a door. Were the Germans down on the doorstep? *Aufmachen, Schnell!"* she heard, remembering when Germans with the police had told them to open the door of their house on Botticellistraat.

"Can you see anything?" Kristiaan asked from the window.

But instead of answering, Reka padded in bare feet to the door leading to the corridor, the corridor to the stairs, the stairs to the stoop. She opened the door a crack to listen for the echo of German fists, but all she heard was a small creak on the floor out there in the dark.

Leonard gently tugged on her arm and pulled her back to take her place. She found the hammer of her revolver and clicked it back. But this was wrong. Germans were never quiet, they didn't care whom they woke. From the street, more voices, one now in Dutch, a woman's voice. The door opened wider and Leonard had his silenced pistol raised high, arm extended, the pistol pointed at the head of the shadow coming through the doorway. Then she recognized its shape.

"Leonard, don't!" she shouted, and there was a bang, not a shot, but of something slamming against the open door, and then a scuffling in the dark.

The flare of a match and behind it she saw Kristiaan's face, and in its feeble light there were Leonard and Kagen, tangled at the open door, their arms and legs mixed, Leonard's pistol resting against the wall. Leonard was the first to push himself from the snarl and the match guttered out. In the sudden dark all she heard was loud panting. Kristiaan struck another and she saw Kagen's face, his patch missing and so showing the dark black hole where his eye should be.

"What the fuck are you doin', sneaking around in the middle of the night?" shouted Leonard. He'd stood up. "If she hadn't yelled, you'd be stiff now." The match went out.

"Yes, what were you doing out there?" asked Kristiaan. He scratched another match and Reka saw Rachael kneeling beside Kagen. She had found his patch, and he slipped its strap over his head and tugged the black cloth into place.

His answer was to reach inside his coat and toss a small stack of pasteboard on the floor. Leonard worked his lighter and the yellow flame danced, but she reached them first. In the background she heard German voices just below their window.

She picked up one of the pasteboard cards. It was an identity card, with a large letter "J" stamped on two corners.

"Where did you get these?" she asked in a whisper. The card's photograph was of a young woman with dark hair. She turned the card over to squint at the name: "Heijmans, Clara."

"We needed identity cards, didn't we?" Kagen asked. He still sat on the floor, his back to the door. Through the doorway she saw the dim shape of Mr. Dijkstra, his white shirt untucked from his trousers.

"They're outside, next door," said the old man. His voice was steady. "What shall we do?" Kristiaan stepped past her, through the door to the corridor, and down the stairs. More German voices with words she recognized. "*Aufmachen, Polizei!*" she heard through the hammering of her heart.

She picked up another card. When she held this one to Leonard's flame, the photograph showed a middle-aged man with short hair and spectacles: "Kogel, Ruben." Another card: "van Os, Abraham." Another: "Roodveldt, Jacob." The last, a second dark-haired woman: "van der Staal, Judith." All Jews.

"We need the cards, yes?" Kagen said quietly from the floor.

"Where did you get them, Paul?" It was Rachael who asked this time. "Paul, where did you get these cards?" Reka looked up from the photographs that looked so little like any of them. Everyone had eyes for Kagen, but Rachael most of all. Her mouth was set in a thin line and she stared at her lover.

"I did what I had to do," he said roughly. "The Jodenbreestraat," he said. "We walked near it when we scouted the route to Muiderpoort."

The Jewish quarter, two kilometers to the west, not far from the Joodsche Schouwburg. Footsteps on the stairs again, but it was only the old man Dijkstra.

"They're leaving. He says they're leaving." Reka listened for a moment, and as her reward, heard boots on cobbles again, a door slam, another, and the catch of a motor starting. She sucked in a long breath and as she exhaled, the flame on Leonard's lighter wavered.

"I don't get it," Leonard said. She looked at him. But he does understand, she thought. She heard another motor whine, catch, and rumble, this one deeper.

"Did you hammer on their doors and show your pistol?" Reka asked Kagen. "Use your German? Did you hurt them?" The light wasn't enough to show more than the outline of his face.

"What happens to them?" Rachael asked quietly, and she pulled her hand away from Kagen's arm.

Rachael must know what kind of man he was. "No identity card means no ration card," Reka answered. "When they run out of food, they'll have to go to the police and say they've lost theirs. They'll be deported on the next transport. Without a card, they can't risk the street. If they're stopped for any reason . . . deported." Deported, deported, deported, Reka sang to herself, like Martin had singsonged, Jew-Jew-Jew.

There was a long silence in the attic, but Kagen broke it himself.

"They'd end up there in any case, wouldn't they?"

That was when Rachael slapped Paul Kagen with her open hand, and the surprised *Duitser* knocked his head against the door. Leonard's lighter snapped shut and the flame went with it.

# PART THREE

# *The Train*

... and he made ready his chariot,
and took his people with him ...

EXODUS 14:6

# Seventeen

## Monday: April 26, 1943

Mouse looked down at the star on his coat. He wondered how Rachael had found thread strong enough to hold it to the cloth. Its weight was like iron, heavy as a manhole cover in a Brooklyn street.

Ten minutes ago he had been all Mouse Weiss. But now he wasn't only himself. Now he was like a penny out of one of those hundreds Little Man had stacked on the scratched table in Bergson's office, just one tiny slice out of something huge. It was a feeling he'd had only twice. The first time had been in synagogue staring out at his foter, who wore that one good suit always and that one homburg with the worn brim, Mouse saying his memorized Hebrew in front of everyone. The other, that had been when the old man gave it up in the hospital, burned bad and too tired to live.

If the stars marked Jews, putting it on made you one, Mouse thought. When he touched the star, it made him remember his muter saying Shema, like Reka had. "Hear, Israel, the Lord is our God, the Lord is

One." And he heard it in his muter's voice as it had been twenty years before and in Reka's as it was now.

He looked up and out this alley's mouth and at the Jews walking by, an endless river of stars. A man in a gray pin-striped suit with a star, a woman in a green and white dress with a star, another woman, thin like a rail and with a star, holding the hand of a little dark-haired girl in a blue coat the same color as the Dutch cops' jackets.

Mouse nodded to Kagen, who hated him with that one eye, and Rachael and finally Schaap, and each of them walked quickly down the alley and slipped into the march for Muiderpoort station. Reka grabbed his hand, hers not shaking now, and took it, and him, into the world of Jews.

A gain," Preuss said. And the Gestapo, he of the too-small ears, swung the steel rod against the little one's arm, that arm stretched out across the tabletop, tied there with thin rope because his hands were too swollen now to fit into the manacles. Joop van der Werf didn't scream; he had run out of them, it seemed. He only moaned and his head slumped on his chest.

"Wake him," Preuss said.

"Hauptsturmführer," the Gestapo man began, but Preuss cut him off.

"Do it," he said. He hated this room, its whitewashed walls that had a sheen here and there of something once wet, now dried.

"He's not going to talk, I'm telling you," said Giskes from his place in the corner.

Preuss looked at the Abwehr officer. Even Giskes thought it futile. But Preuss would not accept it.

His train for Westerbork was to depart at ten o'clock and here it was eight. He'd already telephoned de Groot and told him to manage the march from the Joodsche Schouwburg to Muiderpoort station, and oversee the loading, tasks the detective-sergeant had not before done on his own. Giskes's men waited at Muiderpoort, and his own Kripo and SS were at the Schouwburg to add numbers to those guarding the march. He'd twisted arms and gotten the Marechaussee to double their usual number as security for the transport. He had everything in place except the one piece he needed. The Jews, were they after today's train? Next week's? Next month's?

Everything else had come to nothing. The raid on Wijttenbachstraat, the home once of Vreesje Schaap or Vreesje Ikkersheim, had been a waste of time. He'd watched from the street while Krempel pounded on the door of No. 365, but the Scharführer only managed to scare the wits out of a Dutch mother and her three small children. He'd sent Krempel to rummage through the house on the right, No. 367 and that on the left, No. 363, but the SS found no Jew named Vreesje, no Jews at all, in fact.

But the little Dutchman here knew something, Preuss was sure of it.

"Again," he told the Gestapo once the man had splashed water over van der Werf's head. The tabletop was stained dark from water or blood, Preuss wasn't sure where one ended and the other started.

Joop moaned, said something in a voice so low Preuss didn't catch it. He moved closer to the man at the table.

"What was that, Joop? Tell me what you said."

He whimpered this time, and now Preuss heard the words. *"Mijn lief, Annje."*

Preuss almost missed the name. "My love, Annje," the Dutchman said. Annje. Of course. And he had an idea. Preuss turned to Giskes. "Where's the girl, Visser, the one at the bookshop?"

"The dead one? How should I know? Your Dutch policemen took her away, I suppose. To their morgue, or they've put her in the ground by now." And a look came to Giskes's face, one Preuss hadn't seen before: appreciation. "Your talent's wasted on the Israelites, Preuss," Giskes said, giving a grin. "I never would have thought of this."

Preuss turned to the Gestapo. "Scharführer Krempel is upstairs, in my office. Tell him to fetch the dead girl Annje Visser from the Politie. Their morgue's in that building on Marnixstraat, tell him."

"A dead girl, Hauptsturmführer?"

"If she's in the morgue, of course she's dead, you idiot. Just find Krempel and tell him exactly what I said. The girl from the bookshop, he'll know. And he's to hurry." The man, though mystified, nodded and did as told. He left the door open, thank God, and a whiff of fresh air came into the tiny room. Preuss lit a Nil to chase the stink and looked at his watch: 8:10.

"What if he doesn't know?" Giskes asked.

"He knows," Preuss said, staring at the little one, who again had fallen unconscious. "He's taking this for a reason. Perhaps because of her." He smoked another centimeter of the cigarette. "He knows."

They waited, Preuss smoking one cigarette after another, but Krempel was efficient, and he'd gone through just five Nils by the time the Scharführer backed into the room, holding legs. The Gestapo had shoulders. Between them was a body wrapped in a white drape.

"Put her in that chair," he told them, and though both gave him a look—a look he remembered seeing when he'd told new men in Russia what they were to do at the pits—they did what they were told, and arranged her body in the chair across the table from the Dutchman. "Uncover her face," he said, and Krempel tugged aside the drape until she was revealed.

The Politie's morgue must have refrigeration or ice, Preuss thought. Her skin had gone a gray, true, and she smelled, just the slightest, but she was recognizable. He unbuttoned his tunic breast pocket, retrieved the British banknote, folded it tight into a starved *papirosi*, those disgusting things Naumann smoked. He pried open her lips and stuck the banknote between her teeth.

"Untie him now, and wake him," he said, and stepped back to stay out of the water that the Gestapo threw over the Dutchman, and to admire his work. She would do. His watch read 9:20.

When Joop first opened his eyes and saw the girl sitting in the chair, her head back and her eyes wide, his face showed a split second of joy. But that look vanished as he looked another second and noticed the gray flesh and her stillness and the dark dried blood over her eye and the folded paper between her lips. His face drained its color and his eyes went wide and wider, and he choked out a sob that filled the small room.

He had been right—Visser and Joop had been lovers.

And although Preuss had no experience in this talking, he found the words came easily when he focused on his watch and kept the ideas of Yugoslavia and the Berlin cellars at Prinz-Albrechtstrasse fresh in his head.

"This is what your friends have done," he said in Dutch, dropping his final cigarette to the concrete and pressing it under a boot. He moved to stand beside the dead Visser, but not so close that he blocked the Dutchman's view. "They were the ones who did this. With a pistol that shoots silently. That's what witnesses say. Dutch witnesses." He touched the girl's temple with one finger.

If the man's hands had not been ruined—monstrous things swollen half again in size—and one arm black from the rod, Preuss was sure Joop would have covered his eyes. But all he could do was close those eyes.

"Look at her," Preuss ordered roughly. "The paper in her mouth, do you see that?" Joop opened his eyes and stared at the dead girl. His breath was fast and shallow, and another sob escaped his lips. "It's an English twenty-pound note, folded and stuck in her mouth. It's a sign, we know that. And I think you know who it's from." Preuss pulled the banknote from the bitch's mouth, unfolded it, and leaned across the table to hold it in front of Joop's eyes, like a wall so he could see only the money.

"Oh, Annje," Joop whispered. "God forgive me."

"Which God, Joop?" Preuss asked. Joop didn't answer. "You know who did this, don't you?" he asked. Joop stared at the banknote.

The little man sobbed, lowered his head to the tabletop. For a moment, Preuss thought he'd fainted, or worse. But Joop raised his head again. And at 9:35—Preuss glanced at his watch just then—the Dutchman looked only at the wide-eyed girl, and began to tell them everything he knew.

She held Leonard's hand as they walked down Dapperstraat, turned left onto Domselaerstraat, and made for the Muiderpoort station a hundred meters away. She'd come this way before, holding Mama's hand. But that had been years and years and years ago.

The sun was shining, like it had been that July day. The policemen along the column were the same, and the brick and glass station looked the same, and inside the station there would be a line of passenger wagons, just the same. She didn't know if she could do this again.

The only difference was that Leonard held her hand this time, not Mama, and his didn't tremble.

The Jews were not as quiet as he had thought that day in front of the theater. They talked among themselves in low voices. A mother in front of them, arms angled out to hold the hands of her two sons, neither more than six, spoke softly as they both tried to splash in puddles at the gutter. A young husband, not much beyond a boy, chatted to his even younger wife behind them. An old man with stiff gray hair to their left talked to himself.

It was early, but some Dutch stood on the walk or at the edge of the street opposite and watched while the parade crawled by. Mouse made himself look in the eyes of some of those Dutch, still feeling the weight of the yellow star on his coat. Only one or two dared to look back. Most watched but didn't, like the look he'd given bums on Manhattan streets.

The train station grew bigger and bigger. The cops in their blue and the fewer Germans in gray closed on the head of the column fifty yards away to thread them through a wide needle and into the station. The bag in his right got heavier and heavier.

Reka's hand trembled for the first time as they stepped through the entrance, armed Germans with rifles and submachine guns on both sides of the doorway. "Oh, Leonard," she whispered. The sound of feet on the tiled floor of the station almost drowned out her words. "I don't know if I can do this." She almost stopped, and to get her moving again, he let go of her hand and grabbed her bag.

"Yes you can. You have to."

The seven brown and green passenger cars along the platform looked old and tired, and as they walked up, the cops, still in blue but with loops of gold braid on one jacket shoulder, separated the thick line into groups for each car. Rachael and Schaap and Kagen were sent to the second car. Mouse and Reka stopped at the front step of the third.

"*Zet die koffer neer,*" a cop there said, and Mouse didn't understand. "*Zet er één neer, je hebt er teveel,*" the cop said again, and this time pointed to the bags Mouse held in each hand. "*Je kunt er maar één meenemen, stomme jood,*" and the cop yanked on one of the handles, pulled the bag from his hand, and surprised by its weight, dropped it to the platform. "*Neem jij stenen mee naar het oosten of zo, jood?*" the cop asked.

Mouse looked at Reka, but she couldn't tell him anything. The blue and white striped cloth satchel on the ground was his bag. He wanted to reach and pick it up—that was a fourth of their guns there—but the cop shoved him toward the steps and Reka was right behind him, pushing at him.

"Don't look back, don't look," she said in a nearly silent voice.

The car had tiny compartments on both sides of a narrow hallway. He took the first he found on the right, sat on the wooden seat polished by asses over years, and Reka slid next to him and pushed him right up against the window. She squeezed his hand, which told him to keep quiet. It was good advice. Six others crammed into the compartment, the old man, the young married couple, and the mother with the two little boys. The mother's eyes were big as cups, but the little boys, they chattered as if they were going places.

The guns, he couldn't stop thinking about the guns in that bag on the platform. Not just because they'd lost them, but what would happen when the cops or the Germans opened the bag and rooted down through the clothes on top and discovered the three Webleys, the .38 he'd used to shoot the fat man on Canal, and the Sten in its pieces.

It was hot in the compartment, but the window wouldn't slide down, and Mouse scratched at the collar of his white cotton shirt. They waited. And waited. And even though he didn't like the idea of where this train was going, he wanted it to start moving.

Muiderpoort sighed with its Jews. Preuss stepped into the station, glanced at the line of green and tan passenger wagons along the nearest platform, and knew at a glance that the loading was almost done.

A small gathering of Jews straggled near the second-to-last wagon. The sighs came from the other wagons, already jammed full of Hebrews.

"Looks like we scared them off," Giskes said beside him.

Preuss took in the station—he'd had it cleared of regular travelers this once, worried that the Jews who had guns would hide in the crowds of real Dutch—and saw Marechaussee trolling the platform, Giskes's uniformed men thick here at the entrance, and his Kripo and SS huddled near the locomotive. The black engine creaked and groaned as it built steam. De Groot stood beside the locomotive with a dozen of his policemen, his bulk impossible to miss.

"No, they're here. The little one said so," Preuss said. He and Giskes, with Krempel hard on their heels, walked across the tile floor of the station as the Marechaussee slammed doors to button up the first five wagons: 9:55, that's what his watch read.

"Go find the stationmaster and bring him here," he told Krempel, and pointed to the far side of the station. "Drag him by his collar if you have to. Hurry." Krempel gave him a nod and jogged off.

"They're not going to take the train," Giskes said, waving a hand at the armed men in the station. "It's suicide. They've seen that and given up, I tell you."

"They're already on board, didn't you hear what the Dutchman said?" Preuss asked, striding for the train. They were buried in the body of his Jews, five or six or seven roaches hiding among five hundred. He might not know when or where the boats would come to take off the Jews— Joop had holes in his memory, caused by the steel rod, no doubt—but he knew this.

With Giskes still at his side, Preuss went to the nearest Marechaussee, a weathered man with leather skin and bad, black teeth, who stood at the foot of the rear steps to the second-to-last wagon. Its windows were up and shut, no way for the Jews to jump out, but he was close enough to see them through the glass. A man, his fedora pushed back off his forehead, looked down with an empty expression from the nearest window.

"Almost all counted, sir," said the Marechaussee. "We'll have the count for you in—"

"Unload them," Preuss interrupted.

"What?" the Marechaussee asked.

Was everyone deaf, or only thick?

"You heard me, stop the loading. And those already aboard, pull them out and stand them along the train."

"Sir, I—"

"Drag them out of the damned wagons, can't you hear!" Preuss shouted. "Every last damn one, do you understand?" The ache behind his eyes stabbed sharper and he rubbed the bridge of his nose. He turned and called out in his loudest voice to make it echo up the platform, first in Dutch, then repeated for his own. "Out, drag them out. Every one of them, clear this train." Three Marechaussee edged for this wagon and shouted into it for everyone to come out. A few others up the platform had heard and were doing the same. Doors slammed open here and there.

"What are you doing?" asked Giskes.

Preuss pressed a thumb against one temple. "I know one of them, one of these Jews that the little one named and said was on this train. I've seen her, I know her. I'm going to look at every yid face on this train until I find her. Then I'll put a bullet in her neck."

"Hauptsturmführer," another voice said behind him. He turned to Krempel, who had Kuiper, the Dutch stationmaster, by the sleeve.

"I'm emptying this train, Kuiper. It's not leaving yet," Preuss said.

"Hauptsturmführer," said Kuiper, and his Adam's apple jigged up and down as he swallowed hard. "The schedule—"

"Fuck the schedule," Preuss said. "There are partisans on this train, and I want it emptied."

"Hauptsturmführer, the schedule is already in tatters, what with you clearing the station for your Jews, and . . . you said just an hour." The man swallowed again as if that would make him braver. "If this train doesn't leave now, I'll have to put it on a siding in the yard. God knows when I'll have another open slot." Kuiper swallowed again. "I'll have to telephone The Hague and notify your department there, and they will have to request another schedule, and . . ."

His words faded for Preuss. Zoepf would know, and he'd ask questions. Why did you stop this train when you haven't met this month's quota? And his secret, his and Giskes's, would be out.

"Preuss, send them on," said Giskes, who was quick enough to think those same thoughts.

"Shut up," Preuss snapped.

"Look here, I am an Oberstleutnant—"

Preuss stopped him. "Yes, yes, I know that. But I'm the expert here. Let me do my work, and you do yours."

They locked eyes for a moment, and Giskes nodded, his face pinched even more than usual. Then, without a word, Giskes turned on his heel and made for the entrance where his men waited. Preuss watched him, but Giskes and his men didn't leave the station. He wants his part of the prize, Preuss knew, enough not to give up yet.

The Jews came out of the passenger wagons, a small stream of them from this one, only a trickle from the wagons between here and the locomotive.

"I need just a few minutes," he said to Kuiper finally. "Long enough to get them out of the wagons, take a look at them on the platform, and back aboard. Fifteen minutes. You can stretch your schedule that far without calling The Hague, can't you?" Kuiper thought about it, his Adam's apple slithering in his throat while he did.

"Fifteen minutes, no more. Or I'll cancel this train. I'm sorry, Hauptsturmführer, but I have schedules to meet—"

"Yes, fifteen minutes," Preuss said, and walked as quickly as he could toward the locomotive and de Groot's big shape. Krempel tagged along.

Preuss pulled the photograph of the Jewess Dekker from his tunic breast pocket, fingered it for a moment, and looked at it one last time as he made the last steps to de Groot.

"I'm looking for this one," he said, handing de Groot the photograph. "She's on the train, she and the others." The detective-sergeant looked at the photograph and nodded.

"I've seen her somewhere," he said.

"On the Plantage Middenlaan, six days ago, in front of the Joodsche Schouwburg," said Preuss. "She was with the man who struck your policeman. You saw them both." De Groot nodded again. "This is the one Visser talked about the night she disappeared. Her name is Dekker, Reka Dekker. She means to take a train from us."

"Us" was all de Groot said as he continued to stare at the photograph.

"Start from the first wagon and work back. I'll begin at the rear and work forward," said Preuss. "Look into each face, Detective-Sergeant. She's here."

"Yes."

"They have weapons, and they'll use them," he said. "But I want these Jews in one piece. You understand?"

"Yes," de Groot said one more time, nodding yet again. He looked up and their eyes met for a moment. "Yes, of course."

Preuss looked at his watch. Three minutes of the fifteen Kuiper promised him were gone. He turned and walked to the rear of the train, past the Jews spilling out from the wagons in full flood now under the shouts and blows of the Marechaussee.

With Krempel and the borrowed Kripo and SS around him like a shield, their machine pistols aimed at the Jews lined along the train, he began to look into each and every face.

M ouse had almost dozed off in the warm compartment, one shoulder pressed against the window, the other against Reka. Shouts and whistles came through the window to wake him, and at the same moment a Dutch cop was at the door to the compartment and yelling. The cop's face was furious. Grabbing hold of the mother's jacket, the cop yanked her out of the compartment and down the hall toward the steps that led back to the platform, her two boys wailing after her.

"They found the bag," he said to Reka, but she reached a hand behind her for him to grab, and gripped it, telling him to shut up. They wormed out of the compartment and into the hall, someone pushing at his back, and then they were down the steps.

He saw his bag when they stood on the platform again, backs to the car, second row. The striped cloth was almost hidden under a small hill of suitcases and parcels and boxes and a haversack or two. The old man stood in front of Reka, the boys with their mother in front of Mouse. Reka held his hand, the left one, and clutched it so tight that tears came to his eyes. Not a word, not a sound, she was saying.

And there was the fat Dutch dick in his blue suit. His fedora was pushed back a bit and showed his blond hair, which was damp, maybe sweat. He'd been there when the old woman got her head smashed Tuesday, the same one talking to the rat Annje behind the glass of the café Wednesday. And he was looking for a face.

Reka jabbed him in the ribs and when he looked her way, to his left, he took in the scene. Everybody had been pulled off the train, and cops and Germans stood in a long file along the platform. There. That's who she wanted him to see. Far down the way, near the back of the train almost, he saw a man in gray uniform. Tall but not too tall. It was too far to see a face, but he could see a small black spot on the gray jacket's sleeve. The SD was searching for a face in the crowd of people, too.

The dick, though, he was their problem now. He had something in his hand—it looked like a photograph—that he glanced at it every few moments as he checked the crowd.

Mouse put his right hand inside his coat and laid fingers on the Welrod. There was a cartridge in the chamber, but with what it took to work the action, he'd get off another one or two, no more, before the cops and Germans heard the *phfft* for what it was, or saw theirs dropping. He and Reka would be gunned down in a hail of slugs.

The dick looked at the photograph and Mouse saw him look past the old man and put eyes to Reka. His expression didn't change, but Mouse could tell he knew. And Reka could, too. Her fingers squeezed the blood from his.

Hand tight on the butt of the Welrod, Mouse waited for the dick to point a finger at her. But he did nothing except steal a glance to his right, down the line of the train.

*"Nee, jij bent het niet, he meisje?"* was all he said, again looking at Reka, and then he was gone. In a second he had moved on to the next car. And in another five minutes, the shouting started and the whistles blew and they were all shoved back aboard the train.

She's not here," de Groot said. The detective-sergeant handed him the photograph.

The pain in Preuss's forehead was like a vise made of red-hot iron.

Kuiper coughed beside him. "The fifteen minutes are long past, Hauptsturmführer. Either the train leaves now, this very second, or I must call The Hague for other arrangements," the stationmaster said. He was not swallowing now, Preuss noticed. He's worked up his courage and is drawing the line.

Preuss turned to de Groot. "I'm going to accompany the transport to Westerbork." Perhaps the Jews mean to climb aboard along the way, in a stretch where the train slows, he thought; it's possible that their plans had changed after the little one was captured. "Load your men in the last wagon, then find the commander of the Marechaussee guard. I want his men on the steps of every wagon this time, tell him that."

Krempel's orders next. "Go fetch the Oberstleutnant, tell him we're leaving, and ask him to join me in the locomotive. Then board the guard's wagon, you and your men." The Scharführer saluted and hustled across the empty Muiderpoort toward the entrance, where Giskes still lingered.

Back to de Groot. "Drive my car to Westerbork. You know the way?" The Dutchman's fat face was calm and he nodded, compliant.

Preuss stalked down the platform, past heaps of bags abandoned by the Jews. Reaching the panting black locomotive, he grabbed hold of its short ladder and hoisted himself into the cab, surprising the greasy old engineer and the coal-sooted fireman and the dirty boy who must be the brakeman. He was riding with them to Westerbork, he told the engineer.

"Don't slow this train for anything. All the way to Westerbork, go as fast as the throttle allows. Slow down for anything—a cart across the track, a railyard, a woman whose shoe is wedged into a switch—and you and your children will disappear like summer fog."

The engineer barely nodded, too scared for anything more, and put his hand on the throttle. Giskes climbed into the locomotive, and the train slowly pulled out of the station. Preuss tucked the photograph back in his tunic pocket as the locomotive dragged the wagons out from under the shelter of the station and into the beginnings of a light rain.

The train rocked around the curve, steel squealing on steel. She held on to Leonard's hand, the one with the two raw lines, the stitched wounds that looked like rails.

Amersfoort, Harderwijk, Zwolle, and Meppel had rushed behind them each in turn, and Hoogeveen was the next stop from the signposts that had flashed by outside the window a moment ago. Hooghalen after that, then Westerbork. Another thirty minutes at this speed.

Her heart still hammered in her chest, but not so loud as on the platform or even after the locomotive had first blown its whistle and yanked the train out of Muiderpoort.

The Dutch policeman had stared in her eyes, but he had let her go. He'd done nothing, called no one, even though the pin-eyed Sicherheitsdienst was within shouting distance at the rear of the train. "No, you're not the one, are you, little girl?" was all he'd said.

The train's whistle blew again, two short blasts, as they raced over a crossing. She felt Leonard's shoulder against hers, his fingers around hers. She smelled the faint odor of his American cigarettes on his coat and it made her feel safe.

Reka put her free hand on her coat and felt the outline of the paper she'd carefully folded and placed within its inside pocket. She had not finished the sketch in the attic, but there was enough done to see the sadness she'd put on paper. His eyes, something about the way they went dark from their hazy gray. It was enough, she thought, that she even picked up a pencil. She'd not held pencil or brush since she was fifteen. Reka shut her eyes and remembered how Leonard had looked at the drawing.

Reka opened her eyes and glanced at him. He was unlike any man she'd met. Maybe all Americans were like this? Leonard was strong and willful and proud. He'd looked so fierce that night on the polder when she had thought he was about to pull the trigger of that gun of his.

Afraid, yes—who wouldn't be?—but ready to use it. I am sorry, Papa, Reka told herself, but Leonard would not have said the end was come when his name was called and gone to pack a bag. He would have fought back.

And because they sat close, like two lovers—Reka blushed just thinking that—and because she could pretend that the others packed in the compartment were only travelers, she leaned her head just the slightest toward him. This could have been a train to Brussels or perhaps Copenhagen, on holiday, with her lover next to her.

"Kiss me," she whispered to Leonard, not able to lift her head to look him in the eyes.

He put his hand on her face, his fingers near the scar, and turned her head toward him. She closed her eyes and Annje wasn't there for once and her heart thundered in her chest but not from fright. And Leonard kissed her, softly on the lips, his hand moving across her scar, a chill running down her arms, his hand finding a home at the back of her neck, and he pressed her to him. She opened her mouth to him, their tongues touched once, then again, an inner kiss, her head growing light as she kissed him back, hard and harder and hardest. Her leg trembled, and Leonard kissed her still.

Dully she heard someone in the compartment say, "*Mevrouw, dat is hier niet gepast. Mevrouw?*" the voice calling her a woman, a wife. She ignored it, feeling Leonard's lips against hers, smelling the American smell of him, feeling a warmth as Leonard gently put his other hand on her breast. "*Meneer? Er zitten hier kinderen.*" And the whistle sounded again and the steel wheels screeched and as the train rounded another curve too fast, gravity pulled them even closer.

Reka touched her tongue to Leonard's lips one last time, softly, and she pulled away.

She didn't look at his face, but instead at his hand, which had slipped from her breast and now lay in her lap, that hand scarred with two straight lines. She touched that hand with hers, and their fingers blended again.

Still refusing to look into his gray eyes, she said, "*Ik ben zo bang.*" Then again, now in English. "I'm so very afraid."

Leonard said nothing, just pulled his hand from hers and lifted her chin. He put a finger on her lips.

All the way to Hooghalen at fifty kilometers an hour, and not a sign of anyone but a handful of Dutch children along the tracks near Zwolle. The children waved as the locomotive flew by. He heard no gunshots and not a single Jew dropped out of the train or climbed aboard.

The little Dutchman had been wrong about the transport. Wrong about it all, perhaps.

The train slowly backed onto the spur that went the last five kilometers to Westerbork, and the wagons clanked over the switch. Fifteen minutes later, Preuss leaned out into the rain to look down the length of the train as the gate to Westerbork opened, letting the locomotive huff its wagons into the camp.

"See, nothing," Giskes said, his irritation unconcealed. "I told you, they've given up. We overestimated these people. They've run or gone to ground. Anyway, this is your last train, isn't it? Before Thursday, the date the little one gave you in the cellar."

Preuss pulled his last Nil from the tin, lit it, and blew the smoke out from under the locomotive's roof and into the rain. The engine wheezed to a stop, the tender bucking against the locomotive and making its floor slide under his boots. Preuss turned up the collar of his tunic—he'd not had time to grab an overcoat before rushing from the Euterpestraat—and stepped to the edge of the ladder that led to the ground.

"Where are you going?" asked Giskes.

"I'll be back. My Dutchman, the fat one in the blue suit, should be here with my car. Look for him. We'll drive together back to Amsterdam."

"I asked where you're going, Preuss."

He turned back to the older Abwehr officer. "To the commandant's office, that's where. I've never accompanied a transport and when he hears I've come—and he will—he'll wonder why. I have to give him a reason."

"Don't tell him anything, Preuss, or—" Giskes said.

"Or what? What if the Dutchman's right, and a train is stolen from

Westerbork? The commandant will wonder why I was here, why *we* were here," Preuss said. "He'll start asking questions or say something to The Hague and our secret will be out, my friend."

"These Jews are still in Amsterdam, I'm sure of it. Don't give anything away."

"Don't worry," Preuss said. The beginning of an idea was gathering in the corner of his brain. How to solve two problems with one solution.

He stepped down from the black beast and was wet within seconds.

The commandant's office was a ramshackle wood-sided building that needed new paint and a new roof. A square of canvas was nailed across the ridgepole. Beyond, a bit farther from the gate and this building, but still outside the high wire fence, was a large, single-story house with lamps lighting a score of windows. Most likely the commandant's residence.

Preuss shoved open the door to the office and stamped the water off his clothing. A young man, German, SS but not SD, looked up from behind a slanting desk. One leg of it was shorter.

"Untersturmführer Brumm," Preuss said.

"Yes," the man said, his eyes glancing at the pips and bars on Preuss's tunic collar tab. "Hauptsturmführer, what can I do for you?" Brumm stole a look at the SD stitched to his elbow.

"Preuss, Amt IV B-4, Amsterdam," Preuss said. "We talked on the phone, Untersturmführer. I've come on the transport just now. I want to speak with your commandant."

"Hauptsturmführer?" The man was as thick in person as on the telephone.

"Find him for me."

Brumm tried to smile, but it came out lopsided. He licked his thick lips. Preuss leaned toward the desk. He thought he smelled alcohol.

"I'm sorry Hauptsturmführer, but the Obersturmführer is unavailable. He's with Schlesinger, the camp's Jew administrator, to give him the numbers for the selection." Brumm must be an accomplished drinker; he didn't sound much drunk.

Preuss took pause. His train was safe and sound, his responsibilities ended. He'd seen his transport to the camp personally, and technically the Jews were no longer his problem. And naturally, there was politics to play. If he banged his hand on the desk and demanded Gemmeker, he would be doing more than putting himself in this man's memory. He'd be stepping on toes. Naumann's toes, actually, because Gemmeker and this Brumm and this camp, they were the Brigadeführer's.

He would have to very careful what he said. Enough to justify his ride here with the transport, but not too much that he gave anything away. The earlier idea took shape.

"Tomorrow's transport to . . ." and he couldn't remember its destination, but realized it didn't matter. "What time does the transport leave?"

"Eleven, always eleven in the morning, Herr Hauptsturmführer."

"And guards? How many?"

"I don't understand."

"How many guards on the transport, Untersturmführer? Is that too difficult?" His voice was loud in the small office, but he couldn't help it. The headache was on him.

"Some of the Dutch police, as always, Hauptsturmführer. A few Orpo. I don't know the exact number. Perhaps a dozen, give or take."

"And these guards. They're on each wagon?" Preuss asked, remembering how he had made the Marechaussee huddle on the wet steps of each wagon today.

"No, Hauptsturmführer. In the last wagon, that's how it's done. The Jews are locked into their wagons, naturally." Brumm smiled his off-center smile again. "We've been doing this for some time, you know."

"Yes, yes, of course."

"Is there a problem?" Brumm asked.

It was the question Preuss had expected, and dreaded. He was ready with his answer but didn't get the chance. Obersturmführer Gemmeker, his hair damp even under his peaked cap, stomped into the office. Preuss turned to see the commandant of Westerbork, older, in his middle thirties, a tall man too handsome for his own good, with wide lips and blond hair and a face so oval it might have been drawn by a draftsman.

"What do you want?" Gemmeker asked, looking at him from under meticulously trimmed eyebrows.

———

Preuss was only one rank above him, but to Gemmeker, the Hauptsturmführer played as if he was a dozen. Like God or the Reichsführer himself, coming into his camp and telling him what to do.

He was an arrogant prick, Gemmeker decided, because he wore the SD stitched to his sleeve and had been with the Einsatzgruppen back in the old days. This Preuss was a friend of Naumann's, that new SD ass in The Hague, Gemmeker had heard, so he must be handled with the utmost care and correctness. But he'd also heard the rumors of how Preuss had had a breakdown in '42, been shipped home to hospital to calm his nerves, and landed in Amsterdam last fall only thanks to his friend the Brigadeführer.

The pipsqueak, Gemmeker thought, looking at Preuss. One of the killers who thought himself special for shoving Ost yids into pits and getting his hands dirty. What is he trying to pull over my eyes?

"I've heard talk in Amsterdam," Preuss said, and Gemmeker leaned back in this chair—he'd invited the Hauptsturmführer into his own office rather than remain in Brumm's damp outer room—and lit an Eckstein No. 5. He offered Preuss one of the short, thick cigarettes from the green package, but the Hauptsturmführer looked down his nose as he took one—not good enough, perhaps.

"Yes?" Gemmeker asked. Preuss said nothing. "Hauptsturmführer, this is the busiest day of the week for us, what with the selection before dark and the preparations for the train—" Gemmeker began. Preuss waved him off, the smoke from the No. 5 curling into a tight spiral.

"I realize that, Obersturmführer." Gemmeker didn't miss the emphasis on his rank. "I'll get to the point."

Good, thought Gemmeker. He thought for a moment about Elisabeth, who waited for him next door. No damp floors or wet roofs in the villa, he thought, especially not in the bedroom.

"I've heard talk in Amsterdam about schemes," said Preuss.

"Yes?" Gemmeker smoked more of the Eckstein. He thought of Elisabeth's mouth, how it curled at the corners when she lay on his bed.

"I believe the Resistance means to steal Jews from us," Preuss said. His eyes, too small by one or two sizes, looked hard and eager.

"You're joking."

"No, I'm afraid not. I came on my transport today to ensure its arrival. Yours tomorrow may be at risk as well."

"What talk?" Gemmeker asked. But Preuss's eyes got shifty. Gemmeker stole a look at the clock on the wall beside the door, over Preuss's shoulder. Three. Elisabeth waited for him right this minute.

"The Abwehr," Preuss said. "They've heard rumors."

"The Abwehr?"

"Something the Abwehr heard from its informers in the Resistance, I've been told. By an Oberstleutnant of the Abwehr. Giskes is his name." Preuss said the Oberst's name clearly and slowly. His eyes stayed shifty.

"Rumors? That's all? Rumors?"

"No, not only rumors. You heard about the incident in Belgium last week?" Preuss asked. "Jews escaped a transport from the camp at Mechelen bound for the East." It was news to Gemmeker, but he nodded as if he knew all about it. "This could be like that, that's what the Abwehr say."

"I've been handling Jews here long before you came to Amsterdam, Hauptsturmführer," Gemmeker said. He stubbed the Eckstein into the porcelain ashtray on his desk. "I've never lost one from a train."

It wasn't his intention, but his words made Preuss angry, and for a second Gemmeker thought he would stand, but the Hauptsturmführer stayed in the chair and only rubbed his thumbs on his temples. Ash from his cigarette drifted to his tunic. An oaf, this one was. A postal clerk, that's what he'd heard Preuss had been before the war.

Preuss's voice came out of that small mouth like a snake, coiled and menacing. "If they take your train, Obersturmführer, because you didn't do anything about it, you'll wish you'd listened." That was a threat, clear and present.

Gemmeker leaned forward and put his arms on the desk. The clock behind Preuss read five past three. Elisabeth was not patient.

What kind of game was the postman playing? Warnings from the Abwehr of Jews escaping? Ridiculous. What did the Abwehr know of Jews?

That was Preuss's expertise, wasn't it? But he knew if he let this boor chatter on unchecked, Preuss would tell him what to do and how to do it in such excruciating detail that he would be here for hours. He knew the SD, little men made big by the black diamond. "I'll double the transport guards, how's that?"

"You should also post men in each of the wagons," Preuss said. He doesn't even know his ignorance, Gemmeker thought; he doesn't know the trains from here are of cattle wagons. There was no place for a guard, not unless he stood in the Jews' own shit. On top, perhaps, or perched on the footstep alongside, but what use that when the Jews were shoved inside and the latches thrown? But he nodded, watching the clock's hand click another minute.

"I'll have every piece of baggage searched, put two men in each wagon, guards in the locomotive, too. Will that suffice, do you think?" He tried to make his voice as fawning as his stomach allowed. Preuss finally nodded.

"You'll telephone me of anything unusual?" Preuss asked. Gemmeker nodded, wondering why the man cared. But anything to get this lout out of his office. The clock's hand ticked again.

And finally, finally, Preuss stood and they shook hands—Preuss gripped hard, as if that would tell him he was a man to be reckoned with—and the Hauptsturmführer left his office, tramped through the outer office, and the door slammed open and shut.

"Brumm!" Gemmeker called, and the wide face of Elisabeth's husband came to the door. "Did you hear that, Brumm?"

"The walls aren't any thicker today than yesterday, Obersturmführer," the young man said. He was half in the bottle already, and it wasn't even dinner.

Perhaps he knows about Elisabeth, Gemmeker thought, but like always, he dismissed the idea. He's too dull to know. Gemmeker watched the hand on the clock slip another minute.

"I don't know how we can do what you said, Herr Obersturmführer," said Brumm. "We haven't enough Marechaussee to double the guard. I'll have to call Groningen and ask the Orpo to send more than the five promised. And to search their baggage, we'll have to start that tonight, and we don't even have the selection. Schlesinger's slow in getting his list together, what with the extra this transport. Over two thousand this time."

Gemmeker stood from his chair, pushed the green package of Ecksteins into his trouser pocket. It was ten past three. He felt himself get hard at the thought of Elisabeth, waiting, he hoped, already in his bed.

"No, that's not necessary. I was humoring him. The cheek of that prick, telling us our business. He's cracked again, that's what it sounds like. No, we'll do what we always do—we haven't the men, like you said."

He made for the door. Get past the clock, he thought, and out of the office and into the villa fifty meters away.

"The selection, as I said, it's running behind," Brumm said.

The hand snicked off another minute. Damn. "The Jews that he brought just now," said Gemmeker. "They're in registration?"

"No, not yet, Obersturmführer. Still unloading."

Gemmeker thought for a moment, worrying that the time it took would mean another minute, and perhaps Elisabeth's impatience would win out and she'd slip off that French silk he'd found in Amsterdam last time, and tramp home through the rain and mud.

"Count the ones he brought today, subtract that from the number we're to ship tomorrow, and cut the selection there."

"I don't understand—"

"Put the Jews he brought today on the transport tomorrow, that's what I'm saying," and the clock did move again.

"That's very irregular—"

"I know, I know, but if we can't cut a corner or two, who can? One Jew's just like another, eh, Brumm?"

Brumm struggled with the idea. "What should we do with them tonight? If we don't assign them barracks, where will they sleep? And if we assign them places, but ship them tomorrow, we'll have to rearrange—"

Christ. Did he have to do everything? "Leave them out in the rain, I don't care. Have Pisk put his OD on them, I don't know."

"Obersturmführer?"

"Look, Brumm, just see to it. Yes?"

Again the thought that Brumm knew flicked through Gemmeker's head. Again he set it aside. He needed to get out of here. Now.

And he did, not even bothering to pull on his overcoat, just stepping into the rain. As soon as he'd walked around the corner of the wooden building, he started running like a boy for the villa, its lights golden in the cloud-made dusk.

# Eighteen

If Mouse were any wetter, he'd drown. Rain came down in pails and pots and buckets one after the other, and every time he breathed, it seemed he pulled in enough water to have to swallow or spit.

Reka leaned against him, asleep. Unbelievable. But the others, Rachael and Schaap and Kagen, were wide awake and hunkered under their coats in the heavy rain. Rachael was nearest to him. She'd put distance and her brother between herself and Kagen since the thing in the attic. And when she looked at Kagen, Mouse thought it was like that plug girl who'd stared at him after he'd popped the big man on Canal, scared enough to smile at what she saw.

He'd warned her, hadn't he, about Kagen? But she hadn't listened. Worse, it had turned out they didn't even need the identity cards—no Abraham van Os for him, Mouse thought—and the five Jews back in Amsterdam without theirs would be deported for no good reason. Because the cops had yanked them out of the train yesterday and left them here on the platform, the rain hard enough to soak in a couple minutes. Rather than shove them into the long frame building Reka said was registration, where they were to have their names taken down and pictures made for the camp identity cards, the Dutch cops left and were replaced by Ordnungsdienst, OD, Reka said—Jewish camp cops. The Jew cops— Jews, doing the fuckin' Germans' work—wore long brown overcoats and, under them, green overalls, and above their elbows, white armbands with the letters "O" and "D." The OD made a ring around the platform, shouted odd Dutch with an accent that sounded German. Reka translated for him and Kagen. They were to stay outside in the rain for the night, and in the morning they'd go on another train to continue their journey.

That solved one problem, but made another. They'd get on the train without having to sneak aboard, it seemed, but Schaap and Rachael went witless—how would they find their Vreesje now?

And the hours waiting had been miserable. Mouse had never spent a night outdoors, never, and he was pretty sure few others had, either. The old man who talked to himself coughed so loud Mouse thought he'd die in the rain, though he didn't. The young couple from the compartment were nearby too, the husband giving his wide-brimmed hat to his wife since hers was a little felt circle with a drooping wet feather. Squatting next to them was the skinny mother and the little dark-haired girl he'd seen from the alley. The mother had tucked her kid under the hem of her coat.

"Reka," he said, and gently shook her awake. "Time." She slumped away from him and rubbed the water from her eyes.

Mouse looked at the closest OD, ten yards away, his overcoat wrapped tight. The next was a good twenty yards farther, and in the dark all Mouse could see was a vague shape. He hoped that one's back was turned.

Reka and Rachael behind him, Schaap and Kagen behind them in case things went bad, Mouse stiffly stood and went to the OD. Reka'd said that most of the OD were *alte Lagerinsassen*—German Jews from when Westerbork was a refugee camp and had been filled with those who had escaped from the Reich. Mouse hoped so.

*"Ich möchte um einen Gefallen bitten,"* he said in German, and the OD's head moved. It was too dark to see much of a face.

"What do you want?" the man answered in German, his voice tired, like he'd been asked for favors over and over and over in his life here.

Mouse pulled out five of his last ten Chesterfields from a pocket, holding them under his hand, the back of his hand keeping them dry. He slowly raised his hand—the OD didn't have a gun but he had a wooden club half as long as a baseball bat—until the cigarettes were within smelling distance of the OD's nose.

"Five cigarettes. Deluxe tobacco."

"What do you want?" But the OD took a sniff.

"My friends, the two girls," Mouse said. "They want to go into the camp. They want to see someone they know before we take the train again."

"No one can leave the platform," the German yid said.

"They'll come back."

"I've heard that one."

"We're staying," Mouse said, turning to point to Kagen and Schaap. They'd decided they would have a better chance if only two left the platform, and Reka—she wouldn't say why—said she must go with Rachael. And it seemed to make sense to ask for the women, since they'd be less likely to try something, the OD would think.

"No one leaves."

Mouse touched the OD's hand with the one holding the cigarettes. "These five, and another five."

The OD said nothing for a moment, but looked to his right, toward the next cop. "What else?" he asked finally.

Mouse thought. The soaked coat was a weight on his shoulders, and not just because of the rain or even the yellow star. "Money. English pounds." Nothing from the OD. "A hundred pounds." Mouse did the arithmetic, remembering what Reka had said about how much pounds were worth. "A thousand guilders."

The OD took the five cigarettes from his hand and stuffed them in his overcoat. Mouse gave him his last five and stepped away into the dark, behind Schaap and Kagen.

"What are you doing, gangster?" Kagen asked. "Couldn't make it work?" Mouse thought Kagen might be reaching for his Webley. Start shooting here, and they'd be dead before they could get halfway to the gate or the wire fence. Even Mouse could see that.

"Getting them in the camp." Mouse reached into his coat. The lining was already ripped from when he'd torn it getting to the twenty-pound note he'd put in Annje's mouth. He fingered five of the notes, but changed his mind and pulled out ten. What did it matter, the money? His chance of seeing his bed in Brooklyn seemed so slim right then, it might as well be none.

The ten banknotes he pressed into the OD's hand. "Two hundred English pounds for my favor. That's two thousand guilders. Another two thousand when you let them back onto the platform."

"Maybe I'll have it all," the OD said, sly now.

Mouse leaned in until his face was just a few inches from the dark spot of the OD. "You don't want to do that." It sounded fiercer somehow in the German. *"Das machst du besser nicht."* No wonder the Jews jumped when the Germans yelled.

Maybe the yid hadn't been talked to like that, maybe he just was as scared as every other Jew, his overcoat and armband not enough to protect him, and he nodded. Reka and Rachael, the first giving him a good long look, the second a nod to say thanks, disappeared into the darkness.

D avid," Reka said to the back of the man with the short brown hair. She knew it was he before he turned, but still her heart was large in her chest.

The man looked up from his workbench, and in the early air of the electrician's workshop his breath rose in a small thunderstorm. At first, her brother looked little different. He still barely shaves, Reka thought. But the lines along his mouth and across his forehead were deeper than before, and his skin was parchment thin at his temples. He looked like an old man.

"David," she said again.

He said nothing. But his face changed as she watched, his brow furrowing and his eyes closing and his shoulders sagging. He stepped to her, embraced her so tightly she couldn't catch her breath, and he shook as he sobbed into her hair.

"Don't cry," she said, touching him on the back of the neck as he held her tight to him. "Don't cry."

I can't believe it," David said. "Reka . . . ," and he started to cry again, this time softer than before. She stood near the workbench, no one else in the shop except for Rachael, who was near the door. David sat on an upturned crate.

"Why did you come back?" He wiped his eyes with a dirty rag. "You got away."

Reka looked at him. There wasn't time to do more than simply say it. "We're here to steal the train from the SS. We have boats waiting in the Waddenzee to take us all to England."

His mouth open, David shook his head. "You're mad, little sister," he whispered finally.

"Mama and Papa are dead, David," Reka said. "They went to the East and the Germans murdered them there. That's what they do, the Germans. You know that now, don't you?"

"They can't kill us all," he said, still whispering.

"Yes they can, David. Every one of us who wear this," and she tapped the star that Rachael had stitched to her coat. "It's not just me. Others are helping," she said. "I have an American friend now, David. And Rachael." She nodded to the silent woman who waited near the door. "She's not even a Jew. Before the train reaches Groningen, we'll seize the locomotive. We'll run the train to the Waddenzee, where boats take us to England. It's not impossible."

"They'll kill you," he said. "And everyone on that train if you try to escape."

David hadn't changed in the five months since she'd fled Westerbork. Not one bit. "They'll kill us if we don't," Reka said. "The train is our chance, David. Come with us. Please."

"My name's not on the list . . . ," David started. "They lock everyone not on the list in the barracks, I can't get to the train."

"You must try, David. If you don't . . . please."

Her brother shook his head again. "You'll never get out of the train. They lock the wagons. You'll never get out. And you'll be—" He choked off the words and his tears came faster.

Reka looked again at her brother and changed her tack. "Please, David, help us. We need your help to do this."

But David's face was anything but brave. He still thought the Germans would let some live, and he was afraid he would not be one. David shook his head. "I can't."

Rachael was at her shoulder now. The woman was so quiet. "We don't have much time, Reka," Rachael said. Reka looked to the shop door. The darkness through it was beginning to lose its mystery. It would be dawn soon, and then Appel. They had to search more barracks for Vreesje, then be back to the platform before the camp was awake.

"David," she said one more time. He shook his head.

She was glad that moment that she'd not told Leonard her brother might still be here, afraid he would demand to come, and if David refused, that Leonard would drag him to the train. He'd be caught and end up like Mama and Papa, smoke. She'd been right, and it broke her heart.

All she could think to do was hold him. "I'm sorry, little sister," he said as his tears wet her cheek. "I'm so sorry." That was what Annje had said, Reka remembered, and look where it got her.


Rachael had more luck. When she shouted "Vreesje Ikkersheim?" and "Vreesje Schaap?" into the third dim barracks they'd come to after David's workshop, she got an answer from deep in the wide room with the stacked beds.

And a woman flew into Rachael's arms. Or Reka thought it a woman. She was thin, so thin Reka thought she might circle the woman's arm with her fingers. She'd been pretty once upon a time; the photograph

Kristiaan carried showed a pretty woman with short black hair, a narrow nose, and high cheeks she'd wished were hers. But in the feeble glow of the paraffin lamp near the barracks door, Vreesje was so thin that she looked like a child's stick drawing, lines for body and legs and arms, and an empty circle for a head.

"Vreesje, dear Vreesje," Rachael cried. And the stick woman, her thin dark hair almost hiding her face, wept too. Reka couldn't tell the words, not that she needed to hear.

But after a few moments she said the same thing that Rachael had in David's shop. "We don't have much time."

Rachael talked quickly and quietly to her sister-in-law, the tears not stopping. Reka caught a word or two, "Kristiaan," certainly, and "train." Vreesje looked confused, said something about her mama and papa and "Autje," who Reka remembered was this woman's younger brother. Rachael was shaking her head.

"Rachael, it's time, we have to—" Reka started.

And Rachael turned on her with a look of sudden hate, her mouth almost twisted, her blond hair flying as her head moved. But then it vanished as quickly as it came. She nodded, held a fistful of Vreesje's worn green dress, the woman had no coat, and whispering whispering whispering, used both talk and her grip to pull her out of the barracks.

As Reka stepped into the rain, she heard someone call "Vreesje!" behind her. But she didn't look back.


"Where are they?" Schaap asked for the hundredth time. Mouse shrugged, but didn't take his eyes off the spot between the two buildings where Reka and Rachael had disappeared two hours before. The sun would be up soon, the light was already gray. Five o'clock by his watch. The OD man was looking more nervous by the moment. This would queer soon if they didn't show.

A whistle blew, not something between a guy's lips but a train's whistle, and Mouse and all the others on the platform looked up the tracks toward the camp's gate, which swung open. In the distance, between the thin trees that crowded the rails, Mouse saw a black locomotive, smoke climbing out its stack, backing a long long string of cattle cars toward them. At this end was a passenger car, like the one they'd taken yesterday, brown and green. The cars made clanking noises, knocking against each other as they came nearer.

Mouse realized right away the problem, and it had nothing to do with Reka and Rachael not returned. This train was not like yesterday's, passenger cars with windows they could crawl through and jump to the ground when the locomotive slowed. The Germans would pack them into these slat-sided cattle cars. Once the doors slammed shut, they'd never get out. Not without tools.

Mouse looked again at the locomotive and the smoke rising above it. Smoke.

Before the passenger car reached the platform, Schaap grunted behind him. "There they are," he said in the low voice they'd used all night when speaking English.

Mouse put his back to the train and saw Reka and Rachael—and a woman so thin he thought she'd disappear if she turned sideways in the rain.

O bersturmführer Gemmeker hunched inside his overcoat and carefully stepped around a large puddle. Perhaps there was something to Preuss's warning.

He rarely came into the camp. He let the Jews run things, Schlesinger as Oberdienstleiter, Pisk as lord over the Ordnungsdienst, and stayed out of their way. It meant fewer Germans necessary, which The Hague liked. And kept German hands clean, which he liked. But he thought he'd better check on this transport personally.

The train was already backing into the camp, longer than usual. And he remembered what Brumm had said about two thousand heading East today. But it was just five A.M., his watch said, so they had six hours to pack them in.

He walked along the tracks, trying to stay on the gravel spread beside the ties so he wouldn't have to slop through the mud. There was the crowd of yids already on the platform. They looked drowned. Even those protected by hats had hair that hung down in strings from the rain. Gemmeker looked up—it would rain all day.

He stopped outside the ring of OD in their long brown overcoats and green overalls. No need to get too close; the light was enough now that he could see shapes from here.

"I've had these counted," Brumm was saying. "Five hundred, ninety-two. We're shipping exactly two thousand, one hundred today. I had Schlesinger stop the selection at one thousand, five hundred and eight from ours, as you ordered." Gemmeker nodded, trusting Brumm's numbers. The man was thick, but he kept good track of details.

Half into the platform's wet carpet of Jews, Gemmeker noticed movement. An OD man argued with another Jew. The OD turned his way and saw him, or Gemmeker assumed he did, because the OD quickly turned back to the Jew and raised his truncheon and landed a blow. The Jew staggered back, caught in the arms of another. Next the OD shoved a pair of women. A third stood off to the side, off the platform. That one was blond, which was different for the yids—probably peroxide, a way some Jews took to looking Aryan, not that it worked. The OD lashed out at her and knocked her to the mud.

Nothing unusual in any of this. Jews tried to get onto trains with family all the time, wanting to stay together.

"There's nothing to worry about. Add another Marechaussee or two to the guard detail if we have them. Just get this bunch on the train and out of here on time."

"Yes, Obersturmführer," Brumm said. He'd find Pisk, that ferret of a Jew who oversaw the OD, Gemmeker knew, and shout at him to get the Jews into the wagons and the wagons latched shut.

Gemmeker turned and walked back for the gate on the solid ground of the roadbed. Someone stealing a train. He laughed out loud, startling an OD who was shoving open the door to the closest wagon as the locomotive finished pushing the transport toward the platform and its five hundred and ninety-two yids.

L et them back in, all three of them," Mouse said to the OD.

"No, only two left. Two return. Not three. Two." The German Jew was stubborn. "The numbers must match."

Mouse edged closer. "I gave you two thousand guilders to let them out, I'll give you four thousand to let these three back to the platform." Mouse heard his voice get big, but he couldn't help it. Even with the low clouds and the rain, it was getting light. Another OD would notice something screwy and come to ask cop questions.

The OD retreated a half step. "No, I've done enough. Two. You can choose."

Mouse stepped closer, wanting so bad to pull out the Welrod that he tasted metal on his tongue. The OD backed up again.

"Stay back, stay in your place." And the OD changed his grip on the bat he held in his right hand. He's gonna swing that thing, thought Mouse.

Then the German Jew looked up the train, which was creeping closer, wheels of the cars nicking over the joints in the rails like tick-tocks of a clock. Mouse looked too, and recognized two Germans by their high caps, neither of them the SD fuck they'd left behind in Amsterdam, for the one closest to the rails was taller, the other heavier. When the OD turned back, his face was stretched tight with panic, like seeing the two Germans was enough to scare his wits away. The OD raised his bat, and even though Mouse had thought he was ready, it happened too fast. The club flashed across his shoulder, like a cop's billy but a lot worse. Mouse staggered back, slipping in the mud, and someone caught him.

"Get back in line, damn you!" the OD screamed.

And the OD reached for the three women behind him, intending, Mouse knew, to grab only two. Mouse saw how they were standing. Rachael and the thin woman were closest to the OD, shoulder to shoulder, Reka half hidden behind the wall of them. Mouse tried to get to his feet so he could make sure Reka was one of the two. That was all he cared about.

———

When the Ordnungsdienst in the muddy overcoat and the cudgel in his hand reached for them, Reka thought he was going to beat them, too. Instead, the OD, his face a mix of fury and fright, yelled out in accented Dutch.

"*Slechts twee,*" he shouted, spit flying from his mouth. Only two.

Two what?

As the moment slowed and stopped, Reka realized what the OD's call meant. In the shock of those seconds, she couldn't move, and saw Rachael grab a handful of the stick woman's green dress and wrench her into the OD, who caught her at arm's length and pushed her into the mud at Leonard's feet.

Rachael turned and put hands on Reka's shoulders. "Take care of Mr. Weiss," she whispered. Before Reka knew what was happening, Rachael gripped the corners of her coat and pulled and twisted both at once so Reka lost her footing and went spinning. Not until Leonard picked her out of the mud did Reka know whether Rachael had shoved her at the platform, or away.

Leonard lifted her up and put his arms around her and held her so tight. Behind her, Reka heard the OD's cudgel land, and knew without seeing that he'd struck Rachael. As Leonard crushed her into his sweet American smell, Reka looked at Paul Kagen, who didn't blink once while he allowed Rachael to be left behind.

The mamzer, the bastard Kagen, didn't raise a hand to save Rachael. Mouse couldn't understand any of it, none of it. Let your woman take one in the neck, how could Kagen do that? Give yourself up, for what, a skinny yid you'd not seen in a year, like Rachael just done? Nothing made sense.

Even Rachael's eyes made no sense. She picked herself up, brushed the gluey mud from her coat, and backed away. But it was like her eyes were smiling, like she knew she'd done what she'd come for, and that made it all right. Only when she looked at Kagen did her eyes go cold, like they should, by rights, already be.

The last he saw of Rachael was the back of her head, her blond hair not so golden as that first time he'd seen her in the sitting room on Argyle Street. She was gone between two buildings before he could get untangled from Reka, much less go for the Welrod.

And then it was just shouts and whistles and shoves as the OD closed its net around the platform and squeezed them toward the front of the train. More OD were sliding open the doors to the cattle cars. He held Reka tight to him, picked up the one bag he had left, the one with four revolvers, and went with the flow of Jews.

"Leonard, look, look at the wagons, how many there are," Reka said quietly. He counted as the OD pushed at the back of the crowd. Twenty-one cattle cars and the one passenger car at the rear.

"Yeah. So?" What did it matter, the number?

"There's enough here for twice a thousand. Think how many of us came on the train yesterday, and only six wagons."

"Yeah?"

"We thought there would be a thousand. Not more. We don't have enough boats for everyone," she said.

Fuck. He counted again as they were pushed along.

"We don't have enough boats." Her voice was almost a soft moan.

There was nothing for it now, Mouse thought. "We'll worry about that later. We have to take the train first, don't we? First things first."

The crowd stopped and they stood in front of the open door of a car third from the front. The smell inside was like a circus, hay and animal shit. The mother with the little dark-haired girl was next to them, the young husband and wife in front, the old man who talked to himself behind them. As he looked around, he found Schaap and his skinny wife, and that fucker Kagen. They were just a rank or two behind, pushing for this car, too.

Another OD stood beside the open door, shouting in Dutch. The young husband put his hand on his wife's ass and boosted her into the car, jumped in and reached down for the hand of the little dark-haired girl's mother. Mouse lifted Reka into the car—she seemed light as a dollar bill—and tossed in the bag after. He grabbed the little dark-haired girl by her blue coat and swung her up and in. He put a leg up over the edge. A hand grabbed his and pulled him up, and it was the old man, chattering still.

It was dim but not dark, with light coming through the wooden slats. Mouse didn't try to count the people, but he thought eighty easy, and more climbing in behind him, pushing them toward the front wall.

Then there was the scratching sound of wood sliding over iron and the crash and bang as the door slammed shut. A second later, the clang of metal striking metal echoed through the closed door and Mouse realized the latch had been slapped into place.

And although he was scared, he felt a kind of quiet settle on him. The rub of shoulder on shoulder in the car made him think of how close they had to sit at table for Seder when he was little, and all the relatives jammed into the apartment. For the second time in two days, he thought of the Shema.

Reka's hand found his.

It might have been hours, he didn't know, for time didn't seem to run right in the cattle car. But sometime later the floor under his feet shifted—everyone inside the car moving back and forth like water sloshing in a pan—and with a clank and clank and clank, each fading into the distance down the train, the locomotive pulled them out of Westerbork.

# Nineteen

They started working on the front wall of the cattle car five minutes after the train jerked out of the camp. Without tools, it was impossible. But they tried anyway; Mouse and Schaap put fingers around boards and tried to force them loose, but the nails held.

Reka called out the towns from her spot near the front right corner of the car, where she crouched with her eyes pressed into the gap between two slats. Only when she yelled, "Another twenty kilometers to the switch!" did Mouse think of using the Stens. He dug in Schaap's bag, pushing away the thin Vreesje, and pulled out two of the foot-long Sten stocks. The pointed end of one he jammed in the inch-wide gap between two boards, then pulled down to use the stock as a lever. A nail squealed and the board made a pop. Schaap understood and used the other stock to do the same. But it was hard work. In seconds, Mouse was dragging in huge ragged gulps of air and sweating so that he had to pull off his coat and let it fall to his feet. And in five minutes, they'd managed to loosen, but that's all, just one board.

"*Wat zijn jullie aan het doen?*"

Mouse turned to the voice. Beyond Kagen and past the young couple and the old man who talked, was a guy with a narrow face snarling behind glasses. He called to the rest in the car. "*Ze proberen te ontsnappen!*" Mouse had no idea what he said, but the tone, that was simple. The guy was scared, and he was making everyone else scared too.

"Shut up," Mouse yelled. "Get him to shut up," he shouted to Kagen. But Kagen did nothing.

"*Zo gaan we er allemaal aan!*" yelled the man with the glasses. "*De Duitsers schieten ons allemaal neer!*" His words set off dominoes of pandemonium. Others took up the cry and soon the entire car was shouting and yelling. What the fuck! Mouse thought. They should be grateful, but no, they're scared of being shot by the Germans, maybe for letting others escape. They didn't know they would die no matter what.

"Shut up, shut up, quiet!" he shouted, but no one could hear him. Reka solved the problem by scrambling for their bag and pulling out a Webley. The first gunshot shut them up. Its slug drilled a neat hole in the roof that right away dripped water.

"You stay on this train," Mouse said in English, and he caught Reka's eye and she shouted out a translation, her voice carrying almost as well. "You stay on this train and you'll die."

More craziness in the car. "I know, I've seen pictures!" Mouse yelled at the top of his lungs. Reka translated and it got quieter. "I've seen photographs of where this train ends. The Germans kill us with gas and burn our bodies. Every Jew that comes on a train is a dead Jew!" Reka shouted her Dutch as an echo. The car was silent again, the only sound the wood creaking as the car rocked, and the metal flanges of wheels banging over joints.

"What are you doing about it?" The question was in English, and came from the husband half of the young couple. He was barely twenty, with a long horse's face and a narrow nose.

Mouse wasn't good with words, but he remembered something that

Peter Bergson, the Jew who talked like a rabbi, had said to Lansky in that office above Broadway.

"Jews save Jews, that's what we're doing. Jews save Jews," he said.

"*Joden redden joden,*" the young man said, turning the words into Dutch. "My name is Alder," he said after a pause.

Mouse looked at the rest of the car and used Alder's words. He called out "*Joden redden joden,*" not that loud because he didn't have to. "*Joden redden joden!*" The car was so quiet that the only sound Mouse heard was the wheels on the rails, and he swore, the drip of water through that hole in the roof.

He went back to the wall, levered his Sten stock into the gap, and pulled as hard as he could. Another nail squeaked. Schaap was catching his breath, Kagen did nothing. This would take too long, and by the time he'd made a hole big enough to squeeze through, they'd be on their way to smoke.

"I want to help," someone said, and beside him was a new pair of hands, holding the other stock, shoving it between the boards and pushing down. It was Alder. The board popped free at one end. Two more hands, and Mouse looked up to see the old man who had quit talking to himself. Two more and another two, hands of boys who had stood not far from Reka. Everyone pulled together and with a loud crack, like a branch breaking in a storm, the plank broke in half and came free.

M ouse crouched at the hole they had ripped in the car. Through the yard-wide opening he could see only the car ahead. It was five or six feet away, and swayed to a different rhythm.

"Let me come," Reka said, and fell against him as the car jostled everyone.

"No, we can do it," Mouse said, and their eyes met for a moment. "You need to keep them under control. Kagen doesn't know Dutch." He tilted his head toward the others in the car. He dug in the bag at Kagen's feet until he came up with the map Schaap had made of the tracks, and stuffed it inside his cotton shirt, and out of habit, picked up his wet money coat and slipped that on, too.

Mouse looked at Alder. "You have to help," he said, and Alder nodded like he understood. Mouse took the Webley from Reka's hand and gave it to Alder, who stuck it in his waistband, like Mouse had his Welrod. Alder grinned, a gangster now. Mouse couldn't help but remember Joop and how he'd loved Cagney.

Mouse put his head through the hole and looked down. The coupling where the two cars connected was four or five feet below, and past that all he got was dizzy watching the wooden ties on the track flick by in a brown blur. He looked to the left and saw iron rungs fastened to the outside of the car. Mouse looked down again. There was no way out there, not unless the train stopped or slowed, and they were already past Assen, Reka had shouted a while ago, the one place where Joop said the train went slow enough for that. It would have to be the rungs, three feet away.

Mouse ducked back inside. He wasn't sure this would work, but the rungs were the first step on the way home. So he jammed the Welrod a bit farther into his waistband and told Alder what they had to do. He slipped his right leg through the hole. Alder grabbed his left hand and held it tight, the stitches pulling and hurting like hell.

Blindly he tried to put a foot on one of the iron rungs, edging out more until his right arm and his shoulder, finally his head, popped free. The wind tore at his coat and he was soaked in seconds. He felt a dryness in his mouth, but his foot found a rung and he put his weight on it. His right hand, pressed against the wood of the car, groped aimlessly for another.

For a moment he thought Alder had let go, but he realized it was only Alder moving half out of the hole to give him room to reach. Mouse's right hand waved in the air, he watched like it was someone else's, he tried not to look down. When his hand finally reached the iron, he swung himself over, Alder letting go for good, and he was standing on one rung, his hands wrapped around another. Mouse closed his eyes against the height, then opened them again.

He stepped up and peeked over the top of the car. Just their car, another, and another, he lost track as he counted, but all he saw were empty roofs. He twisted to look forward toward the locomotive, and before he had to shut his eyes against the smoke and rain, he saw it was clear. Two cars between them and the engine.

He hoisted himself up to the roof and lay down flat. He yelled for Alder and the boy popped out, looked up, and saw his face looking down. Alder's leg and arm appeared, and although the boy's foot slipped off a wet rung twice, each time he tried again until he stood on the rungs and climbed to the roof and lay down beside him. Alder grinned, his face as white as flour. Schaap followed them, his blond hair plastered against his skull from the rain. More minutes and he was lying on the rooftop, too, holding tight to a Sten.

Mouse didn't say anything—the rain and the train were too loud—so he just got to his knees, then to his feet, trying to keep them under him on the slick roof as the car rocked. He backed up a step, ran, and jumped over the gap between cars, landing on his feet but having to put out his hands to keep from sliding off. Not thinking—he knew if he stopped to think he'd freeze and drop to the roof and never let go—he crouched and ran the length of the car, jumped, ran again, jumped again, and fell to his knees on the metal top of the tender. Only then did he dare look back for Alder and Schaap, but the boy was right with him, now leaping over the last canyon. Schaap was crawling across the car behind Alder.

They perched at the front of the tender, a small pile of coal on the floor of the locomotive cab beneath them. Mouse saw the engineer's legs, the rest of him hidden by the cab's roof. But below, a hand on a shovel and his face turned up looking right at them, was the Dutch fireman.

Alder jumped down first, Mouse next, each landing on the deck of the locomotive, one each side of the fireman. Schaap tumbled down in a heap, his Sten ringing on the steel floor, and was slow to get up. Mouse yanked the Welrod from his waistband and pointed it at the fireman, made a motion with its barrel, and the Dutchman let the shovel clatter to the steel floor.

Alder had pulled his Webley from his pants but not thumbed back the hammer—he didn't know guns—and Mouse stepped to the engineer, who only now had turned at the sound of the shovel. Mouse stuck the Welrod in the engineer's face, the muzzle just an inch from the Dutchman's sooty nose.

"Tell him to keep going!" Mouse yelled to Alder. The boy translated and the engineer nodded. He didn't take his hand off the lever that must be the throttle. Mouse pulled Schaap's handmade map from inside his shirt, pointed to the spot that marked the place where the tracks split. "Tell him to pull off the main line here!" he shouted to Alder.

Alder talked Dutch again, and again the engineer nodded. Mouse noticed the man's eyes glance at his coat. The star was still there, though he had forgotten it, the weight nothing now. Mouse touched the yellow star Rachael had sewn to his coat and smiled what he hoped was a Little Man smile. It was a badge now, he thought, like being a Brownsville boy.


Preuss stared at the ledger on his desk. He was short for April. The *Aktion* this morning had been a travesty, only thirty-nine.

Even so, he could not keep his mind on the ledger. Instead, his eyes slid to the leaflet he had had printed and posted throughout the city, the one with the photograph of the Jewess Dekker. She taunted him.

Preuss stared at the leaflet, and smoked one cigarette, then another, yawning in between. He had slept fitfully the night before, waking with a pinching headache from a nightmare of snow and mountains and partisans.

"Herr Hauptsturmführer."

He looked up from the end of his cigarette and there was Krempel. He had a blue and white striped cloth satchel in one hand.

"What?"

Krempel didn't say a word, simply dropped the satchel on his desk. Metal against metal sounded from inside, and the way it made the Nil tin bounce, the bag was heavy.

"What?"

Krempel snapped open the satchel, spread its lips, and leaned it toward him. It was dim there, and all he saw was clothing. Rags, perhaps. Krempel reached inside and pulled out a revolver like a magician pulls a dove from his top hat. Its cylinder snicked as he thumbed it. The revolver went on his desk beside the Nils. Krempel dipped his hand in three more times and each time set a revolver on the desk. Two looked new enough to have come straight from the foundry.

Several more trips to the satchel and Krempel had laid six stamped metal parts across the desk. A bar that ended in the shape of a T, a spring and two small bits, and two large, long tubes that looked like gun barrels.

"Where did you find this bag?" Preuss asked as Krempel pieced it together, this puzzle of a gun, and held it in his hands. An English machine pistol, one of those Stens. All of a sudden Preuss wanted a drink. But there was no Pierre Ferrand in the filing cabinet behind him.

"One of the extra bags from the station yesterday. The Marechaussee make the Jews leave behind all but one bag each. There were stacks of them. They took their time going through them, though. Looking for money, I don't doubt." Krempel put the Sten on the desk, just out of reach, not that Preuss wanted to touch it.

The Jews had been on his train; this was their bag. Somehow he'd missed Dekker. Or it was de Groot, that fat bumbler. He'd had the photograph and still missed her.

Preuss looked at his watch. Brumm had said yesterday that transports left Westerbork at eleven in the morning. That was three and a half hours ago.

"Fetch two trucks from the motor pool," he said to Krempel, deciding then what he'd do. He'd tried not to step on toes, but now he would take charge. He'd find Dekker and her gang of thieves. And put Russia behind him. "Have my car brought around. Gather the men, and telephone Marnixstraat and find de Groot. Tell him to come here immediately with his men."

"Hauptsturmführer," Krempel said, and he was gone.

Preuss picked up the handset and told the switchboard to ring the commandant's office at Westerbork. The static on the line was especially loud.

"Brumm here," a voice said, sounding sober enough.

"This is Preuss in Amsterdam."

"Yes, Herr Hauptsturmführer."

"Has your transport left?" Preuss held his breath. If it had been delayed and was there still, this would be simple. He would order Brumm to hold it, drive to Westerbork, and go through the train until he found this Reka Dekker.

There was a quiet on the telephone line, static in the background, before Brumm answered. "Yes, Hauptsturmführer, over an hour ago. Why?"

"Where would the train be?" he asked. "At this moment. Exactly." Nothing was easy. But he still could do this. He'd drive clear to the Reich's border if necessary.

He heard static, or the sound of papers, or both. "I'm not sure, Hauptsturmführer," said Brumm. "We had some delays here, the transport was much larger than normal—" There was a pause. "It's not on priority, Hauptsturmführer, they pull the transports to sidings all the time, and this one was late leaving and perhaps missed its schedule, so—"

"Where?" he asked. Preuss felt a knot begin to grow in his head.

More static or paper. "Winschoten, perhaps," said Brumm finally. "Close to the border, just a few kilometers. Or Hoogezand, not quite so far." Preuss groped a map from his desk drawer and spread it out atop the weapons. Hoogezand he found first, Winschoten next. Both east of Groningen. Three hours and more by car.

"Have you heard from the transport?" he asked.

Again the lengthy silence of static. "No, Hauptsturmführer. I don't think it's at the border yet, as I said."

"You aren't kept informed as to its progress?"

"No, Hauptsturmführer. Once it leaves us, it's in the hands of the railway. First the Nederlandse Spoorweg, then the Reichsbahn. We get a telephone call or teletype when it reaches the Reich, but only because we need to send a truck to bring back the transport guard."

The pounding in his head rang behind his eyes.

"Is there a problem?" Brumm asked. Again the static made it impossible to know if Brumm hesitated, but there was no voice on the line for several seconds until he said, "I know things were done irregularly this transport, Hauptsturmführer, but it was the Obersturmführer's orders that we put your Jews directly on the train. I told him—"

"What did you say?" Preuss asked.

"The Jews you brought us yesterday. We shipped them out straight away, on today's transport. We had trouble finishing the selection and the transport was so large. . . . I knew it was irregular, I told the Obersturmführer this."

Preuss pushed aside the map and two revolvers to uncover his ledger. Five hundred and eighty-seven shipped yesterday, counted by de Groot as they left the Joodsche Schouwburg. But they'd not finished a count in the station, not in his rush to look them over and get them back aboard before Kuiper called The Hague.

"How many of mine?"

Static again. "All of them, Hauptsturmführer. Five hundred ninety-two. Exactly."

The pain between his ears blossomed. Five. He rooted through the desk drawer until he found the blood-spattered list of names little Joop had given up.

|  |  |
|---|---|
| ~~Annje~~ | ~~(K?) Schaap, Kristiaan~~ |
| ~~Martin Visser~~ | ~~Koster~~ |
| Kagen | ~~Keuning~~ |
| Groeneweg | Dekker, Reka (J) |
| Rachael | Mouse |
|  | Vreesje, Schaap/Ikkersheim (J) |

Seven names left. Close enough.

The Jews had wormed their way onto his train between the theater and the station, gotten into the camp, and were now on Westerbork's transport.

"Can you stop the—" Preuss began, but quit. He couldn't admit there was a problem. But more important than that now was his wish—no, it was his right: I am the one who will wring the necks of these Jews.

---

Even though the light was bad and the rain made it worse, Mouse had no trouble seeing the fireman sprint for the brush and trees along the track. Before he could put the Welrod on him, the Dutchman was gone, pushing aside bare branches and ducking under. Fuck.

He'd sent the fireman down the short ladder from the locomotive to throw the switch the engineer said would shift them from the main line onto the spur marked on this map. But once the fireman shoved a yard-long steel bar in a half circle to clang the switch open, and before the locomotive chuffed past, he'd lit out.

The engineer yanked on the big black lever at his side and the train slowed even more. "Shoot him if you need to. You understand?" Mouse said to Alder. The boy, his face now gray from the coal smoke, grinned again and his teeth gleamed. "Stop the engine when you're at those tallest trees up ahead." Alder nodded, fingered the Webley that hadn't left his hand.

Mouse stepped to the edge of the cab, where the short ladder led to the ground. The train clacked over the switch and the locomotive went right. He jammed the Welrod in his waistband, grabbed the ladder, and dropped to the gravel. The train was moving so slowly he only had to run a few steps to keep from falling. Schaap came down the ladder, too, and was beside him.

The train moved too fast to slip between the second and third cars to yell into the hole and tell Kagen to get the fuck out and help. So Mouse counted the cars as they swayed past, wondering if his ears played tricks or if he could really hear voices inside them. Five left before the last car—the one that held the guards, Reka had said—then four, and three, and he edged even closer to the passing wheels and crouched down.

Mouse was scared, a feeling different from when the cattle car door slid shut. The feeling sat at the back of his throat and made it hard to swallow again.

As the passenger car came to them, Schaap reached for the railing along the steps to its front platform and swung himself up. Mouse followed. His heart thumping, Mouse pulled out the Welrod and stepped behind Schaap. The Dutchman's blond hair dripped water onto the collar of his coat. Schaap raised his Sten, Mouse heard the clack of the bolt pulled back, and the Dutchman opened the door.

The car looked like any railway car. A hallway ten feet long passed two small compartments, one either side, and in the open part of the car beyond, pair after pair of bench seats facing each other. Schaap walked down the hallway, and Mouse glanced into the compartments, each empty.

Men in blue uniforms sat in the bench seats nearest them, those facing their way not yet showing anything, and four men in green tunics had their heads together at the back on the right. Mouse heard them laughing. Only one, dressed in green, was standing, and he leaned out a window on the right. Trying to guess why the train was slowing down.

The train jerked once and, close to stopping, jerked again, and Schaap was yelling in Dutch, and the nearest man in blue was putting up his hands. But the one in the seat behind him was reaching for something or trying to put the wooden seat between him and them. Mouse stepped out from behind Schaap, hating the idea, like always, of shooting a cop, but there was nothing he could do. So he shot the guy with the Welrod, the tiny noise of the pistol drowned out by the hammering of the Sten.

The slug caught the cop in the neck and spun him half around. Mouse worked the action of the Welrod—twist and pull and push and twist—and he felt air move as a slug passed his head and smacked into something behind him.

Schaap fired his Sten, the shots strung together in its familiar, choppy ba-ba-ba-ba-bang. Another slug zinged past Mouse and he pointed the Welrod at a Marechaussee halfway out of his seat and shot at him, too.

Shouts and screams, and two more slugs tore into the seat beside him and he felt a sting on his left hand, right behind the twin wounds from Cromwell's teeth. He looked down and saw a small sliver of wood, no bigger than a toothpick, stuck in his wrist.

Mouse didn't duck behind the seats, but stayed in the aisle beside Schaap, the Dutchman's Sten stuttering.

And it was over. *"Hände hoch!"* Mouse yelled in German, telling them to put their hands up, and the ones in green at the back hurried to do what he said. Schaap yelled in Dutch and the Marechaussee still able stuck their hands in the air, too.

Neither he nor Schaap had been hit. In the swirl of the smoke and the long, drawn-out minutes between each second, a strange thought ran through Mouse's head, that it was because of the star on his chest. Like a shield.

The one open window and the breeze through the car cleared the air as the train clank-clank-clanked to a stop, the connections banging. Six blue-jackets, three in green, had hands in the air. Three, no four, slumped in their seats or were motionless on the floor. Thirteen, Mouse thought. Just thirteen guards for a train that held thousands.

Schaap herded the nine through the back door. Mouse followed, but unlike the Dutchman he stayed on the rear platform of the car. Sounds of boots on gravel, and Mouse turned, but it was only Kagen, come through the hole now that the train was stopped, and armed with a Sten.

Schaap lined up the nine prisoners in a ragged row at the edge of the roadbed. Their hands were empty and still above their heads, and some looked like they were ready to shit their pants, especially the three in green coats. One in blue held his arm, and blood showed through his fingers, and another had his hands over his stomach, blood on his hands too, his face as white as fresh sheets.

Mouse looked to the right. Trees there. He looked to the left. More trees. Back the way they'd come, Mouse could see the switch a hundred yards away where the fireman had escaped.

"We can't stay here," Mouse said, calling down to Schaap and Kagen. The Dutchman looked up and Mouse saw his mouth twitch once.

"You did well, gangster," said Kagen, looking up and grinning. Fuck you, thought Mouse.

"What about them?" Mouse asked, nodding to the nine standing along the tracks.

"Kill them," said Schaap. The Dutchman's mouth twitched again. That face, Mouse thought, might scare even Lansky.

Before Mouse could put thoughts in his head and make his mouth say them, Kagen nodded and said, "Yes. The Orpo certainly." He pointed his Sten at the three in green, their eyes glued to the gun. Kagen stood in front of them and asked, *"Gehörst du zur Ordnungspolizei, ja oder nein?"* Mouse looked at the Nazi eagle on the tunics.

Kagen didn't wait for an answer, but slung the Sten over his shoulder, pulled a Webley from inside his coat, and shot the first Orpo in the head, the noise loud here in the rainy canyon between the trees. The German cop pitched off the roadbed, his body slipping down the graded gravel until Mouse saw only the soles of his boots.

Mouse stepped off the platform. Part of him knew this was the right thing to do, but Kagen did this because he liked it. The Webley barked again, Kagen wasting no time.

Mouse pushed past Schaap. "That's enough," he said to Kagen, finally finding a voice as he worked the Welrod's action again to chamber a round. Kagen turned from the two dead Orpo, just wet green uniforms against the gray of the gravel along the tracks. Kagen grinned crazily.

"This is what Jews do with Nazis," Kagen said, that grin still on him. "I have sixteen now, gangster."

Kagen turned and was ready to put the muzzle of the Webley above the ear of the last Orpo, the oldest one, when Mouse grabbed the German's arm. Kagen spun on him.

"Let go of me. This is our business." He yanked free from Mouse's grip, and with his arm straight out like a signpost, aimed the Webley at the Orpo and pulled the trigger. The Orpo dropped to his knees as blood sprayed from the side of his head. He tipped over, and a foot jerked once, twice, and was still. The gunshot echoed off the trees. "Seventeen. This is how real Jews deal with these kind," said Kagen, now looking back at him. "Are you a Jew or not, gangster?"

Wrong, this was all wrong, Mouse thought.

"They're not even German." He looked at the Marechaussee, caught the eyes of one, Alder's age.

"They guard Jews, don't they?" Schaap said from behind him. "They'll be the ones to watch when Rachael's sent East, won't they? Can you tell me they won't? Kill them, yes, I agree. Kill them."

Schaap spoke Dutch loud and sharp to the Marechaussee, and after a hesitation, they began to pull off their jackets. They knew what was coming. The youngest among them, just a kid, started to cry. Mouse wanted to stop this, but he couldn't come up with a reason good enough to get through their hate. What would Lansky do?

Mouse thought he knew: Little Man might agree with Kagen. Mouse would not.

"Don't do this," he said. But Kagen held the Webley loose in his hand, reminding Mouse of Jack Spark and how he'd played with the Welrod that time in the butcher shop. The revolver's muzzle was pointed at the ground, but Mouse knew it could come up in a flash. His Welrod was heavier, and he might not bring it up in time. But Kagen wasn't so sure. The German's one eye took in the silencer.

"*Bist du Jude, Gangster, ja oder nein?*" Kagen asked, and laughed a little laugh that made Mouse feel the cold wet rain all the more. Kagen's question sounded too much like the one he'd asked the Orpo.

Gangster, Mouse thought, stinging now at the word. On the flying boat to England, Kagen had called him the worst kind of Jew. But who was the gangster now?

He shook his head, keeping his eyes on the Webley in Kagen's hand. "No, not your kind of Jew."

The moment passed and Kagen loosened his grip on the revolver, deciding not to risk getting shot by the Welrod. Schaap spoke Dutch and pointed the Marechaussee to the trees twenty yards away. Kagen fell in behind Schaap, the six Marechaussee leading the way.

Mouse flinched when the first shots came out of the trees and scared up a flock of crows, big and black with wings as wide as eagles. In the far distance, he thought he heard dogs barking.

Nothing good ever came from killing cops, he thought as he watched the crows wheel off beyond the trees.

# Twenty

Mouse swung the heavy latch up and over, heard it ring metal on metal, but before he could shove on the door, hands appeared from inside and pushed until the opening was as wide as the door allowed.

"Reka!" he yelled into the cattle car, but the name went nowhere against the wall of bodies that filled the door. "Reka!"

Several people already dangled legs over the lip, ready to jump down to the ground. "No, no, stay, stay!" Mouse shouted, but he didn't speak Dutch and no one listening, it seemed, understood English. Now three or four stood on the gravel, looking confused, looking like they would light out for the trees.

"Get them back in that wagon!" It was Kagen, the fuckin' mamzer, the fuckin' bastard. His English was thick with a German accent, and as skittish as they were, the accent stopped them in their tracks.

"Reka!" Mouse yelled, ignoring Kagen.

"Get them back in there. We're leaving!" Kagen yelled.

"Fuck you," Mouse said. Some of those in the doorway looked like they were getting ready to jump out and join the ones already there. "You tell them."

"*Zurück! Zurück in den Wagen!*" Kagen shouted, and waved his Sten. The German words and the gun scared the shit out of the Jews, who pushed to get away from the open door. Two of the three on the ground started to climb back in.

"Leonard, Leonard!" Reka's voice came from the car, and Mouse saw her face peering over the shoulder of a woman near the door. She squirmed through, popped out, and dropped down. He grabbed her by the shoulders, pulled her to him.

"You are safe," she whispered against his throat.

"Help me close this," Kagen said, and grabbed an edge of the door and started to slide it shut.

"Wait, wait!" Reka shouted, and jumped to the closing gap and yelled again, this time into the dark of the cattle car that smelled like a circus. "Vreesje!" and again, "Vreesje!" A shuffle from inside the car.

And she stuck her hands in the car and pulled out Vreesje, who slid to the gravel at Reka's side. Kagen slammed shut the door and swung down the latch.

"I'm heading to the locomotive," said Kagen. "Get back to the guard's wagon."

Mouse didn't care for the orders, but he knew the last car was the best place for Reka and Vreesje—and Schaap was back there, maybe his wife would make his mouth stop twitching—so he gestured toward the rear of the train. Reka held the hand of the thin woman in the tattered green dress and started that way.

For a moment Mouse was alone. He put his hand on the shut door of the car and felt the wood shiver. Was it him or the people inside?

As Reka shifted in the seat to get a better look at Leonard, she woke Vreesje, who had been resting on her shoulder. The woman rubbed her eyes, those eyes deep in her face. Reka had almost forgotten how little there had been to eat in Westerbork.

Vreesje put her hand on Reka's. Its weight was less than a leaf. "Your name is Reka?" The woman's voice was soft, but fuller than what she expected.

Reka nodded.

"Is he yours?" Vreesje asked. She was looking at Leonard, who sat opposite against the window. Leonard glanced their way, but because Vreesje had spoken in Dutch, he went back to his staring at the raindrops racing sideways across the window.

"I don't know," said Reka. She looked in Vreesje's green eyes, which didn't blink for the longest time.

"The other one, with the patch."

"Kagen," Reka said.

Vreesje looked again at Leonard. "I don't know how to say this . . . ," she began, stopped, then started again. "It's not that I wish you ill, but I don't know you, do you see?"

Reka thought so. "I'm sorry about Rachael," she said.

Vreesje turned to face her, those green eyes looking like small hard opals. "Why didn't . . . Kagen . . . Did he love my Rachael?" she asked.

"I don't know," said Reka, and when Vreesje's hand twitched atop hers, she went on. "I thought so, yes."

"But he . . . Kagen . . . didn't . . ." And Vreesje stopped, this time for good, Reka knew, for she pulled away her hand and placed it in her lap.

"There was nothing he could do," Reka said. But when she reached out to comfort Vreesje, the woman shrugged away her hand and edged toward the aisle. She kicked off her clogs, tucked her legs under her, and curled up on the seat.

Reka listened to the monotonous sound of the wagon's wheels rapping over the joints between the rails for the longest time. Then she picked up the paper and pencil she'd been holding before Vreesje had woken.

Another drawing, this on the back of the first, quick lines was all as the train had rocked. Leonard's face was almost in profile—he'd not noticed her drawing this time—and as she scratched on the paper one last time, around his eyes, she saw they looked not so sad now. At least to her pencil. Reka folded the paper and slipped it inside her coat.

Her hand had been steady while she drew, the fear of trains gone like water steamed from hot summer pavement. It had vanished as soon as the wagon's door slid open and she heard Leonard's voice calling. They had done it. They had done this impossible thing. And every kilometer that went under the wheels was one closer to salvation.

"Reka," Leonard said, his voice startling her. She turned to him. "I have to tell you something . . ." But his voice trailed to an awkward silence. She thought of the kiss they'd shared on yesterday's train, and she felt her face flush.

"That night on the field, when the airplane put us down . . ." His voice disappeared again. She leaned toward him, and gently, for his hand was still bloodied from where she'd plucked a splinter, she rested her hand on his.

"I know," she said, looking at him straight. Even under the grime, his face showed surprise.

"You know."

"I know you were afraid that night. You had your gun in your hand because you were frightened. You ran back for the aircraft, I know why. But you're no coward." And she patted his hand very softly.

Confusion showed through the streaks of rain that lined the soot on his face. But he smiled, a pleasant smile—she could not believe he was a gangster, a killer—and gave her hand a small squeeze.

"We should be in the locomotive," said someone behind her. It was Kristiaan, who looked down at his Vreesje but didn't put out a hand to touch her upturned face. It was as if he'd seen the edge of life and been tempted to take the last step. Kristiaan would never be the same, and every time he looked at his wife he'd remember.

He talked to Leonard. "This is the most dangerous point, Groningen. We must get through the railyard. I'm going to the engine to help. And you should be there, too. The *Duitser* . . ."

Leonard nodded. He understood what Kristiaan meant; Kagen's judgment could not be trusted; the man had shown that plainly with what he'd done in Amsterdam, and in the camp. Leonard gave her hand one more press, looked at her as if he wasn't finished with this conversation, but only asked, "You'll be okay here?"

She nodded, and felt the train slow. He stepped over her feet and into the aisle to follow Kristiaan to the rear door of the wagon. He will look back, Reka thought, he will look back once, even for a moment. That will mean something.

Leonard turned and glanced back at her before stepping onto the platform.


The BMW's single wiper could not keep pace with the rain. "Pull over here," Preuss said, and de Groot turned the wheel and braked the car to a stop. Its interior filled with the light of headlamps as a truck pulled behind them. The sign on the building across the street read POLITIE.

Preuss turned to look back, but saw only the lamps of one truck. "This is Meppel?" he asked, not bothering to hide his irritation. The weather was not cooperating.

"Staphorst," the fat Dutchman beside him grunted. "Meppel's another five kilometers, I think."

"You think?"

"I'm from Amsterdam. This is the middle of nowhere."

"How far from Westerbork?"

De Groot switched on his electric torch and unfolded a map. He studied it for a moment or two, and put a fat finger on the map. "Another fifty kilometers."

"Thirty minutes," Preuss said. He held his watch in the light of de Groot's torch—a few minutes after half-past four. Marta would be wrapping up her work about now. "One of the trucks is no longer behind us. Find out why not," Preuss said. De Groot glanced into the back seat of the BMW where Krempel and the thick-necked Kripo Munkhart sat. The Dutchman pulled at his coat, jammed on his hat, and opened the door. The wind sucked rain into the BMW and wet Preuss's face.

"Foul weather, Hauptsturmführer," said Krempel from the back. "Not fit for dogs or Jews, eh?" Preuss said nothing. Instead, he lit a cigarette. This was what it must be like to fight partisans, out in the weather and in the dark. He didn't like it.

They'd made good time, an hour and a half since they'd pulled out of the cobblestone courtyard of Euterpestraat. De Groot had held his foot on the accelerator and the needle stayed on 80 most of the time, the two Opel-Blitzes keeping pace, at least until now.

Before leaving, he'd lost an argument over the telephone with a Luftwaffe major out at Schiphol who had told him that requisitioning an airplane was impossible, even a small Storch. The rain and low ceiling, sorry, Hauptsturmführer, everything's grounded—perhaps later, when the storm clears. He'd reluctantly telephoned Giskes then, needing more men than he could round up on such short notice. The Abwehr officer was out, so he'd had to be satisfied with leaving word for Giskes to come to Groningen with his men as soon as possible. From Groningen, they could decide which way the train had gone.

The BMW's door opened, more rain blew in, and de Groot's bulk blocked the wind. The door slammed shut. "That's my men in the truck," the Dutchman said. "The driver doesn't remember when he last saw the other, the one with yours."

"Naturally," Preuss said. He stepped out of the car and into the rain and walked across the street to the police station, flicking the half-smoked Nil into the rain.

There was only one Dutch policeman, a Marechaussee, on duty in this tiny town. "I need your telephone," Preuss said in his Dutch, and the policeman grabbed a black telephone and clumped it on the desk. Preuss rubbed his temples, one at a time, then the middle of his forehead. This headache would kill him.

First he telephoned the Euterpestraat, hoping for news of Giskes. But the soft-voiced girl on the switchboard had no messages from the Abwehr. Only from The Hague, Hauptsturmführer, she said.

"Brigadeführer Naumann called thirty-five minutes ago. He was very insistent that he speak with you. I said you were out, and he made me promise that you would telephone immediately when you returned," she said, her Austrian accent making him homesick, like usual.

"Connect me with his office," Preuss said, wondering what Naumann wanted.

"Horst, how are you?" asked the familiar voice after a minute. There was almost no static on this line.

Preuss took a breath. "Fine, Brigadeführer, fine."

"Where are you, Horst? Amsterdam said they couldn't find you, that you'd left in a rush in your car."

"Brigadeführer," he croaked out, his head whirling as he tried to come up with a lie. But it seemed Naumann didn't really care where he was, because he went on.

"I had an interesting telephone call from Untersturmführer Brumm, the adjutant at Westerbork, an hour ago," said Naumann, his voice like oil now.

"Yes, Brigadeführer?" Preuss asked to fill the silence on the line. But he thought he knew where this was heading and wanted to put the handset down.

"Brumm was very upset, Horst. Something about irregularities with the transport today, and how you were in the camp yesterday, and then you telephoned again this afternoon."

"Brigadeführer," Preuss said.

Naumann went on. "Brumm's tattling on Gemmeker, that's what I think. Perhaps Brumm discovered that Gemmeker's fucking his wife, it's all around." God what a mess, thought Preuss. "Brumm said you told Gemmeker yesterday of rumors you'd heard, some cocked-up story the Abwehr whispered to you of Jews being stolen from trains. And you called him again today with more questions about their transport. Brumm was worried about what you said, but Gemmeker refused to take precautions as I understand it, so Brumm telephoned Nieuweschans, where the train was to change crew and guard and locomotive. But it hasn't arrived. It's overdue. He was very upset, Horst. He doesn't want to be blamed for this missing train."

"Herr Brigadeführer—" Preuss began.

"What kind of mischief have you and your Abwehr friend Giskes gotten into, Horst?"

Naumann's slippery voice hurt him, but he swallowed, and using everything he'd learned lying to Jews, and lying to Marta, he lied now. "Brigadeführer, it's as I told Gemmeker. Giskes says he's uncovered a plot to steal Jews, and I have taken precautions, even went with my train yesterday to Westerbork. I told Gemmeker to be on watch, if he didn't listen to what—" That was as far as he got.

"But why all the interest in the Westerbork transport today, Horst? That's what puzzles me." Naumann's voice over the wire was more than oil now; it was like oil on oil. Preuss closed his eyes against the blinding light in his head. The migraine was as in Russia, when he'd stood at the edge of pits and joined in the shooting to set a good example. Nerves, that was what the doctors had said. Nerves and stress.

"I think you neglected to tell me of something, or neglected to tell Sturmbannführer Zoepf. Did you think you could scheme with the Abwehr? *Keep secrets from me?*" Naumann thundered down the telephone, his lawyer's voice like God's judgment. "I told you to watch him, Horst, not *conspire* with him. I told you the Abwehr was filled with *traitors*, didn't I?"

He's fishing, thought Preuss with what brains the headache left him. He's guessing. He doesn't know for certain. I have only to lie this through and things will be fine. Preuss closed his eyes against the pain again. "Brigadeführer, you're wrong. I've not conspired with Giskes, I did what you asked, I only watched him. And when he came to me with his story—"

"*Hauptsturmführer!*" The rank struck him like a slap; Naumann never called him that. "*Don't dare lie to me!*" he yelled. "I have a letter right in front of me, brought from Amsterdam by dispatch rider just forty-five minutes ago. It lays out everything. This Visser woman, your fumbling over her gang of Jews, this plot to steal a train. And boats? *Boats are involved, and you didn't think to tell me?*"

Preuss's voice was little more than a whisper. "Who says this, Brigadeführer? Who says these lies?" It must be Giskes, it could only be Giskes. He betrayed me as I thought to betray him. I'll shoot Giskes myself.

"It doesn't matter, Hauptsturmführer, does it?" Naumann's voice softened. "These Jews are Gemmeker's responsibility once in Westerbork. And so they're mine. Over two thousand on that train, Brumm said. So many lost Jews would do nothing for my reputation, Horst."

"Yes, Brigadeführer," Preuss said quietly, hearing his name again, but knowing it would never be the same between them.

"Find this train of mine. And I will forget everything, for old times' sake. But if you fail . . ." And Naumann's voice faded for a moment before it came back, strong and so completely calm. "I will say that you kept this from me and from Zoepf. That you plotted with the Abwehr to allow this to happen. To give myself and Zoepf the black eye."

Preuss thought he would be sick for sure and so could not stammer out an answer.

"No one must know of this wayward train, Horst," Naumann said. "I want you to take care of this personally. Contact the Orpo in Groningen, my man there is Hassel. He'll keep quiet. But no further. If it gets out—"

"I will be discreet, I promise you." He was ready to put the handset in its cradle with his shaking hand, but it seemed Naumann was not finished.

"There are no shortages of meat hooks in Prinz-Albrechtstrasse, my friend," said Naumann. "I do not intend to dangle from one."

The light of pain shone brighter than the sun inside Preuss's head.

O ut of breath from his dash alongside the creeping train, Mouse barely managed to grab the ladder and haul himself up into the locomotive.

"Thanks for nothing," he said to Schaap, but the Dutchman just blinked. Schaap stood behind one shoulder of the engineer, Kagen the other. Alder had taken the place of the missing fireman and was working the coal into the firebox one shovel at a time.

Mouse poked his head outside the locomotive to look up the track through the rain. He couldn't see much, just rails that bent to the left and out of sight, and brick buildings close to the roadbed.

"Joop said Groningen was where we'd find the line to Uithuizen," Schaap said. Mouse looked back into the locomotive.

"He's the one who knows," Kagen said, pointing to the engineer. Kagen had put on the tunic of an Orpo, and Mouse noticed there was blood on the collar.

Schaap said some Dutch and the engineer turned from his steel chair bolted to the side of the locomotive cab. The engineer's face was like dirty leather, the creases in his face deep enough to hide a roll of dimes, and his gray hair stuck out from under a greasy cap. He kept his hand on the throttle.

"They will have questions in Groningen," the engineer said. He said it in English.

"You know English," Mouse said.

"Yes."

"Shut up, gangster," Kagen said. "What about questions?"

The engineer didn't take his eyes from Mouse's, but he answered. "Every train is on a schedule. Even trains like this one."

"So?" Kagen asked.

"So he's saying they'll wonder why we're not on time, that's what." Mouse kept looking at the engineer. "That when we get to Groningen they'll stop us and ask questions. Right?"

"Yes," the engineer said.

"But Joop said he could take the train through the switching yard without suspicions," Kagen said. The train took the curve slowly. "You know the yard."

"Yes."

"You'll take us, then." Kagen was telling, not asking. "Through the yard, to the track that goes to Uithuizen. Without the station knowing it's this train. Or stopping us." Mouse waited for the engineer to answer. The man looked at him, next at Kagen.

"Why should I? You'll shoot me, like you shot the Ordnungspolizei and the Marechaussee." The man looked at Kagen's green Orpo jacket.

Kagen raised his Sten. Mouse saw its bolt was back. He looked next at the weathered face of the Dutchman. The gun was past scaring him, Mouse knew. The engineer had heard the shooting, maybe even seen Kagen gun down the Orpo. The engineer had nothing to lose. A man like that, if he was brave, he'd be stubborn—Kagen could threaten him from now until next dawn, and he wouldn't listen.

Mouse stepped between Kagen and the engineer. "No one will shoot you, I promise."

"Get out of the way." Kagen, behind him.

Mouse faced Kagen. "Go ahead and shoot him," he said in German, so that the Dutchman wouldn't understand. "Then we're all dead. None of us get out."

"He'll do what I tell him," Kagen growled.

"Or what? You'll kill him? Who drives the train? You can't kill everybody. If you do, we'll never get home. I don't know about you, but I want to get home."

The train swayed on, the only sounds the breathing of the locomotive and the scrape of Alder's shovel. Kagen caught him by surprise by nodding slowly and lowering his Sten.

Mouse turned back to the engineer and said in English, "If you give us away or try to run like your friend," he said, keeping his voice as steady as the look he gave the Dutchman, "I'll shoot you myself. You understand?"

The engineer didn't blink at the words. "The first switch is a half kilometer ahead. Someone must throw the switches as I call them out. But it must be someone Dutch. Workers will be about the yard, and they must hear only Dutch." The skies opened wider, and drops big as marbles pinged off the locomotive. Some tumbled into the cab and sizzled when they splattered against the steel in front of the firebox door.

"I'll do it," said Schaap.


The locomotive slowed, the wheels barely turning, and steam hissed from its sides. Mouse stood at the open side of the cab behind the engineer to see ahead. Schaap had left his Sten and shoved a Smith & Wesson inside his coat and run ahead in the rain. Now he stood by the switch, a three-foot-long steel bar beside a fork in the tracks. At one end of the bar was a painted white circle, closest to the tracks, at the other what looked like a counterweight, a square hunk of iron. Schaap first pulled on the bar, got a different grip, and pushed. The bar swung around and to the right, the circle on its end followed, and Mouse watched the switch in the tracks slam that way, too. Past the switch, an arm high on a pole banged down horizontal, and the light below the arm changed from green to red.

"Why the red light?" he asked, looking back in the locomotive at the engineer. The Dutchman said nothing. "Answer me," Mouse said, but he didn't press it by reaching for the Welrod.

"This section of the track has a train on it now. Ours," the engineer said slowly.

"And who else knows this?" Kagen asked. He moved aside as Alder stepped forward to toss coal into the firebox. "Joop said the switches are worked from the central station. They must have a way to watch where trains go so they can work the right switch."

The engineer took his own sweet time, but finally nodded. "Yes, but we can switch them by hand."

"But they know we're here," Kagen said.

The engineer looked at Kagen, Mouse next. "That a train is on the tracks, yes. When we throw a switch, they know a train is here. But not what train. Not that it is *this* train." He looked ahead by leaning out his window, and shouted some Dutch down the tracks.

Mouse leaned out again and saw Schaap wave, run ahead to the next switch, and like before, push it to the right. The locomotive followed, again bearing right.

"One more switch and we're clear of the yard," the engineer said. He shouted again to Schaap, who reached the third switch, pushed it aside, making the white circle move right, the arm on the pole swing down, and the light turn red. The engineer shoved the throttle forward.

But Schaap didn't come back to the train. Instead, he trotted beside the tracks.

"Tell him to get back here," Mouse said, and felt that prickling on the back of his neck. Just ahead was a long platform. Mouse made out figures standing in the rain shadows at its far end.

The engineer leaned out and called in Dutch. Mouse saw Schaap turn, stumble and fall, but pick himself up. He was near the men on the platform. The train came on.

Kagen crowded in beside Mouse. "Ordnungspolizei," he said. "What are they doing here?"

"Look there," the engineer said, and pointed to a group of men behind the Orpo, twenty or more in a clump, each holding a pick or a shovel or a pry bar, their thin clothes soaked. "Foreign laborers. Poles or Russians. Working the tracks."

One of the Orpo waved as the locomotive chuffed nearer and yelled something Mouse didn't catch. The German cop grinned as he waved, called again, and because they were closer now, Mouse heard him clearly this time. *"Wiedersehen, Juden!"* the German yelled and laughed.

"He means the people in the cars," the engineer said, and Mouse glanced back along the train and saw fingers wriggling through the slats of the cattle car behind the tender.

Mouse turned to look ahead again. Schaap was past the platform now, still in front of the locomotive, but he'd heard the Orpo and turned and stepped backward. And that was when Kagen, who had only been holding on to the edge of the cab and waving at the Orpo, him in one of their uniforms if they could see it, brought up his Sten and opened up. The hammering rocked around the cab and Mouse watched as one, then two of the Orpo went down and the Polacks or Russians, or whoever they were, dropped their tools and scattered.

Movement from the corner of his eye caught Mouse's attention, and he turned from the Sten to look forward and saw Schaap right in front of the locomotive. As Kagen fired the Sten, Rachael's brother pulled the Smith & Wesson from inside his soaked coat.

The Sten banging in the background drowned out Mouse's shout, but Schaap slipped on the wet rail, the locomotive bearing down on him. Mouse yelled to the engineer to stop but there wasn't time for that either, and Kristiaan tumbled backward onto the tracks and was gone under the locomotive.

Mouse heard Kagen tell the engineer to go faster. The Sten was quiet, he realized.

Kagen turned and said, "Nineteen."

Mouse knocked the Sten from his hands and punched him, bang-

bang, once alongside the nose and again under the eye covered with the patch. Kagen fell against the tender and into the coal spilled there, and stared up like he didn't know where he was.

Mouse yanked free the Welrod and, bending down, pressed its muzzle against Kagen's temple. Mouse saw real fright, but he didn't pull the trigger. If he popped Kagen, there was just him and Reka.

Mouse picked up Schaap's Sten from the floor of the cab, backed to the other side of the locomotive, pointing the gun on the groggy Kagen. He tried not to listen to the clack-clack of its wheels as they ground over the joints between the rails.

T he rain fell in wide ribbons that came and went in the sharp beam of the locomotive's single light. Mouse's watch said it was only six o'clock, but the clouds and rain had brought the dark early.

Alder climbed back into the cab—he'd run ahead to throw a switch— and then the engineer pulled the train forward a few hundred yards until Mouse told him to stop. The engine wheezed, steam blew out its side, and the cars behind banged together, the sound fading as each knocked into the next.

"Where are we?" Mouse asked.

"Groot Wetsinge," the engineer answered, pointing into the black to the left. "Just a small village. Winsum is another three kilometers up the tracks. Bigger. Then Warffum, eight kilometers more."

"How far to Uithuizen?" Mouse asked.

"From here, twenty kilometers. Thirty minutes, or longer. The tracks here are old, we cannot go fast."

A small figure hoisted into the cab, pulled off a hat, and twisted the water out of long, dark hair. Reka.

"Why have we stopped?" she asked, looking at Mouse. The light from the small lantern in the cab was enough to show her face.

"We had to throw another switch," he answered.

She hadn't noticed that Schaap was missing. "We must go on. It's already six," she said. "Boersma will be waiting for us at half-past ten, that's when the tides let his boats come close. We have to hurry." Hours still, but the unloading of the train and the loading of the boats might take ages.

"Where's Kristiaan?" Reka asked as she looked at the faces in the lamp's dim light, Mouse and Kagen and the wet Alder and the oil-faced engineer. No one answered her, the only sound the still-escaping steam from the engine. "Leonard, where's Kristiaan?" She'd settled her eyes on him.

"He was switching the tracks. And he . . ." He wanted to tell her that Kagen had caused it. She closed her eyes for a second, opened them, and stared into his.

"He died quickly?" was all she asked.

## Twenty-one

The locomotive's wheels slipped on the wet rails, gripped and jerked the train forward. Another meter, then two and three, closer to the Waddenzee.

Reka felt an emptiness. David had refused to leave Westerbork, Rachael was gone, and now Kristiaan, too. They were so few. They would fail.

All she had now was Leonard. She felt his hand in hers as they stood in the locomotive, huddled under its roof and out of the heaviest of the rain. Only the pressure of his fingers kept her from crying.

Kagen had a dark lump under his black eye patch and a deep shadow across his swollen nose. Someone had struck him. Leonard, she knew, from the careful way he looked at the *Duitser* when he'd handed the German one of the Sten machine pistols a few minutes ago.

She looked at Leonard. He stared up the invisible tracks, seeing, as she had seen a moment ago, only a dim green light in the distance. The coal dust was gone from him, washed off by the rain that slipped under the locomotive's roof, but his cheeks were still dark with stubble.

He was such a dangerous man. That night on the polder came to her again, but instead of remembering that, she made herself remember how they had kissed, how his hand had felt on her breast, how right it felt. She didn't know if she loved him, but she did know that the night was dark and the dark was uncertain. Reka knew she didn't want to die not knowing what love felt like.

But it was Leonard who leaned to her ear, not she to his, and whispered, "I have to talk to you." Reka looked at him, saw his eyes, not gray now but darker in the poor light.

"I'm listening," she said, quiet as he.

"Not here," he said. "Someplace private."

Reka looked around the locomotive cab. Kagen stood behind the engineer, a young Dutchman huffed as he shoveled more coal into the furnace. "The wagon at the rear of the train," she said. The train moved no faster than an old man walked; it would be easy.

He nodded. "The engineer said we have a half hour to Uithuizen."

Without a word to Kagen—she thought he would tell the German that they were going to check on Vreesje—Leonard stepped down the ladder of the locomotive, and she followed, hopping to the gravel along the track. As the rain struck her shoulders, the train rattled by so slowly she knew she could reach out and touch its flank and not worry about it crushing her under its wheels. They waited until the passenger wagon drew abreast, then Leonard swung up onto the platform, held out his hand, and pulled her up.

The wagon was dark. Vreesje she'd left at its rear, and Reka imagined she'd be there still. But Leonard, his hand on her elbow, guided her into the tiny compartment on the right. It smelled like dust, dry even through the rain out its window. He left the door ajar.

They sat on the cushioned seat, their thighs touching. Reka felt her leg tremble, just the slightest.

"I have to tell you something," he said.

But she put her fingers to his lips, as she'd done that night on the polder. This time she wasn't embarrassed.

Leonard was silent and the seconds ticked by in time with the noise of the wagon's wheels on the joints between the rails. And then he leaned toward her, and kissed her.

She had hoped that this was what he had wanted to say.

It was too dark for Mouse to see Reka in the compartment, but he could smell her hair, wet from the rain outside.

When she put her fingertips to his lips and didn't pull them away, he couldn't tell her. Not now. This wasn't what he had planned, but the moment was what it was, and he leaned over, knowing where her face was. He found her mouth in the dark and he kissed her.

He reached for the buttons high on the back of her dress, and the hand of hers that had been on his chest climbed and wriggled under the shoulder of his coat, tugging at it, pulling one sleeve from his arm before returning to lie flat over his heart.

Mouse drew away only far enough so that when he talked, his lips barely brushed hers. "Are you sure?" he asked.

She said nothing, but stood, the creak of the springs in the seat the only sound other than the wheels. Her smell grew fainter and he heard the rustle of clothing; he knew if he stretched out a hand, he would touch her.

"Leonard," she said so softly. "We don't have much time."

Mouse stood then, too, and took the Welrod from his waistband and dropped it to the floor. He pulled off his coat threaded with the British pounds and let it fall. He pulled off his shirt, his well-worn boots and too-thin cotton socks, his muddy, wet pants. He shivered in his nakedness.

This was not how it was supposed to be. His muter was supposed to introduce him to this girl. And he was supposed to meet her parents in their apartment, share coffee and cakes. He was supposed to take her to the pictures, maybe to the Coca for dancing, and months later maybe, he would fall in love. It was not supposed to be like this. But it was.

"Leonard," Reka whispered as the springs creaked again.

He felt the cushioned seat against his shin, reached out his hand and there was Reka, bare under his hand, tiny bumps on her thigh from the chill. She shivered when his fingers moved to the inside of that thigh.

"I'm cold," she lied. And as the train rocked slowly, he found a blanket on the seat and pulled it over them. He lay next to her, both of them on their hips on this narrow bench. She was warm, warmer than the heat of the warmest air rushing by in the subway on the hottest day of August. She reached down and put her hand around him, her hand trembling like it had done that first time on the train.

He put his hand on her bare back and traced a line down her spine until he felt the curve, and pulled her so close their skin melted. Mouse touched her breast, cupped it in his hand, circled its tip with first his finger, then his mouth. "Please," she said. She sounded so young there in the dark.

Reka cried, quietly, when he pushed at her, into her. "*Ga door, alsjeblieft, ga door,*" she whispered. "*Mijn lief,*" Reka said quietly, "*mijn lief,*" again, and he thought he understood the words because they were close to the German. Their rhythm matched the rocking of the train as the car clack-clack-clacked over the joints of the rails, each like a sharp footstep, each a step closer to home. He felt the familiar sudden heat and he strained against her and Reka hissed something in Dutch he couldn't understand. It didn't matter. She could say anything and he would love her.

The wiper was motionless against the BMW's windscreen and the rain made a waterfall over the glass. Preuss opened the door and stepped onto the empty, rain-swept pavement outside the Groningen station. The truck with de Groot's men pulled up behind the BMW and switched off its engine. Preuss tossed his cigarette to die in a puddle. Miserable, this weather was. He walked to the shelter of the dark station's doorway.

Krempel had climbed out of the BMW's back seat and stood beside him. The Kripo Munkhart and de Groot stayed. "Hauptsturmführer?" Krempel asked. "What should we do? Our truck . . ."

Preuss didn't bother to look. His head hurt too much to move it more than necessary. "Go find the stationmaster. Hassel, too, the Orpo. He should be with the stationmaster." After putting down the handset in the police station in Staphorst, he'd telephoned this Hassel, the chief of Groningen's Orpo. He'd told him to send out his men to search for the train, then find the stationmaster and meet him here. "Go. Bring them both." Preuss breathed in the cool humid air, thinking it might ease the pain in his head.

No Giskes, either, Preuss thought, moving his head slowly, wishing Giskes were here so he could put the Walther at his temple and shoot him. He pulled another Nil from the tin.

Krempel was back in moments, followed by a short man in a dark uniform—in full light, it would be the green of the Orpo—and a heavier man, the stationmaster certainly, wearing a white shirt that glowed under a dark jacket. Preuss groped in the dark for Hassel's hand, found it, shook it.

"Leutnant Hassel," Preuss said.

"Hauptsturmführer."

"Tell me you've found the train."

Hassel nodded quickly, his small head moving like a toy's in the dark. "We believe so." That was a cue, Preuss thought, and he changed to Dutch.

"Where is the train?" he asked the stationmaster, not bothering to keep his tone pleasant.

"You understand, I'm not certain," started the stationmaster. Preuss didn't nod; that would hurt his aching head. "The signals show a train on the stretch between Winsum and Warffum."

"How far is that?" Preuss asked.

"Twelve to twenty kilometers. Somewhere on that section of the track."

"And you know this is my train?"

Hassel's deeper voice. "There are no trains scheduled for the line, not this time of night. It must be your train of—" and the Orpo, thank God, was smart enough to stop. "And there's the fireman and the shooting in the yard here."

"The fireman? What shooting?"

"One of the locomotive's crew escaped. He showed up babbling about men with guns who stormed his train, south a few kilometers. When the train left, he came out of hiding and found three of my Orpo along the tracks. Part of the transport guard. Murdered, Hauptsturmführer. And just twenty minutes ago, I was told of a shooting in the switchyard on the south side of the city. They shot two more of mine who watched a work gang of Poles. No question but this is your train."

Of course it's my train, Preuss thought. It's always been mine, even before Naumann had shouted through the telephone.

"I want you to show me where it is now," Preuss said to the station-master, and told Krempel to bring the map and a torch from the BMW. He disappeared into the rain.

"There are no branches on this line? No way for the train to escape?"

"No, Hauptsturmführer," said the stationmaster. "The one line, no spurs, and it ends just beyond Uithuizermeeden, thirty kilometers from here. This is the only way out."

"You can close the line, can't you, stop the train where it is? Do that now." Krempel reappeared and handed him the torch and map. He switched on the light and shone it on the stationmaster's face.

"No, that's impossible, Hauptsturmführer," said the stationmaster, his voice nervous. "The switches are manual on this line, so they can throw them as they wish. It's such a small line—"

"Show me." He opened the map and spread it on the damp pavement in front of the door, squatting down to look, forcing the others to do the same.

The stationmaster pointed to a spot north of Groningen. "Warffum is here, twenty kilometers, your train is here somewhere, between here and here." He pointed to places west and south of Warffum.

"You have a station in Warffum, a man there? Telephone him and tell him to stop the train."

"We have, Hauptsturmführer," said Hassel. Preuss pointed the torch in his direction and saw that Hassel was much younger than his voice. He looked too young for his work, but then, aren't we all too young for what we do?

"He likes his drink, I don't know if he understood," the stationmaster said quietly.

"What did you tell him?"

"Only what I was told. That the SD wants this train stopped."

Preuss nodded. "What about this place?" he asked, putting a finger on the map where the faint rail line came closest to the North Sea. Boats, he remembered. They would want a place where the tracks came near the water. He pointed the torch light in the stationmaster's face again.

"Hauptsturmführer?"

"Stop stalling. You heard me."

"I only meant I didn't understand." The stationmaster stared into the glare of the torch, frightened. "That's Uithuizen. It's another nine or ten kilometers past Warffum. I know for a fact there's no stationmaster on duty at Uithuizen, he took sick yesterday."

Preuss drummed a finger on the map. He smoked the last bit of the Nil and threw it into the rain.

"Hassel, call in your men," he said.

The child shook his head. "My company's scattered across forty kilometers, Hauptsturmführer, and we're not important enough for radios." He sounded apologetic. "They check in by telephone every hour or so."

"Fine, fine," Preuss said, trying to skirt the headache and pull together a thought or two. "Can we block the line between Warffum and Uithuizen?" he asked, swinging the torch back to the stationmaster. "In case this drunk of yours lets it through?"

"Block the line? No, as I said, Hauptsturmführer, there's no way to throw a signal from here."

"What good, exactly, are you?" Preuss asked, knowing his nerves or temper or both were shot. "I want these Jews and their train stopped and all you—"

"Jews, Hauptsturmführer?" the stationmaster asked. His face was all confusion.

Preuss flicked the torch's beam off the Dutchman's face. He'd promised Naumann he'd be discreet.

"Telephone your man at Warffum again. Impress on him the importance the SD puts on this train." And the Dutchman nodded—glad, Preuss thought, to be out from under this conversation—and disappeared into the dark station.

He'd have to do this himself.

Preuss turned to Hassel, hesitated for a moment, remembering Naumann's plea for secrecy. But that was out now, and too late in any case. Better the secret be allowed to escape than the Jews. Better that than the cellars on Prinz-Albrechtstrasse. "Luftwaffe, is there a Luftwaffe airfield nearby? Or boats? What about the Kriegsmarine? Do they patrol the coast here?"

"Hauptsturmführer?" Hassel asked, perhaps not following.

"I want planes to intercept this train as soon as the weather breaks. Boats, too, if there are any. The Jews are trying to flee on boats."

"There's a night-fighter squadron in Leeuwarden, I think. Fifty kilometers."

"Boats?"

"Perhaps in Harlingen or Den Helder. That's eighty kilometers, at least. More than a hundred to Den Helder." Hassel paused. "S-boats, perhaps, at Den Helder. The fast ones. But even they will take hours to arrive."

Preuss took the time to light a Nil, thought some more, put his torch on his watch. Nearly seven.

"I'll leave for Warffum, where we'll try to retake the train, but I'll go on to Uithuizen if necessary. You will wait here, right here in front of the station, exactly here, and when my second truck shows, direct it to go to Warffum, and then to Uithuizen if I've gone on. Tell it to meet me at those stations. And an Abwehr officer, Giskes is his name, tall and older, he may be along with more men. If he shows, tell him to do this as well." He wanted Giskes to come; he wanted to deal with that traitor himself. "Gather your men when they check in, and come to Warffum, then Uithuizen if needed. You understand?"

"Yes, Hauptsturmführer," the child said in his deep voice.

"Talk to the Kriegsmarine in Harlingen or Den Helder. Tell them the SD is pursuing commandos bound for the coast and their boats, and I want them stopped. I don't know exactly where, between Warffum and Uithuizen, somewhere in there."

"Commandos? There are commandos?" Hassel asked.

"Just do what I say, and everything will be fine," Preuss said. "Tell them you have orders from Brigadeführer Naumann in The Hague if you have to. Whatever it takes. But they must start their boats this way." He drew deep on the Nil and watched its ember go from dark to bright red.

"Yes, Hauptsturmführer," Hassel said, sounding unsure, but Preuss thought he would do as told. Hassel stood and saluted, his arm stiff out, but Preuss didn't have the time to reply. He was busy looking at the map.

His finger began at Warffum and traced east along the hatchmark line that was the railway as far as Uithuizen. From there the finger moved north, toward the blue that meant the North Sea. To go beyond Uithuizen was to put more distance between railroad and coast. If they made it past Warffum, they would stop here, at Uithuizen, where the walk was but a few kilometers. Here was his train—and he put the finger on the map— here were the boats, and he shifted the finger. If the stationmaster was right, the train was only fifteen or twenty minutes ahead.

Preuss felt a portion of the ache in his head drain away. He had them. He knew where they were. They would not escape.

In his mind, he imagined the scene that the bastard Giskes had once painted for him. Bands played, flags waved, and the Reichsführer himself pinched his cheek.

R eka wanted to doze in the movement of the train and fall asleep against Leonard, his arms entangled around her, their legs touching from hip to ankle. She might pretend again that this was a train to a different place, and that she lay against her lover or even a new-sworn husband. But Leonard talked and broke the moment.

"I have to tell you something," he said quietly into her hair. She moved her arm to put it on his chest and moved her head to lay it beside her hand. Her heart beat a bit faster, thinking that he was going to say something of how he felt, or at least of what they'd just done.

"I went back to the plane that night because I was going back to London."

"I know," she said. "You were afraid. But not now."

He brushed his hand over her still-wet hair. "You know?"

"Yes."

A long quiet, and his fingers stroked a line on her face, tracing the scar.

"I wanted to keep the money," he said. "I was going back to London with that money."

She remembered the stacks of British banknotes he'd paid Boersma. "Yes, I know about the money," she said.

"You know?" he asked again. He was quiet for the longest time and she felt his heart under her hand and head.

His next words came slow from his invisible face. "I wanted the money. And I was going to kill them so no one could say I'd taken it."

Reka felt the warmth drain away. How he'd looked at her that night on the polder, how that huge pistol of his had looked at her like an eel that would swallow her. She had been wrong. He wasn't only afraid. He'd meant to kill the ones he came with.

"But I didn't, that's the important thing," Leonard said, his words fast as he tried to fill the compartment. "I couldn't do it. That's the important thing."

"But you wanted to," Reka said. She pulled away from him and pushed aside the blanket, sat up, naked in the dark and oh so cold.

"I'm telling you this for a reason," he said and put a hand on her arm. "A reason."

She had forgotten who this man was. She'd made herself forget because he'd held her hand and touched her face and made love to her.

"I want you to come home with me," he was saying, words she would have clutched minutes ago but now wanted to push away. "With the money, things would be different. I want you to come to America with me. I'll leave Brooklyn, we'll go someplace, you and me."

There were two men in this compartment. There was Leonard, the one she knew best. But there was also the other, the Mouse, whom she didn't know. Both killed, but only Mouse was like the *Duitser*, Kagen. Mouse killed for his own reasons.

But which man loved her? And which one did she love?

"What kind of man are you?" she breathed, almost a whisper. "You'd kill your own?"

"You killed Annje," he said. The dark was so cold now. "She was one of yours. We're not so different."

She thought about that for a moment, remembering how Annje pleaded. "I didn't do that for money," she said.

"You're forgetting something," Leonard said in anger. "I didn't kill anyone on that field."

Yes. Yes, that was so. He'd run to his comrades with that pistol and she had seen him point it at Kagen. She had slipped from the dark and he'd turned that gun on her. But he'd stopped. He'd not shot the *Duitser* nor her. He'd not shot anyone. And the thought came to her.

"If I hadn't been there, you would have killed them."

Another long pause, and she wondered if he was thinking of lying.

"Yes, if you weren't there, I would have popped them." It was the truth, she knew. His face that night, yes, the truth.

She put her mind around each one of his words and found a way to say what she felt, what she'd felt, she knew now, since she had first seen his beautiful face. "It was meant then, me being there. We were meant to find each other, don't you see?"

Leonard said nothing, and in the silence there, the time between each clack of the wheels on the rails was longer than the one before. The train was slowing.

"Do you love me, Leonard?" she asked. Perhaps by asking she could find out which of these two men here loved her, or if either did. And find out if what she felt was right, that this was all meant.

A second and two of silence. She asked him again.

"Do you love me?"

"I don't know," he said quietly. His words hurt almost as much as her name had that day spoken on the Appelplatz.

The noise of rails was gone now, just the echo of the wagon bumping into the one before it, or that one bumping into this. The dark compartment rocked one last time and was still. Cold, it was so cold. "We've stopped," she said, feeling blindly on the floor for her damp clothes. She stood and pulled them on.

"Reka," he whispered.

"Who are you?" she asked softly.

She waited, but when she didn't feel his hand on her arm—she wanted so to feel his touch and hear him change his words—she stepped out of the compartment.


R eka didn't remember how she'd gotten from the last wagon to the steaming, still locomotive, but there she was. She recognized Kagen by how he stood. The rain was slackening, but it was still as black as the cellar on Lindenstraat when the light was off.

"Why have we stopped?" she asked the *Duitser*. Ahead she saw a lamp set high off the ground. It glowed red.

"The track ahead is taken," someone said in English, and Reka caught a whiff of oil and smoke. The Dutch engineer. "We have to wait until it clears." Reka listened but couldn't hear the sound of another train. No whistle in the distance, no snorting of an engine. Nothing.

"There's a station," she said, seeing a low block of black at the very edge of the locomotive's lamp. Her mind was mostly blank, but she had to do something. She started walking.

"Where are you going?" Kagen called from behind her. She didn't break stride and his boots made noise on the gravel and he was beside her. "I asked where you think you're going."

"To the station," she said. "We must have the line free, yes?"

Reka closed her eyes and opened them again, but the dullness didn't go away. Leonard, she thought, why couldn't you lie and say you loved me?

They walked to the station, the locomotive's lamp showing them the way. A shade behind a window had not been pulled tight and a bar of light spilled out onto the tiny platform and was enough to show the sign on the brick wall: WARFFUM.

She glanced at Kagen for just the slightest second, and after seeing he held a machine pistol, she pushed open the door and squinted against the brightness. A middle-aged man who reminded her of a younger Papa sat in a chair behind a desk. He looked up as the wind followed them into the room. He swallowed, and Reka watched the apple in his throat move up and down.

"We must have the line as far as Uithuizen," Reka said in Dutch, not wasting time. "Do you understand?"

The man, his face sallow in the light of a smoky oil lamp on his desk, didn't look at her but around her, beside her, as Kagen moved. He stared at the *Duitser*'s machine pistol. There were four bottles, big and brown, standing in a line at the edge of his desk. She sniffed and caught the odor. Beer.

"You are from the Resistance," he said, quietly.

"We have a train of Jews," Reka said. "We are going to Uithuizen. And from there to the Waddenzee, where boats wait for us." There was nothing like the truth, she thought as she watched the man's eyes grow big and bigger in his yellow face. "The Germans may follow us, we don't know. But we must get to Uithuizen. If we don't, the Germans will kill us all."

"The stationmaster in Groningen told me to close the tracks," the clerk said. "On orders from the SD." He picked up the bottle closest to him and took a long drink. "It is only eight kilometers to Uithuizen." So the Germans were after them, Reka thought.

"We have women and children," she said, remembering the people in the cattle wagon. "And old ones. They can't walk all the way to Uithuizen, then to the Waddenzee. We don't have time."

He looked at her, his eyes narrow from either the low light or his beer. "I knew a Jew once," the clerk said quietly. Reka heard voices in the background and she looked over the clerk's shoulder and saw a boxy radio on a table near the wall. It was tuned to Radio Oranje, from England, the Dutch announcer quietly intoning something about Warsaw, something about a ghetto there, something about it resisting still. "Fucking *Duitsers*," the man said. "Always telling us what to do, aren't they? Fuck them." He took another swallow of his bottle. He was drunk.

"I knew a Jew once," he said again. "But the Marechaussee picked him off the street when he went out. I told him to stay inside, but he was an old man. He didn't listen." He spoke more to the desktop than to them.

Reka didn't want to break this man's memory, which seemed to be moving him in the right direction, but there was so little time. "Can you make the line clear or not?" she asked.

Without a word the clerk stood, took hold of his bottle, and made for the door. Kagen pointed his machine pistol, but Reka touched its black barrel with her left hand and pushed it down.

"I'll throw the switch for you," the clerk said from the door. "As soon as the signal turns to green, you can go on. Fuck them, that's what I say." For the first time, his sallow face was split with a smile. He missed a tooth at the top.

"Thank you," Reka whispered.

"Do you think he's still alive, that old Jew?" he asked.

"No," she said. Like Leonard, the truth was all she could say.

The clerk nodded, and disappeared with his bottle into the dark. A minute later, the red signal lantern blinked off and the green lantern blinked on.


Mouse sat on the hard-backed seat next to the aisle. Vreesje was beside him, her head pillowed on a crumpled Marechaussee coat pressed against the window. She was awake, but she'd not said a word since he stumbled through the dark from the compartment. He'd lit the small lamp that hung in a bracket beside the back door of the car. The hell with the light, he thought, let the Dutch look in as they rumbled past, and see a man and a woman at the end of a line of cattle cars.

He looked at the woman who had dragged Rachael and her brother, and so the rest of them, to Holland. She didn't look like much. So thin, so frail. If he pushed on her with his finger, it might punch through, like a pencil through a piece of old, brittle paper.

He had fucked up everything. He had spilled to Reka, thinking she knew what he'd meant to do on that field, when she didn't. And told her his crazy idea that she must come home with him.

The train jerked and jerked again, and the dark scenery moved. A man stood under a small light on the platform of a tiny station, waving a bottle in his hand like he was saying goodbye to old friends.

But she'd been right about one thing. Her being there on the field had done more than stop him from popping the four. Without her, none of this would have happened.

He'd always thought himself lucky. That schvartzer whose Browning misfired a foot from his face; how he'd never been pinched, not once; when he'd found the guinea who'd torched his foter's shop by over-hearing those two guys talk on the subway. But maybe it wasn't only luck. Maybe those things happened for a reason.

It explained things. Like why Lansky sent him here, why the Dutch dick had looked at Reka and let them go, and most of all, why he'd not popped Tootles when by all rights he should have.

Was it God's hand? He'd felt that touch just twice, at his Bar Mitzvah and when he watched his foter die from the burns in Brooklyn Jewish, watched his muter close his old man's eyes. She'd taken a corner of the sheet that he lay underneath, and ripped it very slowly, just an inch or so, and whispered the blessing, *"Barukh dayan emet."*

But this was too much for just luck. Even he could see that. She was meant to be there on that field, to make him hesitate. And if that was right, then he was meant to be here. To do this.

They had made this happen, he thought. This train, everything. Not Kagen, who thought only of himself and counting dead Germans. Not Rachael, who had given herself up for only one. It was he and Reka who had done this. They were the ones who would save them from becoming smoke. And that was more than luck explained. God, maybe. Maybe.

But not everything was meant to be, it seemed. Like telling Reka the truth. I tell her about the plan to pop the four and about the money. But I can't tell her how I feel. Not when she hates me for what I was going to do in that field. Where was God's grand scheme in that?

He noticed Vreesje looking at him. He smiled, hoping it wasn't a Lansky smile. Vreesje smiled back. He bent down to the floor and grabbed Reka's cloth bag, the one with a pattern like a carpet. He stuck his hand in and dug around until he found the ancient pistol Reka had gone for that time when the two of them watched Annje through the window. He pulled back on the automatic's slide to put a cartridge in the chamber, flicked the safety on and held it in front of Vreesje's eyes. "You take this," he said. She looked at him from her pillow of a dead man's coat, but said nothing. "The safety's here," he said, and pushed up on the lever at the left side of the Luger. He pointed the pistol toward the lamp and made a quiet sound, "Bang," but even so, Vreesje jumped. He pushed the safety down, pointed again, but shook his head.

He thought she understood, and he laid the Luger in her lap. "I have to go back to the locomotive. You should have this," he said. "You know, for the Germans. *Für die Duitsers,*" Mouse said, mixing his German with Dutch. "Understand? *Verstehen?*"

Vreesje nodded.

S top here," Preuss ordered. De Groot grunted, but did what he was told. The BMW swerved to the side of the road. Across was the darkened station, and beyond the station, tracks. No train. He rubbed his forehead, pushing back his cap with the death's head as he did. "Krempel, Munkhart, come with me." Down the road he heard a man talking and the snort of a horse, but although the rain had stopped and the clouds looked ready to break, even their shadows were invisible.

He walked to the station, shoved open the door—no one locked doors in this part of Holland, it seemed—and aimed for the chink of light at the end of the small waiting room. He didn't knock, but turned the latch and pushed at the door.

A man, his face yellow from the glow of a lamp with its wick turned too high, sat in a chair. He smoked a cigarette, the pack newly opened on his desk. There were six tall brown bottles beside the cigarettes, another lying on its side. The room stank of beer.

"So, you let them go, did you?" Preuss said in his Dutch. Krempel and Munkhart came into the small office behind him.

"Sorry, what did you say?" the stationmaster asked. He had taken off his jacket—it hung over the back of his chair—and he had rolled up the sleeves of his pale shirt, yellow too in the lamplight, and loosened his tie.

"Doesn't your telephone work?" asked Preuss. "Didn't Groningen telephone to tell you how important it was to stop the train?" He picked up the handset, clicked on the receiver, and heard the open line. Some static, but not bad. Into the phone, he said, "Get me the Luftwaffe field in Leeuwarden." There was a hesitation. "Did you hear what I said? The Luftwaffe. Airfield. Leeuwarden. Now."

"Yes," the girl's voice echoed down the line, her Dutch small and far away.

Preuss looked at the stationmaster again. "This seems to be working. You did speak with Groningen. Yes?"

"I'm sorry, what?" the man asked again. This was a waste of time. He nodded to Krempel, who stepped around the desk and roughly pulled the stationmaster from his chair. But the man held on to his cigarette.

"I am Hauptsturmführer Preuss, Sicherheitsdienst," Preuss said, his words clipped short, even in the Dutch. "I have come from Amsterdam to find a train. That train was here. Wasn't it?"

"Pleased to meet you," the stationmaster said, and put his cigarette up to his lips as if to draw a lungful. Krempel slapped it out of his hand, sparks flew, and the man finally looked like he understood what was happening.

"I knew a Jew once," the stationmaster said quietly as he brushed cinders from his shirt. He was drunk.

"Yes?" a man's voice now on the telephone. German, not the simpering Dutch.

"This is Hauptsturmführer Preuss, Sicherheitsdienst. I'm calling from—" and he couldn't remember the name of this spot on the map. "It doesn't matter. North of Groningen."

"What do you want, Hauptsturmführer?" Preuss imagined a man in a room with windows that looked out over a dark airfield. He sounded even younger than Brumm, that Orpo child, but without the ass-licking tone to his voice.

"There are commandos near here," Preuss said. "Near the North Sea. They're trying to escape. I want planes. Put something in the air, immediately. North of—" He had to think a bit to remember the village. "Between Uithuizen and Warffum," he said, pleased he'd finally remembered the name of this flyspeck. "Directly north."

"Hauptsturmführer, I don't understand, you say commandos?" the Luftwaffe voice asked, confused, but at least paying attention.

"Yes, commandos!" Preuss yelled down the line. "English commandos, dozens of them. They've stolen a train and they're escaping, and I want them stopped. They'll be to their boats soon, and if they get away, you'll wish you'd never heard of me."

"I don't have the authority, I'll have to speak to—"

"Then speak to someone who does. Now!" And he slammed the handset down.

He looked again at the drunk stationmaster. "When did the train leave?" he asked, his voice quieter. The headache was back to its worming. No answer, and Krempel slapped the man full on the face. The stationmaster didn't fall but only wiped the blood from his mouth with the back of his hand. He reached for the nearest brown bottle and Krempel knocked that away, too. It shattered in the corner.

"When did the train leave!" Preuss shouted, and leaned close enough to the Dutchman to smell his last swallow of beer. "Tell me, you Dutch shit, or I'll turn you into a yid." The man's eyes registered something at that. "Yes, you know what that means, don't you?"

"Herr Hauptsturmführer." Preuss turned and saw de Groot. How long had he been there?

"I just spoke to a man on the road," de Groot said. "He claims a train was here just a half hour ago." The detective paused, shifted his bulk behind the braces that showed through his open jacket. He looked excited with his news, whatever it was. "He said, Herr Hauptsturmführer, that everyone but the engineer and the fireman climbed down from the train. And he saw them walk north and west. A half hour passed. And the train went on, empty." De Groot wiped sweat from his forehead with a handkerchief he produced from one of his immense pockets.

Preuss turned back to the stationmaster. "How far from here to the water? Quickly!" he shouted.

This time the addled man answered. "Five kilometers. Nordpolder takes you five kilometers to the dike, yes." He nodded, smiled through his yellow face. The man was missing a tooth, and for that, the smile looked sly. No, it was just the man's drink. "Perhaps you'll find your missing train if you hurry." Another half-toothed smile.

Preuss turned and pushed at de Groot to get him to the door. Krempel, however, called from behind. "What should we do with this one?"

"Never mind him," Preuss said. "We'll pick him up after. He's not going anywhere."

T he BMW bounced over the muddy track. A hundred meters back, Preuss had seen a sign in the headlamps that read NORDPOLDER, but that was when the road was gravel. Now it had changed to just mud and more holes than road. The light from the BMW's headlamps jumped onto the track, then into the sky as de Groot shifted and made the engine whine. Preuss glanced back and saw the thin headlamps of the Opel with the Amsterdam policemen, those headlamps bouncing just as madly.

"Slow down, you'll kill us all," he told de Groot, who eased up on the accelerator. Preuss's kidneys were back where they belonged. "You're sure this is the way?" he asked de Groot. They'd not seen a soul, Jew or otherwise, since leaving the last house of Warffum. Just the pale-and-black flanks of cows standing too close to the road.

"Yes, Herr Hauptsturmführer, the man was very specific." The BMW took another hole, this time the left tire, and Preuss wondered how it stayed on. Water jetting from the pothole caught in the light.

"Slow down, I said."

Another minute and still no sign of the Jews. They could not have gotten this far, not two thousand Jews in just a half hour. He knew how fast they walked, he had marched them from the Joodsche Schouwburg to Muiderpoort station for more than five months, and they never walked this fast.

He was about to shout at de Groot that he'd gotten them lost when the BMW swerved into the largest hole yet. There was the screech of folding metal and the loud report of a tire bursting, and brown water and browner mud coated the windscreen. De Groot slowed the car and braked it to a stop.

"You fool!" Preuss yelled. The BMW limped to a halt, and Preuss flung open the door, demanding Krempel's torch. After walking around the front of the car, he examined the left front tire. The bumper and fender had collapsed into the wheel and shredded the tire.

Preuss was furious, the pain was climbing into his head again. He spit as he yelled in German, his anger making him forget his Dutch.

"You fucking cow, look what you've done to the car!" Preuss paced back and forth in the mud in front of the stalled BMW. "And we're so close." He waved a hand at the horizon, where a dark line, straight as a draftsman's, separated sky from ground. That would be the dike against the North Sea. "You prick, if they get away because of this—"

De Groot squeezed from behind the wheel and stood in the beams of the car's headlamps. "Herr Hauptsturmführer, I am sorry. Really I am. Please forgive me, Herr Hauptsturmführer." De Groot's voice was strong and loud.

And with a flash that he first suspected might be the migraine returned in full—and all that meant, hospital and doctors—Preuss had a thought. A malicious, wicked thought. De Groot never said the formal "Herr Hauptsturmführer."

"What's going on?" he asked quietly, his pacing done. Krempel and Munkhart stood now at the rear of the BMW in the glare of the Opel's approaching headlamps. The truck's brakes squealed and its tires slid for a moment in the mud. As Preuss waited for an answer, he thought that de Groot waited too. The sounds of the Dutch policemen climbing from the Opel-Blitz, that was it. Without turning, Preuss heard the voices of the policemen, all ten of them. That was what the fat man waited for.

Preuss unsnapped his holster and pulled out the Walther. He was calm enough to talk in Dutch. "You let that Visser bitch and the rest of them walk out of the shop on Lindenstraat, didn't you? You let Dekker aboard my train in Muiderpoort. And now you're leading us on a chase."

"You're mistaken, Herr Hauptsturmführer." De Groot's voice came out of the big silhouette that marked his place.

The man's impudence was immeasurable. Preuss pulled back on the Walther's slide and heard it rack a round from the magazine into the chamber.

"The Jews are not out here, are they?"

"I believe they are, Herr Hauptsturmführer," de Groot said flatly. There was enough light from the headlamps to see a sliver of a smile on the Dutchman's face.

"There was no man who saw Jews jump off the train and run for the North Sea. And you were the one who sent the letter to The Hague. You did that before we left Amsterdam. Why did you do it, Detective-Sergeant?"

Preuss heard the murmur of de Groot's policemen behind him, but this was not the Lindenstraat and he was not alone. There might be ten in blue, but Krempel and Munkhart were here, both with machine pistols. The Dutch wouldn't dare.

De Groot must have thought differently, or perhaps he thought his words to Naumann protected him. He shrugged, his big belly casting a shadow from the headlamps. "I am tired of your special methods," he said, spitting out the last in German—*Sonderbehandlung*—the sound hard against the Dutch that it followed. No "Herr Hauptsturmführer" now. "The Jews are one thing, but good Dutchmen . . ." De Groot hesitated. "Good Dutchwomen, too. That is another." Preuss recalled the old woman—it had all started there, this Samaritan streak. "Yes, I sent a dispatch to The Hague. I told your fucking lord and master everything," said de Groot, adjusting his braces once again. "I don't know if the Jews will escape, but I am certain you will not."

Preuss's fury was enough to turn the edges of his vision as black as the muddy track beyond the lights. "You love the Jews," he snarled.

"Only because you hate them," de Groot said.

Preuss pointed the Walther, and even though he was the poorest of shots, he couldn't miss, not with the muzzle of the black automatic only a meter from the fat man's face. He pulled the trigger and de Groot backed away, already dead as he slumped against the hood of the BMW, and like a child's fat balloon losing air, sagged to the muddy ground. In the light of the headlamps, Preuss saw a bright red hole under de Groot's eye.

The black at the edges of his vision faded to a red, the red to pink, the pink to nearly nothing. For a moment he felt content.

"Hauptsturmführer," Krempel said from behind him. And Preuss turned, the Walther still in his hand. De Groot's men stood in a solid knot on the muddy track, backlit by the Opel's headlamps. It was impossible to see their faces.

"He conspired with Jews," Preuss said, loud enough for the Dutchmen twenty meters away to hear. "Get back in the truck."

They began to edge away. How meek, how mild. But they surprised him by taking to their heels and darting into the darkness. "Krempel!" Preuss yelled. And Krempel pointed his machine pistol into the blackness and blazed away, the flashes ruining Preuss's night vision.

It was several seconds before Preuss could see more than bright blotches. Some of the Amsterdam men had run back to the Opel and crammed into its cab while the rest, another three or four, hung on its sideboards. The truck's engine caught, he heard a gear grind and rattle, and mud was slinging from its rear tires as it backed down the road toward Warffum.

Preuss emptied the Walther's magazine, all seven rounds remaining, at the truck but he doubted he hit anything. Munkhart leveled his machine pistol and fired a short burst, but the gun jammed. And Krempel groped for another magazine. The headlamps got smaller, smaller yet, and they swung off the road and lit the grass along the shoulder. It was turning around. Its rear lamps, tiny red specks, were gone a few seconds later.

Preuss's mind went barren then, as if the rage had burned every twig of emotion and left him as a fire does a forest.

"There's a spare tire somewhere," he said flatly to Krempel long moments after they had watched the truck disappear into the dark. "Pull out the bumper and change the tire."

Preuss listened to Krempel and Munkhart swear as they dragged de Groot out of the road, as they tugged at the bumper and fender, and wrestled in the mud with the tire jack. Other than that, the only sound was that of frogs. Hundreds and thousands of frogs chirping and belching and hooting.

He lit a Nil with shaking fingers, the flame of his lighter dancing even though there was barely a breeze. And he leaned over, hands on his knees, the migraine suddenly too much for his stomach to take, and vomited all over his boots.

# Twenty-two

S team dribbled from under the locomotive as Mouse walked up the edge of the train. The clouds were breaking fast now, and the half moon, falling toward the west, made enough light to see Kagen jump down from the cab, another man right behind him. As he got close, Mouse could tell the other was the Dutch engineer.

"There you are," said the German, turning to Mouse.

"We're here?" he asked, keeping an eye on Kagen's hands, but the guy had his Sten over a shoulder. The moonlight showed the small station to the right, but he couldn't see a sign.

"Not quite," said Kagen. "The engineer hasn't any idea where the tracks are—the ones Joop said run to the cannery on the coast." Reka climbed down from the locomotive and stood to the side. He didn't say anything to her, afraid whatever he said would only make things worse between them.

"Maybe there's a stationmaster," Mouse said. He looked that way. The building was dark, and seemed deserted.

"You walk the tracks ahead, see if you can find the switch for the spur to the coast," Kagen said. "I'll see if I can find someone here who knows."

"Sure," Mouse said finally. The engineer climbed into the locomotive and, after some noise there, handed down a metal lantern, a large glass globe with a tin top and bottom. It was already lit. Mouse waited for Reka to say she'd go with him, but she was silent. He slung his Sten and grabbed the lantern from the engineer.

Its light was enough to keep him from stumbling over the rails and ties, and Mouse stepped off.

Mouse held the lantern over the switch. The tracks forked to the left. That was north, he thought. Toward the Waddenzee. They were going to make it. He and his Jews were fuckin' going to make it.

Mouse set the lantern beside the switch and grabbed its iron bar and swung it in a half-circle, pulling it toward him. He heard the switch slam open. The lantern again in his hand, he double-checked to make sure the switch had really thrown, and that the tracks would now bear the train to the left.

He turned, ready to walk the half hour back to the station, but was only fifty yards from the switch when he saw the single eye of the locomotive coming. Kagen and the engineer had figured it out themselves.

The engine was creeping along, looking for the switch he supposed, and he swung the lantern back and forth to signal and the train slowed even more. As the locomotive came abreast, he swung up the ladder and into the cab.

His lantern showed him that something was wrong. Reka cowered in the corner, a fresh mark across her cheek. Vreesje sat on the floor beside her, wearing a dead Marechaussee's jacket, her big eyes staring at him.

And Kagen, he was waiting for him. He held a Sten and in the light, Mouse saw its bolt was pulled back. The Welrod was tight against Mouse's stomach, tucked in the waistband under his coat, and his Sten still over his shoulder. He'd never get to either. Alder scooped another shovel of coal and threw it into the firebox, swinging its small door shut with a practiced move of the shovel, avoiding Mouse's eyes.

"What's going on?"

"Leonard, I tried to stop him—" But Reka didn't finish. She didn't have a gun, Mouse noticed.

"She gave me a tussle, this one of yours," Kagen said. He idly swung the Sten toward Reka, then back at him.

"What did you do, Paul?" Mouse asked, using the German's first name.

"He opened the last ten wagons, and he left them back at the station," said Reka. The red mark. That was where Kagen had hit her. "He unhooked wagons from the train, Leonard. I told him we had more than the boats could carry, I was just talking, Leonard, to see if he had any ideas."

"We couldn't take them all," Kagen said.

"So you left them, like you left her," Mouse said, not caring what the words did to Kagen's finger, that finger on a trigger. "You fuckin'—"

"The SD are behind us, she told me so," Kagen said. That was news to Mouse. "They'll have to stop and gather them up, won't they? It gives us more time to get away. It's a good idea, gangster." Kagen tugged on that patch of his.

"Like leaving her was a good idea."

"And if I'd done something there in the camp, where would we be? With all those policemen, inside that fence, guns everywhere you look. That would have been smart, wouldn't it?"

"Leonard, I'm sorry, I'm sorry," Reka said from her corner.

"We have to go back," Mouse said. "Stop the train, back it up, and hook the cars again. We'll find room for them on the boats, we can do that. Please," he said, begging like he'd never begged, not even to Lansky.

"No. We're getting out of Holland, and those I left behind, they'll help us."

"Stop the train," Mouse said, talking straight to the engineer, but the Dutchman didn't move the throttle lever. Mouse stepped toward the engineer and Kagen made his intentions plain by raising the Sten and aiming it right at his chest.

"Leonard, don't," Reka pleaded.

"You point a gun at me, you'd better pull the trigger," Mouse said.

Kagen laughed. "We need each other, or we don't get home. You said that yourself."

The silence between them lasted a half-dozen shovelfuls from Alder. Finally. "Me and you, we'll take care of this business later," Mouse said. But he tried one more time. "Stop the train," he said to the engineer.

"No, you don't understand," said Kagen. "I'm not going back for those ten wagons."

The Germans took it out of their hands. A rough drone above them, loud enough to hear even over the groans of the locomotive and the scraping of its wheels on the rails, and Mouse leaned out and saw a thin-winged airplane against the moonlight. The moon disappeared, as a bright light—whiter than the sun on a hot August day—hung in the air. A flare. Swinging, falling, drifting under its parachute above and along the train, it cast a camera's flash, enough so Mouse saw fingers wriggling through the slats of the first cattle car behind the tender.

"You want to go back for them now, gangster?" Kagen asked, and laughed again.


Preuss switched off the engine, and the BMW coughed into quiet. The half-moon now clear of the clouds was just enough to show the sign across the narrow cobblestone street. UITHUIZEN.

He opened the door and stepped out. Krempel and Munkhart followed and the doors slammed shut. It was quiet on the street, but he didn't think anyone in this village was asleep. As they'd driven by the houses that surrounded the station, the BMW shaking its bent front wheel, he saw curtains pull aside and faces press against backlit panes. That told him the train was here.

He and Krempel and Munkhart went through the unlocked doorway, the dark waiting room that smelled of stale cigarettes, and onto the platform itself. There it was.

The train sat silent like a thing that had once been living but had given up on life. It was black, and the black stretched into the night so far that the moon couldn't show him its head, only the nearest wagons, empty, and their doors gaping wide.

Even with the two men behind him holding machine pistols, Preuss felt uneasy. It had ghosts, this machine, and he touched the side of the nearest wagon gingerly. Preuss wanted to rant and rave, spit out oaths and call down God himself on this damned train, but he had no energy now. They were gone, these Jews, and with just two men there was nothing he could do. Preuss pinched the bridge of his nose.

He walked along the train, the Walther in his right hand, and as he counted the wagons and looked into each, the open doors, like mouths, mocked him in the moonlight. Bags lay scattered on the ground along-side the wagons, under the wagons, in the wagons, where the Jews had left them.

They reached the front, and saw no locomotive. A cattle wagon, the tenth not counting the guards' at the rear, and then . . . nothing. No engine.

"Hauptsturmführer?" Krempel asked. At first, Preuss was confused, too.

But he began to understand. "Where's the rest of the train, do you think?"

Krempel didn't answer.

"They've cut these wagons and gone on," Preuss said. "They've left half the Jews behind," Preuss said. "See if you can find some. They'll be near, the older ones anyway."

Krempel and Munkhart didn't move, didn't understand. "Look around, there are Jews somewhere." The two nodded, switched on their torches, and went off into the dark. Preuss pulled his cigarette tin from his tunic and lit a Nil. These people were brilliant; they'd sacrificed a lesser part to let the greater escape.

Five minutes was all it took for Krempel and Munkhart to return with a small huddle of Jews, prodded by machine pistols. One, two, five, six, eight of them. Not the best *Aktion* ever, but it was a start.

Preuss went to the nearest, a short, round woman, in the half-moon looking fifty, perhaps sixty. Her hair was white in any case, and her face set in a mask, whether fear or rage, Preuss couldn't tell.

"*Dacht u dat u kon ontsnappen?*" he asked, reaching down and touching her face.

"*Meneer?*" the grandmother asked. But she had understood him well enough. She *had* thought she could get away.

"Do you want us to look for the others?" Krempel asked from behind these representative Jews.

"No, no, I don't think so. Ten wagons, that means there might be eight hundred or a thousand out there somewhere. No, they were let loose to slow us down. Don't worry, none of them will get far. We can round them up later."

"The train, Hauptsturmführer, where's the train and the rest?" Krempel asked.

A light in the distance gave him a good idea. It was dazzling white, and hung low in the sky. He caught the sound of an aircraft engine then, thrumming far away near that light. In its glare, he briefly saw the tiny silhouette of a Storch, the delicate wings and long wheel struts easy to make out. Another flare blossomed, and although it was too far—a kilometer or more, he thought—to see if there was a locomotive and wagons under it, he knew. There were the rest of his Jews.

"Krempel, go drag some of these good Dutch out of their homes. I want to know how to get there." And he pointed toward the flares to the north.

T he locomotive wheezed to a stop, and the engineer jumped down to examine the dark rails. Soon he came back and said they ended here, someone had torn them up, perhaps the *Duitsers*. They were always ripping up things to build their bunkers and traps along the coast.

They were less than a kilometer from the coast, the engineer figured. Mouse told him he was free to go, go, get out of here. The Dutchman blinked in the light of the oil lamp and nodded, but said there wasn't anywhere to go. He waved a hand at first one side of the roadbed, then the other.

Mouse saw his point. There was water along both sides of the train. These polders flood easily when it rains like this, the engineer said.

"I think this is the only way to the coast here," the engineer said, "since I can't walk on water. And if the Germans are back there, they'll shoot me when they come up the track. They'll shoot me in any case, for helping." He didn't bother to keep the bitterness from his voice.

Mouse nodded and jumped down to the narrow ribbon of gravel next to the ties. Another fifteen feet from his boots and there was water. The engineer was right; the Germans would come up the tracks behind them.

Kagen was already swinging open the latch on the first cattle car, metal knocking metal, and hands appeared again from inside the car and shoved the wooden door wide. Behind the German, Alder yelled instructions. Under the half-moon, people surged out of the car, some jumping down, older ones carefully lowering themselves over the edge, mothers passing kids to those below. Bags and old men, satchels and young women, suitcases and middle-aged men in rumpled suits, all poured out of the car in a reverse of the loading in Westerbork. Had that been only this morning?

"Tell them to move away from the wagon!" Kagen shouted to Alder, and the Dutchman translated. "Tell them that they are safe! Tell them we will walk to the beaches, where boats wait to take us to England!" But the crowd of sixty or eighty or a hundred that had swarmed out of the car was impossible to control. It was chaos.

Mouse hated Kagen for a lot of reasons, most for laying a hand on Reka and for leaving half his Jews. But he put those hates away so he could concentrate. He walked down the train until he came to the third car, grabbed the iron latch at the cattle car's door, and swung it up and over.

"Let me help," someone said. Alder. The young husband looked at him for a second, then they shoved at the door and it grated open.

Of all the Jews on the train, these are most my responsibility, Mouse thought, and put his hands out to help them down.

The old man was first, the one who talked to himself. His gray hair was pulled half over an ear, and Mouse saw it for what it was, a hairpiece. The old man clutched his hand, and when Mouse got him to the gravel, he still clutched it with both of his.

"*Dank u,*" the old man said, and Mouse didn't need a translator. He didn't know the Dutch, so he answered in Yiddish, "*A sheynem dank.*"

"*Yasher koach,*" the old man said back.

"Say '*Welkom,*' that's the Dutch," Alder said next to him.

No, Mouse thought, the Yiddish, that's better here. And he held out his hands again and brought out first one, then the other of the boys, who looked tough, like new leather, the ones who had helped pull off the planks. "*Dank u,*" each said.

A skinny young mother next, the one with the little dark-haired girl whom he'd first seen from the alley in Amsterdam. In this light, the girl, not more than four, looked like a miniature Reka. "*Dank u,*" the mother said, and she looked pretty in the moonlight, her thin face smiling. Next the mother with the two little boys who had walked in front of them toward the station yesterday. Even the guy with glasses who had stirred up trouble, afraid that they'd be shot for trying to escape, he said "*Dank u*" as Mouse reached out his hand, which the middle-aged man didn't take.

And Mouse helped down the rest, dozens of them, most saying thanks or sometimes long-winded sentences, like the frail old lady in a man's overcoat who cried and hung on his neck until he pried her off. Mouse helped each and every one out of that stinking animal car.

Leonard stood beside the huge locomotive, its blackness drawing all the light from the bright, sputtering German flare. As the tiny aircraft whirred over the remnants of the train, heading back up the tracks for Uithuizen, it dropped another flare. The light doubled for a moment and showed Reka the profile of Leonard's face as he turned to watch it fly over them.

His jaw was set in a hard line that made his strong chin even stronger. It seemed to her that he was trying to decide.

Reka wanted to move off into the dark toward the boats, which should be there within an hour. But the SD were behind them somewhere; the little aircraft, whose engine now droned in the distance, was proof.

"Leonard, what should we do now?" she asked.

He turned to face her, and the others she had convinced to stay behind, all of them knowing what had to be done but none of them wanting it. Eighteen boys and men.

More long seconds passed, and Leonard put his wrist near his face to see his watch. An hour, Reka knew, until Boersma was to come on the rising tide with his five boats. But an hour was not enough.

"Leonard, what do you want us to do?" she asked again.

"We have to keep the SD from following the others," he said. Those behind her huddled closer, and because they likely knew no English, she translated Leonard's words into Dutch. "We have to stay behind to give them a chance," he said, and she translated that, too.

The flare floated over the train, and there was enough light for her to see his face full now. She nodded, accepting what he said.

"We can use the train as cover," Leonard said. "They'll come along the tracks, it's the only way. If we can keep them here for . . . ," and his voice drifted off for a second. "For two hours, or three, the others can get away." She spoke again in Dutch for those behind her.

"You're right, this is what we must do," she said to Leonard, now in English. Her voice was firm, she heard, but her heart raced. Reka stepped close to him and put her hand to his cheek. *"Mijn lief,"* she said.

That, too, was the truth. She loved Leonard, the one strong enough to do this. It was Mouse she wasn't sure about.

For a moment, he touched her hand with his own. Then he walked to the bags piled near the first cattle car, opened them, and handed out the guns they had brought from Amsterdam. After emptying those, he reached for the stack of rifles taken from the Marechaussee and Orpo guards once on the train.

The light of the flare disappeared as if someone had turned a switch, and all that was left was the half-moon to show them the way to the final wagon of the train. There, Leonard directed where they were to wait with their revolvers and rifles. The young man who had shoveled coal in the locomotive slipped under this last wagon; an old man squatted near the water's edge on the railroad embankment with a revolver; two boys younger than her knelt beside the train.

And they waited for the SD.

———

Preuss sat on the curb, his black boots stretched out on the cobblestones, and looked up at the night sky spread with stars. The moonlight was too weak to hide them all. What was Marta dreaming this moment? He stubbed out his third Nil on the curb beside him.

Although the Storch had sown more parachute flares to the north, it had been twenty minutes since he'd last heard its engine. He didn't want to stand nor climb back into the shaky-wheeled BMW for the drive to Amsterdam, because all that waited there was defeat and Naumann. Even the thought that a thousand Jews wandered the fields and waited for collection wasn't enough to stop his wondering if he'd live to see Marta again.

But the world changed when two trucks, canvas-covered Opel-Blitzes both, rumbled up the street and pulled to a stop opposite. Armed men, Germans all, jumped out of the back of the first Opel, his men; and Giskes stepped out of the second. More men climbed out of that truck, one carrying an MG-42 over his shoulder with a belt of machine-gun cartridges looped around his neck.

"Preuss," Giskes said, striding across the street and extending his hand to help Preuss stand. "Not too late, am I?" The older man took off his cap and brushed back his hair, the gray turned silver by the moonlight.

He'd been wrong about Giskes; it had been de Groot all along. "I'm glad to see you," said Preuss. Now there was the chance he could keep these Jews from swimming for England.

"I had a hell of a time finding this place," Giskes said. Preuss glanced over Giskes's shoulder and saw Krempel forming up the men.

Preuss didn't care about excuses anymore. "Part of the train is here, but its Jews have scattered," Preuss said. "They're not the problem. The remainder of the train went on."

Giskes nodded. "They'll make for the closest stretch of the coast, I suppose."

"I know where they've gone," Preuss said. He nodded to Munkhart, who stood watch over a pair of Dutch, a pale man with an untucked shirt and a bloody nose, a woman, his wife, with feral brown hair and eyes to match. "The stationmaster here, I pulled him from his sickbed. He says there's an old spur line, not used for ten years, that can take them almost to the water. An old cod cannery's there, and a crude harbor for fishing boats. That's where they're headed."

"How many?" Giskes asked, brushing his hair again.

"A thousand, perhaps more, from what they left of their train and what the train held when it left Westerbork." He looked past Giskes at the meager force lined up alongside the trucks. His eight, plus another nine—no, eleven—brought by Giskes. And the two of them. Twenty-one for more than a thousand Jews. "This may not be enough."

"Ah, a Jew here or a Jew there, what does it matter?" Giskes said, and after a moment, began laughing. "I'm teasing, Preuss. Any that slip through our fingers we'll get in the morning. They won't go far."

"Hauptsturmführer, we're ready," Krempel said from beside him. "I've parceled out the ammunition and told them not to shoot Jews unnecessarily. We don't want to waste any, I told them."

Giskes was already heading for the second truck. "I'll lead," he said, calling back over his shoulder as he climbed into the Opel and slammed the door. That was fine by Preuss. "Nothing like a little hunt to get the blood up, eh?" And the Opel bucked into gear and rumbled over the cobblestones.

T his is how you reload," Mouse said to the old man, and showed him how to break open the Webley revolver by pressing the thumb lever on the left, which pivoted the front half down and ejected the spent cartridges. "You stick the new cartridges in the chambers," he told the old man, Simon Levie his name was. He'd fought the English in South Africa, he said, he knew how to fire a pistol, young man. Mouse poured a handful of cartridges into Simon's open palm and told him to aim good, this was all he'd get.

Mouse walked along the track and sat beside Reka, their backs to the large steel wheel of the last car.

"How much longer?" he asked her, but she didn't answer. "Reka, how much longer?" She held up her watch and he flicked his lighter's wheel to strike the flame. Nearly ten.

"Less than an hour," she said.

In the dark, the only sound now was frogs, thousands of them in the water on both sides of the train.

R eka thought of Mama and Papa and David. And Leonard.
Somewhere, far to the East, Mama and Papa were smoke and ash swirling from a German chimney. David, closer and still alive, would be smoke soon, too.

But she was not going to die in the East. She would not end up as smoke. Even if this went wrong, Leonard would see to that. Even if he didn't love her, he'd make sure.

Z *ij komen!"* a voice shouted. Mouse looked up and saw two pairs of weak lights, like headlights, jumping up and down on the track toward them. He heard the sound of motors straining, getting closer each second, and eventually the rough noise of tires thumping over wooden ties.

Fuck. It was the cops.

Hold it, hold it, he prayed, hoping they'd remember not to fire early, but let the Germans come close in the dark. It was their only chance of kicking them in the teeth and making some time for the rest.

But someone spoiled it, like Mouse should have figured, by shooting too early out there in the dark. One shot first, the most nervous of the Dutchmen at the trigger, and then the others chimed in.

Mouse raised his Sten and leaned it against the steel wheel of the cattle car.

P reuss knew something was wrong only after Giskes's Opel drove for the edge of the roadbed and then slowly went on its side into the watery polder.

"Stop!" he shouted to Krempel, but his words were drowned by the shattering of glass in front of his face and the hard drum of hailstones on the hood of the truck. Krempel jerked on the wheel and braked hard, the tires bumping over the ties. Preuss's head flung forward and he hit it on the frame of the door.

"Get out, get out," he yelled, and in a fog—a new headache suddenly competing for the one already there—Preuss slid toward Krempel and tumbled out the door and to the ground. His back was to the truck, the truck between him and the North Sea. The hood took more hailstones, and it was several seconds before Preuss realized that it wasn't bad weather that did the knocking.

There were more than five Jews shooting at him. "Can you see anything?" he shouted at Krempel, who was collecting the men at the rear of the truck.

Preuss carefully crawled on his hands and knees until his face was beside the left wheel of the truck. On the right, Giskes's truck was trying to catch fire, but it was half in the water and the flames were weak. Shapes moved against those flames. More hailstones hammered the high snout of the Opel and Preuss ducked back. Glints of red showed on both sides of the roadbed ahead, separated by a blacker boxy shape that he saw as the rear of the train. Some of the Jews had machine pistols. Incredible.

"Hauptsturmführer," Krempel said into his ear. "What should we do?"

"You don't know?" Preuss said.

"I've not had much practice in this kind of thing, Hauptsturmführer." Krempel, Preuss saw, was as frightened as he was. Easy enough to slap around railroad clerks or drag Jews from homes, but this, this was different.

Preuss remembered some of what had happened on the polder that night when the English aircraft came, and what Giskes had done. "We must get around them. On their flank. Yes?"

Krempel didn't argue, Preuss realized, because he had no better idea. "Yes, Hauptsturmführer," he said, and crawled back to the end of the truck. Soon two men, another two, and one more ran from the fragile protection of the truck, slid down the embankment, and disappeared into the polder's water. The last three, Munkhart and two other Kripo, squatted beside him.

Preuss pulled his Walther from its holster. Jews with guns. How astounding.

T he first truck disappeared to the left as shots shattered one of its headlights; another shot must have killed the driver. Mouse, now kneeling, saw it on its side off the roadbed, its remaining headlight gleaming on the water. He let loose at the second truck, that one still coming right along. The Dutch with revolvers and rifles and Stens joined in, and Reka was beside him, cocking a Smith & Wesson, aiming carefully and getting off one shot after another. The second truck stopped on the track fifty yards away, and it was quiet for a second.

There came a long, deep sound, like a big paper bag blown up and crushed between hands. The fire had reached the overturned truck's gas tank. He could see men moving near the truck, the Germans who had gotten out, but he kept his head down. One of the boys behind him wasn't so bright. He'd gotten excited, and as he yelled in Dutch, the fool stood up, put his rifle to his shoulder, and a moment later he was moaning along the train. Alder squirmed out from under the cattle car, dragged him nearer the rails, and in a minute, had hefted him onto his back. The wounded boy's arms hung around Alder's neck and they disappeared into the dark.

Something sawed the air, and the roadbed at his side disappeared into splinters of gravel and ties, some slugs singing off the rails and sparking into the night. That was more than a Thompson or a Sten, and Mouse tried frantically to get under the cattle car. The saw buzzed again, but it tore up somewhere else. Mouse heard Dutch shouted from the other side of the train.

"They've lost three there!" Reka shouted in his ear. She'd crawled under the car with him.

He wormed from underneath the train and crawled over the gravel, Reka with him every inch. They'd watch this side of the train, someone else, he hoped, maybe Simon, would handle the other. The machine-gun sawed away and its slugs chewed at the train.


We underestimated these commandos," Giskes said. "Jews, I mean. Whoever the hell they are." He lay against the steep bank of the track roadbed. The weak flames from the burning truck were just enough to show the end of the train. An occasional shot disturbed the darkness, but for the most part everyone had stopped firing when he and Giskes had pulled their men back a hundred meters.

Giskes was stuffing a bulky field dressing inside his uniform tunic. There was a dark stain along his side, visible in the moon's light. The Abwehr man sounded tired. "How bad?" Preuss asked, nodding to Giskes's side.

"I'll live. But these commandos . . . these Jews . . . they have lots of guns, Preuss. They're trying to delay us until their friends are gone and safe. We need to get around them, flank them, and get to the water."

Preuss wasn't so sure. Krempel had waded through the knee-deep polder trying to do just that and had come back minus two, both shot and drowned, Krempel said. The Scharführer was shaking when he reported.

Giskes grimaced. "How many have you lost?"

"Two," Preuss said.

"Three of mine, one dead and two burned."

"What do we do?" Preuss asked, counting. They were only sixteen now.

Giskes shrugged. "Regroup and try again. I'll take my men along the bank on the right, you take to the left. The MG-42 can pin them down from the track here."

"Perhaps we should wait," Preuss ventured. "A company of Orpo should be along soon. That's another eighty at least."

"And if the Jews swim to their boats in the meantime?"

Giskes was right. The last thing Preuss wanted was to wade through water while someone shot at him, but Naumann's voice rang in his head and made him brave enough for the moment. Preuss nodded.

"I'll get my men," he said, and crawled off to find Krempel.

---

Mouse relaxed when the Germans stopped shooting and pulled back into the dark. Each minute of silence that moved on his watch was another minute the others had to reach the water.

"Leonard," Reka whispered to him, and he thought she'd heard a noise in the watery fields beside the track again. He listened, but heard nothing.

"An air—" was all she got out, and then the world came apart.

Up the tracks, back the way to Uithuizen and the Germans, he saw something winking low in the sky, green flashes like small, strange matches struck again and again and again. And the airplane, huge, three times as big as that puny thing before, roared over their heads, two engines thundering, propellers silver in the moonlight, and at the same time, shells, not just slugs but like cannon shells, turned the last cattle car into splinters that rained down, more plucking at the gravel and digging holes the size of dinner plates in the gravel yards away, and ripping the train from one end to the other.

Mouse tucked himself against and then over Reka, his arms encircling her and shoving her under him. He pushed with all his weight, as if to put her underground where she'd be safe.

The patter of wood and gravel on his back and shoulders stopped, and when he looked up, guns flashed near the stalled German truck and along the slope of the roadbed.

He was no soldier, but Mouse knew enough to know that they wouldn't hold the Germans here, not now, not with that airplane on them. They had to get away from the train, which was the target. Fall back into the dark and try to hold them off from there.

Mouse grabbed Reka and hauled her to her feet, then went down the tracks, keeping low, shouting to the others to run for the water. He collected each man who could move before following them.

The only time he stopped was at the locomotive, which bled steam and dark oil from the huge holes punched in it by the German airplane. He made Reka wait for a few seconds while he picked up a rock and started scratching into the engine's black paint.

———

T he dike was all that kept them from the Waddenzee. It rose up behind them, the only dry ground besides the roadbed without rails, which was twenty meters to the left. Beyond its bulk, this sudden hill from the polder, was the ocean, she knew, even though she'd not put eyes to it. She could smell it, a low-tide smell of mud and fish and salt.

Reka lay close enough to Leonard to wonder if he could hear her heart strike each rapid beat. In one hand she held a revolver, and the other was wrapped in Leonard's.

She knew now that he had lied to her in the compartment, about how he didn't love her. Ever since he'd covered her with his own body, pressing to drive her into the gravel, she'd known.

"Gangster," a voice whispered in the dark, and Kagen dropped beside them. Reka gripped her revolver.

"What's the news?" Leonard asked.

"The boats came. I don't believe it, but the boats came," Kagen said, his voice louder. Reka's heart thumped a time or two in her chest. She had expected that Boersma would see this through—Leonard had paid him a ransom, promised him another—but to know that the fishing boats were on the other side of the dike was different from expectation.

"They're loading?" Leonard asked.

"Not yet. But everyone's at the cannery, right at the water. And it's perfect. There's still a pier. The boats can pull them aboard like fish from that pier." Kagen hesitated. "Just one problem. Only three boats."

"Three," she said. Even with the ones the *Duitser* had left behind at Uithuizen, there were still too many to crowd onto three boats. "Leonard, we'll have to leave some behind." She regretted her words, honest though they were.

"Shit," said Leonard. "He said five, when I get my hands on him, I'll—"

"It seems I was right," Kagen said in a nasty voice.

Reka looked out over the drowned polder, the moon reflected in its water there. The clouds were nearly gone, blown away by a stiff breeze that sped them across the stars. The train was a distant line of burning wagons. The German aircraft had punished it enough to set it afire.

"You and I, gangster, we'll settle things when we're back in England," said Kagen, his voice changing to something hard but frightened. He echoed what Leonard said in the locomotive earlier; they were making a pact.

That was when Reka knew the truth. He was not two men, Leonard and Mouse. He was only one. And no matter what he said, whether he changed or didn't, she would love him.

Leonard didn't have a chance to answer the *Duitser,* for in that moment the aircraft roared over their heads again, the night made day by one, two, three flares floating in the sky, and sounds of shots broke over them like waves break over sand. A loud roll of gunfire, the sawing of the machine gun, and the polder was lit by a dozen or more winking red and yellow stars as guns blinked in the grasses in front of them. More shots came from the right, at the base of a clump of trees, that clump an island above the water.

The world beat even larger hammers and she put her head in the grass as the German vulture returned. Under the howl of aircraft engines she thought she screamed.


It was the field where O'Brien had set them down all over again, but this time it was made day by the flares, and the bees seemed in the thousands, huge, angry insects raining down as the airplane brushed overhead so low he swore he felt its wind. Mouse buried his nose in the wet roots of the grass at the base of the dike and tried not to think. If he thought, he'd stand up to get the fuck out of here, and end up with a hundred stings.

And as the smaller bullets zinged and zooped past, Alder flopped down beside him. Mouse moved enough to turn his head and look at the boy. He'd taken the wounded one to the water, but he'd come back. More shapes filtered down the slope, too, and Mouse saw what else Alder had done—he'd brought reinforcements, men to pick up the guns dropped by the fallen.

Alder got to one knee and leveled his rifle at the flashes in the grass and in those trees on the right. He sighted the rifle and pulled the trigger and worked its bolt, Mouse seeing each spit of flame. In that second, Mouse felt a sort of pride.

But Alder was too brave or maybe just too slow, and a bee caught him under the chin, another his chest, a third his shoulder, all together like a hive swarming, and he went down in a rag bundle. No time to shout or call out, he was dead when he touched the ground.

Mouse couldn't stop himself, the anger on him so fast he couldn't even think—he'd busted his ass to save Alder and all the others and now Alder was gone, not more than a hundred yards from the water. He stood and pulled the trigger of his Sten until it bucked and jumped in his hand.

Bees struck the ground a few yards in front of him, one slow bee jumped up and stung him down under his ribs, and he fell back into the grass and lay beside the dead boy.

# Twenty-three

They flushed out the Jews who remained beside and under and near the train, found two already dead and three wounded, as well as an untouched boy cowering behind one of the steel wheels. Preuss himself used his Walther like in the old days, the first time since his breakdown when they'd had to bundle him onto a train and send him home to Vienna and Marta for his nerves. One bullet, one Jew, a single shot to the back of the neck. *Genickschuss*. His headache put a hot light behind his right eye as he walked from one Jew to another. He ended standing over the boy who pleaded that he wasn't a Jew, although of course he was, since he had a yellow star on his coat, the idiot.

And then they pushed on, finally reinforced by a squad of Orpo that Hassel brought from Groningen—the rest of his company just a half hour behind, said the bass-voiced child. Only at the locomotive did Preuss take pause as he noticed the words scratched into its black skin. He didn't have to ask Munkhart what they meant this time.

## MEYER LANSKY SENDS REGARDS, YOU FUCK

"If ever I find this Lansky," he said to Krempel, "I will gut him like a fish and make him eat his own entrails."

Krempel just nodded before sliding down the embankment and into the polder's cold water. Preuss followed, soaking both his trouser legs and boots. He had no intention of leading from the front, and splashed behind Krempel to the dry rise near the foot of a high, long, straight hill. The hill, Preuss realized slowly, was the dike between Holland and the ocean.

The Me 110 night-fighter swept overhead, dropped three flares to put the polder in relief and first Krempel and his, next Hassel's dozen Orpo, finally Giskes's on the other side of the raised roadbed, opened fire. The gunfire swelled all along the dike, and Preuss crouched behind one of the too-thin trees on this small island. Krempel raised his machine pistol and let loose a long burst. From the east, a pair of green pearl strings, the beads interrupted regularly by darkness, appeared low in the sky, not much higher than the dike, and stabbed at the ground. The tracers showed where the aircraft's cannons probed. The Messerschmitt howled overhead and the budding leaves on his tree shook like in a storm.

At first Preuss was fine, the sound of Krempel's machine pistol comforting him and the aircraft's cannons seeking Jews. There was nothing to this, he thought, forgetting the other polder and how he'd pissed his leg. But when the Jews shot back, flashes just twenty meters away, he couldn't help himself. He curled around the roots of the tree and flinched at each sound.

That was just before the Me 110 strafed again, the crash of its cannons louder by ten now. Krempel collapsed and fell with his face just centimeters away. He cried out loudly for his mother, then his God, and Preuss reached out and his hand came back wet and warm, blood all over. And Preuss couldn't stay, simply couldn't.

He ran from his island without thinking, not sure the direction except that his legs were weighted and weightless in turn, which must mean he'd shoved them through water back to dry land. He ran to a place where the red flickers were absent. The ground rose steeply under his boots and he lost his hat and he ran only to run faster. No thought of Marta, none of Naumann, not even of Jews. His only thought was of getting away.

R eka pulled aside Leonard's coat and felt for blood, waiting for the slickness that would fill her full of emptiness again. He moaned—so he was alive—but the fear was so large in her throat and mouth. She moved her hands on his chest, feeling for the wound—it had to be here, he'd gone down like he'd been killed—but she found nothing. Her hands were close to his waist and she touched the butt of a pistol. She felt blood, but it wasn't enough to even wet her fingertips. There was no shelter from the gunfire that probed the dike, but she rolled him out of his coat and passed her hands over him again until she found what had happened.

"Leonard, your money," she cried in her relief, as she pulled a bundle of the pound notes from the torn lining. A ragged tear had ripped through half the notes in the bundle. "Your money stopped the bullet," she said. "Look." And she held the stack of paper in front of his eyes.

"A ricochet," he said dully. But he was sitting up.

"Oh, Leonard," she said, and leaned for him, then held him in her arms. He had been dead, she thought, sick inside at the memory of those moments, but now he was alive.

Her tears were masked by the whine of the aircraft over her shoulder again and by the doubling of the gunfire spread in front of the dike. And in the storm, their own fire seemed to slacken.

"It's time for the boats," she said, pulling on his arm and standing him up and handing him his coat, even the bundle of pound notes.

She shrugged the sling of his machine pistol over her shoulder, put an arm around his waist, and as the battle surged forward, she helped him climb the dike, aiming for its summit ten meters above.

I f he lived to be a hundred, Preuss thought, he would never forget this. He had climbed the swell of the dike, his legs weaker with each step, but when he reached its level summit, he forgot his panic in the

wonder of the scene. Below him on the water were two stubby boats rising on shallow swells, both nearing a long pier on wooden pilings.

At the foot of the dike, from right below him to the pier and beyond,
was a huge crowd of people pressed against the water's edge, like ants
afraid of a river.

At least the third boat, two hundred meters off shore, was afire, yellow flames and smoke dark in the hissing light of the two parachute
flares still floating down.

The Luftwaffe angel swept over the water, left to right, its green tracers first lancing into the water to splash in white fountains, then disap-
pearing into the dark mass of the crowd. The Messerschmitt 110's two
engines were loud and quickly gone. He thought the Jews would be
screaming, but they weren't.

That's when he saw the woman, so thin, standing at the brow of the
dike where it began its dip toward the water. Her back was to him; she
watched the boats as well. It was simple to step to her and put the muzzle of his Walther at the base of her neck, the noise of the battle behind
them masking the sounds of his boots in the grass.

"Jew," he said quietly, speaking the Dutch. "Don't turn, don't move."
She held the hand of a child, he noticed only now.

Her reply astonished him. "We've won," she said. Her voice was so
calm.

"Certainly not," Preuss said.

He did the same as with the wounded Jews along the train.
*Genickschuss.* Not a Jew will escape. Preuss pulled the trigger.

She stretched out as if to catch herself with her hands and went onto
her face, head lower than her feet, which moved a bit before going still.
The child wailed.

He was bent over and reaching for the hand of the tiny dark-haired
girl, when something cold touched his own neck and a voice, an old
man's voice, although the gun against his skin was steady, asked in Dutch,
"How does this feel?"

The gun's hammer fell, but it was only a snap. Before Preuss could
turn and wrest the empty gun from the old man's hand, everything went
black as something exploded against the side of his skull.

He would have never made it to the top of the dike without her. Whenever he stopped to catch his breath—the ricochet had punched him hard under the ribs—Reka tugged at his coat and told him to stop complaining and keep moving.

"Oh, Leonard," she said as they came to the crest.

No shit.

One boat was burning a couple hundred yards out. But the other two were snugging against the long wooden pier that stretched like a thin finger into the water. Next to the water, but not yet on the pier, was a crawling carpet of hundreds of people. Not moving. Waiting for some-one to give them orders.

"What do we do?" she asked. She still had a hand around his waist, not that he needed it now, but he hadn't bothered to tell her to let go.

"I don't know."

"You don't know? You always know." Was it him, he wondered, that she was talking about?

And then he did know. They had to get everyone on the boats, and fast. He walked through the wet grass to where the slope started to fall away. That's where he found Simon holding a little dark-haired girl in his arms. There were two bodies matting the grass around him. One was a woman, the girl's mother. She'd been zotzed with a slug in the back of the brain, shot like a guinea dropper might do it. The other was a man, his uniform silver in the moonlight. German. He lay on his face, too.

Simon's hairpiece was gone, and his almost bald head was shiny in the flickers of the last flare. He wasn't talking to himself now.

The noise of gunfire flowed over the crest of the dike like water run-ning uphill. The Germans were close. He touched Simon's arm and told him to come. The old man nodded and he stepped down the steep side of the dike with the dark-haired girl in his arms. Mouse and Reka fol-lowed.

They pushed through the crowd along the shore, no one stopping them, and to the wooden pier. It creaked and swayed under the weight of those few already on it. Two boats, not nearly enough. He glanced back at the dike, at the hundreds along the shore. Then again to the two boats. Three hundred, maybe, they could jam on board, and Mouse bet the boats would barely float at that. There had to be three or four times that many waiting.

The sounds of gunfire on the other side of the dike went faint for a moment. Mouse glanced again at the pier, and the flare's light was enough to show Kagen on the deck of the boat roped to the left side of the pier. Vreesje too; her stick shape was impossible to mistake. Kagen had beat them back here; he'd run as soon as the Germans started that last attack.

Mouse felt too small that moment, not strong enough to be in charge.

"What do we do, Leonard?" Reka asked again.

A heartbeat, two, three, but finally he said, "Take Simon to the boat, the one with Kagen, see? And get on yourself." He didn't want to look at her.

She made him look by putting her hand to his cheek. A flare fizzled into the sea, and it was dark again except for what light the moon and the burning boat made. Her face was just a shadow, but he could see it in his memory. He knew where the scar started and where it ended, how her mouth was thin at the corners, how that face had looked so plain to him the first time he'd seen it, but now that he knew her, it wasn't plain at all.

"No, not until you step on, too. That's a promise," she said.

Mouse nodded, not that she could really see it, and he walked through the mud along the shore and made a point to get close enough to look in the moonlit faces as he held the Welrod in front of him and counted some to the left, they would go on the boats, and more, many many more, he waved to the right using the big mouth of the gun. No one argued or refused to go where he said.

Mouse didn't cry, he'd not cried since his father had given up in Brooklyn Jewish Hospital fifteen years before. But as he said the words "I'm sorry" over and over, not knowing the Dutch so saying in English, he grew to hate those words. Each time, saying it was like tearing another piece off the feeling that God had meant him to be here.

---

T he noise of the German aircraft swelling down the dike made Reka
want to fling herself under the slick wood of the pier.

But instead she dashed to join Leonard—he was parting the crowd,
making the one into two, and she understood. Then, from the corner of
her eye she saw first four, next six, and finally eight pencils of yellow
stab from the water into the air. The racket of guns close, and not the
aircraft's either.

The moon and the blink of the yellow lines were enough to show the
outline of a boat. A boat, but not another of Boersma's. This one was
long and sleek, twice the length of a fishing boat, narrower from back
to front, sharpest there, like a needle.

The yellow lines swiveled as the aircraft neared—she saw its propellers catch the light—and the lines converged to meet in a cone. The
tip of that cone touched the aircraft along its length, drawing out
sparks. But they lingered longest at the left engine, which spit flames.
Part of the propeller spun away.

The German aircraft stuttered like it had struck an invisible limb of
an impossibly tall tree. The howl of two engines was suddenly halved.
The aircraft dipped toward the water but didn't touch the Waddenzee.
It banked out to sea, and although she could follow the fire on its engine for a few seconds, it was gone before she could take another two
breaths.

"Thank God," she said, and followed Leonard's eyes to the boat that
had chased away the Luftwaffe. It coasted to the pier.

Leonard stared at the silhouettes of the men on the boat. "I don't
think so," he said.

D own deep he knew who it was before the motorboat bumped against
the pier sixty feet away. Before the six men stepped from its deck
onto the pier. But the voice coming out of the big round head on the big
round man took him by surprise anyway.

"I told you you would 'ave no idea of 'ow much trouble I was gon'a make on you, didn't I?" Jack Spark's voice was big even here, out in the open where the ocean went on forever.

"Jack," Mouse said, just the one word, while he tried to get his brain unstuck. Five ganefs stood behind and to the side of Spark, them shaking mud off their boots or just standing, holding Stens. They wore loose sweaters over pants, but Spark was still in his cheap suit, even in the moonlight you could see it was cut like crap. His arm was in a sling. So he'd touched him on the field near Biggleswade. That was something, at least.

Mouse lowered the Welrod, which he'd raised as soon as the big man had stepped off the pier. He could shoot Spark, but he'd be dead before he could work the Welrod again. And though Reka had a Sten, she didn't know what this meant, Spark here.

"What's all 'em doin' 'ere, son?" Spark asked, waving his hand at the people spread up and down the shore. "An' where's the midget's packages?"

"Leonard, what's going on?" Reka asked.

"Tommy, take their toys, if you please."

"Right, Jack," and this Tommy stepped through the mud like he was afraid of getting his boots dirty. Mouse handed over the Welrod, watching another ganef on the left who had a clear shot at him and Reka both. Tommy pulled on the Sten in Reka's hand, but she wasn't letting go.

"Leonard, who are these—" she started, but Tommy swung an open hand and slapped her to the mud, wrenching the gun from her in the same moment.

Mouse moved, one step that was all, his fingers tight in a fist, and Jack tut-tutted. "She yer twist and twirl, is she?" Spark asked. "Yer one and only? She called you Leonard, right? On first names now. Thought you went by Mouse."

The motorboat's machine guns opened up again. Four pairs, two pair each side of the low cabin in the middle of the boat, raked the dike behind them. The eight guns would hold back the Germans, at least for a while. The crowd of people had backed away when Reka was knocked to the ground.

"I asked you a question. Where's the midget's packages?"

"Packages?" Mouse asked. He'd never see home now, he was sure of that.

Spark pulled a piece of paper from a pocket of his suit and waved it like a flag.

"Eager to receive thousand packages from Mr. Uithuizen, stop, deal not Jack's business," Spark said from memory. The cablegram Lansky had sent him. "Found this in 'at 'iding 'ole of yours in King's Cross. Lots of ovver things, too. Maps an' charts. Lists an' schedules. Told me just where to find you an' when. An' a little brown book with money numbers innit. Said you 'ad twenty-five thousand quid." Spark crumpled the cablegram in his hand and threw it to the mud. "What's yer midget up to, Leonard? What's his jelly 'ere in 'Olland, eh, this deal's none of my business? Some sort of smugglin'? I said I was owed my slice, so I've come fer what's mine. An' what's mine is all of i' now."

"Jews," Mouse said, knowing he was a dead man breathing.

"Jews?"

"We came for Jews. A thousand of them." Mouse waved his hand at the faceless mass of people who weren't faceless anymore, not since he'd had to decide whom to send left or right.

By now, Reka had picked herself up out of the mud. "Leonard? What's—" The machine guns blasted the top of the dike again and he lost her voice for a moment.

"Jews," said Spark, and shook his head.

"No jelly here, Jack. No geld, neither. All's I got are a thousand Jews," said Mouse, daring Spark to get this over with.

Spark looked around, then down the shore, as if really seeing the crowd there for the first time.

"Jack, we ain't got enuff time to dawdle," the ganef on the far left said.

"I come all the way to 'Olland, spend three thousand quid to have my SOE friends, some of 'Arry O'Brien's friends—you 'member 'Arry, don't you, Leonard? 'E never came 'ome, 'Arry didn't. Three thousand to take me on their little pisser of a nanny, get here fer what's mine, an' all you got fer me is Jews?" said Spark, his voice unconvinced.

"Don't fuck with this, Jack," Mouse said. "You fuck with this, and Lansky won't forget. Bet your life on it, Jack."

Spark didn't say anything right away. He was thinking.

"The midget wants to be a 'ero, does he?" Spark asked. "'E think 'e can be some sort of 'ero to 'is four by twos, is that i'? Get 'imself into 'is yid 'eaven with a good deed?"

"Jack," pleaded the left ganef, "if there ain't nothin' 'ere, we should be off, don't you think?"

"Shut up, Barry," Spark said. The motorboat's guns stuttered again.

"'E thinks 'e can walk aw over me, yer midget does," Spark went on. "But this side of the water i's me, not 'im. 'E 'as no say 'ere. Big mistake, Leonard, 'at's what you and yer midget made."

"You queer this and Lansky will find out, Jack," said Mouse. "He always finds out."

*"You tried to plug me full of 'oles, you and yer bloody Boche friend!"* shouted Spark, his voice louder than the machine guns.

Mouse had always wondered whether he'd be able to keep his eyes open at the last moment or have to close them. His eyes stayed open, but only just. Yet the seconds ticked by and Spark neither reached inside his jacket nor said the word to his boys. He was thinking again inside the big round head.

"Jack, we got to leave," said Barry, the ganef on the left. "The SOE boys said just twenty minutes, you 'member. Jerry's E-boats showin' on their boffin's box. 'Member?"

"I tol' you to shut your mouth, Barry," growled Spark. The big man looked again at Mouse. "The Boche won't stay away fer long. We leave and they'll be in yer lap, won't they?"

"What—" started Reka.

"Tommy, shut 'er up if she says 'nother word, you 'ear?"

"Sure, Jack," said Tommy, and he pointed his Sten at her.

"What do you want, Jack?" asked Mouse.

"Gone to a lot of trouble comin' 'ere, right? I'm out my three thousand fer the trip and then there's my slice."

Mouse understood. He'd done enough deals these four weeks to understand. "Whatever you want, Jack," he said.

"'Ow much ov yer midget's dollars still left, Leonard?" asked Spark, smiling that mean small smile of his.

"Twelve thousand quid," he said, not hesitating. "It's yours for everyone we can get on the boats." He waved his hand to the pier.

"What's one yid worth to you?" Spark asked. When Mouse didn't answer, Spark turned to his ganef. "Barry, a four by two, what's one worth?"

"Jesus, Jack, I don't know. Fiver maybe, not that I'd want one," Barry said.

"A fiver? No, these are more precious, ain't they, Leonard? A oner, 'at's what I think." Spark looked at him. "Each Jew, you pays me a 'undred quid, Leonard. That's . . . ," and Spark paused just a second, telling Mouse that the big man had been doing the arithmetic, "nine thousand quid after you pay my expenses, which means ninety of 'em. You can take ninety four by twos."

"You can't leave them here, Jack," Mouse said, trying to keep his voice free of begging. Spark wouldn't listen to begging. "We can get more than three hundred on the boats."

"Pays the oner, you can 'ave 'nother."

Mouse thought and thought, his brain like the mud they stood in. "Lansky will pay you, I'll make sure he does, Jack. He'll owe you the rest."

"We ain't yids here, son, don't work on credit. No, whats you 'ave is whats you take. An' I 'ope fer their sake you 'ave the money on you or nothin' moves."

"Jack, please," Mouse said, hearing begging now for certain. "You can't leave them, the Germans—" But he stopped, knowing it was useless, and shrugged his arms from his coat and handed it to Spark, who gave it to Tommy. "Money's in the lining," Mouse said, glad then that he'd saved as much for himself as he could, sick at the thought of what he'd not. That thousand he'd tossed into O'Brien's lap, which got burned to ashes, that thousand would have bought ten more.

"Tell you what, Leonard, 'cause I'm so gracious, let you 'ave an even 'undred." Spark paused for a moment as the motorboat's guns banged away again in short bursts. "That's settled, then. But it's all the bloomin' midget's money, ain't it? You, Leonard, what about you? What *you* gon'a pay me fer the trouble *you* made me? Puttin' a shooter in my face."

Mouse looked in those little eyes, barely visible in the moonlight.

Vaguely, Mouse heard scattered shots from the dike behind him. The Germans were there, looking down on them, and a few braved the motorboat's guns.

He started to get an idea of what Spark meant. "You're leaving me, that's what you mean."

Spark laughed. "No, I'm sendin' you 'ome, Leonard, to tell 'at midget what's what. Like a lesson, right? I run things 'ere and if 'e sticks 'is kike nose in anything of mine again, 'e's brown bread. What means dead, Leonard. No, yer gon'a go 'ome, 'cause yer gon'a tell 'im."

Home. Mouse breathed again.

"But you, yer not rich like the midget. 'Ow you gon'a pay?"

"Jack, time," said Tommy. Spark looked at him, nodded, and turned back to Mouse. His words came out quick.

"'Ere's the jelly, then. Same's in the shop on Whitechurch. Same's you gave me. You said to pick 'tween Richie and the Welrod when you 'ad a shooter to Richie's 'ead, now I say you gon'a pick. You can't 'ave both, ain't 'at what you said?"

Spark paused and Mouse caught a quick glimpse of that mean little smile when the machine guns spit again. "You take yer twist," and Spark pointed his one good hand at Reka. "Or you take yer four by twos. That's the pick." His smile was nastier and thinner than ever. "Take 'er and we leave like we've never been 'ere, and the Boche'll be down before you say Bob's your uncle. Or leave 'er, and we stay until you pack yer 'undred on those nannies. But I think just one's those choices what makes yer midget 'appy to see you. Don't matter to me, I 'ave the midget's money, now don't I? What's it be, 'er for all this," and Spark held the coat out, "or the 'undred?"

"You fucker," Mouse whispered, hearing and understanding, but neither really. "You're crazy."

"Fucker, am I? Crazy, am I? You pissed all ovver me, you fuckin' kike wanker," and Spark's voice got lower yet. "Well, 'ere's some of yours back, innit, both you and yer midget, think you can fuck Jack Spark."

"I don't understand," Reka said, but Mouse didn't believe her.

Mouse looked at Reka, turning his back on Spark. He wasn't thinking about Little Man, what he might say if he came back with only one instead of a hundred. Instead, he looked at the people he'd pointed left with the Welrod just ten minutes before.

And thought he wouldn't have to make a choice. There was Kagen, at the end of the pier. Kagen, that fuckin' mamzer, his ace in the hole, Mouse's moyz, as it were. Kagen had the crew from Jack's motorboat in front of him, all five of them hands half in the air.

But while Mouse expected Kagen to add now to his crazy count, like he'd done alongside the train and from the train, Mouse was disappointed. For once, Kagen didn't shoot.

"Mr. Spark" was what the guy said instead of putting daylight into Spark and his boys. "What's going on?"

"The Boche in this jelly with Lansky, too?" asked Spark.

Kagen was quick. He knew from the time in the East End what Spark meant. "I'm no gangster, Mr. Spark," said Kagen, without moving the Sten one way or the other, off Spark's crew or onto Spark himself.

"We're waiting fer Leonard 'ere to make 'is mind," said Spark. He'd not told his ganefs to gun down the German, Mouse knew, because the motorboat's crew was in between. But he still hoped Kagen would see this for what it was and shoot and free him from Spark's crazy choices.

"I have no quarrel with you, Mr. Spark. Kill him if you want," said Kagen, who was paying him back, Mouse understood, for everything all at once.

Spark's barking laugh again boomed up and down the shore. "No, Boche, 'e's gon'a come 'ome with me."

"I'm coming, too," said Kagen, and his Sten slowly swiveled to a space between two of the boat's crew and through that space, to Spark. Mouse knew Spark saw that. "You're not leaving me behind. Not after what I've done."

"What I need you fer? Once a Boche, always a Boche, what I say," said Spark. "You put a shooter on me too, didn't you? Tommy, Barry," Spark said.

"Jack, the nanny's boys are in the way," said Tommy.

"I don't care if they're in the fuckin' way!" Spark yelled. "Do what I tol' you, Tommy!"

"Jack—" said Tommy, but the ganef was smarter than Spark or at least not so crazy, and didn't shoot.

"Mexican standoff, Jack," said Mouse. "That's what we got here." Mouse still thought he could work the angles and get them on the boats. Wasn't that what he was good at, working the angles?

"The longer we wait, Mr. Spark, the closer they get," said Kagen. Mouse heard the gunfire growing behind the dike, too. "There's no time to load them. We're leaving now, you and me, on your boat."

"You fuckin' Boche, I'm gon'a piss down yer throat—" and Spark stopped suddenly. Mouse followed Spark's look.

A shape, less than a shadow, so thin it might have been just a dark line in the moon's half-light, stepped off the end of the wooden pier and took one two three steps to Kagen's back, none of those steps noisy, maybe because the shadow was so very thin. A second line extended from the first and Mouse saw it as an arm.

"*Je hebt mijn Rachael achtergelaten,*" Vreesje said. In her hand was the old Luger of Reka's that he'd given her on the train, telling her it was for the Germans.

The gun went off and Kagen flopped to the mud. Vreesje dropped the Luger. Tommy went to her and picked it up, stuck a boot under Kagen and rolled him over. His Orpo coat was dark at the front. If he wasn't dead, the fuck, he would be soon, Mouse thought. No more counting for you.


Reka didn't cry, she was tough, she had a face like a dropper, didn't she. But Mouse felt his eyes wet. Look at him, the real dropper.

She didn't make it any easier, but then, that wasn't her way. "I want to see America, Leonard," she said quietly. She understood his choice, she'd figured it out through Spark's gibberish, she was smart.

He looked beyond her again at the people huddled near the pier, at Simon who was easy to spot with his bald head and the little dark-haired girl in his arms. Reasons, he thought. He needed a reason. He hesitated, like he had hesitated that day on Canal when he had put his Smith & Wesson in Tootles's face but not pulled the trigger. But this was a different hesitation. Now he took the moment to think of what reason there was to kill a hundred to save one.

One or one hundred, one hundred or one.

"Jack, come *on*," said Tommy.

He looked at Reka and the tears got big enough in the corners of his eyes to slip down his cheeks. His thinking started to nick slices at the edges of his heart. That's how it felt.

"Make yer mind," Spark was saying behind him.

He couldn't look her in the eyes. She touched his hand and she curled her fingers around it and she squeezed his hand. "Don't leave me, Leonard. I don't want to end—" but she didn't finish. Her hand was trembling in his.

"Jew!" Spark shouted.

"Take her," he said to Spark one last time. "I'll stay, Jack, Lansky won't even know what happened here, he won't come after you."

"No. You don't understand, do you? I want 'im to know, right? 'Ow's it a lesson if 'e doesn't know?"

Mouse looked down the shore. He had tried to tell her he wanted out of the business, that was why he had wanted the money. Change has to start somewhere. But it tore his heart from whatever held it inside him.

"I'm sorry, I'm sorry, I'm sorry," Mouse said to Reka, soft so Spark couldn't hear.

"Yes or no, Jew, yes or no?" Spark asked in his big voice.

"Do you love me, Leonard?" she asked, quietly.

"Yes," he said, the answer to both questions. The word gouged out a chunk so large he thought his heart stopped for a second.

He looked in her dropper's eyes. He couldn't lie this time. "I love you," he said.

"Barry, Alf, Reggie, go help 'em get on the nannies, just a 'undred, make sure's you count 'em," Spark's voice said behind him, and Mouse saw the three ganefs slop toward those from Westerbork.

"Have your mama say the Kaddish for me, won't you, Leonard?" Reka asked him. "If you tell her about me, she'll do that for me, won't she? I have no one else . . ."

"I'll say it," Mouse whispered back. "Every day. I promise."

She put her hand on his cheek and brushed away the tear there. "Don't cry, Leonard." Her voice was stronger.

"Call me Mouse," he said softly, and put out his hand to touch the scar bright along her temple.

"I love you, Mouse," she said, putting her hand over his there on the scar. She went into his arms for a moment and he held her close, smelling her smell, the rain still in her long dark hair.

And the ganef named Tommy grabbed him by the sleeve and pulled him away from the woman worth one hundred.

He was Hauptsturmführer Horst Preuss, Sicherheitsdienst, Amt IV B-4, Department of Jewish Affairs, master of Hebrews, Amsterdam's leader of the Tribe. He remembered all this as he came awake, his head beating to the time of his heart. Preuss got first to his knees and, when he'd found his Walther in the wet grass, to his feet. His trousers were damp and he felt the migraine in all its fury.

As the blackness faded, Preuss peered over the crest of the dike and saw the two fishing smacks pushing through the water beyond the pier. A longer, sleeker boat was beside them, looking like an S-boat, one of those fast motor torpedo boats the Kriegsmarine ran, which should have showed by now but hadn't. They were fleeing, with his Jews.

No, not all, not nearly all. He stared at the foot of the dike and saw the dark mass of people there, a congregation of hundreds. They waited for him. He would lead them to their rightful place, by himself if necessary.

Ignoring the spotty gunfire behind him, Preuss stepped down the slope of the dike with the Walther in his hand. When he reached the Jews, they parted for him like the sea for Moses. Preuss smiled at the thought.

Preuss wasn't afraid. These Jews had no guns. He pointed the Walther at the edges of the circle that had opened around him.

"Back to the top of the dike," he yelled in his Dutch, and waved the pistol. "Trucks will return you to Westerbork." He wasn't used to talking to Jews, and perhaps, he thought, that was the reason why they didn't move. So he aimed the Walther and pulled the trigger. A shadow dropped from the wall of people and fell into the mud.

He fired again, and that began to move them. The closest edged away, and a few at the border began scrambling up the dike's slope.

"You have nothing to be afraid of," he called out. "You were on your way to labor in the Reich, that's all!" he shouted. Lies, but the lies always worked.

A short man in a thick coat and no hat, that was all Preuss could see in the dim light, stepped out of the circle's edge.

"Back to your place," Preuss said. But the man didn't do as he ordered, instead walked another step and another until Preuss could see his narrow face and, on his thin nose, spectacles. He ordered again, now in German. *"Zurück! Bleib zurück, du Saujude!"* But that didn't stop the man, and so Preuss shot him, the first missing but the second catching him in the throat and sending him thrashing on the ground.

Someone threw mud, and it splattered Preuss's tunic and struck his cheek. A Jew scooped at the ground, and he shot. Another handful of muck hit him, this time at the shoulder and near his mouth. He tasted the sea, like shellfish gone bad.

And like that moment facing de Groot in the headlamps of the car, the cork on his fury flew as a champagne stopper flies across the room. He pointed the Walther at the wall of Jews and fired once.

A rock struck his arm and knocked the pistol into the mud. The cordon closed, another rock clouted him aside the head where the old yid had hit him, and Preuss went to his knees, his head white and whiter inside from the migraine or the blow or both.

His ears wouldn't work. No, not so. He heard sucking sounds as their shoes moved in the mud and muffled noises as their fists fell on him. He couldn't believe this was happening, and he tried to stand, thinking if he could stand they would obey, but he went instead the opposite, into a ball in the mud. They pummeled and pounded and punched his head and shoulders and back and legs until the world went as black as their hearts.

She had watched while the Englishmen pulled Mouse from her arms and pushed him to the pier, shoved too few people into Boersma's boats, and pressed others onto the deck of their own needle-nosed ship.

Its guns hammered at the dike all the while the boats loaded, even after its own engine rumbled and it pulled from the pier, keeping the Germans at bay.

And the two fishing boats and the one she knew carried Mouse wallowed through the swells and put to sea. She watched the boats disappear into the dark and, as they did, felt the miracle of it all settle a calm on her. The ghost of Mama's hand trembled one last time in hers and was gone.

She put her back to the Waddenzee and stepped through the mud to join the comfort of those Mouse had pushed to the right and away from the pier. Gunshots came from the middle of the crowd, and amid their shouting and screaming, she pried her way to the inner edges of a circle.

And found a man, more a mud-covered blanket than a man, curled at the water's edge, his boots taking the swells as they lapped ashore. Around him was this circle of men and boys and women. A boy standing nearest the blanket held a rock. The blanket moaned, and Reka stayed the boy with her hand. It was a German, she saw—the black diamond on the sleeve, one of the only clean spots left.

She bent down to look closer at the *Duitser* and he moaned again and turned to show his face, a dirty round face, plump along the chin, with pinhole eyes and a wide mouth splattered with mud and something darker. She knew that face. This was her Sicherheitsdienst.

"My Jewess, Dekker," the SD man whispered in Dutch around broken teeth, and in the saying of her name, she thought of the time the OD read their names on the Appelplatz in Westerbork. Even now, names.

Reka touched her coat and plucked at the yellow star, tearing it from the threads. She didn't need this any longer. The star she jammed down the German's throat, pushed it in and shoved until it could go no deeper.

Mouse, she thought, stealing one last glance out to the Waddenzee, but the boats were gone in the darkness. My lover. My betrayer. My teacher.

She leaned closer to the SD and watched while he struggled, but his arms, she saw, had been broken long before. He made soft snuffing sounds and wiggled there in the mud. She held his wet hands to keep them from plucking the star out of his throat, and they trembled in hers, like ghosts.

Reka leaned nearer yet, remembering what Mouse had explained to her as he'd written on the cellar wall and, later, scratched into the locomotive's side.

"*Mouse Weiss doet je de groeten, klootzak,*" she whispered.

T he motorboat plowed through the swells, its guns reversed but silent. They were out of range.

Its decks were hidden under the feet and knees of people he'd touched and pushed toward the pier, every one of those he could find in those few minutes whose faces he remembered helping down from the cattle car. Simon and the dark-haired girl, and the boy whose name he didn't know who lay wounded in the mud, brought there by the dead Alder, and Alder's wife, and the mother with the two little boys, and the old woman who had hugged him so tightly around the neck. He even found the train's engineer with the deep creases in his face, the only one without a yellow star, and took him even so. And Vreesje, who had started it all and ended it all.

Eighty, ninety, one hundred, he'd counted, double-counted, ignoring Barry and the other ganefs who tried to count for him. He'd counted, just like that fuckin' mamzer Kagen, meshuge Kagen, who lay in the mud at the end of the pier where everyone had to walk past him or step over him or maybe put a boot on him stiff there. Count, counted, counting like Kagen, but not.

A white star trailed sparks over the dike and burst into a flower that lit the shore now fading behind them. He looked and looked and looked, but all he saw was a darker smudge against the dark of the dike. Reka was a small part of that darkness.

He held the little dark-haired girl close, having taken her from Simon, who was unsteady as the motorboat rose and fell in the waves. Vreesje stood beside him.

The little girl whose name he didn't know joined him in crying and she jabbered in Dutch, and all Mouse could think to do was to touch her dark hair and say, "It's gonna be okay, it's gonna be fine," in a soft and quiet voice.

He felt a prickling on the back of his neck, and Mouse Weiss looked again toward the shore, but there was nothing but darkness as the motorboat herded the two fishing boats through the cold, cold water of the Waddenzee. He shifted this little girl in his arms and turned to keep her from the wind.

R eka found the pistol a meter away from the dead Sicherheitsdienst. It had been stepped into the mud and gone unseen by the people who had beaten him into a blanket. She scraped the mud from its barrel and grip, and because it was much like that ancient Luger she had once used, she fumbled only a second before finding the magazine release. The metal magazine dropped in her dirty palm and she held it so the moonlight showed inside.

Empty. She pushed the magazine back into the grip and put her thumb on the hammer and gently eased it forward. She wiped the mud from the slide, and pulled it back, so slowly, to peek into the chamber. The moon showed her the one bullet, its copper head clean and its brass body the same.

Reka bent over the *Duitser* again and put hands to his tunic, and in his pockets. But she found no magazines packed with bullets, no more bullets at all. Just one stiff piece of paper.

A star burst overhead to her left and trailed white sparks, and the shore was lit. The paper was a photograph. She held it for long seconds. It was her face she stared at, but it wasn't, not now.

Reka rolled the stiff paper into a tight tube, then slipped it between the parted lips of the dead SD. Like a cigarette, she thought.

She stretched then to take the kink out of her back from the time spent leaning over the *Duitser,* and heard voices calling at the top of the dike.

Smoke. She would not become smoke.

She had told David so long ago that the only thing the Germans left them was to choose the where of their death, and the when. She'd been right, but not quite in the way she'd thought.

Reka pulled the folded sketch from her coat and stared at the portrait she'd made of Mouse on the train, when his eyes had not been so sad.

The star sputtered in the water, and she couldn't decide whether to drop the drawing into the slow waves of the Waddenzee or into her pocket.

It went in her pocket.

Another star flared, again to the left, and whistles blew in that direction. But to her right, it was dark still and there were no whistles or foreign voices calling.

They will come down off the dike and take us away because they can. We let them. But Mouse had taught her different. She would never wait for them to come again. No matter what that meant.

Reka looked up at the stars banded across the sky, too many for the moon to drown, and then at the pistol she held loosely in her hand.

Her only regret was that she was not brave like Mouse, who had saved a hundred.

The crowd around her compacted into a tight tribe, but stayed where it was. Waiting. Reka glanced down the shore, west again, where it was dark and empty, and took a first step.

She would save only one.

# ACKNOWLEDGMENTS

Anyone who thinks writing is a solitary profession doesn't know many writers. We lean on lots of people.

First among those I'd like to thank is my agent, Don Maass, who plucked me from the pile, was enthusiastic from the get-go, and has taught me more about the craft of storytelling in a few months than I thought possible. I'm looking forward to future lessons.

Jennifer Hershey, my editor at G. P. Putnam's Sons, not only took a gamble on a first-timer but was equally vital in turning this novel into what it is. Her eye is sharp, her pencil sharper, and she is all a writer could wish for in an editor.

Claire van den Broek and Matthias Vogel, both of the University of Oregon, translated dialog into Dutch and German, respectively, and saved me from more than a few embarrassments.

My family, Lori and Emily, of course, deserve more credit than can be stated here, but I'd like to especially thank them for living with a writer, and reading the bits and pieces as they came off the printer.

Finally, I want to thank my best of friends, Keith Ferrell, who convinced me that this was all possible.

But leaning on others goes only so far; naturally, any errors are mine and mine alone.

## ABOUT THE AUTHOR

Gregg Keizer lives in Eugene, Oregon. He is a reporter for the TechWeb online news service *www.techweb.com* and is at work on his second novel.